My Bicentennial

Books by Evie Kelley

My Bicentennial
A Mostly True Tale of the Far-Out '70s

Coming Soon!

The Nascent Bloom
A Young Adult Science Fiction Suspense Series

The Nascent Bloom Book I: Caught
The Nascent Bloom Book II: Running
The Nascent Bloom Book III: Home

My Bicentennial

A Mostly True Tale of the Far-Out '70s

EVIE KELLEY

GREAT BROOK PUBLISHING

Copyright © 2025 Evie Kelley

All rights reserved. This book or any portion thereof may not be reproduced, distributed, or transmitted in any form or used in any manner whatsoever without the express written permission of the publisher except for the use of brief quotations in a book review. No part of this book may be used in the formation or use of AI technologies without express permission from the author.

This is a work of fiction. The events described here are imaginary: The names, settings, places, and characters are fictitious and not intended to represent specific places or persons, living or dead. Any resemblance to actual events or persons is entirely coincidental.

ISBN 979-8-9901207-7-8 (Paperback)

ISBN 979-8-9901207-8-5 (E-book)

Cover design and interior illustrations by Hannah Hill

www.hannahhilldesign.com

Dedication

For Bob,
the bestest big brother
a girl could ever ask for

Part One

January 1976

Chapter 1

Are You There, Twinkies? It's Me, Deidre

TELL US WHO YOU *are (maximum 250 words).*

I tapped my pen to the papers on my lap. The first question on State University's application had me stumped. Besides being a girl who had nothing else to do on New Year's Eve but hang out in her bedroom with the cinder block walls painted the grayish shade of a fresh corpse, filling out college applications, I didn't know who I was.

How could I craft a pithy summary of the enigma wrapped in the mystery of the walking disaster known as Deidre Daly in just 250 words?

The basics alone would put me over the word limit.

Seventeen, high school senior, a white girl of average height who wanted to be a writer someday. Gold-rimmed glasses, eyes that changed from blue to gray like a Mood Ring, and dark blonde hair parted in the middle like Marcia Brady. Cursed with freckles *and* pimples. Always joking, even when I shouldn't joke. Poor—not dirt poor, just regular poor—and stuck living with my parents, three siblings, and the world's most disagreeable Chihuahua in the dumpiest public housing project in the dumpiest city in New England.

And as of today when I weighed myself, two hundred pounds.

I'd always been heavy, but it seemed appropriate to reach such a milestone now, minutes away from January 1, 1976, the first day of the Bicentennial year. The United States had made it to two hundred years. I'd made it to two hundred pounds. My own personal bicentennial.

My dad blamed heredity and his side of the family for this dubious achievement. "You've got a fat ass like my mother," he'd say.

Perfectly rude, and perfectly him.

The son of immigrants who'd fled abject poverty in Ireland to come to America and be only mildly poor in Massachusetts, my father wasn't a successful man. He couldn't play sports or ballroom dance, and he was only moderately okay at manufacturing ball valves (whatever those were), since he'd been a line worker at Higgins Manufacturing for forty years without a single promotion, but two things he excelled at were insulting his kids and drinking.

Especially the drinking.

Beer was Dad's booze of choice, chased down by whiskey nips, little glass bottles he stashed behind the baby oil tanning lotion and dead batteries in the cupboard over the kitchen sink. He thought no one knew he hid them there, but everyone did.

My mother was far more supportive (and sober). She used to have a job in an office downtown, where she had to wear dresses and pantyhose and answer phones for a stiff guy named Mr. Allen.

"Male chauvinist pig to the *nth* degree," she'd called him.

Then she took a class at the community college and had her consciousness raised and she told Mr. Allen to take a hike. After that, she wore pantsuits and got a job in our neighborhood, where helping others became her way of life. If a family needed food stamps or rent assistance or a ride downtown for an appointment when they couldn't take the bus, they called Mom to help.

She did her best to help me too. She told me not to let my weight bother me. She said everybody was different, and every *body* was different too. An uplifting thing to say, probably something from that woman's health book *Our Bodies, Ourselves* she'd left in the bathroom on top of the busted radiator, hoping I would read it someday.

But my weight *did* bother me. So did being a fat girl living in a skinny world. And the fact that when someone on TV who looked like me appeared, the trumpet of elephants announced her arrival and the ground shook when she walked. It bothered me that I had to go all the way to Timbuktu to find clothes that fit. And don't get me started on the nonexistence of jeans in my size. Not to mention no guy had ever asked me for a date. Not once.

If I was skinny, my life would be different. Better. People wouldn't tease me or rag on my jokes and say they weren't funny. Skinny girls could do and say anything and everyone smiled and simply said, "Isn't she cute?"

If I was skinny, I'd be popular. I'd wear tight jeans over a stylish bodysuit that snapped closed at the crotch and strut down the school hallway in platform shoes with the other popular girls, cracking gum and giving dirty looks to the dorky kids far less popular than us.

Most important, guys would want to go out with me and I'd have the delicious dilemma of choosing which one I'd let take me to the prom, the Holy Grail of all high school activities. At the prom I might even *do it*. My friend Donna said any girl who was still a virgin popped their cherry on prom night, and I so wanted to be one of them.

If I was skinny.

I tidied the forms on my lap into a neat pile. Somehow I doubted the admissions officers at State University were interested in an essay about my weight woes. Only I was interested in that, and only I could do something about it. I couldn't change much else about my life, not where I lived, or my dad's drinking or his fondness for telling me I had a fat ass.

But I could change myself.

And there was just one way to do that. A course of action me and my love affair with junk food and especially Twinkies loathed above all else—I had to go on a diet.

Oh, I'd made New Year's resolutions to lose weight before, and I'd always given up the first time my stomach growled. *This* time, I wouldn't break my resolution. This time, I'd stick with it. This time, I'd lose weight, a *lot* of weight and get as skinny as Twiggy and wouldn't *that* be something to write about in a college essay?

The bedroom door creaked open, as if a bashful ghost crept into the room. Really just our dog Marco, a tiny brown Chihuahua with white paws, nudging the door open with his nose. The sound of Dick Clark's *New Year's Rockin' Eve* with guests Neil Sedaka and Average White Band followed Marco in, drifting up from the living room downstairs.

The clock radio on the bureau flipped to 11:55. Mom and the current book she was reading had gone to bed hours ago, but the rest of the family were still up.

I supposed I should go down and join them to watch the ball drop, and to see if my father was still awake. My brother Rusty had bet me a buck Dad would be passed out by eleven. I held out hope he'd make it to midnight for once and wanted to find out which one of us was right.

I slid off the bed and tossed State U's application onto the bureau with the forms from the other colleges I couldn't afford to go to but Mom wanted me to apply to anyway. The applications weren't due until the end of the month, plenty of time to finish them later. Plenty of time to figure who I was. In 250 words.

I scooped Marco up under my arm and kissed him on the head as I left the bedroom and hurried down the stairs. He growled. I laughed. A light, tingly sensation sparked in my belly. Anticipation, excitement. At the possibilities of the new year, and the prospect of a shiny new me.

Goodbye 1975, hello Bicentennial year. The year I would get skinny. The year I would change my life.

I *would* do it. I *could* do it.

All it would take was a little thing called willpower.

CHAPTER 2

My Boogie Shoes

I WAS BORN A **Baby Boom** bundle of joy with pink hair on December 26, 1958.

The pink hair eventually changed to blonde. The date of my birth stayed the same, and I'd grown up fervently opposed to the sneaky practice of giving one gift as a combined Christmas/birthday present.

But when I opened the box Aunt Polly handed me on Christmas night, all was forgiven. Inside were *the* coolest pair of platform shoes ever crafted by the shoemaker elves at Thom McAn. A rich, burnt-orange color with long laces and thick, spongy white platform soles.

I called them my marshmallow shoes. They weren't completely broken in and would probably give me blisters before the end of today, but I absolutely had to wear them the first day back to school after winter vacation.

The storm door slapped shut behind me as I stepped outside onto the concrete stoop bordered by metal railings your tongue would stick to in the winter (one guess how I found that out). I clomped down the steps and turned toward the bus stop at the bottom of the hill.

The day was cold, but clear. Sunlight beamed down on the William E. Harrington Public Housing Project, dozens of rectangular brick buildings of six or eight two-story apartments that sprawled over acres of rolling hills, like a child's toy blocks plopped down at all angles. The light warmed the bricks to a rusty red and glinted off the yellow *Fallout Shelter* signs that hung over the cellar entrance at the end of each block.

Overall, a pretty scene. If I ignored the torched mattresses and other junk piled in the clothesline yards, the overflowing trash bins, junk cars parked on the grass, and the broken glass strewn across the pavement of the Tot Lot playground.

And the frequent shrill of police sirens.

I slip-slid down the icy sidewalk, looking forward to going back to school for once. I felt a foot taller and kind of sexy in my new shoes. Thinner, even. Though that had more to do with my new diet. I'd lost one pound since New Year's. One hundred ninety nine. Bicentennial minus one. A triumph to see the number on the scale go down and not up. If not for the Boston crème pie incident over the weekend, I might've lost two pounds or even ten.

I reached the bus stop. The usual gang of idiots waited at the corner, minus the few who'd dropped out of school before Christmas break. The girls wore short jackets that showed off hip-hugger jeans, the boys wore flared polyester pants in a variety of colors so bright the cops could easily spot them at night. Jimmy McMahon and most of his six hundred brothers swarmed a snow pile, making snowballs and hurling them at any target they could find.

No one said hello, not even my brother Rusty. He'd fled the house early, partly because I'd won our bet and he was avoiding paying up, more likely so he could get down here and smoke his morning cigarette. He'd gotten Dad's permission to smoke the second he turned sixteen (Mom refused to discuss it). My old man puffed like a chimney and was happy to have someone joining him in clogging his lungs and stinking up the house so he granted his permission in a heartbeat.

Our ride arrived. Not a cheerful yellow school bus, a lime-green city bus with grimy windows. The vehicle wheezed up to the curb, spitting smoky crap from the exhaust pipe.

Lars Quigley elbowed people out of the way to get on board first. A tall, doughy guy with skin as white as the snowballs the McMahons had splattered all over his coat, Lars was the smartest kid in the Project and always in a hurry to get to school and impress the teachers with his big brain. Rusty let a couple of girls go ahead of him like the gentleman he wasn't, then he flicked his cigarette into a snowbank and followed them inside.

My turn came. Still getting used to my platform heels, I stumbled and tripped on the top step. I pitched forward. My knees met the floor treads with a painful smack. Cold wetness seeped into my purple pants. My macramé handbag swung off my shoulder and the flap flopped open. Pencils, notebooks, and sanitary napkins spilled out.

Behind me, Jimmy McMahon snickered. Some other kids laughed. I flushed, mortified. I guess I wasn't as excited about this first day back at school after all.

I crammed everything back into my bag and hoisted myself up, avoiding eye contact with the bus driver as I passed. A dumpy man of about fifty, Gus had grayish skin, wispy hair, and a perpetual scowl designed to frighten toddlers, puppies, and anyone unfortunate enough to be a passenger on his bus.

Jimmy McMahon and his multitude of brothers squeezed on board after me, the door squealed shut, and Gus hit the gas. I sank into a seat and brushed wet grit off my knees and inspected my marshmallow shoes, relieved to see my doorway swan dive didn't injure them, then I gazed out the window as we raced down the street.

We stopped several more times, at each of the streets that intersected the Project's main thoroughfare, Prosperity Way, and was there a more ironic name for a place where poor people lived?

A thousand poor people, to be exact. Kids, old folks, Black, brown, white, different backgrounds, religions, opinions, and attitudes, but with one thing in common. We were broke. And we knew we were broke. The guy who named the streets didn't need to rub it in.

At the corner, Gus gunned the gas and swung onto the road to school on two wheels, as if trying to capsize us like in the *Poseidon Adventure*. I hung onto the seat for dear life, wondering why my mother always worried about us kids ending up dead from drugs or kidnapped by a stranger when it was more likely Demolition Derby Gus would kill us all taking a sharp corner.

The bus jerked to a stop in front of Northside High School a while later. We poured down the steps and hustled into the school, a series of interconnected buildings laid out in a complicated pattern of corridors I still got lost in, even in my senior year.

Everyone went their separate ways. I headed to my homeroom in B corridor then to my locker to ditch my coat and grab the books I'd need for the first two periods.

I fought the usual battle to open the combination lock. Math and I had long ago agreed to disagree, mostly because numbers got all mixed up in my brain. So I had to turn and turn the dial until the numbers somehow miraculously aligned and the latch clicked open.

I scooped up my books and slammed the door, hoping to get to science class before the bell. I swung around—and almost collided with Stew Baines. Which would've hurt a lot if it'd been an actual collision, since Stew was the height, width, and breadth of an ox.

"Watch it, *Deer-duh*," he said, smirking as he rushed by.

I sent a hearty thanks to the patron saint of baby names that my parents didn't call me something more in line with my current physique, like Peggy or Patty, names that could easily be switched to Piggy or Fatty by dopes like Stew Baines.

And at least they didn't call me something utterly ridiculous, like my sister's friend Rapunzel. Her mother must've been high when she came up with that, especially since Rapunzel had hair so short Prince Charming wouldn't have the ghost of a chance of climbing it.

My platform soles beat a muted *thump-thump* through the hallways and down two flights as I raced to science in the bowels of D corridor. I didn't know what Mr. Meager had done to get himself stuck in the most remote corner of Northside High, but I suspected it had something to do with his love of Bunsen burners and open flames.

"Nice of you to join us, Deidre," he said, shutting the door. A thin guy with bristly hair and skin the color of a cooked salmon, he wore striped bell bottoms every day and boots that clicked on the tile floor.

"Sorry, Mr. Meager. A twelve sophomore pileup in B corridor slowed me down."

He didn't laugh at my joke. He never did. But he expected us to roar and roll out of our seats at his wisecracks, which were basically needling insults. Like Don Rickles, only not funny.

I learned this uncomfortable fact the first day of ninth grade, when he filmed us freshmen getting off our school buses with what he called a video-tape camera, a big, bulky thing he hoisted onto one shoulder. During orientation in the auditorium, we got to watch the fuzzy black-and-white images he'd recorded on a big TV screen.

At first, I was excited, but as I watched each kid spill off their bus, my stomach clenched tighter and tighter. Mr. Meager let loose like a seagull dive bombing a beach picnic, making sure he hit everyone. He made fun of one girl's stringy hair and gooney glasses, joked about a boy's pimples, and groaned like a pervert whenever a girl with big boobs bounced off a bus, making the boys laugh.

"Hey, look at this nut," he'd said as Camille Arundel, who'd lived in the Project then, popped up on screen. "She's a loon for sure."

Camille cried for an hour after that and I'd wondered if Mr. Meager knew her father had been put into a mental hospital.

When I'd stumbled off my bus with my usual grace, Mr. M. had practically bellowed, "Whoa! This one's too big to fit on the TV."

I wanted to cry like Camille. My thighs and butt seemed to fill the whole picture. But Dalys weren't allowed to cry, so I'd lifted my chin and sat stone-faced until roly-poly me exited the screen and Mr. Meager's next victim appeared.

I trudged to my seat at the lab table at the back, breathing in the scent of formaldehyde and other science-y things that turned my stomach. The smells were such an appetite-killer I could easily stay on my diet if I hung around here all day, but that would mean being trapped with Mr. M for hours when I could barely stand being in his company for fifty minutes of class.

My attention drifted as Mr. M explained today's assignment. With my resolution to get skinny sort of on track with that one pound loss, time to put the next step of my plan into motion. Find someone to take me to the prom. Wicked early, I knew, but planning ahead could pay off.

I scoped out the guys in class with a practiced eye. I'd been officially boy crazy since I was eleven and fell for Donny Osmond, a cute teen idol singer with black hair and teeth as big as golf tees. I joined his fan club and they sent a pamphlet listing a selection of records or 8-track tapes I could buy to learn about becoming a Mormon. I thought about buying some if I could find the money, until Mom firmly declared organized religion patriarchal nonsense and tossed the pamphlet into the trash.

That ended my Donny crush and I moved on to real boys. Boys who would probably gag if they knew someone like me was interested in them. But once I got skinny? Well, I bet every one of these guys would line up for the chance to take me to the prom.

I'd entertain offers from each of them. Except Billy Bonner, who everyone called "Boner." Not because his dick always stood at attention, though it probably did since all teenage boys suffered from that affliction, according to Aunt Polly, mother of six of those diabolic creatures (her words, not mine). People called him "Boner" because he did things known as "pulling a boner." He ate dog poop on a dare. Sophomore year, when streaking was a fad, he sprinted down the C corridor completely naked.

Did I want to go to prom with someone who might eat shit and expose himself on the most magical night of the year? I did not. So I immediately scratched him off my list, but the year was young and there were lots of other guys left to choose from.

Mr. Meager said his two favorite words, *Bunsen* and *burner*, so I dragged my brain out of boy-land and got to work, hoping I wouldn't scald my fingers like I did the last time we used those vile implements of torture.

CHAPTER 3

With A Little Help From My Friends

BBY LUNCH PERIOD, MY feet were killing me and I was starving. I couldn't do anything about my blistered toes until I got home, but I could find a cure for my empty belly inside C Cafeteria.

Heat and noise blasted out at me as I entered a spacious, high-ceilinged room painted with the school colors, neon blue and diarrhea yellow. Conversation roared like a jet engine and the place smelled of meat sauce, grease, and too many people crammed together.

Through the grimy windows, I saw the smoking area, a courtyard where kids could blow off lunch to have a cigarette instead. No surprise to see my brother Rusty there.

I stepped into line, grabbed a tray, and slid it along the metal counter as we inched forward. Lunch would be a big test of my willpower. Nothing low-calorie on the menu today, or any day. My choices were greasy Salisbury steak that looked like a hockey puck dipped in tar or equally greasy macaroni and cheese, topped with crumbled potato chips. I could already taste the salty chips, so my choice was made.

"Can you give me a small portion of mac-and-cheese?" I asked the lunch lady behind the counter.

Our definition of small clearly differed. She scooped up a massive serving, her arm bulging with muscles that would make Rosey Grier and my school's entire football team envious. She

15

slopped it onto my tray and added green beans that looked like they'd been walked on. She threw in a pile of peaches in sugary juice for dessert.

Willpower, Diedre. I vowed to eat only a quarter of what she'd given me and slid my tray to the cash register.

I reached into the front pocket of my pants and pulled out a small, square card with my name and school typed on it—my free lunch pass. I handed it to the lady at the register. She held it up to the light, as if checking to see if it was counterfeit. She scrutinized my name and address for about twenty years, then looked from the card to me as if she'd never seen me before.

"Free lunch, huh?"

I cringed. She said the same thing every day, like J. Edgar Hoover grilling Patty Hearst about her life on the run. I glanced around. People stared and whispered. Felt like that, anyway. It always felt like that. As if I had a neon sign flashing P for Poor on my back for everyone to gawk at.

My stomach gurgled from nervousness, with the added bonus of hunger. Maybe I'd eat half of my mac-and-cheese to calm myself down. If I ever got past Commandant Lunch Lady and her almighty hole punch.

She stared at me a few more seconds, then let out an unimpressed, "Hunh," and her hole puncher went *click*. *The* most delicious sound in the world.

Everyone who'd gone through the line steered toward their chosen groups. The jocks sat together. So did the Black kids, the popular girls, and the brainiacs like Lars Quigley. Some of the Project kids huddled together, trying to look tough. The snooty kids from upper Chisholm Road clustered in a group, probably commiserating about being rich, but not rich enough to afford private school.

I used to sit with my best friends I grew up with, Yolanda and Pammie. After Yolanda went to a different school and moved away and Pammie dropped out to have a baby, I didn't have anyone to sit with at lunch.

Until Donna Bellarosa came along.

Donna saw me eating alone one day last fall and plopped down and started yapping. The rest of her merry band of misfits followed—Karen Hakanson, a slim white girl with dark hair as long and straight as Cher's, Barbie Diaz, light brown skin, chestnut hair, flat chest, the opposite of the doll she was named after, and Linda Gordon, who we called Linda G to distinguish her from the four thousand other Lindas in our school.

I carried my tray to the table by the side door and slipped in next to Donna. Today she wore a striped, boatneck body suit and navy blue hip huggers, an ocean of *Jean Naté* perfume, and enough blue eye shadow to paint Van Gogh's Starry Night.

She greeted me with a gushing, "Cool shoes," then returned to arguing with Karen and Barbie over the most engrossing topic of our time, who was cuter, Starsky or Hutch?

Donna's defense of Starsky didn't stand a chance. Karen had never met an argument she didn't lust to win and debated with the velocity of an auctioneer determined to wear everyone out. Barbie tried to enter her TV favorite into consideration, Freddie Prinze of *Chico and the Man*, but she was overruled.

Linda G didn't join in. A curvy girl with pinkish skin and rosy, cherub cheeks, she preferred to focus on her well-thumbed copy of *Gone With the Wind* as she ate. One trip through the Civil War and Reconstruction with insufferable Scarlett O'Hara had been enough for me, while this was Linda G's fourth or fifth time reading the book. I'd tried introducing her to more recent historical fiction like *Ragtime*, but she'd gotten stuck on Rhett Butler and no other fictional hero could get her to break up with him.

I doubted anyone wanted my opinion on the Starsky/Hutch dispute, so I concentrated on my hard won lunch instead. I nibbled on tiny forkfuls of mac-and-cheese, determined to eat only a small amount. A real battle. My taste buds salivated over the greasy cheese and salty potato chips and my stomach begged for me to finish every last bite.

"Something wrong?" Barbie asked, watching me with an expression somewhere between amusement and concern. "You're eating like your food's poisoned."

"Well, it *is* school food. You can't be too careful." I put down my fork. "Actually, I'm trying to go slow and watch what I eat. One of my new year's resolutions is to lose weight. My only resolution, actually."

There. I said it out loud. No turning back.

Donna's eyes lit up. "That's *my* resolution too. I need to lose a *ton* of weight. I ate so much over Christmas I'm as big as a blimp."

Barbie frowned. "That's ridiculous. You're *not* fat."

I concurred. Donna was just a little plump, and in the right place, her boobs. From my limited knowledge of the male of the species, I knew they liked that kind of plump.

"Try holding in your stomach when you walk," Karen said. "My mother says it'll tighten your abdominal muscles and get rid of your belly bulge."

I nodded like, *yeah, great suggestion*, though I'd been sucking in my gut since I was five and knew that trick didn't work.

"She says eating lecithin will peel off the pounds," Karen added. "And having a grapefruit for breakfast every morning will do the same thing. It takes more calories to digest grapefruit than you get eating it. Also, go out in the cold without your coat. My mother says your body burns more calories trying to keep warm than anything else. I bet you could burn a thousand calories an hour if you did that."

Karen's mother sure had lots of advice for losing weight. Would any of it work? I hated grapefruit and never heard of lecithin, and though I could very well die of frostbite by going outside half-naked, I said I'd give all of those a try.

"One thing burns more calories than anything else." Donna wriggled in her seat. "*Sex.*"

Karen flashed a smug grin. "Or so you hear."

Ouch. Donna was still a virgin, which explained her very vocal obsession with "popping her cherry," but did Karen have to remind her in such a snide way? She reminded me too, and maybe Barbie, though I didn't know for sure. Barbie never talked about boyfriends or sex or anything like that. Neither did Linda G. She seemed content with her unrequited love affair with a fictional character and completely uninterested in finding a real-life Rhett to lust after.

The newest girl to join our friend group rushed up and tossed her lunch tray onto the table. Peach juice splattered everywhere.

"Sorry I'm late," Jane Austin said, taking the stack of napkins I handed her and sopping up the mess. "What'd I miss?"

"Nothing important," Karen said. "Where've you been?"

"I got cornered by Mrs. Rosenberg. She's putting together a senior prom planning committee and she wants *me* to run it." She beamed at us then dug into her Salisbury steak. The oily thing skidded away from her fork like it was still alive and trying to escape.

A petite white girl barely over five feet, Jane Austin had brown eyes, chocolate brown hair, and almost the same name as my favorite author. She also had a wicked case of acne. Way worse than mine. Her pimples didn't keep people away, though, and she was super popular. With her dad in the Army and her family moving around so much, she'd learned to out-pep the pep squad and spackle on the charm as thick as cake frosting, leaving everyone with no choice but to be her friend.

Including me.

I gave her a grin like running the prom committee was *the* most exciting thing anyone could ever ask her to do.

Karen snorted, not nearly as impressed. "You're not going to say yes. It's a thankless job, and a big headache."

Jane waved off Karen's gloom. "I don't mind. If I'm in charge, I can run the prom the way I want. There's a lot to figure out. Theme, colors and what kind of music. Band or disc jockey, stuff like that."

Sounded like a lot of work, though she chirped about it like the happiest little worker bee in the hive.

Barbie weighed in. "Hiring a band would be expensive."

"I vote for a deejay," I said, especially if it meant he'd play a lot of my favorite performer, Elton John.

"We can have Minutemen figurines on the tables as centerpieces. We'll get Spirit of '76 bunting, and Liberty Bells hanging overhead." Jane's eyes gleamed with Bicentennial fervor. "And everyone could wear red, white, and blue gowns and tuxes."

Karen scoffed. "That would be hideous."

Barbie frowned. "I like that idea."

"I like it too," I said, as perky as the lady in the *Irish Spring* soap commercial, though I really didn't care. I agreed mostly to stick it to Karen.

"We can discuss everything at the meeting. No idea will be turned away." Jane grinned around a mouthful of peaches. "So what d'ya say, who's gonna join me and help out?" She ran her gaze over each of us, a gleam in her eyes. "Donna? Linda G? Deidre?"

I choked on the last bite of my mac-and-cheese. Jane had joined eight hundred clubs and committees in the three months since she'd moved here, while I'd joined exactly zero from kindergarten to senior year. I wasn't about to start now.

Jane's smile slipped a bit. "C'mon, Deidre. I could use someone fun like you helping me out." She dabbed a napkin to her lips. "All committee members get to go to prom for free."

That sure added incentive to change my mind. I looked down at my empty tray. I'd eaten every scrap, crumb, and morsel of food. So much for willpower. What good would a free ticket be if I couldn't control my eating? At this rate, I'd never reach my goal and get a prom date.

The bell shrilled, saving me from an answer, though I suspected Jane's efforts at persuasion had just begun.

The cafeteria exploded in noise as everyone gathered their things and flew out of the room. We abandoned Jane to finish her lunch alone. Linda tucked Rhett into her knapsack with the more boring books she needed for class and left, followed by Barbie and Karen. Donna and I took our trays to the tray return window.

"I'm glad you're on a diet, too," she said, tossing her wadded up napkins into the trash barrel. "We should go to that new exercise place at the summit. It's for women only, no guys allowed. They've got machines that pound the fat off and you don't have to do any work. The first visit's free, and the membership fee is cheap 'cuz everyone's got New Year's resolutions to lose weight." She slid her tray through the slot to the kitchen. "Let's give it a try, Dee."

I liked that she called me Dee. I liked everything about Donna. She was friendly and kind, with an upturned nose and wavy brunette hair. And she always dressed like a million bucks. The thing I liked best was the way she included me. I didn't want to disappoint her so I said yes, though I could never afford what the exercise place must cost, even the cheap fee.

We settled on a date for our visit then went our separate ways, Donna to art class, me to my locker, to grab my books for the final periods of the day.

Getting to those classes required a perilous trek down a connecting passageway between two corridors. Sunlight spilled through the floor-to-ceiling windows, making the hallway's average temperature about three hundred degrees, so everyone called the passageway the Desert.

Guys known as Desert Rats lined both sides of the hallway, staring at girls and making gross comments. Sometimes I saw Mr. Meager and other men teachers here too, pretending to shoot the breeze with the boys, when they were really ogling the girls.

I moved as fast as I could through the crushing mob. A goony kid in a green paisley shirt nudged a fellow rat and pointed at me, snickering.

"You're fat," Goony Kid threw my way.

My cheeks flamed but no way would I show those judgmental jerks they'd hit the target. "You're ignorant," I lobbed back.

My older brother Jay taught me that comeback. As it was a truth universally acknowledged that bullies and name-callers weren't too bright and wouldn't know the meaning of the word *ignorant* if a dictionary open to the definition smacked them in the face, I'd skedaddled long before they figured out they'd been insulted.

I made it to my next class surprisingly on time, French with Mrs. English. Last period would be English with Miss French. I understood the irony of their names. I *relished* the irony.

I didn't relish French class though. After three years, I hadn't progressed beyond *Je m'appelle Deidre.* You'd think with my French heritage on my mother's side I could speak the language, but nope. It didn't help that Mrs. English's entire lesson plan consisted of her flipping through the newspaper, cutting out coupons and commenting on current events.

Today's topic was the US Postal Service. "The price of stamps is going up to thirteen cents," she said, the newsprint rustling angrily as she turned the page. "It's outrageous."

Nobody cared and nobody listened. Although, I did get a head start on my homework while she sat there reporting the news so the class wasn't a complete waste of time.

The bell finally rang and I moved on to English, my favorite class, even if it wasn't Honors English, where I probably should've been. No Project kid was put in Honors anything, except smarty pants Lars Quigley, who was in Honors everything and was expected to go on to Great Things. The pride of our entire neighborhood rested on that kid's pompous shoulders.

I reached the classroom and squeezed myself into the fat girl's torture device known as the combined desk-chair. Attached to the chair on one side with metal bars, the desk part was barely high enough to fit a toddler's thighs, never mind mine.

Seated and stuck, I flipped *Great Expectations* open to the chapters we'd be discussing today. We'd started the book before winter break and I'd already finished, but I went over the pages anyway while my classmates yapped about what they got for Christmas and how they went drinking at the park last weekend, despite it being only ten degrees.

Ruthie Cullen popped through the door and I watched her slip her skinny butt easily into the desk-chair across the aisle. She had tangled black hair and a beaky nose, and wore a black turtleneck, blue jeans miniskirt, black tights, and cork platform shoes as tall as stilts.

"Whatcha looking at?" she snapped, her voice deep, like Bea Arthur from the TV show *Maude*.

I stiffened. Ruthie didn't live in my neighborhood but she was tougher than any Project kid I knew. She'd have no problem cutting out my heart with whatever weapon she could get her hands on.

In the interest of keeping the peace, I mumbled, "Nothing," and went back to reading about Miss Havisham's ill-fated attempt to light the fire.

Miss French hurried in as the bell rang. The smell of cigarettes and *Breck* crème rinse followed her like a shadow. She had thick auburn hair and looked like Mary Tyler Moore in a belted top and flared pants the color of my marshmallow shoes. The tallest teacher in school, she'd played basketball at Vassar and could've gone on to a sports career if she wasn't a girl. Instead, she ended up teaching high school English to a bunch of non-honors slobs like me.

She took a U-turn before we began our classwork, talking about what to expect in the spring semester. I half-listened, but perked up when she announced, "In March, we'll begin a creative writing unit. We'll be reading and critiquing poems and short stories, and you'll get a chance to write some stories yourself."

Most of the kids groaned but I beamed. I hated poetry with a fierce passion, so that would be no fun. But writing short stories? Yes, please.

I'd only wanted two things in my life. To be skinny, and to become a writer someday. Well, three things if you counted wanting to move out of the Project, but I had no control over that. Dieting I could do. And writing I could do too.

I had no idea where my interest in writing had come from. Mom loved reading, but she couldn't write anything beyond letters to the housing authority, telling them everything they were doing wrong and how she could fix it. None of my siblings liked to write either, only me, which made me the family oddball, the neighborhood weirdo, and even an oddity to my teachers, who preferred students who excelled at long division and regurgitating boring facts instead of writing stories during school.

Now, my teacher was giving permission to write about imaginary worlds *for* class.

I couldn't wait.

Chapter 4

Family Dinner & Other Forms of Torture

"Thought I'd try something new for the new year," Mom said when I entered the kitchen. She poked at some kind of meat smothered in onions and sizzling in the frying pan. "What do you think?"

I didn't know what to think. The onions I recognized. Their enticing smell had invaded the entire house. The meat? Not a clue. "What is it?"

"Liver and onions." She laughed at my grossed out grimace. "What? It's full of protein and nutrients. I read an article that girls your age don't get enough iron and that's why so many in your generation are anemic."

She turned off the gas flame under the skillet. I doubted there would be many anemia-fighting nutrients left. The liver had gone from dark red to gray to charcoal. The onions had blackened too and stuck to the pan.

"No thanks. Not hungry." A lie. A big one. I'd been on my diet for a week and a half and hunger pangs rumbled in my stomach loud enough to break the sound barrier. But I'd lost two more pounds—Bicentennial minus three—and I was determined not to slow the momentum.

Mom's left eyebrow shot up in surprise, like Mr. Spock on *Star Trek*. "Well, hungry or not, you're eating. I will not have you keel over from anemia, or worse. Not on my watch."

Discussion closed, she navigated around our dog Marco, who sniffed the green tile floor for stray crumbs, then she reached into the cupboard above the stove for plates. The overhead light shone on her thick black hair, giving it a blueish sheen. Though I'd been told I had a pretty face, usually followed by *if only you'd lose weight*, I was in no way as beautiful as her—trim figure, perfect eyesight, glowing tan skin, and shiny hair, like my siblings and her parents.

I was as freckled, nearsighted, and dark blonde as my dad's relatives. Dad might've been blond once too, but his hair had turned as white as a cotton ball when he was only twenty, so no one really knew. I liked to imagine he got trapped in a haunted house and the ghosts scared his hair white, though there was probably a more boring explanation.

"Set the table." Mom thrust a stack of plates into my hands. "And tell your father dinner's ready."

I didn't ask why she couldn't tell Dad herself. They hadn't spoken to each other directly since 1968 and I doubted they'd start now. I was supposed to meet Donna at the exercise salon at seven, so in the interest of moving things along, I did as instructed.

We gathered in the dining room of our townhouse-style apartment, a fancy way to describe our two-story box of six small rooms and one bathroom. All of us were home for once, even my older brother Jay, who had a night off from the department store where he worked as assistant manager.

Chairs scraped the tile as we sat at the table Gramps Boudreau had once sliced in half with an electric saw as he cut planks to cover our windows during a hurricane. You'd think Gramps would've known better, being a carpenter and all, but I suspected he was as good at his job as my mother was at cooking.

No one spoke as we ate. Well, Chrissy rarely spoke anyway. A thirteen-year-old carbon copy of Mom, my sister's silence as she ate was nothing new. Neither was my mother's. As soon as her fanny hit the chair, she opened a paperback called *The Princess Bride* and disappeared into the book's pages. Mom was *always* reading. Didn't matter what, romance, mystery, science fiction, she devoured everything, except for snooty literature that was supposed to be good for you, like *War & Peace*.

I usually read too, but tonight I sat down with the thick, spiral-bound notebook Mom picked up at Woolworth's for 79 cents and had given to me for Christmas. She'd written *The Great American Novel* on the front cover in black magic marker. Though I wrote all the time, I hadn't gotten anywhere near completing a novel, great or otherwise. Hadn't finished any of the thousand short stories I'd started either.

Now, with a class assignment as incentive, I swore I'd write the best story I could and finish it too. Something with a Bicentennial theme, perhaps. I took out a pen and flipped the notebook over with the spiral on the right (more comfortable for lefthanded me) and jotted down ideas as I ate.

Or tried to eat. The instant mashed potatoes from our monthly USDA Surplus Food shipment weren't bad, even the charred onions were tolerable, but the liver was as tough as one of my dad's leather work shoes.

Which posed a problem for the old man. He had no teeth and had to gum each leathery piece. His mood, already foul thanks to several beers and a few whiskey nips from his not-so-secret stash in the kitchen cupboard, turned volcanic. He grumbled and complained about every bite. Mom ignored him and I did my best to ignore him too.

Suddenly, the telephone rang.

Everyone jumped. Dad cut off mid-grumble. With good reason. A phone call at any time night or day usually meant only one thing. A bill collector on the other end of the line. A bill collector from Home Loan Corporation in particular. Dad owed HLC gobs of money he never paid back and those persistent bastards (his words, not mine) browbeat anyone who answered their call, demanding their dough, and that's why no one moved as the phone shrilled again and again.

Finally, Mom thrust her book aside with a bleat of annoyance and dragged herself into the living room to pick up on the fifteenth ring. She squeezed the phone's handset, her posture a full body grimace, listening a moment, then her eyebrow shot up in surprise.

"It's for you." She looked toward Jay, sitting next to me at the table. "It's a girl."

Jay's face colored a bright red. Rusty let out a wolf whistle and I got all happy-squishy inside. The way Jay blushed, I suspected this girl on the phone was Someone Special. Someone who understood and appreciated Mom's philosophy that everybody was different, and every body different too. Including Jay.

Born with a birth defect called kyphosis, he had long, skinny legs, curved fingers, brittle bones and a hunched back, like his rib cage got turned sideways. I remembered some jerk at a playground saying Jay looked like he'd stuck a football under his shirt. He'd had a thousand operations at Shriners Hospital since he was a baby to straighten his legs and spine, but the doctors never could make that bump on his back go away.

Mom called him breakable, his bones as brittle as glass. Dad called him a cripple in a whispery voice so low you could barely hear the word. Like, "Jay does okay for a *cripple*." Or, "Jay wasn't drafted for Vietnam because he's a *cripple*." My grandfather called him a lost cause and told Mom to put Jay in a home when he was born and forget him. I called him my sometimes annoying but always funny and devastatingly handsome big brother who deserved a girl who'd like him for who he was, differences and all.

Like maybe this girl on the phone.

"Go on, Jay." Mom held out the handset, a tremble in her voice. "We won't eavesdrop."

Who was she kidding? We had just one phone, a standard black model we rented from New England Telephone because they were too expensive to buy. It weighed a thousand pounds and sat on a bookcase in the living room exactly three feet from the dining room. What else could we do but eavesdrop?

Except, Jay cleverly foiled us nosy Nancys. He hustled over and snatched the phone from Mom, cradle and all, and carried it as far as the cord tethering it to the wall would stretch. He disappeared into the stairwell, where he hunkered down on a step and spoke to his mysterious caller in whispers.

Disappointed, we returned to our meals. Dad went back to gumming his food and bitching. Mom picked up where she left off in *The Princess Bride* and continued to ignore him.

I imagined my parents must've been "someone special" to each other at one time. When they were young. Before kids and the stress of Jay's surgeries. Before the Project and the bill collectors. Before the nips. Before the love that brought them together had faded.

That happy-squishy feeling I'd had for Jay turned sour. A sad, bittersweet emotion tickled my belly instead. I smothered it by shoving a big, gloppy helping of mashed potatoes into my mouth.

A short time later, Mom drove our blue, 1966 Chevy Impala past a boarded up gas station that had shut down during the energy crisis and dropped me off at the strip mall where New You Figure Salon was located.

I arrived a little after seven. Donna hadn't arrived at all. I paced back and forth in front of the salon's entrance, hoping she hadn't stood me up. And trying to keep warm. The temperature had dropped to the teens. The tip of my nose froze and I probably burned a million calories shivering, if Karen's mother was right about that cold-making-you-burn-calories thing.

Fifteen minutes later, still no Donna. People came and went from Gino's Pizzeria on the ground floor. A blast of warmth rushed out each time someone opened the door, beckoning me to come in. So did the tantalizing smell of pizza, setting off a riot in my stomach no leathery liver could ever quell. I got so cold (and hungry) I almost gave in to temptation.

Finally, a metallic green, two-door Ford Pinto sailed into the parking lot and rocked to a stop. Donna hopped out of the car. Relief rushed through me. She *hadn't* stood me up.

"Sorry," she burbled, hurrying over. "I had to finish my chores or there'll be hell to pay when my mother gets home."

I answered with a shrug because I didn't want her to think I was mad at her for being late. Plus, my lips were too numb from cold to speak.

The figure salon took up the strip mall's entire second floor. I followed Donna up a steep, dark flight of stairs and we stepped into a big, bright, and loud room. Exercise machines roared, women wearing colorful Danskin leotards chattered, and "Saturday Night" by the Bay City Rollers played from speakers hidden in the ceiling. The place reeked with enough talcum powder, hairspray, and sweat to encourage my growling stomach to pipe down.

We approached the check-in counter. A prune-faced, fortyish woman in a pink leotard and matching tights bustled over. Her eyes flicked over me, gleaming with so much anticipation I expected her to bang a bell and shout, "We've got a live one here!"

She reined in her enthusiasm to greet us with a mildly inquisitive, "Evening, girls. What brings you to New You Salon?"

"I'm here 'cuz I'm fat," Donna blurted.

Pink lady tittered then gazed at me with a *well, obviously* expression that annoyed me so much I let my speak-now-and-never-hold-your-peace monster out. "Scientists say I have to lose weight or I'll pull Mars out of its orbit. Who am I to argue with scientists?"

She nodded like she hadn't heard anything after *I have to lose weight.* "This is certainly the place to do it." She offered an encouraging smile. "You have such a pretty face, let's make the rest of you pretty too."

I cringed. Cringed some more when she gave us a clipboard to sign our name and Donna scribbled *Linda Blair.* Everyone knew who Linda Blair was, after she got famous spewing pea soup in the movie *The Exorcist.* Donna might as well have written Liza Minelli or Betty Ford.

I wrote down my real name because I couldn't do anything else. Mom had drilled honesty into us kids from the time we were little, though the lessons had yet to get through Rusty's thick skull. Don't lie was one of the rules my mother insisted we follow, along with don't get pregnant (for us girls), don't get anyone pregnant (for the boys), and don't break the law (for Rusty).

And the most important rule of all—don't cry.

Not just a rule, the family motto. A Daly never cries. No matter what happened to tempt the waterworks to flow, a skinned knee, a sad TV show, my dad ragging on us, we weren't supposed to cry. Mom would say, "Don't start or I'll cry too," so we'd swallow the tears and carry on.

Donna and I hung up our coats then Pink Lady led us to the machines. I expected to be moving a lot so I left my marshmallow shoes at home and wore my cheapo (but comfortable) K-Mart brand Trax sneakers, a pair of knit pants, and a baggy tee shirt. Donna wore button-fly chinos, a silky print blouse, jingling bracelets on each wrist, and full makeup, as if heading to a nightclub and not a date with an exercise machine.

"Spend a few minutes on the roller." Pink Lady patted what looked like a giant wooden hair curler. "Then try out the other equipment and an exercise session if you want. When you're done, come see me and we'll have a chat."

Which really meant come back for a sales pitch.

Donna clicked the "on" switch and the machine rumbled to a start. I did the same, and the wooden rollers went *chook-a-chook* into action. Unsure what to do, I copied the woman at the next machine and pressed my thigh to the rollers. They pressed back, massaging my leg like a ruthless baker viciously kneading a piece of dough.

"What's this supposed to do?" I yelled to Donna, hoping she could hear me over the machine and Cher's "Gypsies, Tramps, and Thieves" blasting from the speakers.

"It'll loosen the fat and make it wash away," she hollered back.

I'd never been good at science (Mr. Meager could attest to that), but that didn't seem right. How could the fat break loose and magically wash away? Where would it go? With my luck, my thigh fat would float up to my heart and kill me. I was committed to losing weight, but not *that* committed.

We moved to the next machine, a belt that went around our butts and vibrated our bodies so hard our voices sounded like we were underwater. Next, the stationary bicycle, or the humping bicycle as Donna called it. Leave it to her to make it sound dirty, though the way my back arched and my pelvis thrust upward as the seat and handlebars moved in and out, did feel kind of obscene.

We spent less and less time on each machine as we moved along. We didn't even try the table that wiggled your body like a worm and went right to the floor exercises. I got down on hands and knees and lifted my leg to the side like the other ladies, doing the aptly named "Hydrant." We looked so much like a pack of dogs peeing on a fire hydrant all at the same time, I couldn't help laughing. Which earned me some supremely dirty looks.

Donna flopped onto her back on the cushioned floor mat. "This is boring. Let's go get pizza."

I didn't argue. We snatched our coats and fled, ignoring Pink Lady calling for us to stop as we darted down the stairs. Minutes later, I sat across from Donna in a booth at Gino's with a can of sugar-free Tab in front of me and a hot-from-the-oven slice of pepperoni pizza on a paper plate.

"What a waste of time." Donna bit into her pizza crust with gusto. "I thought that place would be fun, but it's nothing but sweaty old ladies. We'll have to find some other way to lose weight."

Not eating pizza would be a dandy way to do it, but I figured I'd earned this treat. Not from exercising at the salon. I'd burned more calories going up and down the stairs than getting beat up by those machines. I vowed to eat only this one slice, though we'd gotten a large pizza and it would be a battle.

"Are you going to join Jane's prom committee?" I asked, taking a bite and reveling in the taste of cheese and spicy pepperoni tingling on my tongue. Of all the basic food groups, pepperoni was my favorite.

Donna nodded. "It'll be fun. You'll join the committee if I do, right?"

She said that more like a command than a question. When I began hanging out with Donna, I quickly discovered she defined all activities as either fun or boring. I also realized she needed to drag someone along to experience the fun or boredom with her.

With me as her designated dragee, I couldn't say no. "I guess I'll join. Jane says we'll get our prom tickets for free."

"I hope our dates go for free too." Her sunny expression dimmed. "*If* we can get dates." She pushed her plate away. "Ugh, whose idea was it to order pizza?"

Hers, but I neglected to point that out.

"I got an idea." She perked up. "I'll have a Valentine's party at my house and invite a ton of guys. It'll be the perfect opportunity to scope out prom candidates."

"One problem." I plucked a piece of pepperoni off the slice and popped it into my mouth. "Won't most guys have dates that night?"

"A lot won't. They'll want to come to a party with other people who don't have dates and who knows, maybe they'll meet someone special there." She smiled slyly. "*Me* in particular."

"You think of everything, don't you?"

"I do. I'm not as stupid as my father says I am." She dragged her plate toward her and picked up her pizza again. "It'll be the coolest party. We'll have so much fun. Maybe I'll even find *the* guy to pop my cherry."

My nose twitched. She loved that phrase. I did not. Not that I was a prude. I'd known about sex since I was eleven, when Mom sat me down and read a Kotex pamphlet she'd sent away for, complete with illustrations. I'd enthusiastically soaked it up and longed to put my knowledge into practice. So I understood Donna's eagerness to do the dirty deed, but did she have to be so crude about it?

She started on her third slice of pizza and turned the topic to party decorations and who to invite to the big event.

"Oh, and we gotta dress up. I'll wear red, like Cupid. What about you?" She looked me over with a critical eye. "Something to show off your tiny waist, I hope."

"My waist? I wouldn't exactly call it tiny." Just oddly slimmer than the rest of me.

"Are you kidding? You have an hourglass figure, Dee. I'd *kill* to have a waist so small. But guys won't notice it if you don't wear clothes to show it off. You need to wear a tight top to my party, preferably red. Case closed."

Fashion critique complete, she attacked her last slice of pizza.

It took a lot of willpower, but I didn't eat another bite. Valentine's Day was less than a month away. If I might meet a potential prom date and possible cherry-popper at her party, I had to be good on my diet. Especially if I was going to wear a tight top.

Donna's orders.

CHAPTER 5

Where Ambition Goes To Die

MY HOMEROOM TEACHER TOOK attendance then got up from his desk and handed me a note written in the finest penmanship I'd ever seen. Every letter perfectly drawn, perfectly spaced, perfectly slanted. Not a single smudge. Pretty impressive to a left-handed individual like me, who diligently smudged every page as if it was my mission here on Earth.

The words I read weren't nearly as impressive:

Dear Miss Daly,

I would like to speak with you about an important matter. Please come to my office at the beginning of period 7 today.

Yours truly, Eloise Clutch.

Uh-oh. Mrs. Clutch. My guidance counselor. Who I'd been avoiding since freshman year, when I darted into her office when I got sick from my period and needed somewhere to throw up. Unfortunately, the somewhere I chose were her shoes, which I heard were Italian and she'd just bought them. But hey, was it my fault she stuck her feet so close to the trash can and in the line of fire?

The first period bell rang. I fretted about why she wanted to see me all the way to science class. Mrs. Clutch had neither guided nor counseled me on anything my entire high school career. I'd never consulted her when choosing my courses, either. Since I couldn't get into honors classes, I simply chose the ones I felt would be the most interesting, and boy, what a mistake where Principles of Law in junior year was concerned.

Lunch rolled around, much to my empty stomach's relief. I hadn't lost a single ounce in more than a week, so I'd skipped my usual Cap'n Crunch cereal and opted for an allegedly calorie-burning grapefruit for breakfast instead, as Karen's mother had suggested. Well, I ate *half* a grapefruit. My spoon kept hitting juice like striking oil and I squirted myself in the eye so many times I finally gave up.

I chose spaghetti with meat sauce, the less dubious of the delicacies offered today and slid my tray to the register, where my lunch lady nemesis interrogated me for sixteen hours.

I held up both hands in surrender. "If I cry Uncle and confess to the Lindbergh baby kidnapping, will you just punch my card?"

She did, reluctantly, her lips pursed like she'd been sucking lemons for a year. Maybe she had. How did I know what she did in her spare time?

Mentally crowing in victory, I joined my friends at our table.

Donna frowned at my lunch selection. "You should only eat the sauce. Spaghetti is starch and starch has a million calories."

I suspected the sauce had lots of calories too, based on its greasy sheen, but I followed Donna's lead and painstakingly parted the meat sauce from the spaghetti with my fork until they were separated by a thin space on the tray like East and West Germany.

Karen chewed on a brownie and watched with amusement. Barbie watched with no amusement at all. She rolled her eyes and stepped up onto a soapbox like Gloria Steinem to complain about girls never being allowed to be happy with who we were or even eat school lunch without dissecting our food like a science experiment.

Jane arrived late from her twenty thousand other commitments as Barbie concluded her rant and I indulged in my first bite of lunch. A disappointing bite. Tomato sauce without spaghetti was an abomination and not very filling, but in the hope of getting back on the right track with the weight loss train, I ignored the spaghetti calling to me in all its delicious starchiness and pushed my tray away.

Jane inhaled her own meal, chattering about the prom committee with her mouth full. She'd succeeded in recruiting Donna and me, but despite a blitzkrieg of compliments and cajoling, she couldn't get the others to sign on, even with the incentive of free tickets.

"We'll be meeting the first Wednesday in February," she said as the bell rang and we picked up our trays. "We have a full agenda, so don't be late."

I wouldn't forget, and I absolutely would be late. I couldn't help it. *Running Late* was my middle name, or so my grandmother joked. Grandma Boudreau also said I'd be late for my own funeral, though she wouldn't be around to see it, unless she lived to be one hundred and sixty. Not an impossibility, considering she'd been embalming herself through copious intake of gin martinis for fifty years.

Seventh period arrived and so did my appointment. I strolled past the main office and a phalanx of middle-aged white ladies named Edith and Ethel to Mrs. Clutch's small office at the end of Guidance Row.

She sat behind an old-fashioned, heavy-looking wooden desk, with a spider plant and a dozen eight-by-ten pictures of identical looking blonde boys with bowl haircuts on top. She wore a flowered dress with a lacy collar and smelled like the Aqua Net hairspray she used to cement her blondish-gray hair into place. A pair of glasses dangled from a beaded chain around her neck.

"Deidre Daly?"

She mispronounced my name as *Dee-dree*, her voice going low on the *dree*, like a foghorn, and she eyed me with a pinched expression that said she hadn't forgotten about me barfing on her shoes. Not for one second.

"How are you?" She directed me to a metal folding chair beside her desk.

The chair creaked as I sat. "I'm okay." As long as this chair didn't collapse.

She pulled a manila folder from the top of a big stack and flipped it open. "How's your family? Your mother and father and…" She balanced her glasses on the tip of her nose and skimmed the papers in the folder. "Your brothers? What're their names?"

Was this a test? Start simple with my brothers' names and move up to more complicated questions like how much do you weigh and how many nips can your father consume if he's riding a train going fifty miles an hour?

"Your brother Russell? He's a junior?"

Her thin eyebrows went up and I could almost see the wheels turning in her head. Deidre, seventeen, Rusty sixteen, both of us born in December, barely a year apart. Irish twins some people called that. Including my father, who'd laugh like a loon after he said it.

"And your older brother, Jeremiah Junior. I remember him," she said, her voice grim, like how could I not remember your odd looking brother?

Unaware of my sudden urge to kick her in the shins, Mrs. Clutch flipped through the pages, making increasingly dismayed clucking sounds. I craned my neck to see my grades, the page that elicited the majority of the clucks. Finally, she closed the folder and sat back. Her chair creaked as loud as mine and I pictured both of our chairs collapsing like a skit on *The Carol Burnett Show*.

I laughed. Couldn't help it. I *always* laughed. I laughed when happy or nervous, even when sad. And always, always at the most inappropriate moment. I bet never being allowed to cry had something to do with that, as if the held-in tears had to find some way to bust out and chose laughter as the way to go.

Mrs. Clutch's eyebrows shot up again, but thankfully she ignored my giggling. "Dee-dree, I called you here today because time is short and we need to talk about your future plans."

"You mean, my plans after graduation?" Why hadn't she dragged me in here to talk about this sooner? "That's simple. I'm going to college."

Something few Project kids did. Something no one on either side of my family ever had. I'd be the first, thank you very much.

She blinked rapidly, as if I'd announced I was going to fly to the moon. "Do you mean you plan to attend secretarial school?"

"Why would I do that? I can't type and looking at shorthand characters makes me dizzy." Plus I was way too heavy to be dandled on the boss's knee, which everyone knew was part of a secretary's job. My mother found that out the hard way. "I'm going to *college*, college. I want to be a writer." I said that proudly and loud, to make sure she heard me.

"Oh dear." She released a gusty sigh, like *writer* was the most problematic career choice she'd ever encountered. "I'll be honest, Dee-dree. College isn't the best path for you. Your grades... They simply aren't good enough. Frankly, I doubt any college would accept you."

A lava rock seared my belly. Was she saying I was too dumb to get into college?

"But it's always been my dream." My mother's dream, actually. Mainly because my grandfather wouldn't let *her* go. She wanted to be a journalist, but Gramps said girls didn't go to college, they got married. Sometimes I thought Mom's obsession with me furthering my education was an intricate revenge plot to get back at Gramps, with me as the weapon.

Mrs. Clutch sighed again. "An admirable goal. But in my experience, young people from that neighborhood don't do well in a university environment."

I flinched. *That neighborhood.* Two words I'd heard before to describe my home, in exactly that way. Two words smug people like Mrs. Clutch with her Aqua Net hair and fancy Italian shoes said in their oh-so-patronizing tone because people from *that neighborhood* were stupid as well as poor and would never figure out she was looking down her nose at them.

"So, I shouldn't even try?"

She heard my anger. I could tell by the way she rapidly tapped her pen on the desk, as if signaling for help in Morse code. "Certainly you may *try.* You'll need to fill out the applications. Quickly. The deadline for most schools is the end of January. That's creeping up."

"Already finished." A gigantic lie. The application to State University and the other colleges my mother wanted me to apply to sat atop my bedroom bureau where I'd abandoned them on New Year's Eve, lonely, neglected, and nowhere near complete.

"Did you fill out the FAFSA too?"

"The what-sa?"

"The financial aid forms," she said patiently.

I shook my head and she let out another windy sigh. I sure wouldn't want her around in a blackout because she'd blow out all the candles.

"You'll need financial aid forms to supplement your applications." She pulled a packet of papers from one of the metal inbox trays lined up on the windowsill. "In addition to government grants, some colleges provide aid and scholarships for people from your background and living situation, although..." She peered at me over the top of her glasses. "Those slots are limited and reserved for only the most competitive students."

The lava rock in my stomach sank all the way to my ankles. *Most competitive* meant a pompous boy with perfect grades named Lars Quigley. He'd scoop up every available grant and scholarship on his way to Harvard or Yale or whatever snooty school threw open their doors to welcome him, leaving the rest of us in *that neighborhood* in the dust.

She stood and pushed a fistful of FAFSA into my mitts. "I wish you luck, Miss Daly. But please, don't get your hopes up."

I dragged out of her office, too bummed out to go to English class for the final minutes of the period.

On the school bus, I gazed out the window at the big houses that flashed by as we zoomed toward home. Mrs. Clutch had gotten me to doubt myself even more than usual, a major feat since self-doubt was my constant companion.

Deidre Daly, average student, average SATs, average grades, average everything except my weight. Nothing to make a college admissions officer jump to stamp YES! on my application.

And what if by some miracle I did get accepted? How would I pay for it?

I took out the financial aid forms I'd jammed into my coat pocket and skimmed the crumpled pages. My gaze stuck on the words *Family Income*. I didn't know the exact amount Mom and Dad made. Barely enough to scrape by. Low enough to need government surplus food and free school lunch, not low enough to be eligible for Welfare, like other families I knew. Maybe too high to qualify for any aid and scholarships Lars didn't snag for himself.

I wanted to bawl but I laughed instead. A bitter, *we are not amused* laugh. Maybe I should leave those college applications sitting on my bureau uncompleted. Save myself the cost of postage stamps.

Mrs. Clutch said it herself, why bother to get my hopes up?

❋ ❁ ❋ ❀

"I'm wicked cold," Chrissy said, stamping her feet for emphasis.

Of course she was cold. We stood outside on a bitter January Saturday, near the Suds 'n Fluff laundromat at the front of Foley Plaza. The sun blazed from a cloudless sky but did little to lift the temperature above twenty-five degrees.

"Imagine how cold the real soldiers must've been," I said. "They had to drag those cannons all the way from New York to Massachusetts."

I nodded toward Adams Street and the men reenacting General Knox's troops bringing the artillery surrendered at Fort Ticonderoga to Boston. A dozen cannons supported by wheeled gun carriages rumbled over the pavement as they passed. The men pretending to be Revolutionary War soldiers looked cold too, in their Colonial Army garb—knickers, stockings, and tri-corner hats. Two young men playing "Yankee Doodle" on fifes marched at the front, their long hair tied back in a ponytail with a piece of white linen.

"I guess so," Chrissy grumped. "But why couldn't they do this parade when it's warmer?"

That was a lot of words for my sister. I owed her a full explanation.

"They're trying to be historically accurate. The British had planted themselves in Boston and weren't going to leave. George Washington needed ammunition right away to help push the Redcoats out. So as soon as Ticonderoga surrendered, the soldiers marched through the winter of 1776 to get the cannons to Boston."

Chrissy yawned. She wasn't as excited by history as me. She'd never read any of Mom's Victoria Holt or James Michener books and she never went near anything with romance in it. She liked to read of course. My mother would've returned her for a refund if she didn't. But Chrissy preferred books about animals and women scientists to the swoony adventures I gobbled up.

I glanced back to Mom, standing with my brother Jay several feet behind us. Jay worked at Cully's department store on the other end of Foley Plaza as assistant manager. He'd taken a break to watch the reenactors with us. He wore a winter jacket and a scarf. Mom wore a speckled gray wool coat but no hat. She never wore a hat. I suspected she liked to show off her shiny hair without a single strand of gray, though she'd turned fifty last fall.

I'd given her the financial aid forms as soon as she got home from work last night, along with Mrs. Clutch's dire news about my prospects for college.

Her response? "Horseshit."

She rarely swore, so I knew she was really mad. Like, march up to Northside High and demand my guidance counselor's resignation mad, which she might have done if the school wasn't closed for the weekend.

She'd channeled her anger into badgering me to finish my applications while she filled out the financial forms. She hunkered down at the kitchen table and I tucked myself into a corner of the couch.

Dad turned his attention from *The Rockford Files* on TV to peer at me from his Archie Bunker chair across the room. "What're you doing? Writing one of your stories?"

I scowled. He'd reached the four beers, several nips, and a slurred voice portion of the evening, but I heard the mockery in his question loud and clear. "I'm filling out college applications, if you must know."

He snorted. "You got high hopes, Deidre."

I shrugged, though he'd hit a nerve. After my downer of a conversation with Mrs. Clutch, I barely had hopes at all, high, low, or in between. But I dutifully completed the forms, cobbling together an essay about my unspectacular academic life and how living in the Project sucked, but that's the way it is, as Walter Cronkite would say, so pretty please let me go to college and fulfill my mother's fondest dreams.

Then Mom and I sat together at the table as she signed her name, swearing under penalty of death and dismemberment that everything she'd written on the forms was true.

We'd taken my applications to the post office in the flatiron building downtown this morning. I watched the lady behind the desk stamp each envelope and toss them into the mail bin, my future setting off on a perilous journey with an uncertain outcome, like Frodo and his ring. Would I make it? Would any of the colleges take a chance on me? Or would I fall into Mount Doom and be lost forever?

The cannons passed and so did the stragglers at the end. One of the reenactors, a guy of about twenty, waved and blew a kiss. Chrissy waved back but I was too embarrassed.

Jay pushed through the slush toward us, Mom at his side. "C'mon. We're going to Sam's Bakery for donuts. My treat."

My stomach said *yes please*, but my brain slammed the brakes. Guilt warred with my want-to-be-skinny ambitions as we walked past the plaza's many stores toward the bakery.

Mom fell back to walk beside me. An Agatha Christie paperback peeked out of her coat's pocket. Christie had died a couple weeks ago and Mom had chosen to mourn her by re-reading every one of her books, from *The ABC Murders* to *Witness for the Prosecution*.

"Stop worrying, Deidre." Mom looked at me, her eyes hidden behind cat's eye sunglasses. "You've been fretting since we left the post office."

"Fretting is my favorite pastime. I could make a career out of it."

"Well, stop." She playfully bumped her shoulder against mine. "You'll get in. You'll see. All those colleges will accept you and you'll have the happy problem of deciding which one to go to."

I accepted this with a grunt. I was beginning to think I had as much chance of getting into college as I had of going to the prom with the most popular boy in school.

Maybe I would have a donut. Or two.

To cheer myself up.

Part Two

February 1976

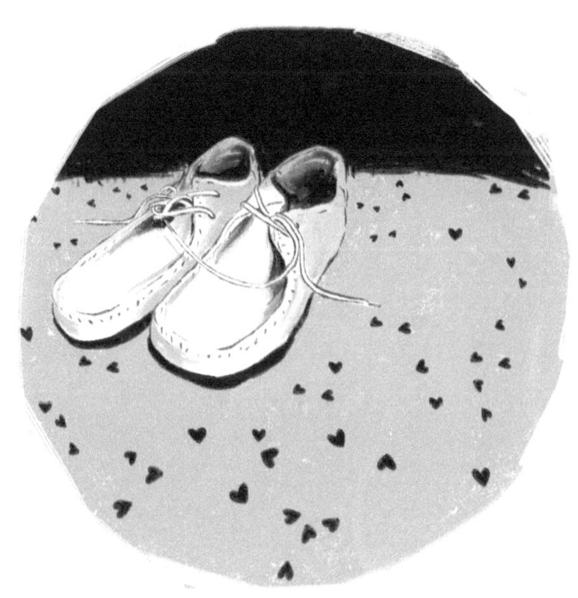

CHAPTER 6

The Third Period Period Incident

Seven pounds.

I'd lost a grand total of seven pounds since New Year's. Bicentennial minus seven. That should've made me happy. It didn't. The weight was coming off too slow. If I kept downing donuts and foraging in the kitchen cabinets for Twinkies and Ring-Dings and other sweet snacks, I'd never hit my goal by May.

It had snowed overnight (*after* the groundhog had predicted an early spring, the liar), and the sidewalk was slippery, making my trek down the hill treacherous. I got to the bottom as Demo Derby Gus fishtailed up to the bus stop, cranky, out of sorts, and feeling a headache coming on.

Homeroom and the first two periods dragged, and by the time I hurried on to third period, my temples throbbed. People pushed against each other in the hallway. I kept my eyes glued to the back of the guy in front of me, hoping today would be Deidre-is-invisible day, when this really cute blond guy who looked like Parker Stevenson stepped into my path.

I stopped my headlong rush and his face erupted in a dimpled smile that would make any normal girl's heart go pitter-pat but only managed to ping my suspicions. I read Stephen King's horror book *Carrie*. I knew cute guys didn't talk to girls like me unless they had something nefarious in mind.

"Yes?" I asked warily.

"Hi Miss Dolan," Cute Guy said. "I forgot my Paul Revere project at home. I was supposed to present in class today, but if it's okay, can I do it tomorrow?"

This? Again? For some reason, kids mistook me for one of the school's social studies teachers, Miss Dolan. She had a small waist like me, wore gold-rimmed glasses like mine, and had straight, blonde hair parted in the middle, also like me.

And there the resemblance ended. We weren't the twins from *The Parent Trap*, girls who looked so much alike they could switch places and nobody blinked. For one thing, Miss Dolan was *much* older than me (thirty, at least). She also had clear skin, was only a little plump, and had a weird habit of roaming around the school, staring at her feet as if she expected them to tell her the meaning of life.

So why did kids in her classes who should know what she looked like stop me in the halls, thinking I was her? Did she ever get stopped on her way to the teacher's lounge by people who thought she was me?

The whole thing would've been screamingly funny if I wasn't in such a foul mood. "Oh, that's too bad," I said, adding a fake smile. "Don't worry your pretty little head. Bring your project in when you can."

Cute Guy dimpled like crazy, blurted a relieved, "thank you," and hurried his cute fanny away.

I felt kind of bad about tricking him but put it out of my mind and continued on to cooking class, where our teacher Mrs. Baker greeted us with a cheery smile as we filed in.

"I've got a treat for you, girls." She wore a yellow dress and a frilly white apron, and she held up a well-used Betty Crocker cookbook. "Today we're making chocolate cake. From scratch."

She spoke with breathy glee, as if every girl in America would be guaranteed a successful life if we simply mastered this important skill.

She separated us into two groups at long tables on the cooking side of the room. Sewing machines and ironing boards took up the space on the other side. I'd taken sewing as an elective sophomore year, a bad choice that ended with my iron bursting into flames, a visit from the fire department, and me banned from handling any combustible appliances for the duration of my high school Home Economics career.

Mrs. Baker organized us into groups of four. She teamed me with Robin Samaria, Cindy Soderman, and a girl named Jessie Moron, and, honestly, if there was any last name just begging to be changed at Ellis Island, that was the one.

I hung back while my teammates circled the measuring cups and the mixing bowl like vultures inspecting a kill. Cindy even had vulture talons, long, sharp fingernails painted as red as blood. Jessie measured the flour and dumped it into the bowl. Robin followed with the sugar and chocolate powder.

Normally the chocolate smell would make my mouth water. Not today. Cindy cracked an egg. It plopped into the batter with a soft *thup*. Slimy goop dripped from the eggshell like spit. A sour wave of nausea rose up and my belly roiled. When Cindy crunched the shell to bits in a measuring cup with one of her vulture fingernails, I gagged.

Another egg went into the mix. Crack, *thup*, slimy drool. *Crunchhhh* into the measuring cup. My stomach flipped over and over like gymnast Olga Korbut going for Olympic gold.

Then...

Something worse. Something terrifying. A giant fist wrapped around my uterus and squeezed so tight my breath cut off.

Holy crapola. My period.

I winced and braced my hands on the table for support until the cramp subsided. No wonder I felt so moody and mad all morning. My damned period. I called it MDP for short and not "my friend" like some girls did. This belly-squeezing, blood-shooting, bloat-inducing, nauseating thing was no friend of mine. Excruciating and one hundred percent unexpected, because if I had a clue it was coming, believe me I would've skipped school and stayed home in bed.

Another hard squeeze gripped me, like someone trying to wring every drop of juice out of an orange. MDP had arrived more than a week early, and it'd arrived angry. Sometimes, my cramps were light and didn't bother me much. Other times, like now, they hit so hard it felt as if I was in labor with a fifty pound baby.

I kept spare sanitary pads in my pocketbook, but I didn't have spare anything else, like underwear. I had to get to the bathroom before the flood began and I bled through—*the* most humiliating thing that could ever happen to a girl in school.

"What's wrong?" Robin asked, gaping at me in horror. Probably from the sight of me sprawled across the table and practically drooling.

I peeped out of the crook of my arm. "Mrs. Baker, can I go to the bathroom?"

"*May* I go to the bathroom, Deidre," she said, smoothing her apron.

I groaned. This was no time for the grammar police. "May I go? Please?"

She sighed her permission and I rushed out so fast I forgot to get a hall pass. My handbag bounced against my hip as I raced down C corridor, aiming for the girls' bathroom at the end. I darted past the open door of Mr. Aboody's typing class. The *clackity-clacking* keys of thirty typewriters pounded into my throbbing brain.

I choked back a sob and kept moving. I hadn't gotten far when the next cramp struck. My belly contracted in on itself like a collapsing star. I gasped for breath. My legs trembled and my ears rang with a hollow, high-pitched shrill. Needles and pins prickled along my scalp. I went clammy all over. My fingers tingled. Fear folded over me, killing all other sensation.

I'm going to faint.

My brain droned like a hive of bees on the attack. Spots popped in front of my eyes and my knees turned to jelly. My vision closed, drawing me into a dark tunnel.

The bell rang as everything went black.

I woke up, stretched out on the cold and gritty floor. A murmur of anxious voices whirled around me. I swept the cobwebs from my brain and opened my eyes to see... Shoes. A *lot* of shoes. Every kind and every brand. Lace-up Oxfords, platforms, boots, and a variety of sneakers.

My cheeks burned. I'd fainted before, but always at home with only our dog Marco to see me flopped on the floor like a beached whale. Not with the entire school for an audience.

The sea of soles parted and a pair of brown penny loafers with shiny pennies in the slots stepped into view. Mr. Anger, the vice principal. A squat, roly-poly man with a fondness for plaid suitcoats with elbow patches, Mr. Anger bent down and helped me sit up against the lockers. The cool metal felt good against my sweaty back.

Mr. Anger said something. He had a whispery voice as soft as a pillow and I couldn't hear a single word.

"What?"

"I said, what happened? Are you on drugs? Are you pregnant?" This time he spoke loud enough to be heard down the hallway and halfway across the city. The crowd of gawkers broke into a hubbub of speculation and snickering.

I cringed, thinking I might faint again. How could I tell him I passed out because of cramps? How could I utter the word *period* in front of all these people? "No. I'm...I'm fine. I just need to go to the bathroom."

He took that with a nod and gripped my arm with both hands to help me up. I didn't have the strength to stand and he couldn't lift me. He looked around, a little frantic, then his eyes lit up.

"You. Come help this poor girl up," he said.

By *you* he meant one of the male gawkers, who pushed his broad shoulders through the crowd and two seconds later, I was on my feet. I wobbled, still woozy and weak-kneed. The gawker put his arm around me to hold me up. I trembled again. Not from fainting this time.

The object of my most secret desire held me in his arms.

Carl Werzbicki. The dreamy guy with an old man's name. The most popular boy in school. The guy I'd had a crush on since freshman year.

Big, broad, and muscular, he looked like actor Jeff Bridges, with blondish hair, blueish eyes, and the most scrumptiously kissable lips. He played offensive tackle on the football team and actually looked good in his letterman's jacket and not like a dopey jock.

Carl always had girls fawning over him and I doubted he'd ever noticed me. But he noticed me now, in all my hall-fainting, blobby splendor. I was as pale as a ghost, not to mention sweaty and let me say, whoever invented polyester should be shot at sunrise or sooner. The fabric didn't breathe, like cotton. Every part of me dripped with perspiration. My pants and blouse stuck to me like an onion's skin.

"Are you feeling better, dear?" Mr. Anger asked, his voice soft again.

"Much better, thanks." Except for wishing the floor would split open and swallow me whole.

He scooped my handbag off the floor and handed it to me, then turned to Carl. "Escort this young lady to her destination," he said, like I was waltzing off to a ball and not the toilet. The bell signaling the start of the next period rang and he swung on the spectators. "Move along, people. You've got classes to get to. Don't be tardy."

The crowd dutifully dispersed, laughing and whispering as they did so. Mr. Anger flashed me an encouraging smile, then he and his penny loafers tiptoed away, leaving me alone with Carl.

"Where to?" he asked.

Speech failed me so I pointed like a big dummy and he steered me down the corridor. He kept his arm around me the whole way. Not a tight hold, but tight enough. I feared I might faint again.

At the bathroom door, he released me with a simple, "Feel better," then he left.

I watched him go, my insides in an uproar, and not completely due to MDP. My hero. My glorious object of desire. Not that I could ever reveal that desire to him. He would never feel the same way about someone like me, especially not after my belly flop today.

Carl probably thought me the grossest girl on the planet, while I found him the most magnificent man in the world.

CHAPTER 7

Get A Job

I MANAGED TO MAKE it through MDP alive, though scarred forever by the humiliation of fainting in public.

Worse, fainting at *school*. In front of Carl, of all people. I skipped school the rest of the week, hoping the incident would die down and not live forever in Northside High infamy.

I'd like to say I did something productive on my days off, but I didn't do anything beyond trying (and failing) not to think about Carl, trying (and failing) not to eat too much, and generally moping about the catastrophe that was my life.

On Saturday, Mom got sick of my sulking and hauled me off the couch and told me it was time I got a job. Jay had called to say he'd heard the motel at Foley Plaza was hiring. They were desperate for help on the weekend shift, and I should apply *now*.

I had no chance to argue. When Mom and Jay teamed up to do something, it got done. And that's how I found myself in the lobby of the Eden Motor Lodge, filling out an application to be a chambermaid while Mom waited in the car, reading Ursula Le Guin's *The Dispossessed*.

The manager, a tall Black lady wearing a nametag that read Valerie, was with a customer so I waited in a chair by the picture window with the motel's name painted on it in cursive letters.

I moved an ashtray off a pile of magazines and thumbed through *Newsweek*, *Life*, and a copy of *People* from last August with my favorite singer, Elton John, on the cover. I picked that one up, eager to read about what *People* claimed was "Elton's New Look," though his goofy hat, platform boots, and big glasses with gold palm trees on the frame looked exactly like his old look, so I doubted I'd learn anything new.

I didn't get far into the article when the customer handed Valerie some bills and lit a cigarette on his way out the door. She placed the money in a metal cash box and it disappeared under the counter.

"Are you Jay's sister?" she asked, looking me over.

I looked her over, too. A little taller than me, she had ebony skin, a glossy hairdo like ladies wore in the 1950s, and she wore an elegant navy blue pantsuit.

"Yup. It's me, in the flesh," I said before I could stop myself. This was no time for joking. I needed to start earning money for college (*if* I got accepted) and I'd been afraid to apply for a real job (because why would someone hire me?) long enough. I approached the counter and deepened my voice to a serious setting. "I mean, yes, I'm Deidre. Jay said I should fill out an application 'cuz you need help."

She laughed, a hearty chuckle from down in her belly. "Do I ever."

She handed me the form. I picked up the pen connected to the counter by a thin chain and scribbled down my information, trying desperately to recall my Social Security number. I was supposed to memorize that sucker years ago, but the numbers floated around in my math-addled brain like slippery minnows, refusing to be caught.

I handed her the paper. She barely looked at it before sliding it into a desk drawer, then asked, "Can you start next Saturday?"

My eyes popped. "You mean I got the job?"

"Yeah," she said, like I was doofus for even asking. "The hours are six to noon, Saturday and Sunday, sometimes a little longer depending on how long it takes to clean the rooms. You're in luck. The minimum wage went up at New Year's to two dollars and thirty cents an hour."

Wow. Since the tender age of ten, I'd had jobs that paid fifty or seventy-five cents an hour, babysitting, walking dogs, shoveling snow off sidewalks and front stoops. One summer I'd earned a dollar a day for emptying an old lady's commode she had to use because the bathrooms in the Project were on the second floor and she couldn't climb the stairs fast enough when she had to go. But I'd never earned that much money per hour. Pretty soon I'd be swimming in cash.

"You'll need to wear a uniform." Valerie moved to a cabinet on the back wall and took out a dress. "You look like a size eighteen."

More like a size twenty, but I didn't argue that point since I'd only been hired five seconds ago. I unfolded the dress she handed me and gulped. Not just a uniform, an *ugly* uniform. A sickly shade of green, with a white ruffled collar, white trim around the short sleeves, and an attached white apron with a pocket like a kangaroo's pouch. Old fashioned, and did I mention ugly?

But... For two dollars and thirty cents an hour, I'd wear a burlap sack, no matter how snug.

Clutching my new uniform, I shot out the door and across the parking lot to our car. I hopped in and Mom closed her book, raising an inquisitive Mr. Spock eyebrow. "Well? What happened?"

I beamed. "You don't have to worry about paying for college anymore. I got the job."

My enthusiasm for my new job dimmed considerably when my mother dragged me out of bed at five-thirty on Saturday morning. Far too early for a night owl like me.

After breakfast of a handful of Cap'n Crunch cereal, I quickly brushed my hair but didn't skimp when it came to my teeth. Mom took us to City Hospital Dental School downtown because it was free and, believe me, we got what we paid for. I brushed and re-brushed every single tooth with the determination of a girl who never wanted to go back to those sadists ever again.

Mom dropped me off at Eden Motor Lodge on the dot of six. Still dark outside, and cold, but the motel lobby was bright and warm, smelling of coffee and laundry detergent. No Valerie behind the desk this morning. Hector, the overnight manager, greeted me instead. Scrawny, muscular, with a tattoo of an anchor on his forearm, he looked up from his newspaper long enough to mumble hello and point me to a door off the lobby into the motel's main corridor.

I'd never been in a motel, much less stayed in one, and was disappointed by what I saw—a long hallway with a thousand identical doors except for the numbers, tan wallpaper, and a brownish-red carpet that seemed to absorb all the light and every bit of life of anyone who walked down it.

Soapy smells, the sound of clean towels thump-thumping as they rotated in the dryer, and the tinny beat of Aretha Franklin's "Respect" playing on a transistor radio greeted me when I got to the laundry room.

So did a familiar face from the Project, Camille Arundel, who'd cried when Mr. Meager said she looked crazy on the video we saw the first day of freshman year. She sat on top of a washing machine, swinging her legs and chewing gum. A dark haired girl of eighteen, she was a little shorter than me, a little paler than me, and a lot thinner than me. She also looked way better in her ugly uniform.

"It *is* you." She hopped off the machine, her clunky black work shoes hitting the floor with a thump. "I heard Valerie hired a sucker named Deidre Daly and wondered if it was you. You'll be sorry, I'll tell you that."

"Camille. Haven't seen you in forever. How you doing?" A loaded question with her. She'd earned her neighborhood nickname, Hurricane Camille, because she was always stirring up trouble.

"Doing good. You knew the state emancipated me after my mother threw me out?"

I nodded, though I'd heard a different story. At fifteen, she attacked her mom with the sharp end of a broken ketchup bottle, an incident that got her hauled off by the cops, a visit to juvenile court, and a year at Our Lady of Perpetual Regret Reform School for Girls. And banned from ever seeing her mother again.

"I'm on my own and couldn't be happier." She snapped her gum. "I been working here a year now. I've got a new boyfriend. His name is Mack and he drives a Mack truck, isn't that a scream? We should double date sometime."

It'd have to be a blind date, because only a guy who couldn't see would double date with me. That popped into my head, but I shut my mouth before I said it. Why did I always feel the need to insult myself?

"Yeah, maybe we should," I said. "And maybe we should get to work, right?"

She agreed with another crack of her gum.

She turned off the radio and pushed a wheeled cart out of the laundry room and into the main hallway. The cart was stuffed with towels, tiny soaps, and toilet paper rolls, and the wheels squeaked like outraged mice. I worried the noise might wake people up but Camille didn't care. She shoved that squeaky thing forward and banged on doors to see if the room was empty, shouting, "Chambermaid. Are you decent?" at the top of her lungs.

Only a few rooms were unoccupied at first, so Camille had plenty of time to show me the ropes. I didn't have to be a brain surgeon to figure out what to do, anyway. Change the sheets, wash and dust tabletops, pick up trash, vacuum, and scrub the bathroom. The same chores I did at home, only grosser and smellier (especially the toilets).

The only part I had trouble with was the laundry. I sprinkled too much detergent into the front-loading washing machine and soapsuds bubbled through the door onto the floor.

I freaked out, fearing Valerie would yell and call me stupid. Like Dad did when I burned the fish sticks I'd cooked for dinner while Mom was at one of her tenant meetings. Like Gramps when I'd accidentally locked the keys in his car and he had to force open the triangular vent window and use a coat hanger to jimmy the lock.

Camille shrugged at the escaping bubbles. Cool as a cucumber, she tossed a towel on the floor to soak up the wet suds that oozed across the tiles.

"Our little secret," she said, pressing a finger to her lips.

As more people checked out, we worked our way along the corridor to get the rooms ready for the next customers, or "guests" as we were supposed to call them. My back grew sore from bending over beds and my energy drained. I worried I'd be completely wrung out by Donna's Valentine's Day party tonight.

Camille seemed to have an endless supply of fuel, like OPEC. She folded sheets and snapped wrinkles out of towels at an impressive speed, chattering the whole time.

"I'm living in a rooming house on Elm Street with a bunch of creeps and divorced dads. I'd get my own place if I had enough for first and last month's rent and security deposit. I work here in the mornings except Mondays and at the minimart by the drive-in theater in the afternoons. It's still not enough money. My boyfriend Mack's on the road a lot so he could crash with me if I ever get an apartment. I wonder what he got me for Valentine's. Flowers?

I hope it's a ring, though I doubt it. He said he had enough of marriage the first time around and won't make that mistake twice."

I soaked it all in, thinking there was a heck of a lot more to being emancipated besides getting kicked out of your mom's place.

We were almost done when a skinny guy with a beard and a cap with a trucking company logo on it came out of a room carrying a big suitcase with silver snaps.

"Here you go, sweetheart," he said and held out the room key. I reached for it and he let it drop. I bent to pick it up and he slapped me on the fanny so hard I yelped.

He laughed and Camille giggled, but as soon as the side door closed behind him, she turned to me. "Fucking dirty old man. Bet he didn't even leave a tip."

I rubbed my sore butt. This might not be the best job after all.

CHAPTER **8**

Willpower

THAT NIGHT, JAY LET me drive to Donna's house. Which he probably regretted when I swung our Impala around a corner too wide and the car ended up on the opposite side of the street.

"Pick a lane and stick to it, Deedee," he said. Though he sounded pissed, I knew when he used that nickname he wasn't.

"I'm trying." I turned the wheel toward the correct side of the road, a hand-over-hand struggle in a car with no power steering. "This thing's like driving an ocean liner."

"As long as it's not the Titanic we'll be okay."

I loosened my grip on the wheel a smidge. I got my learner's permit when I turned sixteen but with a requirement of thirty hours of class instruction and six hours road time—both of which cost money I didn't have—I still hadn't gotten my license more than a year later.

Now that I had a job, I could save up for driving school. Until then, I needed to practice and that required a licensed driver by my side. Jay was the only one who fit the bill. Mom nearly put her foot through the floor slamming an imaginary brake when I drove with her.

My father never got his license because a fortune teller once warned him he shouldn't drive. I suspected his brothers paid the fortune teller to say that as a prank. Or maybe she got a whiff of

63

Dad's whiskey breath and decided to do the world a favor and keep him off the road.

"Give her a little gas," Jay coaxed as we crept up a hill into a development of homes built after World War Two and named for the generals who led that war, like Patton and Marshall. "We don't want to roll backwards."

I tapped the gas pedal and we shot forward. I tittered like a nervous chickadee.

We finally made it to Donna's, a white ranch-style house with black shutters tucked among a hundred similar style houses along MacArthur Way. I even managed to park between the other cars lined up by the curb.

"You did good," Jay said. "Even if you almost steered us into a snowbank."

"Almost? I'll try harder next time." I glanced toward Donna's house. The lights in the windows shone out into the chilly night. Black Sabbath's "War Pigs" rocked from inside, along with the chatter and laughter of dozens of voices. My pulse picked up. I'd been so excited thinking of this party I hadn't considered the reality of actually going to it. "Jay... I'm worried no one will talk to me."

"Then you talk to them. Be yourself. They'll come around. If all else fails, spit in their eye."

I grinned. That was a Dad-ism, his way of threatening revenge on people who pissed him off. Which was practically everyone.

I got out of the car. Jay got out too and moved to the driver's side. "Have fun. I'll pick you up at midnight."

"Where're you going?"

"Out."

"Where, out?" And with whom? The girl who'd called him several times since January?

He raised an eyebrow, a Mr. Spock quirk like Mom's. "Just out."

He slid into the driver's seat and the Impala puttered off before I could press for more. He wouldn't answer anyway. Like all of us Dalys, he kept his secrets locked up as tight as he did his emotions, and those he kept locked up like Fort Knox.

I turned toward the house. I'd never been here before and wasn't sure which door to go in. I mentally tossed a coin and chose the kitchen entrance next to the driveway on the side. The wooden steps creaked as I climbed them, adding to my nerves. I peered through a window framed by lacy white curtains into a kitchen filled with lime green appliances and a small dinette table at the center of the room.

Donna sailed into the kitchen. She wore a red halter top, dark blue jeans, and red platform shoes, and she carried an empty tray that she tossed into the sink.

I tapped on the window.

"You *finally* got here." She snatched open the door and tugged me inside a steamy hot room that smelled like tomato sauce and Cheetos. "Why'd you come in this door? You're so weird, Dee."

Being called weird bothered me, but I pretended it didn't. "That's me, I guess. Weirdra Deidre."

I tossed my coat onto a chair at the table then smoothed the tunic-style top I'd bought at Cully's last week, using Jay's store discount. Dark blue, with long sleeves and a wide belt, the blouse's silky fabric (well, polyester) draped over my hips and hugged my waist and breasts in a slinky way.

"What do you think?" I spread my arms and spun in a circle.

Donna squealed. "*That's* what I meant about showing yourself off. Ooh-la-la those boobies."

I flushed, both pleased and disconcerted. She twisted the top off a quart bottle of a drink called Tango and shoved a *Flintstones* grape jelly jar into my hand. The bottle clinked against my glass as she filled it to the brim.

"Something to get the party started," she said and poured one for herself. "Don't worry, it's diet. Vodka has no calories, and the Tango's sweetened with that Saccharin stuff." She raised her glass, and after a cheery, "Bottoms up," she chug-a-lugged like nobody's business.

I sniffed the drink. It smelled like a bag of spoiled oranges. I sipped. Tasted like that too, a gross orangeade and vodka combination even my dad would turn his nose up at. But Jay told me to have fun and everyone knew drinking at a party was essential to having fun, even if I was under the state's legal drinking age of eighteen.

So... When in Rome, do as the Romans do. Though the Romans probably had some nice tasting wine to guzzle and not orangeade and vodka.

The Tango both burned and tickled as it flooded down my throat. I'd barely eaten anything today and the liquid hit my mostly empty stomach with a sharp splash. Within seconds, the vodka flushed through my veins, encouraging me to relax.

Donna smacked her lips and poured another for each of us, repeating her previous guzzle.

"Are your parents here?" I asked, drinking slower this time.

"No, they're out...somewhere." She filled her cup for the third time. "Did you hear what happened? Miss Dolan fainted in the hallway last week."

I nearly spit out my Tango. Before I could confess the truth, Donna darted over to a giant pot of meatballs simmering on the stove. She put down her glass, threw off the lid, and spooned meatballs the size of softballs into a serving bowl.

"Hurry, put these on the dining room table." She stuffed the bowl into my free hand and gave me a shove toward the kitchen doorway. "Everyone's waiting, and they're starving."

Including me, especially with that delicious Italian restaurant smell teasing my nose.

The hum of conversation turned up to a roar as I waded into the party. The smell of beer and cigarettes engulfed me. So did a hungry horde as I plunked the bowl onto the table with the other refreshments.

I squeezed out of the mob before I got crushed and stepped down into the sunken living room, a spacious area lower than the rest of the house.

Heavy drapes the same burnt-orange color of my shoes bordered the windows and shag carpeting covered every inch of floor. Red and white streamers dangled from the ceiling and Valentine's hearts were taped to the walls. Albums, 8-track tapes, and 45s littered the floor in front of the stereo console, waiting for their turn to be played when David Bowie's "Fame" finished pulsing from the speakers.

I wandered around, sipping my drink, unsure what to do. People drank and mingled and chattered. Some I recognized from school, a lot I didn't. I spotted my lunch friends Karen, Barbie, and Jane, but Linda G had wisely chosen to stay home. A place I began to think I should be.

I returned to the food table, where I knew I'd be most comfortable. The horde had decimated the meatballs and fled the scene of the crime. I looked over the remaining snacks. Potato chips, cookies, Valentine candy hearts, tuna salad sandwiches slathered in mayo. All the bad stuff that tasted so sinfully good.

Willpower, Deidre.

But I had to eat *something*. Warm and woozy from the Tango, my head tingled with an alcohol buzz. I didn't want to end up like that girl Karen Ann Quinlan, who starved herself and didn't eat for days. She went to a party and popped so many pills and drank so much she fell into a coma she had no chance of waking up from and now her parents were suing her doctors to let her die and wasn't that the scariest thing ever?

I stepped back from those morbid thoughts and moved to the fruit and vegetable end of the table. No one had touched a single one of the grapes, mushrooms, and tiny tomatoes heaped on a platter.

I picked up one of the tomatoes. I'd never seen one this small. It was adorable. I popped it into my mouth and bit down. The thing exploded inside my mouth. Outside, too. Globby tomato goo shot out like a rocket ship hurtling toward the horizon. The horizon being the wall, where it hit with a splat.

"Got away from you, huh?"

I froze. The guy who'd spoken leaned against the wall a few feet away, his thumbs hooked into the belt loops of his jeans. About six feet tall, he wore a sweatshirt with *Saint Stephan's Basketball* on the front and the sleeves pushed up. He had a slender build, deeply tanned skin, brown eyes, brown hair, tangled like the wind had gone mental on it, and a face that was all angles—sharp cheekbones, solid jaw, tilted eyes.

Not Cute-with-a-Capital-C like Carl Werzbicki, or even conventionally handsome. More like stunning. In an odd way.

"How long were you standing there?" I asked, my face going hot.

He pushed off the wall and ambled closer. "Long enough." He had a nice voice. Mellow, a little sexy, but not *too* sexy.

"You can't take me anywhere," I said, watching the goo slowly slide down the wall.

"I'll help get rid of the evidence." He grabbed a napkin and scrubbed away the mess. He got most of it and a few flecks of wallpaper too. He wadded the napkin and, with a jump and a toss like he thought he was Kareem Abdul-Jabbar, he threw it into a nearby trash can.

He turned back to me. "Hi, I'm Will."

I gulped. If he said his last name was Power, I'd die right here, right on this spot.

"Will? As in Shakespeare?"

"As in Will Hovey. I'm not as brilliant as that other Will." He added a soft *yip* like an exclamation point.

Will Hovey. A rich person's name if I ever heard it. What did he want with me? "I'm Deidre, of the County Mayo Daly's, by way of the potato famine." I winced as the words tumbled from my mouth. I had no idea how to talk to guys. Or any human being. "You come here often?" I added, desperate to recover from the fumble.

He hesitated, like I was Woodward and Bernstein and had asked him to spill classified information. "Only when there's a party. How do you know Donna?"

"From school." I picked up another small tomato and bit into it. This time I managed to keep the juice inside my mouth. Most of it anyway. "How do you know her?"

"I don't really. We go to the same church. So you go to Northside High?"

I thought I'd clearly established that fact but confirmed the information again to be on the safe side.

"I go to Saint Stephen's," he said and another yip slipped out.

"Good to know. I thought you might have stolen that sweatshirt."

"I did steal it. I'm the famous sweatshirt thief everyone talks about."

I blinked in surprise. The boy was quick. "Saint Stephen's is a Catholic school. I'm Catholic too." Well, I used to be. We went to church every week before my mother gave up on religion altogether and let us sleep in on Sundays. "I bet you know all ten commandments."

He grimaced in mock alarm. "Is this a test?"

"More of a pop quiz."

"Damn. I didn't study." He laughed, showing a bright smile that had never set foot inside the Sadistic Dental School at City Hospital downtown. "You know something, I like the cut of your jib."

I flushed. That sounded like a compliment. Having received so few of them, I couldn't be sure. "Jib? What's that mean?"

"It means you're cool. It's a sailing term. My family sails. Every summer and sometimes in the fall when the weather's good. We have a boat. Do you sail?" He spoke in a rush punctuated by another of those intrusive yips. Could he be as nervous as me?

"Sadly, no. Unless you mean sailing across the room when I trip over my own feet."

That earned me another laugh. He started to say something else when Donna wafted up to us, looking wobbly, probably due to yet another glass of Tango in her hand.

"Hey Will. I see you met Dee." Her gaze lingered on him before she turned to me. "What're you two talking about?"

Half annoyed, half relieved she'd busted in, I shifted position so our duo conversation could become a trio. "Will said he goes sailing with his family. They own a boat."

"You do?" she cried. "My dad used to own a boat, but he sold it to buy his Cadillac."

Will mumbled a vague response then he clammed up. So did Donna, letting her eyes do the talking, eyeing him like a prime cut of beef. He studied the refreshments on the table as if trying to memorize every piece. I scrambled for something to say. While Will seemed to fear talking, I feared silence. I needed to jump in and talk and talk and *talk* to fill the tiniest pause in a conversation, like a record with its needle stuck.

Jane breezed up, saving me from a fatal chattering fit. A girl named Marilyn followed and our trio became a quintet. A pretty girl with golden hair and a mouth shaped like a trapezoid (the only thing I'd learned in geometry), Marilyn wore tight jeans and the newest fad in shoes, Earth Shoes. Made of a soft fabric like Moccasins, they sloped down at the heel, designed to stretch your calf muscles while you walked.

She spoke to Will like they were old friends and maybe they were since she announced to anyone listening she attended Saint Stephan's sister school, Holy Mother of God. Which was something Mom always said when our dog Marco pooped in the house and she accidentally stepped in it.

"Marilyn says they're putting on *Jesus Christ Superstar* at Saint Mary's this spring and they need actors," Jane bubbled. "Anyone want to audition with me?"

"I already signed up to audition." Marilyn picked a non-existent piece of lint off her patterned blouse. "*I'm* trying out for the lead."

"You mean Jesus?" I said. I couldn't help it.

Will won my gratitude for eternity by laughing at my joke. Marilyn's expression went cold. Barbie and Karen showed up, saving me from her wrath. Everyone shifted to let them in and our group became a... What? A sextet? An octogenarian? I had no idea. Any number higher than five and I was lost.

Karen demanded to be filled in and Jane zoomed through an explanation. "You've got to try out, Will," she announced when she finished. "There's *lots* of roles for boys."

Donna perked up at the B-word. "We'll be there." She laced her arm through mine. "Dee and I wouldn't miss it."

I lifted an eyebrow. It'd be nice if she asked me first, though my answer would've been yes anyway.

"Will?" Jane prodded.

"Uhh..." The room seemed to fall quiet, except for Three Dog Night's "Mama Told Me Not to Come" on the record player. Will eyed me, then he shrugged. "Guess I'll check it out."

He ended with a yip and Karen's eyes narrowed to slits, like a hawk zeroing in on its prey. Will ducked his head. I couldn't tell for sure in the low light, but I thought he blushed.

"I need a drink," he said hurriedly then was gone. Marilyn chased after him.

"What's *wrong* with him?" Karen demanded.

I bristled. I'd heard that tone before. That *who is that freak* note in a person's voice when they first saw Jay. It made me sick. And it made me mad. "There's *nothing* wrong with him," I snapped. "He's got a speech thing, that's all. Like a stutter or something."

Karen's gaze homed in on me. "You *like* him."

Heat crept up my face, all the way to the roots of my hair. I did like him. Mostly because he was someone I could actually talk to, someone who laughed at my jokes, and liked the cut of my jib. And pretty sure I'd seen him checking me out. Well, he checked out the other girls, too, because that was something guys did, but to have a guy look at *me* for once like I might be attractive and not a big slug gave me a thrill, so...

Sure I liked him.

I just couldn't admit that out loud.

"That's not the point," I said. "*You* shouldn't make fun of people you don't know." That came out odd. As if making fun of people you did know was fair game.

Karen scowled and I braced for an argument, which I was no good at. I always folded like a piece of tissue paper in the opening round.

Fortunately, Queen's "Bohemian Rhapsody" came on. Donna squealed, "I love this song," and tugged me toward the living room to dance. I forgot about the *sunken* part of sunken living room and Will almost got a major demonstration of my ability to sail as I tripped on the way down.

Donna pushed me into the gyrating mob. Everyone sang along, shouting "Scaramouche" and "Galileo," jumping and swaying. I sang too, though fear of imminent floor collapse under my weight kept my jumping to a minimum.

Elton's "Saturday Night's Alright for Fighting" rocked from the stereo next and the party really took off. Song after song played. The crowd got louder. Jane made the rounds, chatting with everyone. Karen and Barbie knocked back *Miller Lite* beers while arguing over which car was cooler, Corvette or Camarro. Donna hunted for the perfect cherry-popping candidate, flitting from boy to boy like an indecisive bee.

And I danced. Full of inhibition-killing and allegedly calorie-free Tango, I didn't worry about the floorboards anymore (well, only a little). I boogied to Billy Preston's "Will It Go Round In Circles" and sang along to Helen Reddy's "I Am Woman" and hopped and bopped to a ton of other songs until midnight arrived.

The cold air hit me as I went outside to wait for Jay, using the front door this time. Will sat on the low step, no coat or hat. The storm door clicked shut and he swiveled to look at me.

"You're leaving?"

He was truly the King of Obvious Observations. And very good-looking. "Yup, I'm Cinderella and it's time to go. My pumpkin is due any second."

A grin tugged at his lips. "Where you headed?"

I hesitated. *Where you headed* meant where did I live. I didn't want to tell him. Mostly because saying I lived in the Project embarrassed me. A whole lot. So I answered with a vague, "Oh, down there," and tilted my head toward the south of the city.

I gathered my long coat over my legs so he couldn't see the way my polyester pants stretched over my thighs as I sat down beside him. He smelled like Coke and clean cotton and a hint of Hai Karate aftershave. "What about you? Where do you live?"

He hesitated like I had, though I thought the slight pause was to control his speech rather than embarrassment. "Up there," he said finally and jerked his thumb toward the north side. The rich side of the city.

We gazed at each other a moment. KC and the Sunshine Band's "That's the Way I Like It" boomed from inside the house. Will had nice lips. Really nice lips. Kissable. I bet they tasted like cotton candy. Warmth rippled through me. *Don't even think about it.* He'd never kiss a girl like me. Besides, I knew what *up there* meant, he knew what *down there* meant and never the twain shall meet.

The storm door squeaked open and we both jumped. I looked back to see Marilyn poke her head out.

"Will, aren't you cold without your coat?" she asked, her eyes on me.

"No." He shivered, the big liar.

Her trapezoid mouth drew down and she disappeared back into the house like a gopher into its hole. He watched her with a scowl.

"Okay, let's hear them," I said.

He turned back to me, his expression much friendlier. "Hear what?"

"The ten commandments."

"Hate to disappoint you. I know only five. Proving I'm pretty bad at Catholic-ing. What about you?"

"Let's see." I tapped my forefinger to my chin. "There's pride, envy, sloth... No, wait, those are the seven deadly sins. Apparently I'm bad at Catholic-ing too." Our Impala chugged up the street. Too bad. Things were getting interesting here on the stoop. "Well, there's my pumpkin."

"See you at the auditions?" he asked as I stood.

"If you're lucky."

He chuckled and said good night. I walked away, tempted to leave behind one of my marshmallow shoes so he could chase after me with it, except I wasn't Cinderella and no way was he Prince Charming. Well, he was too good looking and too nice not to be *someone's* Prince Charming.

But I doubted he was interested in being mine.

Jay hit the gas and steered the Impala toward home. His favorite song, "Suite: Judy Blue Eyes" by Crosby, Stills, & Nash drifted from the 8-track tape player he'd bought and somehow figured out how to install under the car's dashboard.

"Did you have a good time?" he asked, taking a corner with ease.

"I did." I covered my mouth so he wouldn't smell my Tango breath.

"Did you have to spit in anyone's eye?"

"I did not. I actually had fun."

So much fun, I practically floated through the door when we got home. This had been a good night. A *really* good night. I'd talked to a nice guy without embarrassing myself to death. I danced like a fiend and probably burned ten thousand calories. And I'd discovered a delicious new kind of tomato. So, all in all, a success.

I didn't notice the weird quiet of the living room until Jay stiffened. The lamp over Dad's chair was on. A cigarette smoldered in the ashtray and the horror movie *The Invisible Man* played on the TV at a low volume. A crash and the shattering of glass from the kitchen cut through the stillness. We both dashed in that direction.

We found Dad, bent over the sink, hands gripping the edge, a broken nip bottle at his feet. He wore only his underwear and a tee shirt, exposing knobby elbows and knees and skin as white as the snow outside. His neck wobbled, so weak and rubbery it could barely hold his head up. His lips spread in a gummy grin and he laughed. Not a happy laugh. One of those guffaws that end in a sob.

And then he threw up in the sink. Mostly.

Jay let out a soft cry. My stomach clenched. So did my chest and I struggled to breathe. How much did Dad drink tonight? Thirty-six beers? A hundred nips? *Happy Valentine's Day, Mom.* Thank the stars above she'd gone to bed.

"Help me get him to his chair," Jay said, reining in his emotions and seizing control.

I nodded dumbly and took one of Dad's arms, Jay grabbed the other and we carry-dragged him to the living room. Dad's arm trembled, feeling fragile under my grip, his skin sweaty. His bare feet tripped over themselves as he tried to walk and his head lolled.

"You don't like your old man," he slurred, his bloodshot eyes finding mine.

"Not at the moment." Had I ever liked him? Maybe, when I was little, when he'd chatter and sing and take us trick-or-treating and play with us kids like a real father. Before booze took over his life.

Jay shushed me. He never said a bad word about Dad or anyone. I had trouble being so nice.

We settled Dad into his chair as carefully as handling an egg. The TV *Guide* magazine with Redd Foxx from *Sanford & Son* on the cover disappeared under his butt. His eyes rolled back in his head and his eyelids slammed shut.

Passed out, not dead, though deep down I wished he were. And not for the first time. Guilt and shame followed that nasty thought, with more guilt for my own drinking tonight. I sent up a *Hail Mary* and a mental plea for God's forgiveness for both, despite being bad at Catholic-ing.

"I'll clean up. You go to bed." Jay pointed toward the stairs. "Don't tell Mom what happened. She doesn't need to know."

I nodded and did as instructed. I always did what Jay told me to. He was so wise. It struck me that I didn't really know him. With all his surgeries, he'd been in the hospital and away from home for months and months, missing Christmas and Easter and years of school, too. He never had a normal childhood. He only had this—responsibility. Taking care of us like he was the dad of the house.

A gush of sadness flooded me. I wondered if Jay knew Gramps had pushed Mom to put him in a home when he was born. I hoped he didn't. I only knew because I overheard Mom and Aunt Polly whispering about it once. With everything else weighing on Jay's bony shoulders, knowing a secret like that would probably crush him.

All traces of my earlier good mood crumbled. Tears pushed at my eyes, egged on by the alcohol pricking my emotions. *Dammit, Deidre.* Dalys weren't supposed to cry, but I sure risked doing that now.

I went upstairs and waited until Jay finished cleaning up and toddled off to bed, then I snuck back down to the kitchen. Willpower went out the window as I raided the cupboards for the one thing that could plug the waterworks and hold those tears at bay. The only thing that could make me feel better.

Food.

Chapter 9

The Belle of Saint Mary's

Mom put dinner on the table, sat down, and disappeared into the pages of Erica Jong's *Fear of Flying*.

Tonight's offering was one of my favorites, creamed tuna and peas, accessorized by a platter stacked with toast, tilting like the Tower of Pisa. I'd fallen off my diet with a spectacular crash these last few days, and this tempting creamy concoction would seriously challenge my efforts to get back on.

I did my best to nibble on tuna and toast as daintily as Chrissy did. Rusty wolfed down his meal like he had an important gang meeting to get to. Dad had survived his booze binge of Saturday night with little remorse. He clanged his silverware and banged his beer can on the table, spoiling for a fight.

"Mom, can you give me a lift to Saint Mary's Church after dinner?" I asked, hoping to get out of here before round one began.

She looked up from her book and raised an eyebrow. "Why on earth do you want to go there?"

"Don't worry. It's not for Mass or anything. The church is putting on a musical and I'm going to..." I trembled at the thought of performing on stage in front of a bunch of people but I took a breath and *whooshed* out the rest. "I'm going to audition for a part."

Proving they were the yin-and-yang of parenting, Dad let out a derisive snort while Mom cheered.

Not long after, she dropped me at Saint Mary's, in a parking lot large enough to land a 747. A large, elegant brick colonial house where the priests lived stood at the far end of the lot.

The church itself was closer to the street. A simple building of white clapboard, it had a sloping roof and a steeple that reached up to the sky, but not too far up. *The* perfect metaphor for the Virgin the church was named for—allowed to be part of the action though never able to climb as high as the male players.

I entered the side door onto a landing between two flights of stairs covered with yellow linoleum. One set of stairs climbed upward to the church proper, known to all good Catholics as the nave. The other stairs led to the basement level. For a second, I felt caught between heaven and hell, which would be purgatory, I supposed.

When voices rose up from below, my choice was made. *Hell it is.*

My marshmallow shoes thumped as I ventured downward. I passed through a set of double doors into a cool, musty-smelling, spacious function room. Photographs of priests from days gone by hung along cinder block walls painted pale pink. A small stage occupied one end, with a pass-through window and a door into the kitchen at the other. Metal folding chairs and tables were set up along the perimeter. A heavy curtain had been drawn across the stage, the bright green fabric splashed with giant yellow flowers exactly like a dress I saw Karen Carpenter wear on *American Bandstand*.

A lot of people were here. Donna, who'd goaded me into coming tonight, was not among them. I saw Jane with a gaggle of girls near the stage, including Will's friend Marilyn I met at the party. Will was here too, hanging out at one of the tables with some other guys.

I'd normally join the girls and hope one of them would talk to me but Will saw me and waved me over.

"You decided to come," he said, continuing to excel in the obvious observations department. He wore a dark blue long sleeve shirt, faded jeans, and leather construction worker's boots the color of an acorn, with the laces untied. His hair was a tangled mess and he leaned against the wall as he had at the party.

"I didn't have a choice." I peeled off my coat and threw it on an empty chair. "Donna talked me into it. She has a way of getting me to agree to anything. I hope she never asks me to rob a bank with her."

He laughed and I laughed because he laughed. He had a nice smile and magnificent eyes, an unusual shade I hadn't noticed in the low light at the party. Pale brown, almost gold.

"Deidre, yip, this is Pete." Will nodded at a broad-shouldered guy with reddish hair and a green-and-white striped shirt, seated with his feet up on the table. Then he gestured to a bunch of other guys and tossed out so many names I'd never remember them all.

"Holy mother of god, is all of Saint Stephan's here tonight?" I cracked.

Will laughed again and I decided I could get to like this guy. More than I already did.

"Saint Mary's doesn't have enough guys to fill the roles," Pete said. "We get extra credit for participating in this horror show."

"Your name's Deidre?" a guy named Barry said. Tall, thin, with a trimmed beard and mustache and long brown hair past his shoulders, he looked up from his seat at the table with inquisitive blue eyes. "Never heard that name before. It's a nice one."

That got me flustered, being unaccustomed to guys uttering my name in any way except as an insult. "Oh, ah... I'm named after a woman from Irish legend who was so beautiful she had to be hidden away so men wouldn't go to war over her. Not that I'm beautif— I mean, uh, I could never make men go to war. Not even a light skirmish. Ha-ha."

Before I could dig myself in any deeper, Donna popped into the room and steered our way. She held her coat over her arm and as usual, she wore a stupendous outfit, a V-neck patterned blouse with a thin belt, crimson flared corduroys, and a pair of buckled wedge platform shoes that clip-clopped rhythmically as she walked across the floor.

"What are you all talking about?" she asked after introductions were made. She sized up each of the guys with as much interest as they looked her over. She checked out Barry the longest.

"Deidre was telling us a story about her Irish namesake," Will said.

I would've described his expression as impish, if someone with his bone structure could pull off such a look. Surely my own expression betrayed my delight at his teasing, based on the blush I felt burning my face.

Donna squinted. "What does that mean?"

No one enlightened her, as a clatter from the stairwell announced the arrival of our director. A big guy with a barrel chest and a thick, bushy beard, he whooshed into the room like an astronaut propelled by his own atmosphere.

"Greetings, thespians," he cried. "Get ready for the theatrical experience of your lives. The one, the only *Jesus Christ Superstar.*"

He ended this show-stopping declaration by throwing off his heavy parka jacket. I half expected he'd be wearing robes or a Pontius Pilate get-up underneath, so my heart sank to see only a plaid shirt and brown corduroy pants.

Bushy Beard introduced himself as Ralph Puck, a graduate student in theater at nearby Winslow College, then he gestured for us to gather round. "Bring it in, gang. Let's rap."

As we moved to do as instructed, I caught Will's eye. "Let's rap? Who says that anymore?"

Will grinned, a smile that faded when Bushy Beard demanded we go around the group and say our names and a few interesting facts about ourselves. When it was his turn, Will spoke slowly and deliberately, letting out only one yip. A couple kids snickered and I gave them a death glare. Marilyn did too.

I already knew Will liked to sail, but tonight I learned some new things. He was a junior, would turn eighteen soon (which meant he must've gotten held back in school), and he loved history, movies, and reading all kinds of books, activities my mother would wholeheartedly approve. And so did I.

My turn came. "I'm Deidre Daly, a senior at Northside High. I wear a size nine shoe and my hobby is standing on one leg on a rocking chair on Saturdays." That earned me some laughs and a frown from Marilyn, probably appalled to hear I had such big clodhoppers for feet.

We finished our introductions and Bushy Beard moved on. "Before we audition, we're gonna do an exercise so I can assess your skills and what you can bring to the show."

Given my dislike of exercise, that sounded painful.

"We'll start with—"

The thump of footsteps on the stairs announced the arrival of Carl Werzbicki, who stumbled into the room as if someone had pushed him. My heart leapt and my curiosity flared. What was Joe Cool football god and all-around popular guy Carl doing in a church basement with a bunch of theater nerds?

"Get in here, big guy." Bushy Beard gestured and Carl squeezed into the circle between two girls. "Glad to have you with us. What's your name?"

"Carl, but everyone calls me Werz," he said in a voice so slick and smooth Bushy Beard let out a gooney giggle.

"Okay, Werz. You can start. If you could be any animal in the world, what would you be?"

I doubted Carl (I refused to call him Werz and no one, not even him, could make me) expected this kind of question. He quickly recovered the fumble and said, "A gorilla."

Will rolled his eyes like, *duh, obvious choice* for a behemoth like Carl but our director chuckled in approval.

"Excellent. Excellent," he said then proceeded to go around the circle, having each of us choose an animal.

Jane said parakeet. Will went with a tiger. Fitting choice, given his tiger-like eyes. Marilyn tried to say tiger too but changed to a cheetah when Bushy Beard told her to choose something original. Barry, who stood about six feet four, said, "Giraffe, of course," and everyone laughed. For some reason Donna blurted, "Boa constrictor."

"A goose," I said, the first creature I could think of that wasn't a hippo or elephant, thank you very much.

Bushy Beard then had us *be* our animal and everyone went around growling or barking while he watched us as if trying to see into our souls. I honked and flapped my arms like wings. I would've felt like a fool if everyone else didn't look as dumb as me.

Except Donna. She hissed seductively and undulated her body from top to bottom, guaranteeing the attention of all the male lions, tigers, and bears, oh my.

Finally, our intrepid director clapped his hands as if turning us back into people again. "Alright. Let's take ten. We'll audition and cast the roles when we get back from break."

Several people stepped outside to smoke. Others went to the bathroom. Donna and I joined the Saint Stephen's crew at their table. Marilyn did too. An odd twinge flashed through me as she flew straight to Will. Were they dating?

Something hotter flashed through me when Carl strolled over. He wore a black tee shirt that showed his muscled biceps, tight,

tight blue jeans, and a burning smolder that practically melted me through the floor.

Donna threw her shoulders back and asked the burning question of the ages, "What are you doing here, Werz?"

Not a single R appeared in that sentence, thanks to her Massachusetts accent. We all had that accent, dropping Rs where they should've been and adding them where they shouldn't. Not Will, though. I suspected he'd had voice lessons or something.

"My old lady's in the church's women's guild," Carl said. "She twisted my arm." He sounded annoyed, though I thought doing what his mother wanted him to do was kind of sweet. He scanned the group gathered around the table then his gaze settled on me. "Hey, Deidre. No more passing out in the hallway, I hope."

He knew my name. He'd pronounced it wrong, but still... Copious blushing ensued, followed by my tongue firmly tying itself into a knot. All I could manage was a feeble stream of vowels and consonants and an awkward headshake.

"Dee!" Donna bounced on her toes like Tigger, a miraculous feat in platform shoes. "You didn't tell me you passed out at school."

"You did? What happened?" Marilyn's eyes dug into me, like a reporter hot on a story.

Everyone pasted their gaze on me, eager to hear the sordid details of my C corridor belly flop. A riptide of embarrassment coursed through me as I scrambled to come up with a convincing lie. Why couldn't girls just admit they had their period instead of acting like it was a deep, dark secret to be ashamed of?

Saved by the director again. He called for us to gather by the stage and asked who wanted to audition first. Donna raised her hand to the sky and launched into a boisterous rendition of "Mary Had a Little Lamb" when he told her to sing.

Will moved up next to me. He smelled nice, like Lifesavers candy and soap. "What part are you trying out for?" he asked.

"Well, my singing can crack windows from here to Boston. My dancing would kill Fred Astaire. We'd have to pay the audience to get them to watch my acting. So, I think I'll audition for the lead."

"You're a shoo-in for Mary. Everyone'll just have to cover their ears."

"That'll help. What about you?"

He sobered. "I plan to lurk in the land of extras."

"Oh. I'm sure I'll be in extra land with you." I would've said more but Marilyn flashed me a supremely frosty look that said *shut up* loud and clear. So I shut up.

"Thank you, Donna," Bushy Beard said when she finished her song. "That was...interesting."

Barry went next. Chills danced up my spine when he sang. No surprise he landed the lead role right away. He was really good. And a dead ringer for Jesus, with his tall, slim build and long hair. Well, the Jesus you see in movies, anyway. My friend Yolanda once said the real Jesus was Black and not a white guy like in *The King of Kings* or other Hollywood films. That made sense, but since no Black kids came to audition for the part, or any parts at all, or even went to this church, Barry got the role.

The other roles were soon cast. Marilyn landed the part of Mary, much to Jane's disappointment. Pete landed the pivotal part of Peter, who denied Jesus three times. Jane and Donna got a few singing lines and Will and I ended up right where we wanted to be. In the ensemble, in the background, doubling as stage crew.

The biggest surprise was Carl. He could act and sing as well as Donna, which meant not at all, but he sure had stage presence.

"Huzzah! We've found our Judas," Bushy Beard cried in delight.

He then called for us to "bring it in" again and we ended the night with a cheer. Carl erupted in a "*Wahoo*" that shook every stained-glass window in the church.

Dismissed, we mobbed up the stairs and spilled out the side door, babbling in excitement. Some people dashed to their cars. Others searched for their parents waiting for them in the parking lot, motors running and chugging exhaust into the chilly night.

A dark-haired man in a suit and with a steely set to his jaw stuck his head out of the window of a giant black car that looked expensive and new.

"Come on, Will, move it," he yelled in an *I mean business* voice.

Will shot him a glare then aimed a gloomy look at me. I frowned. I'd figured rich kids had their own cars and didn't need to rely on their cranky fathers to haul them home. But nope. There he was, climbing into the car as if going to his own execution. Marilyn got into the back seat and I watched the vehicle glide away.

A second later, Carl tore off in a squeal of burning rubber in a beat up Buick Skylark. A few minutes after that, Mom swung our equally beat up Impala into the parking lot.

"Dee." Donna poked me in the back. "Can I bum a ride with you?"

I wasn't about to say no. Most everyone had left. How else would she get home? She'd have to take two buses then walk from the bus stop to her house in the dark. Every Project girl knew, and probably all other girls knew too, you didn't risk walking home in the dark if you could bum a ride from a friend.

I sank into the front passenger seat while Donna scrambled into the back.

"Thanks for the lift, Mrs. Daly," she said, pushing books and magazines aside to clear a space to sit. "You look nice tonight."

"Thank you, Donna." Mom sounded suspicious, like when Rusty's friends tried to suck up to her. She looked at me. "Sorry I'm late."

"That's okay." She'd probably wanted to finish a chapter and lost track of time.

She left the parking lot, turned onto Adams Street, and headed for Donna's. "So...how did it go?" she asked in her cautious voice, like she expected a disaster of biblical proportions. Entirely possible, I supposed, since we'd been in a church.

"It went great," Donna chirped.

"I got the role of third wailing woman on the right," I said. "Plus I get to pull the curtain ropes. An important job."

Mom murmured her congratulations and I sat back with a sigh. A strange excitement tickled my stomach, like Christmas Eve when I was younger.

This show promised to be something special. Despite my jitters around Carl and general nervousness about performing on stage, for the first time in my life, I felt like I fit in.

Part Three

March 1976

CHAPTER 10

Doctor Crabby Explains It All

"SLIDE DOWN. FURTHER. FURTHER. No, further."

The doctor's voice grew more impatient which each "further" he bit off. I declined to inform him "farther" was the proper word for this situation, and also that if I slid any further *or* farther, I'd fall off the exam table and onto the floor. Or on top of him.

After I'd fainted at school, Mr. Anger called Mom to express his concern. I could only imagine the vice principal's whispery voice asking if I was on drugs or pregnant and my mother's not-so-whispery response about how it was none of his business then slamming down the phone and making a doctor's appointment, because me fainting in school was absolutely *her* business.

That's how I ended up in the gynecologist office at the Project's free clinic on a Tuesday after school. I'd never been to a gynecologist, though I knew what they did and I expected my visit wouldn't be fun. I hadn't expected it to be so creepy, with me wearing nothing but a johnny, my feet stuck in metal stirrups, a nurse hovering like a gargoyle, and Doctor Crabby sitting on a low stool between my legs, sticking his nose in my crotch.

Eager to get it over with, I scooched my bottom as close as I could to the exam table's edge. The paper covering the vinyl crinkled beneath me and stuck to my back. I focused on that, rather than the doctor sticking his finger into my vagina and wiggling it around as if hunting for a spot on a beach ball that had sprung a leak.

"Yes?" he barked. Not at me, at the nurse who'd tap-tapped on the door and popped her head inside to ask a question.

The nurse got her answer and left. Doctor Crabby's finger left my vagina too. I let out my breath, about to unscootch from the table's edge and sit up, when round two of the exam began. The gargoyle nurse handed him a device called a speculum that looked like a metal duck beak or maybe a space alien's torture device. Whatever, he slid that cold thing inside me, something went *click, click, click* and I tensed as my vagina yawned open.

"You might feel a small pinch," he said, words he no doubt said every day and words he no doubt knew were a lie, because, yeah, that was no small pinch.

Another tap-tap on the door, another of the fifty nurses who bustled about outside poked her head in.

"This is a busy place," I said after the doctor answered her question and the door thumped shut. "Will the pizza guy drop by next?"

Doctor Crabby grunted something that might have been, *I don't appreciate your sense of humor* and removed the speculum. I let out my breath again and unscootched.

After I got dressed, my mother, who'd been in the waiting room reading *Looking for Mr. Goodbar* (a book *not* about candy, believe me), joined me in the doctor's office to await his verdict.

We sat in green plastic seats in front of a long metal desk covered with medical charts and files. The health center had opened only a year ago in the old janitorial building when the city built the housing authority a shiny new maintenance facility down the street. This office must've once been a mop closet because it smelled like dirty water and ammonia and other cleaning fluids used to wash floors.

The door clicked open and the doctor stepped inside, wearing a white coat and a gloomy expression. He perched on the corner of his desk and faced my mother. "Mrs. Daly, we'll have to wait for the results of the pap. Right now, I see nothing to give me concern. Your daughter is primarily healthy."

My mother nodded, looking relieved. So was I, but I wished he'd said that to me instead of acting like I wasn't even in the room.

He tented his fingers in a thoughtful pose. "I believe Deidre's fainting spells and intense cramping is caused by poor dietary habits and, more specifically, her weight."

My belly fluttered unhappily. Was he saying my period's vicious attacks were all my fault?

Mom's eyes went all squinty. "Are you sure?" She employed the doubtful voice she'd perfected during dozens of consultations for Jay's surgeries. "Perhaps she simply needs more iron. Her condition could be caused by anemia. Or something internal. I've read that the Pill can help relieve—"

He held up a hand. "Let's not get lost in speculation. What Deidre needs is to drop some weight. She needs to cut out sweets, starch, and fatty foods. Eat cottage cheese and get plenty of exercise. It's a simple matter of diet and discipline. Calories in, calories out. Trust me, losing weight should cure those cramps. She'll feel much better." He swiveled, finally looking at me. "Best of all, you'll look better, too. I know how important looks are to girls your age."

It was after four when we left the clinic, Mom clutching her green vinyl pocketbook, me clutching a food pyramid pamphlet and a calorie counting guide.

Clouds had rolled in, with dusk not far behind. Men and women in work uniforms and heavy coats trudged along the sidewalk, the first shift coming home from the factories down the street. A city bus stuffed with passengers huffed by. Across the way, people lined up on the steps of the neighborhood center, waiting to get inside and vote in today's presidential primary the newspapers had dubbed "Super Tuesday."

"Well *that* was fun," I grumbled as we walked up Prosperity Way toward our street.

Best of all, you'll look better, too. What Doctor Crabby really meant was pretty face, unpretty body equals ugly, ugly Deidre.

Only one way to change that, something I'd failed at miserably these last two months. I'd hit the halfway point between New Year's and prom and had only lost a paltry ten pounds. It wasn't enough. As much as the doctor's sniffy attitude irked me, he was right. I had to cut down and work harder if I had any hope of ever losing weight.

"I'm sorry the exam was uncomfortable," Mom said, misinterpreting my scowling sarcasm. She gave me the Daly version of a heartfelt hug—a quick pat on the shoulder. "The exam's part of being a woman, I'm afraid. And in case you're worried, that's not how..." She cleared her throat uncomfortably. "That's not how it feels when you have sex."

I smothered a groan. This conversation had taken an awkward turn.

"Sex is a whole different feeling. If you're with the right person, and using proper birth control, of course, sex is..." She sighed. "It's so, so *right.*"

Her expression turned dreamy and I wanted to launch myself into space. She had four kids, and might've had ten more, she liked to say, if the Pill hadn't been invented, so there was a time "it" must've been right with my father. An activity I did *not* want to think about. Not now, not ever.

Her wistfulness evaporated as we reached the corner. A group of guys with ratty beards and straggly hair hung out near the cellar entrance of the next block. One of the gangs that infested the neighborhood. There were dozens of them, both white and Black guys, jerks who'd dropped out of school and had no place to go and nothing to do but sniff glue, go to war with each other, and harass every innocent passerby who dared to get too close to their precious turf.

It wasn't fully dark yet, so we were safe enough. Still, Mom nudged my elbow to steer me across the street. She picked up the pace.

I moved faster too, trying to decide what was scarier, the prospect of a run-in with one of these gangs at night, or the lingering mental image of my parents having sex.

I helped Mom make dinner when we got home. Baked beans, hot dogs, and moist, molasses-scented brown bread for everyone else, a healthy, low-calorie meal for me. Following doctor's orders, I whipped up an orangey mixture of chicken bouillon, water, and carrots, the whole soupy mess thickened with a sprinkling of flour.

Mom's squinty look made a return appearance as she watched me pour the concoction into a bowl, her expression somewhere between dismay and disapproval. Couldn't blame her. The orange slop looked like baby poop. Even Marco turned his nose up at it. He sniffed around under the table for more palatable scraps as we ate and avoided my chair altogether.

Dad spooned beans into his mouth and gazed at us around the table, his expression three nips and three beers giddy. "What a homely bunch of kids you turned out to be," he said, as if we had a choice in the matter. He added a laugh the mean girls at school could've learned a thing or two from.

Mom closed her book—another Agatha Christie—and pushed her plate away, her expression tinged with disapproval. "Deidre, finish your dinner, or whatever you call that mess. Unless you prefer to be late for play practice?"

I did not. I quickly downed the second of two bowls of carrot sludge, though it didn't fill me up much and I was still hungry when Mom dropped me off at Saint Mary's.

Bushy Beard was late. Naturally, we goofed off. Some of the boys roamed around, rattling off lines from TV commercials, like "Mama mia that's a spicy meatball," and "I can't believe I ate the whole thing." The Holy Mother girls had found some Jiffy Pop popcorn in the kitchen and Jane helped them figure out how to light the stove to cook it.

I joined my friends at the long table by the wall. *Our* table, as I'd taken to calling it.

Pete had brought a battery-operated radio the size of a toaster from home. He turned it on, and while Rod Stewart croaked through "Maggie May," Pete played a game of solitaire as Barry offered suggestions to help him cheat. Will read a book while leaning against the wall. He seemed to enjoy leaning against walls. He also seemed to enjoy leaving the laces of his boots untied. They dangled like dead snakes.

Donna perched on the tabletop. "I'm s-o-o-o bored." She latched her gaze onto Barry and stretched her arms over her head. She wore a slinky dress and knee high leather boots as sleek as Will's were scruffy. Apparently none of the guys she'd flirted with at her party fit the bill for cherry-popping bliss and she'd moved on to Barry. Who ignored her most thoroughly.

In the kitchen, the Holy Mother girls let out a cry of success and the room filled with the smell of popcorn that made my mouth water. I heard Marilyn's voice in the group, on her own for once and not playing Will's shadow.

I went over and leaned against the wall next to him. My empty stomach gurgled like water swirling down a drain. "Hello, William."

I spoke really loud to cover up the sound. "Ready to break a leg tonight?"

Using a finger to mark his place, he closed his book and gazed at me, the corners of his eyes crinkling. "Not literally, I hope."

"Wiseass." A wicked nerdy wiseass with his books and his geeky beige tee-shirt with brown chest pockets and the unique way he always made me laugh. "What're you reading?"

He turned the book, showing me a dark blue cover with a red silhouette of a dancing soldier and the title *Catch 22* in bold, white letters.

"Oh. I don't know that one. Is it good?"

"Yeah. It's set in World War Two. It's funny and sometimes absurd." His eyes crinkled again, a most disarming smile. "Like you."

"Oh, dear. I hope that's a compliment."

His smile became a frown. He began to answer when Donna hissed for my attention.

"Dee, look." Her eyes lit up, boredom and Barry forgotten, as Carl trotted down the steps and into the room.

I perked up too, and my insides tingled alarmingly. I remembered what my mother said about finding the right person. Did my giddy reaction mean Carl was "it" for me?

"*H-e-r-r-r-e's* Judas," Will announced, like Ed McMahon on the *Johnny Carson Show*. Make that a bitter Ed McMahon.

"That guy kills me," Barry/Jesus said.

Carl pasted on a lazy smile and strutted over to the girls now gathered by the stage and eating their popcorn. He hadn't spoken to me or even seemed to notice I existed since our first rehearsal, but he sure noticed the other girls.

Well, why not? They were all skinny. And all, weirdly, named after flowers. Rose, Iris, Lily... A whole floral garden attended Holy Mother of God. How non-flower Marilyn got accepted to that school baffled me, unless her middle name was Petunia or her father slipped the Mother Superior a bribe to get her in.

Anyway, Carl's dedication to flirting with those girls annoyed me. What did he hope to accomplish? Didn't he know Catholic girls were notoriously prudish and fully dedicated to hanging onto their virginity until marriage? And didn't he know, if he ever turned his lazy smile my way, it could be an entirely different story?

I caught Will eying me in an odd way, as if I were a particularly tricky math problem that had no answer. I ducked my head, hoping he hadn't noticed me drooling over Carl.

Bushy Beard rushed into the room then. A cloud of cigarette smoke and the sharp scent of his cologne rushed in after him.

"Let's get to work, people," he said and clapped his hands impatiently, as if we'd all been late and not him.

CHAPTER 11

Old Friends, New Lives & the Space Between Us

ON MONDAY, I DRAGGED myself out of bed and trucked down to the neighborhood center in the early light. Mom worked the free breakfast program there three mornings a week and she roped dutiful daughter me into coming and helping out a couple times a month.

The yummy smells of eggs, pancakes, syrup, and bacon greeted me and my empty stomach when I stepped into the all-purpose room, the heart of the neighborhood center. Chairs scraped the floor, voices babbled, and the song "Spinning Wheel" blared from a radio, echoing off the high ceiling.

Kids of all ages, from toddlers to junior high and even some high schoolers gathered here for what would likely give the lunch lady at my school a fatal stroke—eating a totally free breakfast on the government's dime.

I headed for the kitchen, where a dozen volunteers and a few paid staff whipped up breakfast each weekday morning. I cut the line at the service window to see what they wanted me to do and was put on cleanup duty. A fortyish woman wearing a colorful V-neck top called a dashiki thrust a plate loaded with a towering stack of pancakes in my face.

Tempting, but I shook my head. I'd been exercising, lifting soup cans like barbells and pacing the living room while watching *Welcome Back Kotter* and that new show *Laverne & Shirley* until

99

Dad yelled at me to be still or he'd brain me. I got more exercise at rehearsal and at work every weekend. I ate nothing but carrot soup until my pee turned orange and I still hadn't lost a single pound since my visit to Doctor Crabby.

So nope. No breakfast for me.

The kitchen crew had wisely kept my mother out of the cooking process. I spotted her on the other side of the room, on cleanup detail like me. She tossed dirty dishes and silverware into bins on a metal cart, then wiped down tables with enough vigor to peel the linoleum off the top.

I found a cart and got to work. I wiped spilled juice off the floor. I helped some of the little ones spread jelly over their toast and resisted licking my sticky fingers. I checked the clock. Roughly fifteen minutes until Gus would screech the school bus to a stop outside. Ten minutes more work, one minute to hit the bathroom, then out into the cold to catch my ride. Several hours until lunch. My stomach rumbled. Would I make it that long?

"Deidre."

I looked up from my chores. "Pammie?"

On the windowsill in my bedroom, there stood a picture in a tarnished metal frame. Three ten-year-old girls, three best friends—Yolanda, a skinny Black girl with a confident smile and light brown skin, Pammie, a shy white girl with ash blonde hair in pigtails, and me, freckles, upturned nose, plump cheeks. My mom had taken the picture. The flashbulb's flare shined on Yolanda's forehead and turned my eyes to red orbs like the devil.

Yolanda had gotten a scholarship to a fancy prep school and her family moved shortly after to a three-decker apartment house near the school.

Pammie hadn't been as lucky.

She sat alone at a small table with a cup of coffee, a half-eaten plate of eggs, and a cigarette clenched between two fingers. A baby carriage stood beside her chair, one of those big, bouncy carriages from the 1950s that had seen better days. The chrome wheels were rusted and a cloth canopy as frayed as the cuffs of Pammie's blue jeans.

I hadn't seen her since she had her baby. Well, since long before that, when she decided chubby, bookish me wasn't cool enough for her and she started hanging out with the girls who ran with the gang on her block.

"How are you?" I asked. Dumb question. She was tired. I knew that from the circles under her pale blue eyes and her dirty and limp ash blonde hair. I supposed I'd be tired too, if I had a baby to take care of.

She let out a heavy sigh and lifted one shoulder. "I guess I'm okay."

I dropped the washcloth into the water bucket on my cart and went to check out the creature inside the carriage. About six or seven months old, she wore pajamas and a pink knitted hat and wiggled and coughed and squinched up her little face, clearly unhappy.

"She's cute." I couldn't remember the kid's name. How was that for a friend?

"Yeah. Cute." Pammie took a slow drag on her cigarette and looked me over. She centered her gaze on my face. "What ya been up to?"

How could I answer that? The three of us had once been as close as sisters, spending nearly every day together. Now, we'd grown so far apart, I couldn't think of anything to say that would interest her.

I settled for a vague, "Oh, you know, the usual."

"Writing your stories." She blew out a cloud of smoke. "Dreaming."

She sounded like my guidance counselor. Or my dad, telling me I had high hopes, and not in a *good for you, kid* way. What was wrong with dreaming? Pammie had dreamed once. She wanted to be a model, like Cheryl Tiegs. She was pretty enough, despite not having the height.

The baby fussed some more. Pammie growled impatiently then reached out and jiggled the carriage. It didn't help. The baby whimpered, which quickly turned into a wail and believe me, that kid was tiny, but her crying could wake the dead.

"Jesus Christ, this kid." Pammie stabbed out her cigarette in her half-eaten plate of eggs and rocked the carriage harder. It bounced and the wheels squeaked. The kid still howled and thrashed around. Pammie leaned over the carriage. She pressed in real close. Then she shouted, "Shut up!" right in the kid's face.

The baby did not shut up. She just cried and cried.

And then... Pammie did too.

My chest went tight and I got all jumpy. I wanted to run away. As fast as I could. Strike two in the bad friend department.

This was why Mom had always told us everything about sex. And why she'd been such a stormtrooper about birth control. She didn't want me or Chrissy to end up like Pammie and the other girls I knew, high school dropouts stuck with a kid and not knowing what to do with it. Or end up like Mom herself, with four kids and no money, and lots and lots of problems.

Suddenly, my mother was there.

"Okay, girls, what's the fuss?" She scooped up the crying kid and cuddled her, eyeing her with a tender smile. "My, aren't you the sweetest thing." She shifted her gaze to Pammie's tear-streaked face. "Do you remember that time you and Deidre babysat the Perez twins? Must've been, what? Four, five years ago."

Pammie scowled, but she nodded.

"Those rugrats had such terrible diaper rash." Mom swayed, gently bouncing the baby up and down, back and forth, calming her crying a little. "Deidre called me that night, freaking out. She didn't know what to do. But *you* did. You took care of those kids beautifully. You were stressed, but you did it. Remember that?"

Pammie dragged her knuckles across her leaking eyes and nodded again.

Mom lifted the baby and sniffed her butt. "Ah, there's the problem. We've got spare diapers in the ladies bathroom. Want me to change her?"

"I can do it, Mrs. Daly." Pammie swiped away the last of her tears and stood. She took her daughter and tucked her gently against her shoulder, holding her with one arm, the baby's head nuzzling her neck. She pushed the bouncy carriage with her free hand, weaving through the tables toward the bathroom. She didn't look back.

"Mom, you saved the day." How did my mother get to be so amazing? If the Dalys weren't so allergic to displays of affection, I would've given her a hug.

"I solved one small problem. That girl has a lot more." She watched Pammie cross the room, her eyebrows drawing down, frowning. "Girls like her can be so foolish. They think a baby will make them happy and give them the love they desperately want. They don't realize how much work children are. Especially when they don't have any help." She sighed. "I hear there's a program at the Y downtown that gives young mothers the support they need. I'll see if I can get Pammie into that." She turned to me. "As for you—"

"Yeah, I know. Birth control."

"Yes, that." She tucked a strand of my hair behind my ear and smiled, something she didn't do much. At least, not lately. "Also, eat something. Dieting is all well and good, but I do *not* want to get another call from your school telling me you fainted again."

✳ ✿ ✳ ✿

The morning zoomed by and lunch rolled around. After an unexpectedly brief scuffle with my pal at the register, I took my tray to our table. Karen had stuck her skinny butt into my usual chair next to Donna. That irked me, but I didn't say anything as I squeezed behind her to take a seat with my back to the wall. Everyone was here except Jane, who was probably retiling the school's roof or finding sixteen more clubs to join and would arrive later.

I dug into my meal. Mom's wisdom paid off. Because I'd had a full breakfast, I didn't go wild now, eating slowly and getting full before I'd even finished.

"I've got news." Linda G looked up from her tuna sandwich and *Gone With the Wind*. "I got accepted to Mount Holyoke."

"That was fast," Barbie said. "I thought most colleges didn't let you know until next month."

Karen scowled. "You applied to only one school and you got in? Did you bribe someone?"

"Maybe I'm just brilliant," Linda said coolly.

"Sure you are." Karen clenched her jaw like my dad did when he was in a bad mood and looking for a fight.

Barbie threw down her fork and picked up the challenge. "Why do you have to be such a pill all the time? A large pill you need a whole glass of water to swallow."

Karen swung on her. "What's wrong with you? You on the rag?"

I rolled my eyes. Because any girl who states an opinion or disagrees with someone *must* be on the rag. Of course I didn't say that. I shrunk into myself and let them bicker and battle as I did at home when tempers flared.

"That's got nothing to do with it." Barbie's eyes spit fire. "Can't you ever just stop? You're always so critical and judgmental of everyone. God, you're exactly like your mother."

That did it. Karen went as hot as a kiln fire. "Don't *ever* fucking say that. My mother's nothing like me. She's...she's..."

She shoved her tray and it skimmed across the table, smacking into mine. Then she jumped up so fast her chair flew back and banged to the floor. The room went silent, followed by a buzz of speculation and all eyes following Karen as she raced across the room and out of the cafeteria. As the door swung shut, I saw her bomb into the girls' bathroom.

"I bet *she's* on the rag," Donna said with a weak laugh.

"She's *always* like that." Barbie snatched up her fork. "I've known her since kindergarten. Her mother's a Miss Perfect controlling bitch and Karen's following in her footsteps. Always picking people apart. Nothing and no one's ever good enough for either of them."

Jane arrived, late as usual, asking what she'd missed. I didn't stick around to help fill her in. I brought my tray—and Karen's—to the tray return and left.

I hesitated outside the bathroom door. Should I go in and see if she was okay? My mother would. Like with Pammie this morning, she'd zoom in and demand to know what was wrong, and how she could help. Karen would fall into her arms and spill her guts.

Me? What could someone who avoided confrontation at all costs do to help a Miss Perfect controlling bitch in training who would probably tell me to mind my own business anyway?

In true bad friend fashion, I chose not to take the risk. Pondering the mysteries of the universe and cranky girls who may or may not be on the rag, I went to my locker, then on to French class. The period dragged as usual, but afterward I made it through the leering mob of guys in the Desert unscathed and un-insulted, so things were looking up.

The day got even brighter when I got to English. Miss French breezed in after the bell rang and strode to the front of the room. She picked up a piece of chalk and it screeched on the blackboard like a train derailment as she wrote *Creative Writing Assignment* in blocky letters.

I straightened up so fast I nearly cracked my neck. Karen's outburst, Pammie's woes, and everything else flew from my mind.

"I know you've been waiting for this one," Miss French said, as if speaking directly to me. "But before you write a story, you'll need an idea of how themes and imagery work, so we'll read excerpts from great literature."

A majority of the class groaned. I joined them. Great literature did *not* mean we'd be reading *Jaws* or any spicy romance books like *Sweet Savage Love*, that was for sure.

"I promise it won't hurt too much," she added with a chuckle. "As we progress, we'll put into practice what we learn in our classwork. Your first assignment, a short story, will be due in two weeks."

I nearly died from glee. And anxiety. I'd been noodling on my Bicentennial story about a girl living near Concord Bridge at the start of the Revolutionary War forever, but it'd stalled out, lost without a plot. Could I whip it into shape in two weeks? Or come up with something new?

Ruthie Cullen wriggled in her seat across the aisle. "What do we write about?" she asked, kind of whiny.

"Use your imagination. As long as there's no swearing or sex in it, of course."

"Hell, where's the fun in that?" Lawrence Tetro said and I envied the big laugh that got.

A skinny girl with curly hair that looked like pinwheels raised her hand. "Does it have to be a short story?" Anne Albright said. Quite dramatically, I might add. "Because I've already written a novel. May I turn that in?"

A *novel?* A ravenous green-eyed beast called jealousy instantly consumed me. Anne had penned an entire novel and I struggled to get beyond page two of my story.

"Oh," Miss French said, as surprised as me. "See me after class and we'll discuss it. Now, let's get started by taking a look at the structure and themes of the short story 'A&P' by John Updike."

She picked up a stack of papers and began to hand them out. I took my copy from her and sniffed it. Everyone did. No one could resist the hot, inky smell of freshly mimeographed paper, as satisfying as a hit of an addictive drug.

Miss French started to read. I had no interest in Mr. Updike's tale of a teenage grocery clerk's unfortunate effort to impress girls in bathing suits. I wanted to hear more about Anne's novel. I wanted to hear more so desperately that I lingered after class. I took my sweet time packing up my books, determined to eavesdrop on every word.

"Now..." Miss French leaned her butt against her desk and folded her arms. "Tell me about this novel."

Anne grinned. "It's a hundred and ten pages and it's called *Adventure at Almacks.* It's a Regency romance." She breathed that last sentence with all the fervor of a devoted Georgette Heyer fan.

"Interesting." Miss French kept her tone neutral. "Turn it in when the assignment's due. I can't promise I'll have time to read the entire novel. I'll look at the opening pages at least."

Anne turned to leave, looking disappointed. I couldn't blame her. If I'd written something so long and put in so much work, I'd want Miss French to read the whole thing right now.

"Can I read your book?" I blurted as Anne passed me, not even slightly hiding my eavesdropping now. "I'm a writer too and I love historical romance and the Regency is one of my favorite time periods. I'd *love* to read your story."

Anne lifted her nose so high her nostrils would've gotten sunburned if we were outside. "No. What a weird thing to ask."

She sailed through the door and I snatched up my handbag. My cheeks roasted, stung by such a bald rejection. And my own foolishness for opening my big mouth. Why was everything I did or said weird?

Through the classroom window I saw Gus slap the school bus doors shut and tear off at lightning speed.

And to top it off, I'd missed my ride home.

Chapter 12

Do You Know Where You're Going To?

I brought my notebook to rehearsal that night, planning to work on my story during our breaks. I might not have time before my assignment was due to write a novel like some snippy people I knew, but I sure could finish a short story.

All I needed was a beginning. And a middle. And an end.

Not to mention a plot.

Bushy Beard threw a wrench into that plan. He suddenly realized the show was a little more than a month away and he put us to work the second he arrived, insisting we rehearse straight through without a breather.

Barry and Marilyn had their parts almost completely memorized. The rest of us stumbled around, bellowing the songs out of tune, while our director played his guitar and yelled directions nobody listened to. Will and I hung out in the back and I got to see that million dollar smile more than once as he laughed at our theatrical disaster, especially Carl's performance.

"If Judas had to sing for his last supper, he'd starve," he said.

Impressive how Will never called Carl by his real name. "He's not that bad." Well, he was that bad. His singing could break eardrums and his acting stunk, but he sure looked nice stomping around the stage, giving Jesus hell.

Will's mood darkened. I didn't get to ask what bee had gotten into his bonnet because the church's resident priests came into the basement to watch us rehearse and everyone sobered fast. We finished practice on our best behavior and when we broke for the night, the priests introduced themselves.

One of them had white hair, twinkling blue eyes, and was so old I suspected he'd known Jesus personally. The other priest was half his age, thin, with black-rimmed glasses, and a sober manner. The kids from Saint Mary's greeted Father Old like he was Bing Crosby, with fawning smiles and peppy hellos. No such adulation for Father Young, though. Only wary glances and gloomy silence.

When we broke for the night, the Fathers, or whatever you call the plural of two priests, asked us to join hands for a prayer. Father Young took a boy's hand and the kid cringed like the man had cooties. Donna shoved between me and Barry so I was stuck holding her hand and a kid named Stanley's sweaty paw. Carl and Will were on the other side, with Marilyn between them.

I bowed my head to pray, like everyone else. As Father Old droned on, I wondered why prayers were always about dying and the reward waiting for us on the other side while we barely celebrated being here on Earth.

The priest finally wrapped it up. An explosion of noise followed our halfhearted "Amens," as everyone rushed to get their coats and leave. I'd draped my coat over the back of a metal folding chair at our table. I snatched it up too fast. The hood snagged on one of the legs. The chair flipped backwards then crashed to the floor with a *twang* that shot throughout the room.

The buzz of chatter abruptly cut off. Everyone turned to stare at me, even the priests. Then it started, a slow-clap round of applause that rippled around the room like a taunt. I flushed, burning from head to toe.

I bent to pick up the chair but Will got there first. He righted the chair and scooped up my coat. Then he helped me put it on, as if he thought I was his grandma.

"Thank you, sir," I said, heat searing my face again. "You are a gentleman and a scholar."

"Oh brother," Marilyn muttered, but Will laughed and that was good enough for me.

Outside, people were leaving. Will wasn't laughing now as he went to meet his executioner, I mean, got into the car with his father. He eyed me through the window with a shrug and a *woe is me* expression as their fancy car pulled away from the curb.

A second later, Carl's Buick peeled out of the parking lot with a Holy Mother girl named Rose snuggled next to him on the front seat. My heart upended and so did my theory about Catholic girls and their dedication to virginity. Rose sure looked eager and willing to be kissed and maybe more before he dropped her off at home.

"You need a ride?" Donna asked, strolling up to me, tying the floppy belt of her plaid, knee-length coat.

"Sure. My brother has the car. I'm supposed to go to his store and wait for him to close up." Which wouldn't be for almost two hours. "If you can give me a lift, I'll be glad to get home earlier."

"Oh, sorry, I wasn't offering. My mother took our car. She has her so-called bridge club tonight and left me with no way home. Again." She released an angry sigh. "I bummed a ride from Marilyn. I'm sure she'll take you home too."

She tugged me over to Marilyn, who stood by the curb, yammering a mile a minute with her school friends.

Donna butt in. "Deidre needs a ride. I told her she could come with us."

Marilyn sniffed in surprise. Or maybe offended that Donna would offer rides in her car to any slob that came along. But she was trapped, and her reluctant, "I guess so," told everyone in a twenty mile radius she knew it.

Donna beamed. "Thanks. You're a peach, Mar."

Mar's face squinched in distaste at the nickname. My face fell when I got a look at her car. Huge, almost as fancy as the family hearse Will rode home in.

Donna jumped into the back, leaving me with the honor of sitting up front. I sank into the leather seat, guessing this was Marilyn's mother's car by the old lady perfume smell and the polka-dotted plastic rain bonnet from Woolworth's on the dashboard.

The engine purred to life and Marilyn rolled to the parking lot exit. I thought she might pick up speed once we turned onto Adams Street. But...nope. She drove as slow as an elderly sloth. Cars tore past us and honked their horns.

She looked at Donna in the rearview mirror and said, "Should I drop you off first?"

Donna didn't answer. She sat back with her eyes closed, snapping her fingers and singing along to "Black Water" by the Doobie Brothers playing on the radio, in her own little world. Marilyn steered toward Donna's anyway.

Donna snapped out of her daze with a gasp when we reached her house and she spotted her mother in the driveway. She leaned against the Pinto, smoking and looking pissed. She wore a slinky leather trench coat over palazzo pants and the kind of shoes a woman would wear to a nightclub and not her bridge club. Delicate, with pencil heels.

"There you are," her mother shrilled when Donna cringed her way out of the car. "Where the hell have you been?"

"At Saint Mary's, Mum. I *told* you a hundred times—"

"I'm locked out of the house. I've been waiting for an hour. Open up."

The rest got cut off as Donna shut the door and we drove away. I glanced back and saw her mother slap the back of her head then push her toward the steps by the kitchen door. She shoved so hard Donna almost fell. I winced. Not the first time I'd seen a kid smacked around by one of their parents. The first time outside the Project, though.

The Beatles' "The Long and Winding Road" came on the radio. Marilyn turned down the volume and glanced at me. "Where to now?" she asked.

The moment of truth had arrived and I had to tell her. I hemmed and hawed before finally getting it over with.

Her eyes went as round as Frisbees. "I didn't know you lived in *that* neighborhood."

I nearly burst into flames with embarrassment. "Yeah, ha-ha. All my life."

"But...uh...I can't drive you all the way down there. I'm...I'm running low on gas."

I glanced at the gas gauge. The needle pointed at F for *Full* like an eyewitness pointing out the accused in court.

"I can pay you if it helps." Well, sort of pay her. I had exactly thirty five cents in my pocket. Which would buy half a gallon, and that wouldn't go far in this gas guzzler.

She turned a pleading gaze on me. "Look, Deidre, I'll be honest. My parents would kill me if I drove anywhere near the Project. You understand."

I heard fear in her voice, touched with superiority. I understood only one thing. Marilyn was too scared to drive into the place I called home. And it filled me with shame.

"Do you have enough gas to get me to Foley Plaza?"

Cheering up, she let out an eager, "Yes," and we headed back where we'd come from.

I fished around for something to fill the silence that followed and latched onto the only thing we had in common. "How long have you known Will?"

A tiny wrinkle creased her smooth forehead. "I've known him forever. We went to Hammond Elementary together."

Oh. The Richie Rich grammar school, in the Richie Rich land of upper Chisholm Road. Where snobby white people lived in big houses with three bathrooms. Where sirens meant the cops were on the way to save a kitten stuck in a tree and not coming to bust up a riot or beat the living crap out of some innocent bystander like in my neighborhood. The place that spawned stuck-up girls like Marilyn who thought their shit didn't stink.

The place Will called home.

Surely he was different. He was nice, not snobby. He didn't care where I lived. Well, I couldn't be entirely sure he knew I called *that neighborhood* my home, but if he did it wouldn't matter.

I hoped.

"That's cool," I said. "Will's a good guy."

"Yeah, he's nice. Kind of shy, but that's understandable, with his problem."

Problem. Like he needed to be fixed. Like something a girlfriend would never say about a guy she was dating. But for some reason, I had to know for sure. "So, are you and Will, like, going out?"

"Of course not." She flashed me a narrow-eyed glance. "Why do you want to know?"

She sprinkled a ton of suspicion into that question. I didn't want her to think a chubby Project girl like me was interested in him, so I shook my head and clammed up. I stayed quiet for the rest of the ride. Marilyn didn't volunteer to talk either. Her body language spoke volumes, though.

She didn't like me. Not one bit.

Ten minutes later, she dumped me at Foley Plaza across the street from Saint Mary's and I vowed I'd walk home barefoot in the pitch dark with the Hound of the Baskervilles nipping at my heels before I ever bummed a ride with her again.

The automatic door slid open like the doors in *Star Trek* as I stepped into Cully's Department Store. Warm and stuffy, the place smelled like hot dogs and fries and other yummy things for sale at the lunch counter in the back. Shiny new ten speed bicycles were on display by the front windows. Rows of fluorescent lights ran the length of the ceiling. One of them flickered, winking from light to dark as if keeping time to the song "December 1963" playing on the store's overhead speakers.

I went to the bathroom then wandered the aisles, checking out the toy and shoe departments, the electronics area with TVs, tape decks, and 8-track players of all brands, and shelves heaped with everything a shopper could possibly need. I pored over racks of women's clothing. I found a couple of blouses that would show off my ooh-la-la boobies and I would've bought if I had more than thirty five cents in my pocket. Perhaps I could put the tops on Layaway and pay a little each week.

I finally spotted Jay, talking with a short Black woman with a plump bottom and a short Afro hairstyle. She touched Jay's arm and I saw something I didn't often see on my brother's face.

A smile. A big, genuine smile.

I rushed over. "I'm here," I blurted, getting a better look at Jay's companion. About the same age as him, twenty-two, she had a smooth complexion, a button nose, long fingernails painted red, and thick, silky eyelashes Donna would kill for.

"Thought I'd see you earlier," Jay said and I shrugged, declining to go into the Marilyn saga. "This is Shirley." He blushed a becoming shade of pink. "She works here."

Well, obviously. Her Cully's uniform of crimson polyester pants, tan blouse, and a barber pole striped vest gave her away. I couldn't help a grin as I said hello. Could Shirley be the girl who'd been calling Jay on the phone?

Jay dug into the front pocket of his corduroys and pulled out a buck. "Go hang out at that snack bar until we close. And stay out of trouble."

I gave him a salute and did as commanded.

It had been a stressful day, so I ordered the French fries as a reward. To offset the calories, I got a Tab to drink. I opened my notebook and took out a pen. Though tempted to jettison my Revolutionary War concept in favor of a story about a snooty girl from a ritzy neighborhood driving her car into a ditch, I stuck with my original idea.

A while later, Shirley stopped by. I swiveled on the stool and looked up at her. Not very far. She was tiny, about five feet. She carried a stack of boxes labeled "The Authentic All-American Bicentennial Puzzle" with an eagle and the stars and stripes on the cover.

"Let me guess. Jay hasn't said a word to you about me," she said.

"Nope. He's always been secretive. Won't give a hint about what he got you for Christmas, and he'll never, ever tell you what he's thinking."

"I'll see what I can do about that."

"Are you...dating?" The idea filled me with joy.

She mimed pulling a zipper over her lips, then wiggled her fingers in a sassy wave and walked away. I watched her go, my anger at Marilyn forgotten, my spirits soaring.

This was big news. Big, *big* news. *Man Walks on the Moon* news.

Jay had a girlfriend.

CHAPTER 13

One Joke Over the Line

MDP ARRIVED OVER THE weekend for the briefest stay in history. A two day visit, no cramps, very light flow and see you next month. It was a March Miracle.

I'd been (mostly) sticking to my calories-in, calories-out regimen and had lost three more pounds for a whopping total of thirteen—Bicentennial minus the thirteen colonies. Seemed Doctor Crabby was right that dropping some weight would ease my period's bad symptoms.

That would've put me in an excellent mood forever if my pulse didn't already thrum with excitement to turn in my short story.

I eagerly placed my three handwritten pages torn out of my notebook into a metal box on Miss French's desk. Some others had typed their stories and put them in folders with clear covers. Anne Albright offered up her precious novel in a three ring binder, with *Adventure at Almacks* written in magic marker on the front.

The only one left was Ruthie Cullen. She bent over her desk, scribbling furiously, trying to finish her story before Miss French came in. I fought the urge to peer across the aisle and peek at Ruthie's paper. For three seconds. She'd written in large, blocky letters, anyway, easy to read without spraining a muscle when I craned my neck to look.

I got up and went downstairs the smorning.

117

I slammed on the brakes and didn't read another word. *The smorning?* Did she mean *this morning?* How did Ruthie get to be a senior and not know that was wrong?

Of course, not everyone had a mother whose eyes popped when you made such an egregious mistake. Or a mother who would insist she learn words like egregious. I considered telling Ruthie how to correct it, but she rushed up and slammed her story into the box and her fate slipped out of my control.

A tingle rushed through me as Miss French whooshed into the classroom a second later. I called my story "The Battle" and had my heroine waving goodbye to her Minuteman boyfriend as he rode off to fight at Concord and Lexington. It came out good. *Really* good, and I knew Miss French would think so too.

"Settle down," she said. "Let's begin today by looking at T. S. Eliot's 'Love Song of J. Alfred Prufrock.'"

She started passing out assignment packets. My spirits drooped. I'd poured my soul into those three pages and she didn't even glance at the box on her desk. *What did you expect, dummy?* For her to read all the stories right now? Anne's *Almacks* opus alone would take a week to get through.

Sighing in major disappointment, I took the mimeographed paper Miss French handed me and gave it a good sniff. Then I sat back to read some poetry, the thing I hated most of all.

Bushy Beard got a phone call from his wife and had to leave, so rehearsal ended early Tuesday night. Which meant people without cars got in line at the payphone in the kitchen to call home for their rides to come early (including me). After that, Father Young came in and shooed us out of the basement, telling us to wait outside.

"Can I bum a ride off you?" Donna asked as we climbed the steps to the door.

"Sure." Though still miffed about her role in the Marilyn debacle last week, I decided to be magnanimous in my forgiveness. "Um, where are your parents? Why don't they pick you up? I never see them." I'd never even met them, except for the brief and troubling glimpse I'd gotten of Donna's mother smacking her the other night.

"My dad works a lot of crazy hours in the emergency room. Mostly broken bones and stitches. He says you wouldn't believe the weird shit people do to themselves. My mother..." She stopped on the landing and drew me aside. "Honestly, I think she has a boyfriend."

"A *boyfriend*?"

She shushed me. "Keep it down. I don't know for sure, but she's always complaining my father doesn't pay her any attention, then she goes out I don't know where and is gone for hours. What else am I supposed to think?" Footsteps sounded on the steps from below and she grabbed my arm in a tight grip. "Don't tell anyone. Promise me you won't."

I promised, royally shaken up, but Donna stepped outside with a carefree smile, as if she hadn't just revealed such a painful secret.

Lots of people were still hanging around outside. Jane chatted with Marilyn and several others near the door. I frowned at Carl, who toddled off to his car, his arm around a different Holy Mother girl tonight, Lily this time. Will sat on the stone wall that ran between the sidewalk and the parking lot, hanging out with Pete and Barry.

Donna towed me toward them. "What're you guys talking about?" she asked, her hungry gaze on Barry.

"The future." He touched a lit match to a cigarette and a soft crackle filled the air as he took a deep drag. "In twenty four years it'll be the year 2000. A new century. Freaky, huh?"

"What d'ya think that'll be like?" Will said, eyeing me. "Utopia? Or chaos and robots running the world?"

"Good question. I'd like to say things'll be hunky-dory, but you know how people are, so... Robots. *Killer* robots. Danger, danger, Will Hovey."

"Dark and cynical, Deidre Daly. Don't you think we humans stand a chance?"

"You maybe, Will. The rest of us are toast, but you're too perfect for the robots to mess with."

"Perfect?" He laughed. Loud. So loud, Marilyn broke away from her conversation and snapped her gaze toward us. "Deidre, you know I'm not. Far from it."

Pete butt in with, "Besides being chased by robots, where do you think we'll all be by then? I'm going to Vegas. I plan to be a star poker player and make lots of money."

"I can see that," I said. "I bet Barry will be a famous Broadway star." That cool fellow nodded, like my prediction had no choice but to come true. "And I see Will as a businessman in a big office with a big desk."

Will's mood abruptly flipped from sunny to stormy. "Hell no. That's what my father wants, not me. I think I'll go to clown college."

Bitterness seethed from every word. Fearing I'd upset him, I quickly turned to Donna. "What about you?"

"*I'm* going to be the first female president of the United States."

Pete heehawed like a demented donkey. "We'll be totally fucked then."

Donna stuck her nose in the air. "It'll serve you right when I'm president with my picture on all the money and *you* won't be able to spend a dime without looking at my face."

"I'll vote for you," Barry said and she beamed.

One of those Volkswagen hippie buses painted with flowers that were all the rage a few years ago puttered into the parking lot. Pete's mom waved from behind the wheel. Pete vaulted over the wall and sprinted to the van. Barry stubbed out his cigarette and followed him. They shouted goodbye as they both piled in.

With her current object of desire gone, Donna drifted toward the remaining boys, leaving me and Will to entertain ourselves.

"Do you really want to go to clown college?" I sat down next to him on the wall. "Is there even such a thing?"

"If there is, I'd be terrible at it. I was just clowning around."

"*Groan.* You should have to pay a fine for that pun." I turned a little so I could face him. "I hope I didn't piss you off earlier. You know, when I said you were going to be a businessman. I was kidding, but typical me, I always take the joke one step too far. You seemed kind of mad."

He flinched in surprise. "Mad? At you? No. I was just feeling sorry for myself. Pissed at my father, not you. He's been bugging me about where I'm gonna go to college." He grinned, not amused, more like rueful. "I'm sorry. It's not your fault."

That was a new one on me. Not the father-annoying-his-kid thing, because I was a seasoned pro in that arena. My dad didn't give a shit where—or if—I went to college. The *not your fault* part was new. I thought everything was my fault. Maybe I shouldn't.

"Why not tell your dad you'll go to school where *you* want to go?" That advice earned me a supremely skeptical *yeah, right* look. "Okay, if that's too tough, just spit in his eye. That's how we Dalys settle our disputes."

"That's an interesting solution. Knowing my father, he'd spit back."

Will followed that with a yip. I'd gotten used to the sound, but this one was different. Until now, his vocal tic came out a clipped, tight bark, as if he tried really hard to hold it back. This little yelp was an almost relieved *I'm letting it all hang out and it feels great* sigh. Like he felt relaxed enough with me to do that and, man, did that give me a thrill.

"So what's your deal?" He gave my knee a friendly pat. "You didn't say what you'll be doing in the year 2000. What's in your future?"

"Well, it's kind of silly." I began warily. Anne Albright's snippy disdain still burned in my mind. And Mrs. Clutch's pessimistic attitude and Dad's teasing and all the doubts that greeted me whenever I told people what I wanted to do. "I think I'd like to be a writer."

"A writer?" His eyes widened. "Like fiction? Really? That's not silly, it's great. You're so funny and creative. I'm sure you'll be a big success."

"Oh." That floored me. A glow of pride flushed through me. I should've known Will would get it. "Well, thanks. I love writing stories and I write all the time, like Jo March and John-Boy Walton, and what does that say about my chances when my literary heroes are fictional characters who spend more time bickering with their siblings than writing, and I'm babbling, right?"

"Only a little." He flashed an impish smile and my embarrassment quickly ebbed. "How long have you been writing? What do you write about?"

"I've been writing since, like, forever, and I write all kinds of things. Romance, science fiction, and historical stories. I just wrote a story about a girl who lives in Concord during the Revolution."

"Nice. Historical fiction. My favorite. Next to sci-fi. I'd love to read it."

I blinked rapidly. Did he really say that? A giddy shiver raced down my spine, followed by a surge of dread. For some odd reason, Will's opinion mattered more to me than anyone else's. What if he didn't like my story?

"Oh. Ah..."

Mom and our Impala rolled into the parking lot, saving me from answering. The tires squealed softly as she swung the car around and pulled up next to the opening in the wall. Donna raced over, thanking my mother a dozen times for giving her a lift as she dove into the back seat.

I stood and said goodbye to Will. At the car, I opened the front passenger door and paused with one leg inside to look back at him. "Remember what I said, spit in his eye."

He didn't hear me. Freed from her talkative captors, Marilyn had fooped to his side and claimed his attention.

Chapter 14

The Thing With Feathers

"THIS JOB SUCKS ROTTEN dick," Camille said as she threw on her bulky winter jacket and led the way out of the motel.

I followed her out the door, agreeing heartily. No one had slapped my bottom since that first day, but I almost wanted to go back to babysitting or emptying old lady Grissom's poop pot over the grossness of a chambermaid's job.

Especially after I got my first paycheck and discovered the bitter reality of take-home pay. Taxes and Social Security and other stuff had eaten up so much of what I'd earned it almost wasn't worth it to go to the bank and deposit my check.

Outside, Camille swung toward me. "Wanna go to Thom McAn? I need new shoes. These are beat." She stuck out her foot, showing me her scuffed and worn black work shoes.

"I should say so. You look like you've been running up mountains, with all your heart and *sole*."

My joke landed as flat as a pancake. Camille barely had a sense of humor, never mind an appreciation for puns. Especially puns as terrible as that one. But she was nice in an oddball way and I didn't mind spending time with her outside of work.

Misty drizzle spit from the sky as we set out. Foley Plaza was designed in the shape of a giant horseshoe, with the parking lot in the middle. Cars ignored the lot's marked lanes and zipped in all directions, threatening to crash into each other like bumper cars at the amusement park. Saturday shoppers crowded the sidewalk, ducking in and out of all the shops and slowing us down, but we finally made it to Thom McAn, a brightly lit store smelling of shoe leather and stinky feet.

A clerk in a pale blue sport jacket and a wide, clip-on purple tie hustled over to us. "Is there something I can help you find?" he asked, sounding not at all sure he'd be successful.

Camille tried on every shoe in the store, complaining about the cost, finally settling on a cheap, serviceable pair of clodhoppers.

While the salesman rung up her purchase, she wandered around, gazing enviously at the boxy handbags and lace-up leather boots with platform soles. I looked at the shoelaces, almost tempted to buy some as a joke gift for Will who never, ever tied his own laces.

The rain had picked up by the time we left the store. We dashed down the sidewalk to the Kwik Kup Luncheonette, a long, narrow restaurant squeezed between a record store and a TV repair shop. Kwik Kup had Formica tables, a small kitchen in the back, and walls painted orange, like Jay's store and every other store and public space these days. Forget red, white, and blue, orange seemed to be *the* color of the Bicentennial year.

A silver-haired waitress took our order. Minutes later, Camille dug into a BLT and crispy French fries, with ketchup on the side in one of those small, pleated paper cups. I picked at a salad of limp iceberg lettuce and tomatoes sliced so thin you could see through them. Dry, no dressing. Not very satisfying, but after my recent three pound loss, I'd cut down even more on what I ate, hoping to double or triple that number.

"I've *got* to get out of that rooming house," Camille said. "I got crabs from sitting on the toilet and one of the divorced dads keeps bugging me. He says no one understands him. As if I would." She scraped a piece of lettuce off her tooth with a fingernail painted purple. "I'd like to move but I'm flat broke. And I haven't heard from Mack in two weeks. Man, that guy's a heartbreaker. Playing games, telling me he needs me one second, giving me the cold shoulder the next. He's a lot like my ma. I can't shake him, though. You'd know what I mean if you ever had sex."

I choked on a mouthful of Tab and so much heat flooded my face I could've reheated Camille's coffee.

She laughed. Not a mean laugh, more like teasing. "It's so plain you're a virgin. Well, don't be in any rush. It's not everything it's cracked up to be. It's like riding a different horse every day. Sometimes it's wild, sometimes not. Sometimes it hurts. With Mack, anyway. He makes me do it, you know, when I don't want to."

I listened in fascination mixed with horror. Sex in the more randy books I read seemed like the most delicious thing, with the girl always getting a screaming orgasm at the end. Not to mention she and the hero lived happily (and orgasmically) ever after. Fiction of course, though I hoped real life might be something like that, especially if, as Mom said, I found the right guy. And not someone like Mack, who sounded like an ass.

"Maybe it's good you haven't seen him for weeks," I said. "You deserve a better man than that."

"I don't know." Her voice trembled. "I love him, you know?"

Like my mother loved my dad? Or at least, she must've loved him once, in the beginning, when they met at Dad's factory. She was a secretary and he'd find excuses to visit the third floor steno pool, cracking jokes and waggling his eyebrows, making all the girls giggle. Then he'd wait outside for hours after his shift ended to walk Mom to the bus. One day he invited her out for a beer (an example of foreshadowing if there ever was one), and the rest was history.

"Hey, look what I got." Camille had placed her coat on the seat beside her. She licked mayonnaise from her fingers and reached into one of the pockets and pulled out a pair of suede gloves with the price tag still attached.

My eyes widened. "Did you steal that?"

"Shh." A devious sparkle glinted in her eyes. "That's *our* little secret."

Our little secret was all fine and good when I put too much soap in the washing machine and bubbles spilled across the floor. This was altogether different. She must've snatched the gloves while the salesman filled out the sales slip for her shoes. I hadn't even seen her do it. What other things had she five-finger-discounted?

"Camille, you shouldn't have done that. What if you got caught?" I heard my mother's warning voice in those words, but really, Camille wasn't a juvenile anymore. If she got caught stealing now, they wouldn't send her to reform school. She'd go to real jail.

She set her chin. "Don't be so uptight. That shoe store makes tons of money, they're not gonna miss this one thing. Besides, I *need* these gloves. They're for my ma." She stroked the soft suede with a greasy finger. "They're for her birthday. She likes gloves and I'm gonna give them to her if she'll let me see her."

She sat with her shoulders hunched, her expression broken and forlorn. Lost.

My salad turned bitter in my stomach. Though we Dalys had our fights and our problems, we had each other, for better or worse. Camille was alone. Alone and unhappy, abandoned by her parents and trapped in a dumpy rooming house with crabs on the toilet seat, a shitty boyfriend, and two dead-end jobs.

Maybe I could do something to help her. I'd been a failure in the friend department so far, this was my chance to break my losing streak. "You know, sometimes my mom helps people find places to live in her work. I could ask her if she has any ideas for you to find a new place to live."

Camille perked up. "Really? If I could get out of that hellhole, that'd fix everything. I could find a better job, make more money. Mack would like that, for sure."

She pounced on the rest of her sandwich with renewed vigor. I sat back and watched her eat, happy and impressed with myself for making her feel better.

I'd given her a crumb of hope, and sometimes a crumb could go a long way.

After lunch, Camille and I hoofed it to the bus stop by Liggett's Drugstore at the end of Foley Plaza. Rain fell in buckets and we both got drenched by the time Camille hopped her bus going downtown and I boarded the number 26 toward home.

I got off at the bottom of my hill, glad I always wore my cheapo Trax to work and not my marshmallow shoes. A torrent of rainwater rushed down the sidewalk like Niagara Falls, soaking through my sneakers the instant my feet hit the pavement.

I trekked upward. Kids played outside on the patchy grass quads between the blocks, laughing, splashing in puddles, undaunted by the wet weather. The adults weren't as adventurous and had shut themselves inside. Their voices and the sounds of TVs tuned to an afternoon movie or a late season NBA game drifted from the apartments. The song "Freddie's Dead" thumped from an open upstairs window.

I spotted my brother Rusty and some of his pals trooping across the street to the brook, to smoke pot or sniff glue or whatever nefarious activities they got up to on a Saturday afternoon. My sister Chrissy and her friend Rapunzel had tied a piece of clothesline to Marco's collar and taken him for a walk. Or tried to. The dog stopped every two feet to sniff the slimy worms that always suddenly appeared on the sidewalk in a spring rain. No amount of tugging on his rope could encourage Marco to move.

I waved as I passed them and sloshed up onto the stoop to enter the kitchen through the back door.

"Take off your shoes," Mom called from the living room. I couldn't see her, but I could hear her. "I'll have no wet shoes in the house."

I didn't see why not. The floor was already a mess of dirt and grime. A little water might help to clean it up. But Mom's rules were Mom's rules, so I kicked off my sneakers into a pile by the door and padded across the kitchen in wet socks.

Dad's head popped up over the back of his Archie Bunker chair like a turtle peeking out of its shell. "You got a letter. It's from a college you applied to."

"What? So soon?" Barbie said most colleges didn't make their final decisions until April. But... Linda G had heard from Mount Holyoke last week. And she'd been accepted. Excitement roiled in my belly. Maybe I'd been accepted too. "Is it from State U?"

I flung my coat and handbag onto a chair and raced into the living room. I ferreted through the pile of bills and other mail on the bookcase near the window until I found the envelope. Not from the state university, but from a small college in New Hampshire.

Mom pulled her nose out of a book called *Shōgun* and looked up. Dad worked half days on Saturday and had been home for a while. He held a beer, a cigarette dangled between his lips, and he watched me tear open the envelope with glassy eyes.

I took out the letter with shaking hands and skimmed the three short paragraphs. *Thank you for your application...we regret to inform you....*

My hopes snuffed out in an instant.

"Sorry kid," Dad said. "Told you not to get your hopes up."

I grimaced. Like rainy days and Mondays, my dad always knew how to get me down.

Mom closed her book and gazed up at me. "Listen, Deidre. This is just one rejection. You applied to a lot of schools. You might not be a Rockefeller or live in a palace, but you're someone any college would be thrilled to have. You're smart. You have talent, and an abundance of moxie. The next letter could be a yes. The next one *will* be a yes. You have to have hope. You still have a chance."

And my mom always found the way to let the sun shine in.

I crumpled the letter, choosing to shut out Dad's negative waves and adopt her glass-half-full optimism. "I've got moxie, Mom? Really? Who do you think I am, Shirley Temple?"

She offered one of her rare smiles. "Don't be a wise guy. Go on, go change. You look like a drowned rat and you're dripping all over my floor." She leaned back against the couch cushions and got lost in the adventurous tale of seventeenth century Japan once again.

I did as she ordered. Mom's rules were Mom's rules.

CHAPTER 15

Bad Day At Northside High

I PUT THAT GLASS-HALF-FULL attitude to the test a few days later. A whole battery of tests, actually.

Test number one came when I stepped on the bathroom scale to weigh in. Down only one pound this week. One measly pound. Bicentennial minus...whatever. Bad at Math, remember? Bad at losing weight too, apparently. Why couldn't I drop five or six pounds every week instead of a lousy sixteen ounces?

Chrissy banged on the door for me to hurry up. I pictured her in the hallway hopping around like a rabbit, trying to hold it in. We called that the Daly Dance, a sad fact of life in a house with only one bathroom.

I quickly brushed my hair and teeth then traded places with her and went to our bedroom to make my side of the bed. I'd picked up the habit from Mom, who never showed much interest in tidiness anywhere else in the house, but she made her bed every morning.

"It's the only thing about the day you can control," she'd say, wise words that would turn out to be true words today.

I tucked in the corner of the top sheet as I did at the motel a hundred times a weekend and pulled the frayed quilt up over my pillow. Chrissy didn't need to make up the other side. She slept on her back as straight as a corpse and when she slid out of bed in the morning, the blanket settled back into place as if she'd never been there at all.

I placed my hairbrush in its spot on the windowsill next to the picture of me with Pammie and Yolanda and finished getting dressed. When I put on my marshmallow shoes, a shoelace snapped as I tied it. Test number two.

I tore through the junk-filled drawers and kitchen cabinets looking for a replacement but found none, so I made do by tying the broken lace together then hurried to the bottom of the hill to catch the bus. Which was late. Very late. Even with Gus's lead foot on the gas pedal, the homeroom bell had already rung when I got to school.

The day didn't get any better. My locker combination gave me the usual trouble and I swore I'd take an axe to it before the end of the year. Turning away, I slammed so hard into Stew Baines, my ears rang.

I'd barely recovered from that, when a broad shouldered mob in the hallway nearly knocked me down. The football team, both Black and white guys, the only integrated group in our school, charging up the corridor on their way to a brawl or maybe to lift up a friend's car to help change a flat tire.

Carl led the way. I waved. He did not. In fact, he looked right through me. That stung. Couldn't he at least wave back or even acknowledge my presence with a grunt? Would it kill his Joe Cool, popular guy reputation if he spoke to a mousy blob like me for a half a second?

Needless to say, my upbeat mood plummeted and by the time I got to my least favorite class—gym—that glass had gone from half full to mostly empty to tipped over and spilled all over the floor.

Still, I muddled through. I squeezed myself into my one-piece cotton romper gym suit (believe me, cotton is not as amiable as polyester in the stretching department) and lined up alphabetically in rows on the cold and dusty gym floor with the other girls.

"Today we're going to play volleyball," our teacher, Miss Swett said when she finished taking attendance. A solid woman with a face like a squashed potato, she wore a field hockey uniform year round and paced in front of us, spinning a white ball on her fingertip like she was Meadowlark Lemon of the Harlem Globetrotters. "Let's choose up sides."

Choose up sides. The three worst words anyone in gym class could ever hear. The worst words any Phys-Ed teacher could ever say. Words they probably learned in *How to Torture Unpopular Kids Especially the Fat Ones 101* while in gym college.

Miss Swett selected her teacher's pets as team captains, Robin Samaria and Carol Havakian, and the torture began. Both captains called out the names of every girl in class except mine. Linda Dawson was one of the first picked, a logical choice because of her height, but how could barely five foot tall Cindy Simpson be chosen before me?

The teams grew. Girls jumped up when they heard their name and took their place on either side of the net, until I sat alone on the gym's parquet floor. I thought I couldn't sink any lower until I caught Carol gazing longingly at the trash barrel near me, probably wondering if it could spike a volleyball.

Finally, she gave up. "Come on, Deidre," she said with a reluctant sigh.

I joined the team just as reluctantly. Carol started off with the world's most perfect serve and the game was afoot.

The squeak of sneakers and the spank of palms hitting the volleyball filled the gym. So did cheers from some of the girls encouraging each other, even when they whiffed a set-up or missed the ball. They called each other by strange nicknames that probably made sense to their in-crowd but went over my head, like, "You've got this, Square Root" or "Good job, Featherhead."

Our team captain had a vicious competitive streak. Carol dove for the ball like she played in the Olympics and not twelfth grade gym class in a second-rate city's third-rate high school. She jumped in front of me every time the ball arced in my direction.

"I *can* hit the ball, you know," I grumbled.

As the longest volleyball game in history wore on, my gym shorts rode up to my crotch again and again, with the intention of giving me a spectacular wedgie each time. My inner thighs alternately chafed or stuck together. And the score climbed to an unimpressive tie of two to two.

My turn to serve finally came a minute before gym period ended.

"*Don't* screw up." Competitive Carol's eyes dug into me, threatening bodily harm if I missed. I glared back, vowing to get my revenge on her and all her descendants someday, if it was the last thing I ever did.

I stepped to the line, holding the ball in my sweaty palms. I prepped to serve. The entire team swiveled to watch me. High expectations. High hopes.

I took a breath and swung my arm with all my might. My wrist smacked the ball with a stinging splat. The ball flew. It arced only a little and cleared the net by a mere inch. It caught the opposition by surprise. Caught me by surprise too. I gaped, along with everyone else, as the ball fell between the gap in our opponents' front line and bounced to the floor.

Point to Deidre Daly. We won the game.

A couple girls slapped me five and I almost died from satisfaction at the way Competitive Carol's eyes popped. Smirking, I blew on my fingers and brushed them on my shirt like they do in the movies.

Revenge wasn't exactly sweet, but pretty damned close.

Fresh from my volleyball triumph, I ate a big lunch to celebrate, including one of the school's signature brownies, loaded with walnuts and grease and as heavy as a brick. I'd earned it. For winning the game, and for breaking the bad day curse. Uncomfortably full, I toddled off to the rest of my classes in a slightly better frame of mind.

Until Miss French wafted into seventh period English and began to pass out a stack of papers.

Oh goody. What literary thing were we going to discuss today? How Fitzgerald learned to put nouns and verbs together? Robert Frost's controversial opinion on the iambic pentameter? Exploring Hemingway's lifelong objection to adjectives? Or the thousands of other writing tricks male authors used on their road to fame, fortune, and becoming part of the English class curriculum for the rest of time and why-oh-why didn't we ever read something written by a woman?

"I've had a chance to read your stories," Miss French said. "I've selected some of the best and we're going to read them out loud today."

I sat up straight. Was my story one of them?

Miss French handed me a thick packet, the paper still warm from the mimeograph machine and a little wet from where she licked her thumb to separate the pages. Excited, I scanned the stories. Five of them of varying length, some typed, others handwritten, with the author's name blacked out on each.

Five stories, and none of them mine.

My spirits sank to the center of the Earth and kept going.

Miss French leaned against her desk and read my classmates' work out loud while we followed along. She put real drama into each word and acted out the dialogue. Wrapped in my own stunned disappointment, I barely listened. They may have been good stories. Probably were. Full of metaphors and allegories F. Scott Fitzgerald would salivate to hear.

But they weren't *my* story.

"We'll have a chance to read more in a few weeks," she said when she finished. "Your next assignment is due soon, the first of April. Get those creative juices flowing."

The class ended. Miss French circled the room, returning our stories. She dropped mine face down on my desk then made a quick getaway. I didn't touch it. I just stared at it. The indentations of the words I'd so carefully chosen were visible through the paper.

The bell rang. Taking a breath, I flipped the pages over.

You can do better, Miss French had written. *More emotion.* In case I didn't get the point, she'd underlined the word *emotion* three times.

Right next to a big, fat, ugly C.

I had zero interest in the prom committee meeting after school. The conversation swirled around me. Ideas proposed, discussed and amended, adopted or rejected went in one ear and out the other.

You can do better.

More emotion.

What did that even mean? How could I write something with emotion if I didn't have any? Well, emotion I would never admit to. I kept those pesky feelings buried so deep pirates with a treasure map and a treasure sniffing dog couldn't find them.

I sat at a table in the back of Mrs. Rosenberg's history class, doodling in my notebook. Trying to come up with ideas for the next writing assignment, something that would be better.

Something that would get me a grade higher than a C and convince Miss French I was a good writer. Convince myself too.

"—don't you agree, Dee? Dee?" Donna called from the front of the room. "Are you listening to me?" She perched on Mrs. Rosenberg's cluttered desk, waving around a quill pen with an enormous feather she'd plucked from a pencil holder.

"Sorry, what?" I muttered.

Donna sighed. "I said, Jane wants people to wear red, white, and blue to the prom, but some people don't look good in those colors. Me, for one. I prefer purple."

"Uh…" I stammered, trying to conjure up an opinion for a topic I didn't care diddley squat about.

"It's the Bicentennial," Jane said. "Let's celebrate in a big way. We'll look great."

Donna groaned. "We'll look like a marching band."

"This is the United States of America," a girl named Ellen Gallogly said firmly, as if we'd all suddenly forgotten where we lived. "People should be able to wear whatever colors they want."

"Don't get your Betsy bloomers in a twist." Jane held up both hands, struggling to calm and cajole at the same time. "Nothing's decided yet—"

She snapped her mouth shut and Donna leapt off the desk when Mrs. Rosenberg abruptly appeared in the doorway.

"Don't mean to interrupt. Just need to get something from my desk."

She glided into the classroom. A slender, regal woman in her fifties, with darkish hair in a flippy-do style like Betty Ford's, she wore a simple green cotton dress with elbow-length sleeves that revealed a number tattooed on her left forearm.

"This is the reason I've not only *chosen* to teach history," she'd say, showing the tattoo to students on the first day of classes each semester. "It's why I *have* to teach history."

And why she was the best teacher in the school.

The desk drawer squealed softly as she opened it and removed several bulging folders. "How's the planning going?" She peered at Jane over the top of her glasses. "Is there anything I can help you with?"

"No, no," Jane chirped. "Everything's going great."

Mrs. Rosenberg bought that lie with a pleased-as-punch nod and the bickering continued the second she left the room.

After the meeting ended, I walked with Donna to her house. She chattered the whole way. We passed a playground as we turned onto MacArthur Way and I spotted Barbie and Competitive Carol sitting on the swings, engaged in what looked like an Important Conversation. I waved to Barbie, not to Carol, wondering what Barbie could possibly have to talk about with my volleyball nemesis.

We reached Donna's a few minutes later and entered through the front door, prompting memories of Valentine's Day and meeting Will and dancing like crazy. We moved to the kitchen, which smelled nowhere near as delicious as it had the night of the party. It reeked of celery and stale cigarette smoke instead.

"I'm starving." Donna circled the kitchen, flinging open cupboard doors and banging them shut in rapid succession. "Want a Fluffernutter?"

By that she meant a sandwich of peanut butter and super sweet Marshmallow Fluf, spread over soft-as-a-pillow Wonder bread. Ten thousand calories, at least, and even worse for my diet than the brownie I had at lunch. But I didn't say no. Because I was feeling low and sulky and mad at the world and that would be the most delicious pick-me-up.

Donna whipped up two sandwiches with the speed and skill of a master chef then tossed the sticky knife into the sink with a clatter. She set the plates on the kitchen table, along with a bag of Cheetos and a bottle of Tango. Licking peanut butter off her thumb, she sat down.

"Why did we ever join prom committee? It's so boring." She bit into her sandwich and washed it down with a gulp of Tango. "Jane's acting like a little Napoleon. I'm wearing purple to the prom no matter what color she says to wear. Purple's my favorite and it looks good on me."

"She's just trying to get into the Bicentennial spirit."

"Who cares about that? I want to wear what I want to the prom. My mother's gonna take me to Newbury Street in Boston to look for a dress. My father will pay for it. All I had to do was lay a guilt trip on them both for never being around." Donna laughed, a truly diabolical sound. "If I can't get them to buy me a car, I'll get the most expensive gown I can find. And it's gonna be purple."

I had to hand it to her. Guilt was quite the motivator. Pretty sure it motivated me in just about everything I did.

When we finished our sandwiches, Donna sat back and gusted an unhappy sigh. "Ugh. I'm so full, I'll never be able to fit into *any* gown I try on." She dug a handful of Cheetos out of the bag. "Have you thought about what you're going to wear? Or who you're going with?"

"Oh, I'm entertaining multiple offers. Can you believe Prince Charles and Burt Reynolds got into a fistfight over who I'll choose?"

"Stop it, Dee. You're always ranking yourself down. You can find a date. Not all guys will be interested in you, but some will. You're nice, and you've got such a pretty face."

Oh dear. Had she really said that? On the bright side, she didn't add *if only you'd lose weight*, and maybe she hadn't even thought it.

"What about you?" I asked. "Do you have anyone in mind?"

She picked up a Cheeto and moved it in the air, as if writing a name. "Oh, there's a certain someone in the play I'm looking at."

Not Barry. After flirting with him for weeks, she seemed to have lost interest in him. Or, rather, he'd shown no interest in her so she'd abandoned the chase. Maybe she meant Carl. She sure had a better chance of snaring Mr. Lazy Smile Football God than me. At least he'd noticed she was alive.

"You should come check out the guys where I work." She polished off her drink. "I bet one of them will go with you if you ask."

"Me ask him?" With the exception of Will, I could barely speak to a guy without tripping over my tongue. How could I ever get up the nerve to do something like that?

Donna pouted. "I can't *force* a guy to go with you. I'm trying to help, but you're not making it easy."

I sighed. A huge one, full of self-pity. A whole stack of *whys* piled up in my mind. Why did this prom thing have to be so complicated? Why couldn't some guy swoop in and ask me to go with him? Why couldn't I write a story that would get me an A? No, I didn't care about the grade. I wanted to write a story so good Miss French would read it to the class.

"I'm sorry, Don. I appreciate your help. I'll stop by sometime when you're at work and get a look at your guys."

Her expression turned to sunshine again. "That's all I ask, my friend."

CHAPTER 16

The Strange Case of the Blobby Bells

"GLAD YOU COULD JOIN us, Deidre," my homeroom teacher Mr. Nutley said, stealing a page from my science teacher's *Snide Remarks for Tardy Students* handbook.

Sure I was running late. I had an excuse this time. I'd stayed up wicked late working on a new story, scribbling, crossing words out then tearing the page out of my notebook and starting all over again. I didn't get much sleep, with the added bonus of a Fluffernutter hangover making me move with all the speed of a lethargic slug today.

I muttered an apology and flopped into my seat in the second row. I perked up when I spotted a bunch of small white boxes lined up on Mr. Nutley's desk. Our class rings had arrived. A hum of excitement cut into the usual homeroom hubbub as our teacher began to call out each recipient's name alphabetically, like doing rollcall at dawn. When they heard their name, each of my classmates went to get their ring.

"Margie Dalton?"

Margie sat in front of me. She bounced up and hurried to the desk. I was next. I started to get out of my seat when I heard, "Isaac Dawoud."

I froze. Isaac sat behind me. Mr. Nutley had skipped me. Why? I'd filled out the order forms last fall like everyone else.

I'd thought no way would we be able to afford the ring, but Mom had somehow found the money. She *always* found the money. Despite Dad and his nips and his habit of borrowing money we couldn't pay back. Despite all of us, especially Rusty, growing like weeds and needing new clothes on a weekly basis and gas hitting a new high of sixty cents a gallon, and everything else putting a strain on our miniscule bank account, my mother found a way.

Mr. Nutley called out more names. The number of boxes shrunk until there were only two left. Where was my ring? Did they lose it? I was about to panic when, "Deidre Daly."

"Why were you were out of order?" he said when I reached his desk, like it was my fault.

Back at my seat, I opened the box. Margie spun around to watch as I slid the ring onto my finger. For the first time in my life, something I tried on fit perfectly. Gorgeous too. The band was pale gold, with the words *Northside High School* in tiny letters circling the oval-shaped, cobalt blue stone. I lifted my hand to catch the overhead light. The stone sparkled like blue fire.

"Nice," Margie said. "Wait, what's that? On the side."

She held her ring next to mine and I saw what she meant. Our class had ordered a special design in honor of the Bicentennial. Little gold Liberty Bells dotted each side of Margie's ring under the words, *Class of '76.* The bells even had a little crack in them, like the real Liberty Bell. On my ring, no bells, no little crack. Instead, two gold blobs.

Two. Gold. Blobs.

How did that happen? Had I checked a box on my ring order that said, *I don't want shiny Liberty Bells like everyone else. I prefer two blobs, thank you very much?*

Margie frowned. "That's so weird."

I laughed. Because what else could I do? Margie sure hit the nail on the head. The ring was weird and so was I. Blobby Bells and

Weirdra Deidre. We fit together like sugar and spice. Like Butch and Sundance. Like peanut butter and Marshmallow Fluf.

The bell rang and homeroom ended. Everyone gathered up their things and sped off to first period. I didn't move. I sat there and gazed at my ridiculous ring. I could peel it off my finger and stick it at the bottom of my handbag. Hide it away with the lint-covered Lifesavers and rubber bands I kept in there for some reason, never to be seen again.

Instead, I would wear it with pride.

"Why not drive a little slower, Deedee? I've got time." Jay made a big show of checking his watch, a Timex with a round face, big numbers, and a black wristband. Mom had bought it for him to replace the watch that had been stolen the last time he was in the hospital. "I don't have to be to work for three more minutes."

I glanced at the speedometer. "I'm not driving *that* slow."

Well, yes I was. Jay had let me drive to the church to drop me off for rehearsal even though he was running late for work, and I'd rewarded him by crawling along at a speed only slowpoke Marilyn could appreciate.

I pressed the pedal, giving the Impala a little more gas, and we rolled up Adams Street at a faster pace. "How's things with Shirley?" I asked, looking at Jay in the passenger seat.

"Fine." He twisted the radio dial, turning from John Denver crooning "Rocky Mountain High" to a news station. "Keep your eyes on the road."

I clucked in mock aggravation and a bit of real annoyance. Apparently, *fine* was all I'd be getting out of him. My curiosity about him and Shirley had reached cat-killing proportions but my button-lipped brother wasn't about to satisfy my nosy interest by spilling any beans.

We made it to the church with no major incidents. I hopped out and watched Jay wheel the car around and out of the parking lot back onto Adams Street. He smoothly cut across four lanes of traffic to the Foley Plaza entrance.

I hoped to be as comfortable behind the wheel someday as he was. He drove with the skill and confidence of Mario Andretti at the Indianapolis 500. I had no idea how he'd managed to learn to drive and finish high school when he'd spent most of his teenage years flat on his back, recovering from surgery. Most of his younger years, too.

Determination, I guess. And glass-half-full optimism. Always.

Rehearsal was already underway when I went inside. I slipped into my spot in the back and waved to Donna and Jane, then sidled up next to Will.

"What's new, pussycat?" Yeah, I said that, because, as had been firmly established, I was first and foremost a weirdo. Fortunately Will was a weirdo too. A wonderful weirdo who appreciated my oddball sense of humor.

Marilyn didn't. She swiveled to eye Will and me like a teacher who'd caught her students cheating on a test, promising severe punishment later. I gave her a monumentally insincere smile, then I got to work.

I threw myself into my role with the scenery-chewing energy of ten Grinches plus two, excited and happy to be here.

After my bad day yesterday and the ring disaster today, I needed a picker-upper and these hours I spent at Saint Mary's every Tuesday and Thursday night always delivered. I got to have fun and not think about the outside world. Not prom or college rejections or my half-finished story due tomorrow. Not ridiculously blobby class rings, or even my weight.

I could hang out and just be me.

I glanced at Will next to me, swinging his arms and pretending to sing. And I got to be with him.

Bushy Beard seemed to be having fun too. His version of fun, anyway. He paced in front of the stage, gripping his guitar and barking directions.

Tonight, he focused on the show's stars.

"Stop. *Puh*-lease stop," he hollered, racing up the steps to the stage and stomping over to Carl. "You're doing it all wrong."

I got his point. Carl had buckets of stage presence, and looked excellent in his flared jeans, but he kept messing up his songs like he'd forgotten how to speak English.

Carl didn't get the point, though. He adopted one of those *wanna make something of it?* looks guys get when someone tells them they're wrong. He added a puffed-up chest for good measure. Bushy Beard wisely backed off and called for us to take a break before he got tackled.

Pete brought out his radio. It crackled and whined as it warmed up and soon, The Guess Who's "American Woman" blasted from the speaker. Some of the guys tossed around a Nerf football. The girls swarmed around Carl by the stage. They consoled him, telling him Bushy Beard was a meanie and his performance was great. Carl lapped up their gooey gushes and pandering praise like a fat cat lapping up cream.

"The Hustle" came on next. Squealing, the girls abandoned Carl. They jostled each other as they raced to the center of the room and formed several lines. For some reason, only girls loved line dances like "The Hustle," and, except for me, only girls seemed to know how to do them.

Oh, and Barry. He not only knew the dance, he got out front to lead the group. He wore a blue paisley shirt open at the collar, brown platform shoes, and beige pants with sharp creases that moved as fluidly as he did. Marilyn step-step-turned beside him with equal elegance, a grace I envied and would need all the determination in the universe to achieve.

I watched them dance for a bit then shifted my attention to Carl. He sat alone on the edge of the stage and looked royally pissed about it. Should I go over and say hi? This was my chance to be alone with him, to get him to notice me at last. What would I say? *I think your acting stinks worse than a dead skunk in the middle of the road, but gee you're cute?*

My feet made the decision for me. They moved. Not toward Carl. Toward Will.

He hung out at the opposite end of the room, where he indulged in his favorite pastime, leaning against the wall. He held a book by his side, his gaze on me as I approached.

I leaned next to him. He smelled nice. He always smelled nice. He wore his usual jeans, a Led Zeppelin concert tee shirt, and his boots with his laces untied.

He nodded hello. "You didn't join the dancing."

Another of his obvious observations. I should probably start keeping count. "Uh, have you seen me dance? I've got two left feet. Not even Gene Kelley pushing me around in a fancy gown can make a dancer out of me."

"I *have* seen you dance. You're good. Better than you think."

"Oh." He sounded so earnest and complimentary, I almost looked over my shoulder to see if someone else had entered the conversation. "I learned everything I know from watching *Soul Train.*" I put my hands in my pockets. Then I remembered I had no pockets and slid my hands down my hips like I meant to do that. "So, when do you think our director will have a nervous breakdown? Before or after the show's final curtain?"

"If Judas can't figure out his ass from his elbow, I'd put my money on tonight."

I grinned, though the joke of him calling Carl *Judas* all the time had begun to wear thin.

He shifted his book from one hand to the other. "Have you heard from any colleges yet?"

"Just one. They said thanks but no thanks. The rest..." I shrugged, not so sure I wanted to hear from the rest. Probably better to get no response than to prove my guidance counselor—and my father—right by getting an unequivocal *no*. "I'll hear from them in April, so I guess I'll just have to wait."

"Don't sweat it. You'll get a yes. Probably yesses from all of them."

A delicious warmth surged through me. Speaking of picker-uppers. Will had a way of always boosting me up, always making me feel hopeful, not cynical. Well, Mom did that too, but she was my mother and she had to do that. It was required by law.

"Will, have I mentioned how good you are for my ego? You should follow me around all day saying things like that."

He laughed. Another thing good for my ego. He got my jokes *and* he rewarded me for them, with a laugh or a chuckle, sometimes even a guffaw. He was the best audience a girl could hope for.

I glanced at the book he held. "Is that a new book? What is it?" He had a terrible habit of folding the cover back so you couldn't see the title.

He lifted it and fanned the pages with his thumb. "*Slaughterhouse Five.*"

"I've never read that one. What do you think of it?"

"I haven't decided yet."

"Well, with that title, I doubt there'll be a happy ending."

He laughed again then glanced toward the front of the room and his amusement fled, like flipping a switch from day to night. He adjusted his leaning position a little to turn and face me. "Deidre. Can I ask a question?"

I would've replied with something funny, like, *you just did* if he didn't suddenly sound so serious. "Sure."

"Do you think—" He paused. A long time. Followed by a rueful-sounding yip. "I guess... I mean, do you need a ride home after practice? My father's picking me up."

I hesitated, and the fact that I hesitated indicated how much I liked Will and wanted to say yes. But not with his grumpy father behind the wheel, driving me into *that* neighborhood or anywhere else. Mr. Hovey seemed to resent having to give his own son a ride home, never mind Bertha Butt from the Project.

"Thanks for the offer, but I'm going to Foley Plaza across the street to meet my brother. He works at Cully's. He'll bring me home when he's done work."

He nodded, his posture as stiff as starch. "Be careful. It's pretty dark out there."

Bright, bright streetlights powerful enough to shine all the way to the moon ringed Foley Plaza, so, not exactly pitch dark, but his protectiveness touched me.

"I will. Will," I said with a bubbling laugh. The corners of his eyes crinkled.

"The Hustle" ended to a round of applause from the dancers. Peter Frampton's "Baby I Love Your Way" took its place, filling the sudden silence between us.

"Look, the ten commandments." I pointed to a poster hanging on the wall behind us and ran a finger along the *Thou Shalt Nots* printed in gothic letters. "At last, our chance to learn them and show we're better at Catholic-ing than we thought. I'll take the ones about murder and coveting. You take the defying your father one."

He didn't pick up on the hint. His gaze centered on my hand instead. "Is that a class ring? Is it yours, or...?"

Suddenly self-conscious, I zipped my hand behind my back. "Yeah it's mine." I mean, who else's would it be? "I got it yesterday. It's...not exactly perfect."

"What do you mean? Show me."

Heat crept up my neck. "Promise you won't laugh?"

"Why would I laugh?"

"Because..." I brought my arm around slowly and held up my left hand. "There's supposed to be a Liberty Bell on each side. Instead of a bell with a famous crack in it, I got blobs. And...there it is. I knew you'd laugh."

Will suppressed his chuckles (not very successfully) and inched closer. He tucked his book into his jeans' pocket and took my hand, lifting it so he could get a good look. His palm touching mine was warm, strong. The heat creeping up my neck shot all the way to my scalp.

He turned my hand to examine both sides of the ring's band. "They don't look like blobs." His breath brushed over my knuckles. "They look like yellow sand dollars. See the pattern? It fits you. Unique. One of a kind, you know?"

He lifted his gaze and our eyes met. His smile faded. So did mine. The overhead light glowed on his hair and his angular face. His tiger eyes gleamed as bright as the gold on my ring. My belly fluttered. The warmth that rushed through me earlier turned scorching, a heat that rippled from deep within me. A fiery rush of anticipation and awareness that I liked but bothered me at the same time.

The Frampton song ended and an older tune, "Dancing in the Moonlight," piped up. A lively melody with a happy tempo that skipped around the room. Full of pep, and not the *full of pep* my grandma meant when she said, *Deidre you're too full of pep*, like I gave her a headache.

This pep was light, joyous. Fun.

Like Will.

Like how he made me feel.

Giddiness tickled my spine. My spirits flew as high as the sky. All my life I'd felt guilt or shame, awkward and inadequate. Weird. An unimportant blob. Anxious and worried. But when I was with Will, I felt...

None of that. I felt like a person. Like a unique, one of a kind, comfortable in my own skin, human person.

How had I never realized that before?

"Alright, people," Bushy Beard called out. "Bring it in. Time to get back to work."

Will broke off his gaze and released my hand, casual, calm, as if nothing seismic had just happened between us. Maybe he didn't feel it. I sure had.

We walked together back to the stage. I took my place beside him with the rest of the ensemble for the second act, not at all surprised to find my admiring attention had turned away from Carl.

To focus on Will.

CHAPTER 17

I Woke Up In Love This Morning

I WENT TO SCHOOL, chipper and cheerful. Not even my locker up to its usual tricks or my daily run-in with Stew Baines could dim my spirits.

"Watch it, *Deer-duh*," he said as he flew past.

I declined a retort, though the thin worm of a mustache that had sprouted above Stew's upper lip practically screamed for a zinger.

My new crush on the most perfectly perfect boy in the world had something to do with my bouncy mood.

No, not exactly *new*. I must've liked Will from the beginning but being on the dense side, I didn't realize it. And, like Elizabeth Bennett's feelings for Mr. Darcy in *Pride & Prejudice*, I was in the middle before I had a single clue what my heart had known for a while.

Giddy and grinning, I sailed through my morning classes and bopped into the cafeteria to the tinny disco beat of "Fly, Robin, Fly," thumping from someone's transistor radio. I pushed my tray down the counter to the register, singing along.

Even Checkpoint Charlie was in a good mood. She punched my free lunch card and let me pass with only the briefest interrogation.

Gripping my tray in triumph, I scooted to my table, feeling like this was my lucky day.

151

Donna eyed me in horror as I sat down. "Is *that* what you're wearing for the yearbook photos?"

I gulped. My luck had run out.

"That's *today*?" I'd completely forgotten a photographer would be taking pictures of the clubs and sports teams for the yearbook today. Each group had been scheduled at a different time, which explained why Jane was a lunch no-show. She'd probably been posing and saying cheese since the homeroom bell had rung this morning.

I looked down at my blouse. With everything else in the laundry, I'd worn one of my oldest smock blouses, a hideous green thing with balloon sleeves and baby ducks all over it. The top's only saving grace, it hugged my waist, accentuating the one wee part of my figure.

"Meet me in the bathroom before pictures," Donna said. "I'll do your makeup." She wrinkled her nose at my blouse. "Hopefully distract the camera from *that*."

I agreed and dug into my meal, a relatively healthy green bean salad, pears, roasted potatoes, and barbecued mystery meat, minus the bun, wondering if I could turn my top inside out and hide the ridiculous ducks cavorting on the front.

Linda G pushed back her chair and stood. "Gotta split. Got stuff to do." She picked up her tray and left.

"What's going on with her?" Karen said when she was out of earshot. "She ate lunch in five seconds. Now she's gone."

"She left early yesterday too," Donna said. "I think she's got a boyfriend."

I raised my eyebrows. "How do you know that?"

"She wears makeup now. She never did before. And she doesn't smell like her grandmother's underwear drawer anymore. She's wearing *real* perfume. Charlie from Revlon. I'm sure of it. My nose never lies."

"Your nose knows," I said, shifting to watch Linda glide out the door. She seemed to float in that way girls do when they had someone special on their mind. Had she abandoned her fictional boyfriend Rhett for a real boy?

Had I done the same?

Because face it, Carl as the object of my desire had been just that, an object. Someone pretty to look at and fantasize and dream about. A ridiculous dream, too. Wasn't the unpopular high school girl falling for the unattainable football player the oldest cliché in the book?

I'd gotten to know Will as a person. A brilliant, amazing, and wonderful person. Shy, awkward, sometimes moody, but always adorable. Soft-spoken, when he spoke. Hated to tie his shoelaces. A guy I could laugh with and talk to about anything including the Ten Commandments and what had I been thinking getting into *that* topic when everyone knew there were three things you were forbidden to talk about in polite conversation, religion, politics...

And sex.

Heat spread through me, infusing every pore. *Oh, Deidre.* Don't even think that word and Will at the same time. I may have fallen for him, but he was just a friend. A friend who liked me as a friend and that was it.

That. Was. It.

The sooner I got that through my thick skull, the better.

"Hold still," Donna ordered after she nearly poked me in the eye with her mascara brush for the fifth time. "How can I fix your face if you keep wiggling like a worm?"

Fix your face. According to the general consensus, my face was the only part of me that didn't need fixing. Except for my pimples and they were almost completely gone. I attributed that success to washing my face six thousand times a day more than cutting down on the four basic food groups of sugar, fat, grease, and Twinkies.

I held still as commanded and she moved in for another go at my eyelashes.

The C corridor girls' bathroom wasn't the fanciest spot to be getting my face fixed. Or the cleanest. The place smelled like pee, the floor was perpetually wet in one corner, and someone had beat up the Modess sanitary napkin machine and it hung on the wall by a metallic thread. Girls came and went like Grand Central Station. Stall doors squawked open and shut. Toilets flushed with a *whoosh*, accompanied by the occasional sound of puking, though I might've imagined that.

Donna bit her bottom lip and concentrated, staring into my eyes as if staring into my soul as she worked. She finally grunted in satisfaction and stuffed her mascara back into the bag she'd tossed onto the counter between the sinks.

Why she felt the need to tote her entire supply of makeup to school when she got up every morning at four to do her hair and makeup, I did not know. I supposed I was lucky today that she did.

She turned me to the mirror. "You look so pretty."

"Do I?" I couldn't see it. Especially in this egregiously ugly duck smock.

"Stop it, Dee. You're gorgeous and you know it. Now for some lipstick. Pucker up." She aimed a stick of Maybelline at my mouth, an anemic red that looked more orange than coral.

"No thanks." I put up a hand, blocking her. "I'd rather go without."

Makeup complete, we left the bathroom and found the photographer at the end of C wing, where the rest of the prom committee had gathered. He told us to line up on the stairs to the second floor, four of us on each step. Jane and Donna hustled to the front. I climbed upward to hide in the back. An automatic reaction.

The photographer spent a hundred hours getting us arranged. "Crunch in together," he said, followed by, "You in the third row, tip your head up." Everyone twisted and turned, forming neat rows and perfect poses.

"You up there in the nosebleed section," he called. "Hey, blondie."

I looked left and right to see who he meant, then pointed to myself and mouthed, "Me?"

"Yeah you. You've got such a pretty face, why're you hiding it? Move down front."

I shifted from foot to foot. A dozen excuses not to move sprang to my un-lipsticked lips, most of them smartass variations on *my fat ass (and the rest of me) won't fit in the frame if I get closer.* I remembered what Donna had said about me putting myself down. I'd done that to myself for far too long. I let other people do that, too. I'd let my dad and the jerks calling me names batter and bruise my self-esteem.

I needed to stop it.

I'd been trying hard (mostly) to create a new me. Dieting and exercising and focusing on my outside. Time to work on the inside. To be good to myself mentally as well as physically. To be like Jay and not let the bullies and name-callers or anyone else get me down. To never again give anyone—including me—the power to put me down.

I took a deep breath and did as the photographer asked. I inched my way down the steps and pushed in at the front next to Ellen Gallogly, a girl as skinny as a pencil.

When the photographer got a good look at me, he didn't laugh or make a grossed-out face or tell me he'd made a mistake and that I should return to the shadows.

He flashed a thumbs up.

He futzed with his camera a little more, then, "Alright, ladies, we're ready. Everyone look at the camera and say cheese."

I threw back my shoulders and smiled as wide as the Grand Canyon. I didn't even suck in my gut. Something new and proud and happy gushed through me.

I'd finally, for once, stepped out of the shadows and let the world see *me*.

And it felt amazing.

Part Four

April 1976

CHAPTER 18

Turn the Beat Around

"Miss Dolan, wait."

A mousy kid, probably a freshman, chased me down five feet from the cafeteria. I stopped and turned to face him with a rueful sigh. Couldn't *anyone* in this school tell Miss Dolan and me apart?

"I'm going to miss class today," he said. "I know we have a test but I have an orthodontist appointment this afternoon." He offered proof with a grin, showing me a mouthful of braces so shiny I was nearly blinded. "I'm being dismissed and my mother's picking me up, so I won't be in class and will need a makeup test." The words sprinted out of his mouth in a rush that left him breathless.

Left me breathless too. And conflicted. It was April Fool's Day. Pranks were allowed today. I had every right to say, "Go with my blessing, my child," and send the kid on his way. But... I didn't do it. Instead, I patiently explained to the boy I wasn't Miss Dolan and never would be and then we both moved on.

I attributed this new, more mature attitude to my new, purposeful way of thinking. No more negative thoughts about myself. No more blobby blob from Blobville. No more beating myself up and putting myself down. And most of all, no more back-and-forth between starving myself then stuffing my belly so full I felt I'd explode.

I vowed to get off that rollercoaster and take control. It wasn't about dieting to get a prom date or fitting into a slinky gown

159

(though that would be great). It was about being positive, looking forward, glass not just half full, but all the way full. And trying to be the girl I felt like when I was with Will.

Me. And comfortable with that.

I entered the cafeteria and picked up a tray, getting into a long line to get lunch. At the register, the Spanish Inquisition's most ferocious interrogator pounced on me.

"Free lunch, huh?"

"Actually, they pay me to eat this slop." I gestured to the crusty-looking ravioli, limp broccoli, and carrot-studded Jell-O mold on my tray. "It's a struggle, but I'm up to the task."

Okay, maybe there'd be some backsliding on my road to maturity. Guess I was a work in progress.

The lunch lady grumbled but she punched my card and I headed for my table. As usual, everyone but Jane was here. It struck me we were both always running late—the tardy twins—except Jane had important things making her late, while I just got distracted and ran out of time.

I took my seat and applied myself to my meal, with a plan to stop eating when I felt comfortably full, rather than stuffed.

I picked up my fork and speared the limpest piece of broccoli ever grown. Something greasy dripped off it, a substance that might have been butter but would need a full battery of tests in Mr. Meager's science lab to confirm. Calculating the millions of "calories in" eating that goop would entail, I ate only one piece and turned to the ravioli.

We chattered amiably as we ate, with the exception of Karen, who bitched about the weather and the food and why did she have to use a slide rule in Calculus when kids at other schools got to use those newfangled calculators. Finally, Barbie sighed in annoyance and told her to cool it.

The high point of lunch arrived shortly before the bell—Jane and her adorable new Dorothy Hamill haircut. Dorothy had skated her way to a gold medal in the Winter Olympics in February, but her real achievement was her hairdo. The whole world went gaga over the style, a short and fluffy wedge cut, shaped like a mushroom cap.

"Do you like it?"

A chorus of *ooohs* and *ahhhs* answered her question and even Karen kept the criticism to a minimum. Jane had been taking something called tetracycline for her acne and her pimples had all but faded. With her new hairstyle and a bright smile, she beamed like the sun at high noon.

Later, I pushed through the crush in the Desert on my way to English, clutching my new story. Story number two, due today.

Hopefully, Miss French would like this one better than the last. I'd ditched my Revolutionary War heroine and written about one of the soldiers escorting the cannons to Boston in 1776 instead. Cold, far from home, and scared of the battles yet to be fought, he blubbered like a baby. How was that for emotion?

I spotted Carl, hanging out at the end of the corridor, tossing that lazy smile at the girls he deemed worthy. He didn't look my way and I didn't care. I sped past him without a blip to my heartbeat or a spike in my temperature. I had a different boy on my mind now.

And all this time I'd thought Donna was the fickle one.

Mom had a tenants' council meeting that night so she couldn't drive me to rehearsal. Leaving her and her rabble-rousing cohorts to their ongoing struggle to overthrow the Housing Authority or at least get them to pick up the trash by the brook that had piled sky high, I hopped the bus.

The last wisps of sunset spread a pinkish glow across the sky when the bus doors squawked open and I got off at Saint Mary's. The air held a touch of spring warmth, unusual for this early in April. Everyone took advantage of the nice weather, hanging around outside until it was time to go in.

I spotted Will right away, sitting on the wall with our other friends. My feet barely touched the ground as I sailed over to join them.

"If Ford hadn't pardoned Nixon, he'd be in better shape for this election," he was saying as I reached the group. He sat with his arms crossed over his chest. He wore a nylon jacket and his usual jeans, and he did a "hey there" lift of his chin when he saw me.

A horde of butterflies danced in my belly, but I played it cool and returned a casual wave.

"Ford's mistake is Carter's gain," Barry said. He stood nearby, smoking, looking sharp in green polyester pants and a silky blue shirt splashed with morning glory flowers. "I'm pulling for the peanut farmer."

Donna yawned her opinion of the presidential race. She perched on the wall beside Will. Marilyn sat on the other side, wearing a dark blazer and a slit skirt that showed a lot of leg for a Catholic girl. Jane paced the sidewalk like she had ants in her pants, her expression frighteningly glum.

Marilyn nudged Will's arm with her shoulder. "Did I tell you I'm going to London for Easter vacation?"

Easter vacation. Better known to those of us in the secular world as April school vacation.

"London?" Donna said. "You traitor. It's the Bicentennial, you should stay in America."

"I'm going as far from my parents as I can for vacation," Barry said.

Pete sat cross-legged on the ground, dressed in a sweatshirt and plaid Bermuda shorts like my gramps. "I'm right there with you, brother." He reached up and he and Barry slapped palms.

"Think I'll head downtown to see the sights," I said. "I hear they're tearing down the old Woolworth's. Wouldn't want to miss that."

Will's lips twitched. "Living dangerously, Deidre."

"What about you?" Marilyn gave Will another shoulder bump. "Sailing in Newport?"

He looked at her and something flashed between them. Something private, a shared memory I could never be a part of. I burned up inside, right to cinders.

Jealous? Sure. Just... I didn't know what to be jealous of. They weren't going out. At least, Marilyn said they weren't. And they didn't act like they were a couple. Maybe Will wished they were. That would be a big April Fool's on me. I didn't expect him to like me the way I liked him, but I hadn't considered he might be into someone else. Particularly her.

"No sailing this vacation. I'm going on a college tour with the family."

Will made that sound more like a death sentence than a fun trip, though who was I to judge? We never did anything as a family, fun or otherwise. And we certainly never went on vacation, unless you counted driving around the countryside to get out of the neighborhood during the summer riot season, and we didn't even do those trips any more since the energy crisis had raised gas prices so high.

Will shrugged. "It's gonna be a wasted trip. If my father gets his way, I'll end up at Boston College."

Barry snorted. "Boston College? Haven't you had enough of Catholic school?"

"That's what my dad wants. BC's his alma mater."

"Will's brother goes there now. It's, like, the family school," Little Marilyn Know-It-All added.

I scowled. "Do you *want* to go there?"

He met my eyes, his expression clouded. "I don't know. Maybe. Guess I've got no choice."

"Come on Will, there's always a choice—"

"That means you'll be away for your birthday." Marilyn nudged his arm again. She certainly was touchy-feely tonight. That bugged me. And so did not knowing Will's birthday was coming up or that he had a brother.

"I'm going to El Paso," Jane said, her voice flat, zero pep.

Marilyn's upper lip curled like a Christmas ribbon, and with her trapezoid mouth, that was quite a feat. "Ooh, sounds like fun."

I narrowed my eyes. If I didn't dislike her already, that superior sneer would've sealed the deal. I aimed a much friendlier gaze at Jane. "Why El Paso?"

"We may have to move again. We're going there to scope it out."

"What?" Donna cried. "Who's going to run the prom committee?"

Did that matter right now? Jane had more important things to worry about, like packing her stuff and leaving. Leaving us. *Her friends.* I gazed around the group. With the exception of Miss Marilyn, they'd all become my friends too and I knew I'd hate moving away and leaving them.

Then it hit me. After our performance, there'd be no more reason for us to hang out and I'd lose them anyway. Including Will.

Jane shrugged. "I'm an Army brat. I gotta go where they send my dad. I got no choice."

Serious words. True words. Jane had no choice. Will had no choice. I didn't either. I didn't choose to live where I did. I didn't choose to have parents who shared a name and a bunch of children but were separated by a wall as thick as the one between East and West Berlin. I sure didn't choose to have pudgy thighs and a big butt. Even my future was out of my hands, as I waited for an envelope with a yes or no to come in the mail.

"Well, I'm going to miss you, a whole lot," Donna said, as if waving goodbye to Jane this very moment.

A black VW Beetle with a dent in the door and a piece of rope tied around the side mirror to hold it on rocked and rattled into the parking lot. Our director hunched behind the car's steering wheel. The windows were rolled halfway down and "The Age of Aquarius" from the musical *Hair* blasted out of the car. Bushy Beard sang along at the top of his lungs.

Barry tossed his cigarette to the grass and ground it under his foot. "Come on, kids, it's showtime," he said, and our troupe trooped inside.

CHAPTER 19

Our Little Secret

"UGH. I AM NOT a morning person."

I handed Camille a clean-smelling top sheet, still toasty warm from the dryer. My positive new attitude sure didn't extend to getting up at five in the morning on a weekend to go to work. My eyes were still sticky from sleep and cobwebs muddled my mind, despite being up for hours.

"Neither am I." Camille flapped the sheet open with a snap of her wrists and it fluttered down on the double bed like a feather in a gentle breeze. We each took a side and together we made the bed in two seconds flat. "I hate my alarm clock and want to bash it with a hammer when it goes off."

"When I become a famous writer and have lots of money, I'm gonna sleep until noon." I smoothed the tiny wrinkles to make the sheet perfectly, deliciously flat. "I'm going to hire a maid to clean my toilet so I'll *never* have to do that job again."

"And I'll come live with you." Camille punched the pillows to fluff them up. "That reminds me, did you talk to your mother?"

"My mother?"

"About finding me a new place to live."

"Yeah. She's working on it." A lie. A big one. I promised I'd talk to my mom the day I got my first college rejection. Camille's housing problem and everything else had vacated my mind that day and I forgot all about it.

"Oh," she said, disappointed. As if she knew I lied.

She didn't speak again as we finished the room. I fretted. What a shitty friend I turned out to be. The shittiest friend on the planet, in fact. Unable to help Pammie when she needed me, too scared to ask Karen what was bugging her, and so focused on my own drama I broke a promise to Camille.

The cart's wheels squeaked as I pushed it down the hallway toward number 116, the next room on the list. I scooped up a pile of fresh towels and waited for Camille to unlock the door.

"Can you handle this one alone?" She gave me the key. "I'm gonna go out for a smoke."

Might as well smoke inside. The smell of cigarettes reeked throughout the building. Hoping to ease my guilt, I eagerly agreed and she took off.

I stepped into 116 and instantly regretted letting her go. The place was a disaster area. Newspapers and magazines were strewn about. So were paper cups, plates, and pizza boxes, some containing stale slices with congealed cheese and bites taken out of them. The bedcovers were stained with something sticky and gross, the sheets ripped, and a lampshade obliterated, as if someone had punched it to death.

And the smells... Sick-sweet pipe tobacco, pot, rotting food, stinky feet, and my favorite, poop.

Holding my breath, I dove in. The sheets I threw into the rag pile. Everything else went in the trash. I found what looked like a shriveled balloon that I knew really wasn't next to the bed. I picked it up, pinching it gingerly between my fingers and added it to the barrel.

Afterward, I washed my hands a thousand times and started on the next open room. Camille still hadn't come back. How many damn cigarettes was she smoking?

I finally went hunting for her. I poked my head out the rear door at the end of the corridor. I saw a stack of abandoned truck tires and lots of litter, but I didn't see her. The day was warm and sunny, maybe she'd ditched work and gone home. Which would royally piss me off if she had.

Back inside, I strode down the corridor and turned the corner into the lobby. The clock on the wall over the registration desk read ten minutes till nine. The night manager Hector usually knocked off at eight forty five. Trudy, the lady who worked on Sundays so Valerie could have a day off, came in at nine. We were supposed to tell anyone who walked in during those fifteen minutes to wait, since no one would be at registration.

Except, someone was there today.

I heard her before I saw her. The metal cashbox clanked onto the counter, followed by the whisk of the key turning in the lock. The lid squeaked open. Camille reached in and scooped up a pile of bills. She stuffed them into her apron pocket then went fishing again. Coins jingled, following the bills into her pocket.

I'd caught her with her hand, literally, in the till.

She looked up and our eyes locked. She put her finger to her lips. "Shh. Our little secret."

After work, I trucked across the shopping center to Liggett's Drugstore to see Donna. I'd promised her I'd stop by and scope out the coworkers she thought would be great prom dates, something I'd been putting off for weeks. Might as well do it now, though my thoughts were as far away from prom as Pluto was from the sun.

An anxiety storm raged in my belly. Camille didn't speak to me for the rest of our shift. She didn't have to. Her expression said everything. An icy look, colder than a glacier. A look I'd seen around the neighborhood before. From the vicious punks guarding their corner, from that guy who sold tabs of acid out of his rusting station wagon near the brook, from Rusty sometimes.

A warning. A threat. Squeal and... Well, I didn't want to find out what came after *and...* so I would keep my mouth shut.

I reached Donna's store, wicked hot inside and wicked busy. "Kung Fu Fighting" bopped from the overhead speakers. A sizeable crowd pushed small carts through the aisles under sale signs for chocolate Easter eggs and that other kind of egg—colorful, plastic containers you cracked open and a pair of L'eggs pantyhose popped out.

Donna stood at one of the cash registers at the front of the store. She wore a rusty-red jumpsuit and her hair pulled back by rectangular barrettes. Her fingers flew over the keys as she rang up a shopper's items at lightning speed.

"Have a nice day," she chirped, handing the customer his purchases in a plastic bag. She noticed me and mouthed, "Hang on. My break's coming up."

I roamed the aisles while I waited, squeezing between shoppers, checking out the shelves of Yardley oatmeal soap that smelled so good and Dr. Scholl's wooden sandals that looked so uncomfortable.

When she was free, Donna drew me behind a cardboard cutout of Mr. Whipple warning shoppers not to squeeze the Charmin toilet paper. We peeped over Mr. Whipple's shoulder and Donna pointed out the prom potentials. Two worked the registers, the third stocked boxes of Colgate toothpaste onto a shelf across the store.

"They're college guys," Donna whisper-squealed, like that was a big deal. "They're more mature, you know."

I doubted college boys were any more mature than the high school variety. College guys had started that dumb streaking craze a few years ago and I'd heard frat boys could consume booze in quantities so vast it'd make my dad jealous.

Still, I checked out each guy thoroughly, feeling like a contestant on *The Dating Game*. Not that Bachelors One, Two, and Three were what I would call a dream date. Well, that wasn't fair. There was nothing wrong with any of them except they weren't a certain guy whose name began with a W.

And I wasn't exactly a pinup girl myself. Would any of these college guys even want to go to prom with me (if I could find the courage to ask)? What if they all said no? Three strikes and I was out.

Dejected and a little panicky, I did what Scarlett O'Hara and I did best. I put off until tomorrow what I didn't want to do today. I promised Donna I'd seriously consider each candidate, then I ducked back out into the sunlight to catch the bus home.

CHAPTER 20

Just My Imagination (Running Away With Me)

"Ooh. Look at her, sneaking off," Donna said, after Linda G wolfed down her meal and left halfway through lunch period. Donna swung toward me and waggled her eyebrows in the ridiculously suggestive fashion of Groucho Marx. "She's got somewhere important to be."

I waggled my eyebrows right back. "Or someone important to see." Someone who could make her normally rosy cheeks flush as scarlet as the sunset and rush out of the cafeteria in a flutter of expectation and smiles.

I knew how she felt. I had someone important to see too, tonight at Saint Mary's. *If* he showed up. Will had missed the last rehearsal and it seemed as if the sun had forgotten to come out. Yeah, a little dramatic and a lot cliché, but fitting given the height to which my crush on that boy had soared. I thought about him all the time and fluttered as giddily a Linda G in anticipation of seeing him again in just a few hours.

But first I had to get through the rest of the day, which dragged by, especially French class. Mrs. English pored through the newspaper, clucking about unrest abroad and another plane being "skyjacked" and ordered to fly to Cuba, then finishing the news roundup with the piddling chances the Red Sox had of getting to the World Series again this year like they did in '75.

English finally rolled around. Miss French sailed into the room a few minutes late, carrying a stack of papers. My pulse raced, and not just from thinking about Will. She had our stories. Could mine be in that pile this time?

She handed out the packets. I skimmed through the pages and my shoulders drooped. Nope. It wasn't.

This time, I followed along intently as Miss French read the stories aloud. I tried to determine why she'd chosen each one, and what particular flair the writer had used to capture her interest. I didn't get it. I thought my story was as good as theirs, with ten times the emotion. What was I doing wrong?

She passed back our graded papers at the end of class. She dropped mine on the desk without a word, though she caught my eye for a flash before moving on.

Bracing myself, I turned the pages over. B-minus. She hadn't underlined anything this time but her comments were clear. *Better*, she'd written. *You're almost there. Work harder. Capture more emotion.*

Later, after the final bell rang, I rode the bus, zooming toward home. The weather was warm, the first nice day of spring. A bus-windows-open kind of day. Everyone on board shouted and laughed and bounced around with spring fever as we barreled along, making so much noise I thought Gus's eardrums would burst.

I tuned out the noise and pulled my story out of my handbag. I went over each page again and again, frustrated and discouraged. I'd worked harder on this story than any other. I'd worked to capture more emotion, too. And clearly I failed.

The reason why piped up in my head, that unhelpful little voice that always came calling in times like these. *Because you're not a real writer. Because you don't have the skill, or the talent. You don't have what it takes.* Followed by, *eat twelve Twinkies, you'll feel better.*

Yeah, no. After all this time I knew I wouldn't feel better. That B-minus and self-doubt and all my other problems would still be there when I finished stuffing myself, with the added bonus of being sick to my stomach. And mad at myself for losing control.

Instead of beating myself up, I should take a tip from Jay. He'd been through a lot—way more than me—and he always managed to shove back those negative noises. He fought against the doubters and the name-callers and even our own father and everyone else who told him "you can't" when he knew he absolutely could.

Well, I could do that too. I'd gotten that taking better care of myself and eating right thing on track, now to get this writing thing nailed down.

I stuffed my story back into my handbag. I'd throw it away and start fresh. Before class ended, Miss French had assigned us one more story, due before April vacation. Two weeks. Plenty of time to work harder, to capture more emotion, and to write something new. Something that would prove I could do it.

I'd prove I was a real writer. To Miss French, to the rest of the class, and especially to my harshest critic—me.

❉ ✿ ❉ ✿

Carl bashed into me for the fifth time. This time I lost my balance and nearly crashed to the floor. He caught me just in time. Much to my relief and our director's frustration.

"Come on people, get it together." Bushy Beard ran a hand over his weary face then gestured to Barry and Carl. "You two. Let's rap. We've got to get this scene straightened out."

Carl let me go with an annoyed grunt, then stomped off stage right. I watched him go with a bemused grin, remembering the moment he held me in his arms after I fainted all those months ago. Then, my insides had exploded with joy. Now, nothing. How times had changed.

"Might as well go home," the reason for the change said, suddenly beside me. "Judas will never figure out how to put one foot in front of the other. No amount of stage directions will help."

That came out surprisingly bitter, but I murmured in agreement, seeing Will's point. Carl kept flubbing his movements, going left when he should've stepped right, causing chaos downstage and considerable pain for me. You'd think a football god who fancy-footed all kinds of complicated plays into the end zone would be able to get the moves right. His mind just wasn't in the game.

Or any game, it seemed. Including his favorite pastime, flirting. Carl still hung out with the girls, soaking up their compliments as if he were the Emperor of Broadway accepting his rightful due, but he seemed to have lost interest in the chase. No hovering around the girl he deemed worthy of his attention, no smoldering, no whispery sighs or sultry smiles.

Had he met someone special? Had he been bitten by the fidelity bug and renounced his flirtatious ways for good?

While Carl and Barry conferred with our director, the rest of the cast gathered in groups or darted outside to smoke. Pete fired up his radio and pulled out a deck of cards. Marilyn practiced her solo. Jane hung out with the other girls.

Will might've wanted to use the time to crack open whatever book he was reading, but I saw an opportunity for a few minutes alone with him and took it. I followed him down off the stage and over to our table. He leaned against the wall (where else?), so I did too.

"I'm glad you made it to tonight," I said, excited, but playing it extra cool. "When you missed rehearsal on Tuesday, I thought maybe you ditched this *way* off-Broadway disaster for another show."

"Couldn't be helped." He scooped a hand through his hair, tangling it more than usual. "One of my father's college buddies was in town. I had to hang out and hear stories about the old days over highballs and fondue. My dad wants him to give me a recommendation to Boston College."

"Sounds painful." At least from the gloomy way he put it. And it explained his bitter attitude this evening.

He gave a grim laugh. "It sure was." He hooked his thumbs in the belt loops of his jeans and flicked me a sidelong glance. "Hey, I wonder if you want to, ah..." He cleared his throat and began again. "Have you been writing? How's the Revolutionary War story coming along?"

"It's not." I sighed. "I gave it a merciful death, with a twenty-one gun salute and a grave six feet deep. The story just didn't work. And by that I mean, it was complete crap. Now I'm in a bind. I've got a story due soon for English class and I don't know what to write. It doesn't have to be a masterpiece, just something my teacher will like. Or *anyone* likes. But I don't have any ideas."

He turned to face me, hesitating as he always did before speaking. "They say write what you know." He held up both hands, stopping my objection before it began. "Yeah, that's a cliché. I guess I mean, why not try writing what you *want* to know. Something you want to understand."

I blinked, impressed. "Write what I want to understand," I repeated softly. There were a lot of things I didn't understand but wished I did. Like, everything. "That's kind of brilliant."

He flushed but didn't look away. His gaze stayed on me a long time before he spoke again. "You might get a story idea from the movies. I'm going to see *All the President's Men* on Saturday. It just came out. Think you'd, yip, like to see that?"

Surprise flooded me. Delight floored me. Was he asking me on a date? I opened my mouth. Nothing came out. Absolutely nothing.

"I mean—" He looked down at his boots and his untied laces with an enormous amount of interest. "I thought you...ah, I thought everyone might like that movie, you know?"

Oh. My delight turned to dismay. Everyone. As in, Barry and Pete and Marilyn, everyone. Not me alone.

"Well, I have to work in the morning," I said. "What time's the movie?"

"What's going on?" Donna slinked up to us. No other way to describe the sultry way she moved. Her gaze bounced back and forth between Will and me. "What're you two being so secretive about?"

I cringed at how she said that, like we'd been making out when that was the last thing we could've been doing. Will liked me, but he didn't like me in *that* way. How could I have thought he was asking me on a date?

"Will wants to get *everyone* together to go to the movies on Saturday," I said, because of course I couldn't ignore her question or her curious eyes that always had to butt into my business.

"*All the President's Men.* Bijou Theater. Downtown," he bit off as if trying to save time by deleting prepositions.

"Sounds fabulous," Donna cooed. "I'm in."

CHAPTER 21

Popcorn, Previews & the Date-Not-A-Date

SATURDAY, MOVIE DAY. A good news, bad news kind of day.

The good news, I'd lost five more pounds. Refocusing how I ate and being more consistent with exercise since the beginning of the month had paid off. Maybe there was something to this whole taking care of myself thing.

The bad news, my damned period had decided to make its monthly appearance a few days early. No cramps, thankfully, and a light flow, but seriously, if there was a god, he had to be a man. A lady god would never allow MDP to come when you had a busy day of work followed by a date-not-a-date with a guy you liked. Come to think of it, a lady god would never give girls periods at all.

God or no god, I thanked whoever had invented the adhesive sanitary pad, freeing me from the thirteenth century torture device known as the sanitary belt I'd worn after MDP had arrived when I was twelve.

The elastic belt went around my waist, with metal tabs that looked like buckles dangling down in the front and back. The pad was the size of a Clydesdale horse, complete with a long fabric tail on both ends that threaded through the buckles to hold it in place between my legs.

177

Uncomfortable, unsightly, and unbelievably annoying, especially when the back buckle broke and I had to use a safety pin instead and frequently stabbed myself in the butt.

I moved quickly at work, trying to get Camille to move fast too. I hoped to finish all the rooms well before our normal time of noon. I was supposed to meet Will (well, Will and *everyone*) at the movie theater at two and didn't want to be late. It'd be a crunch to get home and change then get to Donna's house so she could drive us downtown.

Camille didn't cooperate. She dragged her feet, folding towels and vacuuming each room at turtle speed. The bus bringing me home poked along too and the minutes ticked away. Even my father conspired to slow me down.

"C'mon, hurry up," I shouted, banging on the bathroom door. Dad had been in there for a hundred years. I had the outfit I'd picked out last night slung over my arm, a flowered blouse that clung to my curves and a pair of brown knit pants that hung kind of loose.

Dad finally opened the door and stepped out, drying his face with a towel. The scent of his shaving cream canceled out his usual whiskey and cigarette smell.

"You shave once a year and you have to do it now, when I'm in a hurry?" Not true. He shaved every day because that's how men did it in his day, before all those hairy hippies came along. He used an old fashioned straight razor, sometimes shaving while stinking drunk, and how he hadn't slit his own throat before now remained a family mystery.

"You got a hot date?" he said, followed by a raspy *haw-haw-haw*. Good thing he laughed at his own jokes since no one else did.

Swearing I'd someday own a house with a shower, I took the world's fastest bath. I doused myself with deodorant and baby powder, dressed quickly, and knocked on Donna's kitchen door twenty minutes later.

"Get in gear, Don, we're running la—"

I gulped when I saw who opened the door. Donna's mother. She wore a coral-pink shell top, tight blue jeans, and her dark hair teased into a towering bouffant like women wore a decade ago. She smelled like the entire Filene's perfume counter and carried a glass filled with a reddish-brown liquid with a sweet and boozy scent.

"Oh. I'm Deidre, Donna's friend." I giggled awkwardly. "Well, you must know that. Who else would I be? The friendly neighborhood prowler?"

Her upper lip lifted in a sneer she must've learned from Marilyn, or vice versa. "Yes. Donna's told me about you."

She gestured for me to come in. I did, but barely, hovering just inside the door. Her jeans strained against the seams as she settled into a chair at the small table. She swirled her drink and the ice cubes clinked.

"Where're you girls running off to?" she asked with little interest.

"Ma, I already told you." Donna's heels clacked on the linoleum as she huffed into the kitchen. She wore a geometric-patterned red and black shirt with collar points as sharp as arrowheads and jeans almost as tight as her mother's. "We're going to the movies. I won't be back till dinner, not that you care. C'mon, Dee."

Donna snatched a set of keys off a wall-mounted key holder shaped like a squirrel and breezed by me out the door.

I followed her, and so did her mother's voice. "Don't do anything I wouldn't do."

"Which is absolutely nothing," Donna muttered, stabbing the key into the Pinto's ignition. She put the car in gear and we were off. "Just ignore her. She's moping. My dad put his foot down about her going out all the time." She sighed. "I wish they'd get a divorce and get it over with. Did you know my dad's practically living with a nurse from his emergency room? You're lucky. Your parents are normal."

Normal? My eyes went so wide, if I'd been wearing a monocle it would've dropped into my drink. My parents were the furthest (or was that farthest?) thing from normal. Then again, so were hers. Was there really such a thing as normal?

Donna had a lead foot heavier than Gus. She zoomed us downtown with time to spare. The temperature hovered around fifty, cloudy, with a threat of April showers on the way. Our shoes scuffed across the sandy parking lot to the Bijou Theater, a weather-scored brick building that had once offered Vaudeville and stage shows and now featured movies on three screens.

The theater lobby smelled of popcorn, Raisinets, and other tempting stuff. I spotted Will right away and my heart swelled like a rowboat on a wave. He stood with the rest of *everyone*—Marilyn, Barry, and Pete—at the concession stand. Will's hair flew around in its usual tangled mess and he wore jeans and a green crew neck tee shirt.

"Did you want anything?" he asked after smiling his hello. He held a box of popcorn and a soda I thought was Coke by the color.

I eyed the kid in the red-and-white striped smock behind the counter like he was selling botulism and not such delicious treats. Buttered popcorn was super fattening and had a bad habit of sticking to your teeth, but it tasted so good. I figured a small bag wouldn't kill me, not after those five pounds. I said yes and couldn't help a giddy grin when Will turned down the dollar I offered him and paid for my popcorn and medium Tab soda himself.

Like a real date.

Except for *everyone* surrounding us.

We crowded onto the escalator up to what used to be the balcony before they chopped the main theater into a trio of screens to make more money. Pete led the way, with the rest of us crowded behind him.

"Been meaning to tell you how much I dig your shoes," Barry said. He walked up the stairs, keeping stride beside me on the escalator gliding upward, a cigarette smoldering between his fingers. He tipped a glance down at my marshmallow shoes. "They're groovy."

I laughed. "Groovy? Who says groovy anymore?"

"I do."

Oh, to possess one iota of Barry's coolness. If I called something groovy, everyone would laugh, and not the good kind of laughter.

"Use Kiwi shoe polish on them if you can get some," he said. "Keeps the leather fresh."

"Thank you, Mr. Shoe Expert."

I managed to dismount the escalator at the top without dropping my popcorn or falling on my face. Barry put out his cigarette in the standing ashtray by the theater door and exhaled his last puff as we moved inside.

Not many people were here today, so we had our choice of seats. After much scrambling and a little squabbling, we decided to sit in two separate rows, one behind the other, so we could talk. Then the complicated politics of who would sit where began. Will somehow got sandwiched between Marilyn and Donna before I could even try to sit next to him. I took a seat on the end, with Barry beside me, next to Pete.

The lights faded. I loved going to the movies and I loved this moment the most, when the theater went dark and the first images flickered onto the screen. Opening a book to the first page felt the same way. An escape into another world, to not be mundane Deidre Daly with mundane problems, if even for a little while.

The previews came on. I sipped my Tab through a straw and (almost) forgot about Will behind me as an announcer boomed, "Coming soon to this theater." First up, *Ode to Billie Joe* (good luck turning a song into a movie), followed by a guy running up steps and getting beat up in a boxing match in a movie called *Rocky*, and finally a scary horror flick, *The Omen*.

"*Eep!*" I cringed down in my seat. Barry and Pete laughed. So did Will. I shot him a mock glare over my shoulder. "I hate creepy kids," I said. Especially ones that stared silently with bug eyes like Damien in the preview. Like Chrissy did sometimes after she swiped a bunch of sips from Dad's beer.

Will leaned forward and touched me lightly on the shoulder. Delight and agony went to war in my belly.

"Repeat after me," he said. "It's only a movie."

"So you say." I turned to face forward as *All the President's Men* began, thinking I wouldn't be scared to watch *The Omen*, if Will sat by my side.

The first hard cramp came when Deep Throat told Woodward (or Bernstein, I couldn't be sure which was which) to follow the money. MDP suddenly turned from mild-mannered Bruce Banner to the Incredible Hulk, squeezing my belly as if wringing the life out of it. I squirmed in my chair, breathing through the pain as best I could, hoping none of my movie companions would notice my discomfort.

After the second soul-draining contraction, I didn't care who noticed. I had to get out of there. "Excuse me," I groaned and fled.

I aimed for the women's bathroom. Another roaring cramp attacked my gut and my knees turned to jelly. I groaned. Greasy popcorn and sugar-free Tab sloshed around in my stomach, threatening a return appearance all over the carpet. My old friends, needles and pins, stabbed my skull. My ears clanged. My limbs tingled. The next step in this exciting adventure—fainting.

"Holy mother of god."

I needed to sit, and I needed to sit right *now*.

I found a convenient wall and sank down to the floor. My butt met a wet patch on the carpet. God was *definitely* a man. A real bastard to let MDP land on me like Dorothy landed her house on that wicked witch. Hard, fast, and with maximum damage. Today, of all days.

I drew my legs up and stuck my head between my knees to keep myself from passing out. I took deep breaths and tried not to panic, cursing Doctor Crabby and every gynecologist who'd ever stuck a finger into a girl's vagina and told her she'd be fine if she'd only lose weight.

"Deidre?"

I glanced up. Will.

Dear Jesus, why me? Was it asking too much not to have the objects of my desire stumble upon me at my most embarrassing moments?

"Deidre, what's wrong?" He sounded scared.

I thumped my head against the wall. "Go away, Will. I'm just a little tired."

He did *not* go away. In fact, he sat next to me, pulling his knees up like mine. He wore Puma sneakers today instead of boots. Good shoes for running. I wished he'd use them to run away from me as fast as he could.

"Did something...happen?" he asked.

Oh lord, yes. A million answers flashed through my mind, all of them lies and all of them stupid. I sighed. Might as well tell him the truth. A boy wouldn't die if he heard a girl had her period. At least, I hoped not.

"It's a...girl thing. I get super bad cramps with my...my time of the month and sometimes I faint. I half fainted today and I had to sit down and that's why you see me here."

"Fuck," he breathed, an exclamation more outraged than stunned.

For some reason, that cheered me up. "Yup. One of the burdens of being a girl, I guess. I feel better now. Go back to the movie. You don't want to miss the exciting conclusion."

His eyebrows drew down in an *are you kidding me?* scowl. "I *know* how it ends. We lived through Watergate, remember?"

"Sure." I didn't remember much beyond a break-in at the Watergate hotel and Nixon flashing twin peace signs as he made his escape from DC.

"Can you stand up? We can go back inside together."

I nodded and he helped me to my feet. Upright, the blood rushed from my head and I sagged. He caught me, throwing his arm around my waist to support me. I caught his clean scent, felt the warmth of his body, and the strength of his arm holding me. Not gingerly, as if I might give him a disease, like Carl when I'd fainted in school. Will's hold on me was solid, reassuring.

Like someone I could count on.

Someone I could depend on.

He held me that way all the way back to the theater. At the door, the giant's hand reached inside me again and shook me like a ragdoll. Groaning, I pulled from his embrace and fell against the wall, hands clutching my belly.

"Bullshit you feel better. I'm taking you home."

The theater door whooshed open. Music and Dustin Hoffman's voice rolled out of the darkness beyond. And so did Marilyn. Her gaze bounced from Will to me, flopped against the wall, then back to Will.

"What's wrong?" she demanded.

"Deidre's sick."

"Sick? Or drugs?" Her voice went whispery, like she didn't think I'd hear her from three feet away.

Will frowned. "She's not feeling well. I'm gonna drive her home."

"Drive her home—? What about me, how will I get home?"

"Donna will take you." Several more involuntary hiccups rushed from Will's lips. I could feel his anger. Marilyn felt it too. She snapped her trapezoid shut and went back into the movie without saying another word.

A soft rain fell as we left the theater and moved toward the parking lot. Will walked beside me, hovering as if he feared I'd keel over.

I hesitated when we approached his father's Lincoln. "You know I live in the Project, right? Do you really want to take this beauty down there?" Most people in my neighborhood were just trying to get by, but some might see swiping a fancy car like this as a way to get by faster.

He gazed at me with an odd expression. "Of course I do." He opened the door and swept his hand in front of him like Cary Grant in an old movie. "Please, get in."

He didn't die when I told him about MDP, I supposed he could handle a trip to *that* neighborhood, so I slid into the car. He held the door and closed it too. I felt like a princess in a fairy tale. With an ogre stomping around inside my stomach.

The car started with a purr and rolled toward the exit, as silent as the dead of night. Our Impala would've announced our departure with a roar and lots of *pow-pow* explosions from the muffler.

And our car wasn't nearly as fancy as this. Automatic windows, glove compartment with the word *Continental* written across it in elaborate letters, and the *most* comfortable seats in the world, tan-gold leather so soft and smooth the slightest left turn would send me sliding directly into Will's arms.

I quickly banished that scorching image. This was hardly the moment to be thinking about kissing Will. "This is a nice car," I said, an understatement if ever there was one. "How's the mileage?" After the energy crisis, everyone asked about a car's mileage.

"Ten miles to a gallon. Eleven if we're going uphill."

"Is that good?"

His eyes crinkled. "No."

Another cramp hit. Not as intense, but still a belly-buster. I leaned back and closed my eyes, trying to relax through the pain.

"You okay?" His voice tightened with concern.

"I'll live," I murmured.

He switched on the radio and turned the station from classical music to Top 40 hits. Earth, Wind & Fire's "Shining Star" murmured from the speaker. Will steered onto the highway, headed toward the city's south side. He sped up, driving fast as boys liked to do, not reckless, as jerks liked to do. We fell into a comfortable silence. The windshield wipers whisked over the rain-spattered glass, almost keeping time to the music.

"Did you hear? Barry got into State U," he said after a while.

"Cool. I bet he'll major in theater. I'm still waiting to hear from them. Maybe that's a bad sign."

"Maybe a good sign. Could be they're saving the best for last."

The best? As in, me? He was just too, too terrific for words. "Careful, Will. Someone might accuse you of being an optimist."

One side of his mouth tugged upward. "Optimist? No, please. Anything but that."

I laughed. "What about you? I mean, college-wise. Have you considered State U instead of applying to a school you don't want to go to?" His expression darkened and I kicked myself and my big mouth. "Forget it. That's none of my business."

"It's okay. That's what I like about you. You speak your mind. Unlike me. I have trouble speaking at all." He paused a moment, then, "You don't notice it, do you?"

"Notice what?" He shot me a *please don't* look and I put the joking aside. "I noticed at first. Not much now. It's part of you and who you are." I thought of Jay. "You know, my mother can be a pain sometimes, but she's pretty smart about some things. She says everybody's different and that's a good thing. The world would be pretty boring if we were all the same."

"I wish my parents were as easygoing. You know the real reason they want me to go to Boston College? So my brother can keep an eye on me. My dad wants me to work in his company for the same reason. They want to protect me."

"From what?"

"The world. Rejection. Embarrassment. Pick one." He blew out a heavy breath. "This thing I have... It came on when I was, I dunno, four? I can barely remember a time without it. It's called a chronic vocal tic. I call it Grendel, like in Beowulf. It can't be stopped and resents being held back. It needs to bust out or I'll explode. My father, he's worried." A bitter note crept into his voice. "He's always worried. About what people will think. How they'll think about me, about him, and that's why..."

"Why he wants to control your life."

Mr. Hovey might benefit from a long talk with my mother, who'd insisted Jay, her "different" child, be treated like anyone else. And anyone who took issue with that... Well, that was *their* problem. Including Gramps. She told him exactly what he could do with his plan to put Jay in a home.

"What about your mother? Does she want to control your life too?" Or did she just go along with her husband as women often do?

"My mother..." His voice softened. "She worries in a different way. She's from France, grew up during the war. She saw people like me taken away and never seen again."

"Oh, Will. That must've been so hard for her." Tears poked at my eyes and I blinked them away. Damn you, MDP for making me so emotional.

"Yeah. Grendel was bad in the beginning. I couldn't control myself. At all. My mother never forgot the war and what happened. She was scared. I was scared. I was teased all the time. I felt wrong. My parents didn't know what to do. They sent me to doctors and therapists for years, hoping to cure me." He watched the road, his expression serious. "It's supposed to go away eventually. It's gotten better as I've gotten older. I can control it." On cue, he yipped. "Mostly."

I felt wrong.

My heart hurt to hear him say that. And that his own parents made him feel that way, no matter what their motivation. To hear him say he'd been bullied and ridiculed by the same kind of ignorant people who teased Jay. It also touched me that he trusted me enough to talk about it.

"Will... What does it feel like? Grendel, I mean. You said you can't help it and it has to bust out. What's it like?" A couple seconds ticked by. He didn't speak. "Sorry, I guess that's kind of a rude question. And weird to ask." A Weirdra Deidre thing to ask.

"Weird?" He flashed that million dollar smile. "It's *great*. No one ever asks that. Most people ignore my tic. Or turn away and ignore *me*." He drummed the steering wheel with his thumbs. "It feels like...like water pushing against a dam. The longer I hold back, the more it needs to burst through. The thing is, when I don't fight it and let it out, I feel good. Relieved. Not everyone understands that when I first meet them. I'm just this scary guy barking at them."

He spoke in a just-the-facts-ma'am tone but I suspected more complicated emotions lurked beneath the surface. "Now I get why you didn't want a speaking part in the show. I'm glad you came to audition anyway."

"I wasn't going to until…" He let that hang as he hit the blinker and turned off the highway at the Adams Street exit. "When I told my parents I was gonna try out, man did they explode. They didn't want me to do it. My father said no, flat out. I said I was doing it, and they eventually backed off."

"Will Hovey, you *rebel*. You defied your parents. Which commandment did you break for that one? Now, all you need to do is tell you father to back off where you go to school." And what Will did for the rest of his life.

"Or spit in his eye."

I giggled. Something I didn't do often, or at all, because, really, me giggle? He made me so…happy. Then a cramp came on, reminding me not to get *too* happy.

We reached the Project, far too soon, and cruised along Prosperity Way. The rain had let up and the brick buildings looked stark under the cloudy sky. A group of guys, both Black and white, played basketball in one of the paved play yards. The funky tune, "Love Rollercoaster" dueled with ABBA's "Mamma Mia" cranked up on portable radios. No dumpsters were on fire, no gangs brawled with each other, and only one cop car prowled the streets.

The place looked almost normal. Ordinary. Nothing to be ashamed of. The blood-sucking zombies Marilyn feared would come out of the shadows to eat her then steal her wallet if she drove me home were nowhere in sight. Just regular people enjoying a peaceful spring evening in an ordinary blue collar neighborhood that happened to have a chain link fence topped with barbed wire surrounding it.

I glanced at Will out of the corner of my eye. Did a kid from upper Chisholm Road see it that way too?

"My street's the third one up on the left," I said. "Which is conveniently called Third Street." He turned at the corner and the car climbed the hill effortlessly. "Will… What do you really want to do? You've mentioned what you don't want to do, and that's cool. But where do you see yourself in the year 2000?"

He hesitated only a moment. "Not working for my father, that's for sure. He helps men with money make more money. I want to do something that helps people who need real help. People like I used to be. People trying to deal with something they don't understand."

His answer didn't surprise me, and it bowled me over at the same time. An admirable and completely Will kind of goal. "My mother does that. Sort of. She helps people get food and complain to the housing authority. Maybe she could give you some advice."

"Could she tell me how to get my father off my back?"

"Watch out!" I cried. Rusty flashed into sight, riding a banana seat bike he'd swiped from somewhere. Will swerved in time to avoid mowing him down. I stabbed the automatic window button and it whisked downward. I stuck my head out. "Get out of the road, dumbass."

"Fuck off," Rusty spat. He deployed his middle finger and pedaled away.

"Do you know that kid?" Will asked.

"Nope." I leaned back against the seat. "I just know he's a dumbass."

He snort-laughed. "See, you speak your mind."

"Sometimes too much. Or so I've been told. Stop here. I live over there at the end of the block."

Will slowed and swung the car around. A *major* feat—the Lincoln was wide, our road was not. He parked at the curb and leapt out, coming around to open my door. Delighted tingles rushed up my spine. A girl could get used to such princess treatment.

I got out and he glanced toward my apartment as he closed the car door. "Is this your place?"

"Yeah. I'd invite you in, except..." Except, my dad could be passed out on the floor and my mother with her eyes pasted to a book, ignoring him. And a dog peeing on the rug because everyone forgot to take him out. Letting Will drive me home was one thing, having him meet my family would be an embarrassment too far. "I have a story to write and..." I pressed a hand to my belly and winced, though the worst of my cramps had faded. "Thanks for the ride, and thanks for not dying when I told you about you-know-what."

"You're welcome."

He didn't move, just looked at me like he had a hundred other things to say. My breath went shallow. I wished all of those hundred things had to do with him putting his arms around me again, but I knew they didn't.

"Well...bye," I said. Most reluctantly.

He blinked, then started back around the car. "I hope you feel better." Another pause, another long look. "See you at rehearsal."

I waved as he drove off, though I doubted he noticed. I turned toward the house, my heart full. I'd let Will help me today. I let him see where I lived. I felt (sort of) comfortable enough to tell him about MDP. He felt comfortable enough to share his troubles with me.

So strange. I'd never had a guy friend before. And certainly never a guy as honest and nice as Will. I liked that. I liked everything about him.

He was my friend. But I wished he could be a whole lot more.

CHAPTER 22

We're Going On A Guilt Trip

WORK WENT FAST THE next day, Palm Sunday. Not many truck drivers or businessmen were on the road this weekend and needed motel rooms to stay in, only some grandparents come to visit their families for Easter week.

We moved quickly, cleaning each room separately. Camille alternately snubbed and snarled at me, still mad at me for catching her stealing. I pretended I didn't notice and got on with my job. We finished early. I threw on my raincoat as I darted to the front office and the door, with Camille on my heels.

I blinked in surprise to see Valerie behind the check-in counter on her day off. She wore a lacy white cardigan over a flowered dress and a broad-brimmed white hat, as if she'd stopped by on her way to church. She spoke in a quiet voice to Trudy, who ran the show on Sundays.

"Deidre, wait," Valerie called. "I'd like a word with you."

I stopped my headlong rush, alarmed at the serious note in Valerie's voice. Camille kept moving. She shot me a warning glare as she shoved open the glass door.

It had rained off and on since Will had driven me home yesterday, with the faucet turned on high at the moment. Camille instantly got soaked when she stepped outside. Through the rain trickling down the window, I could see Mom in the parking lot, waiting for me in the car.

192

I approached Valerie at the desk. "What is it?" I twittered with nerves. "What's wrong?"

"It's come to my attention that money's been going missing from the register on weekends. A little bit here and there, it adds up over time. Do you know anything about that?"

"Me?" I cried. Like, was I the culprit? Because of course all Project people were thieves.

Her expression softened. "Child, I'm not accusing you. I have a suspicion of where the money's gone to. I'm only asking what you know."

That didn't reassure me. I chewed my bottom lip, verging on panic. Camille taking the money was our little secret. I wasn't a snitch.

"What aren't you telling me, Deidre?"

She had a penetrating stare, like my mom, maybe like all mothers, installed in them the second they popped out a baby. I could never lie to Mom and I couldn't lie to Valerie. Though Camille would hate me forever and never speak to me again if she found out I squealed on her, I told Valerie what I'd seen.

Afterward, I dashed through the rain to the Impala. Mom closed Anne McCaffrey's *Dragonsong* and placed the book on the seat between us when I got in.

She started the car. "How'd work go today?"

"Work was good," I muttered, feeling like a traitor. Feeling like Judas.

"That bad, huh?" She aimed the car toward the shopping center's exit. "I know it's not the glitziest job, and heaven knows you get paid peanuts. At least it's teaching you responsibility."

"Yeah, responsibility." And how to turn on your friends.

Over the next two days, I fretted about Camille and my betrayal. Thought about Will almost as much. Thankfully, school flew by on Monday. On Tuesday, I spotted Linda G at the end of B corridor—with Stew Baines.

Well, well, what an interesting development. She clutched her stack of books to her chest, gazing up at Stew's towering self with a dazed smile. Stew looked equally discombobulated and so very adorable. What an odd couple, though Stew's recent addition of a Rhett Butler mustache could explain some of the attraction.

I ducked my head and rolled on to French class, pretending not to see them. If Linda had wanted us to know about Stew she would've trumpeted the news every day at lunch. Let her keep her sweet secret.

"It seems the government's going to reform the food stamp program," Mrs. English said, glancing up from her newspaper. "I approve. There's too much fraud in the system."

Finally, one of her in-the-news stories I knew about. Mom had been in a tizzy over the plan to cap income levels for people eligible for food assistance since the story broke.

"Typical politicians," she growled. "Plenty of money for bombs, nothing for hungry children."

Dad had agreed with Mrs. English, muttering about people mooching off Uncle Sam. I decided *not* to mention that he said that while he ate a sandwich made with the block of cheese we got free from the government each month. I simply rolled my eyes and declared irony officially dead.

Tuesday night arrived, time for rehearsal. My heartbeat conducted a furious symphony as I stepped into Saint Mary's, excited to see Will. I hurried downstairs and spotted the gang at our table. Barry, Pete, and Jane sat playing cards. Donna leaned against the wall next to Will. He waved and I returned a cool nod, though my pulse zinged.

Before I could get two steps into the room, Bushy Beard yelled for us to get into place for act one. Everyone scrambled to get organized. The Holy Mother girls surged toward the stage as one entity, Marilyn at the center, with Carl hot on their heels.

Tonight was our last rehearsal before the Easter break and school vacation next week. With our performance date the week after that and precious little time left to practice, Bushy Beard frantically tried to whip our band of amateur thespians into something more professional. Or at least less amateurish.

For the first half hour he worked with us on the scene where Pete as Peter denies Jesus three times. Pete kept laughing, which pushed our director into freak out territory. I understood his agitation. Betraying a friend was serious business. I ought to know.

I passed the time by practicing my most important role, opening and closing the curtain. I hung on the ropes, tugging idly. After a few minutes, Will stopped by. Marilyn watched him stroll over, then turned a narrow-eyed glare on me as if I'd lured him to his doom like a siren from *The Odyssey*.

"How're you feeling?" he asked in a low voice.

"Much better, thanks." We exchanged glances I could only term as *sharing a secret*.

"Did you get your story written?"

"No." I sighed. "Still not sure what to write about. Nothing's really clicking. It better click soon. The story's due on Thursday."

"I'm sure you'll figure something out." He shuffled his feet. "Thanks for listening the other day. I've decided to talk to my parents and tell them how I feel and ask them to back off. Still going on the college tour, though. The plane tickets are bought. The hotels are booked. Can't cancel now."

"Oh. Of course." The idea of canceling plane tickets or even going on an airplane made my head spin.

He frowned. "What's wrong? You seem down."

I traced a finger down the braided surface of the curtain rope. "I'm pretty sure I got my friend fired from work."

His eyebrows flew up. "What happened?" I told him about Camille and his eyebrows climbed higher. "Sounds like you had no choice. She was stealing. Don't blame yourself."

"William, don't you know blaming myself is one of my favorite pastimes?" I tried to make that funny, but it came out grim. And slightly self-pitying. "I feel so guilty. Like, I wish I could've done something to help her instead of snitching on her. She needed a place to live and I blew her off. Her life's been so shitty. Oops—"

I covered my mouth but too late. The profanity had already flown out.

"Swearing in church, Deidre? Jesus wept. Say twenty Hail Mary's and call me in the morning."

He was trying to cheer me up. Trying, and succeeding. Because why wouldn't I cheer up when I was with him?

Bushy Beard clapped his hands and called for our attention. We went back to work.

The evening ended with the usual chatter and chaos as everyone bolted up the stairs. I said a breezy goodbye to Will as we left, not letting on how much I'd miss him the next two weeks. It almost felt like I wouldn't see him again for two years.

The next day, I plopped on the couch with my notebook as soon as I got home from school, determined to get my story written. *Needing* to write it, actually—it was due tomorrow.

My father didn't help my efforts to concentrate. He parked his butt in his chair and watched TV at a loud volume. As Richard Dawson and Betty White cracked dirty jokes on the gameshow *Match Game '76*, Dad swigged beer and snuck sips from the nip bottle he thought I didn't know he'd stashed in his pants pocket, but of course I did. We all did.

Afternoon turned to evening and I still had nothing but a blank page. The rest of the family trickled in. Chrissy had been at Rapunzel's working on a school project. Mom got home from her daily battle with The Man and his bureaucratic nonsense (her words, not mine). Rusty banged into the house a minute later, demanding to know when supper would be ready.

In the spirit of procrastination and to shut him up, I went to help Mom cook. And by *help* I meant monitor the pork chops sizzling in the frying pan so they wouldn't get overcooked and turn into petrified rocks.

Suddenly, a sound like a battering ram beat against the back door. Mom and I bumped into each other trying to get there first. I won. I swung the inside door wide and gasped to see Camille through the screen door, standing on the stoop.

"Valerie fired me." She glared at me, her eyes as cold as dark blue pebbles. She smelled like my dad after a date with a dozen nips and her small body trembled with rage. "You told her about the money. You snitched on me."

I cringed. What could I say? It was the truth.

Mom stepped in front of me. "I don't know what this is about, Camille, but you should go. Come back when you can speak rationally."

"*She* knows what it's about." Camille stabbed a finger at me, cowering behind my mother. "You're a fat, fucking backstabber."

That triggered Mom's squinty look full force. "I do *not* appreciate that language, young lady. Please go. Leave now, before I call the police."

Behind us in the living room, Chrissy leaned over the arm of the couch, her eyes wide. Rusty stood as rigid as iron, flexing his fists.

Dad swiveled in his chair to watch the show like a boxing match he'd bet money on and couldn't wait to see who won.

Camille pinned her glare on Mom. "Fuck you. You can't tell me what to do. You're not my mother."

"No I'm not. And you're not a child. You're eighteen and should know better. Now, go on. Come back when you're sober."

"Deidre, your mother's a bitch."

"At least she cares about me," I snapped. "Why don't you go yell at your own mother?"

"Shut up, you fat fuck. You think you're so perfect."

Ouch. Not really.

"That's enough out of you both. Deidre, go back into the kitchen." Mom urged me to do so with a push and turned back to Camille. "And *you.*" Her voice got deadly quiet, a stern, icy tone that made us kids and housing authority officials and anyone with any sense shiver in terror. "You'd better leave, or I *will* call the police."

Seconds ticked by. Tension crackled in the air as Camille froze in place, her body coiled for attack. Finally, she hurled one more, "Fat fuck," in my direction and stomped off our stoop. Mom stood like a sentry in the doorway, watching until Camille disappeared down the hill. Then she closed the door. And locked it.

My hands shook all through dinner and I could barely eat. A mix of fear and guilt bubbled in my belly. No one spoke. Even my father kept quiet, though he sliced his pork chop into little bits before angrily shoveling in each piece.

Later, I sat next to Chrissy on the couch while she and Dad watched an episode of *Good Times* on TV. Neither laughed. Not once, not even when JJ hollered, "Dyn-o-mite," Dad's favorite part of the show. Rusty wolfed down his meal and took off to parts unknown the second he finished. Mom cleaned up in the kitchen, dishes and pans clattering.

I picked up my notebook. Time stretched out. The pink of sunset faded and night darkened the sky. I stared at the lined paper. No words came. My mind wouldn't focus. My story ideas fled. Even Will faded from my mind.

All I could think about was Camille. Her anger, her heartbreak, and what I'd done.

A sudden wail of sirens pierced the night, followed by the squeal of tires as a police car tore up our street. Not an unusual sound around here. And neither was the thunder of feet pounding the sidewalk that came next. Half the neighborhood racing past our apartment to see what was going on. A fire, a gang fight, a drug bust. A kid falling out a window or even a birthday party gone awry (which happened more often than you'd think).

When I was younger, I joined the mob scurrying to the scene. Doing my best to keep up with Pammie and Yolanda running ahead of me. In the winter, the buckles on our boots jingled as we ran. In the summer, our rubbery thong sandals flip-flopped madly on the pavement. Even now I'd sometimes rush after police cars or firetrucks with the rest of the crowd, my curiosity popping.

Not tonight.

I froze in place on the couch, seized by dread and an ominous foreboding. When the front door banged open and Rusty charged in moments later, I knew what he was going to say.

"Mom, mom. You gotta come. It's Camille."

My mother didn't hesitate. "Stay here," she said to no one in particular and darted out the door.

Rusty followed in a flash, and after many agonizing seconds of indecision, so did I. I threw on a jacket and hurried out into the night, fearing for Camille. What had happened?

"Your mother said stay put," I heard Dad yell as the screen door slapped shut behind me.

Up ahead, I saw Rusty and Mom, lit by the streetlights. Mom had pulled her hair back into a ponytail. It bounced furiously as she rushed along the sidewalk. Several blocks up our street, the lights of a police vehicle flashed with a gloomy starkness, bathing the brick buildings in blue and red.

A crowd had formed outside the block where Camille's mother lived. Black, white, young, old, everyone in a twenty block radius had spilled out to see what was happening.

The door to the end apartment stood open. Angry voices erupted from inside. Camille's mother yelled something. Camille yelled back, her tone full of fear and anger. Panic. Two cops shoved into the apartment. Both white, one older, one young. Real young—he wore a uniform so crisp and new I suspected he'd started on the job this morning.

"Calm down, miss," the older cop said. Ordered, really, like he was Camille's father and wasn't going to put up with her nonsense anymore.

A hushed quiet, then, Camille's shrieks tore through the night. A rock clogged my throat and my stomach filled with acid.

Mom saw me and edged closer. "I told you to stay home."

She snapped to attention at movement from inside the apartment. Everyone did.

The younger cop backed through the doorway, carrying Camille by the legs. The older cop held her upper body, his hands under her armpits. She thrashed about, like a fish caught on a hook. The older cop lost his grip. Camille's hands were cuffed in the front, giving her the chance to grab the door jamb. The younger cop tried to break her hold, pulling and pulling her legs, as if she were a sticky piece of taffy that wouldn't come free.

"Put your back into it, rookie," a guy in the watching crowd called and some people laughed.

"Mommy," Camille screeched, hanging on tight. Her mother crept up behind the older cop and peered over his shoulder, crying, shaking.

I tasted bile. Guilt crawled up my throat. This was my fault. I'd gotten her fired. I'd snapped at her, goaded her. *Why don't you go yell at your own mother?* Camille wouldn't have bothered her if I hadn't pushed her. If I'd been a better friend.

"I'm sorry," I yelled. "I'm sorry, Camille."

Mom spun on me. "Stop that. You're not making this situation any better. Please go home."

I swallowed a sob and lifted my chin. I was *not* going home. I normally did what my mother told me to. Followed her rules. Not now. This was *my* mess.

"Drop her," the older cop growled and his partner released Camille's legs. She banged to the stoop with a thud.

The older cop leaned in and wrenched her fingers loose from the door jamb. She screamed. The rookie watched, as horrified as me, as his colleague seized the handcuffs and spun Camille around then dragged her off the stoop and over the grass to the squad car. He tugged open the back door, snatched her up and threw her into the rear seat like a sack of potatoes. She howled and cursed the whole way.

The rookie followed and shut the door. He gazed at Camille through the window, his expression inscrutable. Sorrow, maybe. Touched with confusion, even disgust.

"Welcome to the project," someone yelled and pitched a beer can at the rookie's head. He ducked then hopped into the squad car, in a hurry to get away.

A moment later they were gone. The flashing lights lit the buildings and flickered over the crowd's faces, then faded. People shuffled away and the night went quiet, except for Camille's mother's sobs.

"Rusty," Mom called and pointed toward home. He groaned but went. She eyed me. "You too."

Trembling, I shook my head. "Mom, it's all my fault."

"Sweetheart." She slipped her arm around my shoulders. "It's not your fault. If it's anyone's fault it's mine. I yelled at her when I should've helped her." She tightened her arm around me and urged me to start walking. "I'll see what I can do for Camille in the morning. It won't be much. She's such a fragile thing. The system ignores girls like her and they get lost in the shuffle."

Fragile. A sad word that fit her well. "She's a good kid. She just does some bad things."

"I know. She just wants to be loved and that's the one thing her parents can't give her. Or won't."

"Like Pammie having a baby." Like Will, in a way, who could only get his parents' love and approval if he agreed to live the life they wanted for him.

"Yeah, like Pammie. Like too many other people. People who do all sorts of things to fill that need for love, that emptiness in their lives. And sometimes, like Camille, the choices they make suck."

When we reached home, she turned to me before we went in. "Now, I want to hear you say it. You had no control over what happened. It's not your fault."

I dragged a knuckle under my eyes, wiping away the tears I wouldn't let fall. "It's not my fault."

"Extremely unconvincing, but good enough."

I gave a slightly hysterical laugh and pulled her into a hug so tight she groaned. I loved her so much. She was always, always there for me. She saw me, even when I thought she'd gotten lost in her books and didn't notice. She protected me and she even understood me in her own way and I loved her, more than anything in the world.

And she loved me. Unconditionally.

Chapter 23

Martinis, Muumuus & Turning the Page

I DROPPED MY STORY into the bin on Miss French's desk the next day. I stayed up wicked late to finish it and paid the price. I yawned through all my classes and almost fell asleep in French while Mrs. English yammered on about the Soviet Union's recent nuclear testing and the stock market climbing over one thousand. One thousand what, I didn't know.

I also didn't know if my story was worth the lost sleep. I had no idea if what I'd written was any good or if anyone would like it. But I liked it. And that was all that mattered.

Friday, Good Friday, we had the day off school. I slept late, did my sit-ups and soup can barbell curls, went for a long walk, then I listened to Elton's *Goodbye Yellow Brick Road* album on the record player in my bedroom while reading *The Wolf & The Dove*, one of Mom's spicy historical romances. I'd read the book three times and still couldn't decide what I liked best, the brooding hero, the historical details, or the sex scenes (okay, the sex scenes).

What I tried not to do was think, though my busy brain wouldn't cooperate. My thoughts repeatedly strayed toward Will, the brooding hero if I'd ever seen one. And there was no way I could stop myself from thinking about Camille.

At work Saturday, I found it impossible not to think about her. The motel was unusually quiet. Empty, hollow, like a funeral home with no mourners. I didn't make eye contact with Valerie and went right to the laundry room to stock my cart.

"I'll give you a hand," she said, coming in. She picked up a stack of towels and stuffed them onto the cart's middle shelf.

I dropped a bunch of tiny soaps into a glass cup. "I'm sorry again for not telling you about Camille—"

"Let's not dwell on that. Your mother called and told me what happened. I'm sorry the situation got so out of hand."

"Me too. Camille's a good person deep down, just messed up."

Valerie let out a long sigh. "Child, we're all messed up in our own ways."

I pushed the cart out of the laundry room. The wheels squeaked, a creepy sound in the quiet hallway. "Do you think they'll send her to prison?"

"I don't know. I fired her but didn't report her theft. I suppose it depends on if her mother pushes for punishment." Another sigh. "She was a good worker. I hope she can find peace." She gave me a wan smile. "Now, what do you say we get to work?"

Valerie knocked on the door to 101 then fit the key in the lock. She helped clean the few rooms that had been occupied overnight and let me keep the tips.

"My Lord, do I ache," she said when we finished. "There's a reason I gave up the lucrative world of chambermaiding." She massaged her lower back. "The sooner I hire new help, the better."

❉ ✿ ❉ ✿

On Easter, we went to dinner at Mom's brother Wilfred's house. Dad didn't go with us. No surprise. He hadn't gone anywhere except to work and Brennan's package store in over ten years so why would he break tradition and join us today?

Uncle Wilfred lived far from the Project, in the sleepy suburb of Oakhurst. Jay dropped us in front of a big Colonial house with a trimmed hedge and a white picket fence right out of a storybook, then he left, saying he'd be back with a surprise.

I had a good idea what surprise he meant. Introducing his girlfriend Shirley to the whole family at once didn't seem like the wisest idea. Maybe he thought of it like going to the Sadistic Dental School to have a tooth pulled. Just get in the chair and get it over with.

I followed Mom, Rusty, and Chrissy into the house through the side door, carrying a fruit salad, the one food-related thing Mom could make without destroying.

Inside, the family gathered in a large room split by an arch between the parlor and dining room. The hardwood floors gleamed so bright I could see my reflection. I could almost see myself in the clear plastic that covered the furniture, too. The potted Easter lilies were also plastic. They stood on either side of a whistle-clean brick fireplace my aunt and uncle never used.

"Happy Easter. Christ is risen," Gramps said.

Grandma echoed his greeting and they lifted their martini glasses. They didn't fool me. They'd raise a glass to anything and everything, including the sun coming up each morning if they didn't sleep until noon recovering from toasting the sun going down the night before.

Mom greeted her parents with her usual stilted hello. She took after Gramps in the good bone structure department, but the resemblance ended there. A midsized man with a barrel chest and a fondness for loud sports coats, his hair had abandoned ship long ago. His nose listed to starboard as if trying to follow his hair. Grandma wore her dressiest *muumuu*, a floor-length, bright pink Hawaiian dress that clashed with her orange-red hair and hurt my eyes.

Mom slipped away to the kitchen to help Wilfred's wife, Aunt Sigrid, with dinner, though hopefully not help too much. Chrissy found a big book on the coffee table called *The Bicentennial Almanac* and tucked herself behind an armchair out of sight. Various cousins roamed about, all boys and all extremely hairy.

Rusty's ability to disappear failed him as Uncle Eddie, Mom's other brother, cornered him in the dining room to talk about the weather. A legitimate topic—today had dawned hot and now pushed ninety degrees.

"There's an exceptionally strong high pressure front pushing this heat in," Uncle Eddie droned. "With the sun and the lack of shade, it feels like a July heat wave."

The sweat rolling down my back and making my lavender button blouse stick to my skin had already alerted me to that fact.

"You remember Joe Carlsson?" Uncle Wilfred said, huddling with my grandparents by the fireplace. "His jewelry store was robbed. By one of his own employees. And get this, she's a woman."

"That's what happens when women get jobs." Gramps munched on the olive he plucked from his martini. "Should never let 'em work."

"What about Irene?" Grandma said. "She's got a job."

Gramps sliced a look toward Mom, setting plates and silverware on a table with so many leaves inserted to make it longer, it stretched from here to Canada.

"Irene *has* to work," he said. "You know that."

That stuck a plug in the subject. Anything to do with my father put a plug in any conversation, even if they didn't mention his name.

Aunt Polly sidled up to me. Petite and trim, she wore a satiny blue pantsuit, matching shoes with pencil heels, and, for some reason, a silver blonde wig over perfectly serviceable brown hair. Mom's younger sister, she'd been married and divorced three times.

"I like getting married," she'd say with a saucy smile. "I like getting divorced even better."

She looked me over, head to toe. "You look different," she accused. "Have you lost weight?"

"Yeah, a little."

And by *a little* I meant a lot. I'd lost four more pounds, for a grand total of twenty four. Must've been all those soup can curls and long walks, or laughing and goofing around with Will, or worrying about Camille. Or simply having a better attitude. Whatever, I'd dropped down to 176, a nice Bicentennial number. My hips and thighs had shrunk enough that my pants hung loose. Even my butt had slimmed down some.

Aunt Polly sipped her drink and surveyed the room. "I see your father found a way to stay home again." She spoke as if she wished she'd done the same.

"Yeah, well, you know he's got a busy schedule." I frowned. "Sometimes I wish my mom would get a divorce like you did."

She pursed her lips. "It's not as simple as that. What would he do without her and you kids? Where would he live? What would she do for money?"

My chest tightened, part sadness, part frustration. Questions I'd never thought of and had no answer for. It always came down to money. I suspected Dad would be fine without us. He could live in a rooming house like Camille's with the other divorced dads and he wouldn't have to put up with his homely kids hogging the bathroom or getting in his way when he went to the cupboard for his nips.

But...money.

Aunt Polly took my hand and gave it a squeeze. "Don't be too hard on him. He does what he can, considering his..."

She left the rest unspoken and went to free Rusty from her talkative brother. I knew what she wanted to say. Considering his alcoholism. The ugly word no one in my family ever uttered out loud. The word that bound us and separated us at the same time. The one fact of this life I actually understood.

More martinis were poured from a pitcher and conversation flowed. Chrissy remained among the missing. Rusty and our hairy cousins found a Superball somewhere and hucked it around, aiming for vases and the other breakable knickknacks my aunt and uncle brought back from their one trip to Europe. Where in Europe, I didn't know. They just said, "When we were in Europe..." and "Our tour guide in Europe said..." in a bragging way designed to activate Mom's squinty look.

I went to examine the snacks set out on a card table. I avoided the M&Ms and focused on the veggies. My mood picked way up when I spotted some teeny tomatoes and thought of Will. *Cherry tomatoes*, I'd learned those things were called. How dumb was I that I didn't know that?

Through the window, I saw our Impala pull up out front, followed by a two door, metallic-green AMC Gremlin. Shirley got out, dressed in a salmon-pink dress, tan shoes and a floppy-brimmed hat like Mia Farrow wore in *The Great Gatsby*. Jay took her hand and they strolled up the brick walkway to the front door. My blood rushed in excitement and a little bit of dread. My brother's surprise had arrived.

"Hello, hello," Jay called, as he escorted her inside. "This is my friend, Shirley. Shirley, this is everyone."

The place went quiet. Eerie quiet, like one of those frontier ghost towns in an old movie. I almost expected a tumbleweed to roll across the parlor. Everyone stared at Shirley in various stages of shock that ranged from alarm to delight. The only one not surprised was Mom, because she'd known. Probably from the beginning. Jay never shared anything with anyone, but Mom he talked to.

Shirley circled the room, shaking hands, as if she were Henry Kissinger at the Paris Peace Accords and *détente* was her middle name. Her smile perked with life. I kept my eyes on Gramps, the guy who wanted to put Jay in a home because he was different. Would he sneer or snub Shirley because she was different too? He'd gotten used to Jay, could he get used to his grandson's Black girlfriend?

"It's nice to finally meet you, Mr. Boudreau." She gripped his hand a beat longer than she had the others. "Jay's told me so much about you."

Gramps puffed out his cheeks, completely disconcerted. Or completely smitten. "Jay said only good things I hope." He reached for the pitcher perched on the mantelpiece. "Wanna martini, little lady?"

I cringed. She was a little lady (short), did he have to point that out?

Shirley didn't bat a single long eyelash. "Thanks, maybe next time."

Instead, she accepted my cousin Artie's offer of a Coke, Jay's drink of choice, and Aunt Sigrid announced dinner was served.

Chrissy crawled out of her hiding place, chairs scraped the floor, and conversation picked up. Shirley fielded world-shatteringly important questions like, "would you prefer ham or lamb?" (lamb) and "could you pass the mashed potatoes?" (why, yes).

"Tell me, Shirley..." Uncle Eddie sliced a piece of ham as thick as the earth's crust. "How long have you lived in the Project?"

I slapped my forehead. Of course. She was Black. Black meant poor. Where else could she live?

"That's quite the assumption, Mr. Boudreau," she said, words that held some censure, a little mirth, and a smattering of *what a bonehead.* I bit back a laugh. This little lady could take on every single one of my racist relatives with one arm tied behind her back.

"I live right here in Oakhurst. Grew up in town, over on Hickory Lane."

"You did?" Aunt Sigrid's eyes popped. "You must know the Minton family."

"Of course. I went to school with their daughter Leslie. Mr. Minton and my father are lodge brothers."

Chrissy looked at me and feigned a huge yawn as talk turned to the Oakhurst Masonic Lodge, the country club, the local Boy Scout troop's popcorn sales, and an endless game of *do-you-know-so-and-so*.

One way to bring people together, I guess. Bore them to death.

The public library's downtown branch looked like a giant gray sugar cube on the outside. Inside, it resembled a massive beehive, with five floors open in the middle and rows of bookshelves lined up on each floor like the cells of a honeycomb. The place was stuffy, not very crowded, and smelled like my mother's idea of heaven.

I went to find Donna, who'd called and asked me to meet her here today. She had a paper for English class she had to do research for and she needed me to help her with her work. Or, more likely, to avoid it. I jumped at the chance. April school vacation dragged on and on. Besides my daily walks, reading, and missing Will, I had nothing else to keep me occupied.

I found Donna on the first floor by the windows. Karen and Barbie had joined her. They sat on the other side of the table, bent over open books and encyclopedias, scribbling and taking notes like crazy.

I plunked my pocketbook on a chair, waved hello, then went to the card catalogue, a row of squat wooden cabinets with tons of small drawers stuffed full of index cards.

Mr. Meager had assigned us a term paper in science as part of our final grade and I had to find a topic. I figured I'd do some research while I was here and could utilize more modern resources than our ancient set of encyclopedias at home, published before science was even invented.

The musty-scented index cards pointed me in a thousand different directions, until I stumbled upon the perfect topic and hurried up to the second floor to pore through the stacks. I returned with a bunch of books that klutzy me dropped onto the table with a crashing thump.

"Do you have to be so loud?" Karen said in a harsh whisper, practicing for her future job as a librarian, complete with prune-faced expression.

Barbie eyed her with a scowl. "Do *you* have to be so crabby?"

Apologizing, I borrowed a pen from Barbie, grabbed some scrap paper I found near the microfiche machines, and plopped down and got to work.

One of the books I flipped through had information on chronic verbal tics. I spent some time reading up on the subject, learning about Will's condition from a more clinical perspective, before moving on to the topic I'd selected for my science report. *The* perfect subject to get me into Mr. Meager's good graces and possibly earn me an A—the history and use of the Bunsen burner.

Linda G shoved through the library doors a while later and flew across the room toward us. She wore tan flared pants, a minty green top with bell sleeves, and an eager expression that shouted, "I have news."

"I had sex last night," she blurted the second her fanny hit the chair.

That *was* news. Linda G had seemed the least interested in "doing it" of any of us, and here she'd gone and done it with a month to spare before prom.

"Congrats," Karen said, sounding bored. Or superior. I could never tell with her. "Who's the lucky guy?"

"Tell, tell," Donna demanded. "We want to hear every dirty detail."

"Not *every* detail," Barbie said. "Some things are meant to be private."

One detail I wanted to hear (and Mom would want to hear too)—did they use protection?

"His name is Stew Baines," she breathed. "We went to Firestone Park in his father's Rambler. We had a picnic on the grass. We made out for a while. He said do you wanna, you know. I said, uh-huh and we did and it was..." She sighed and hugged herself. "It was romantic and beautiful."

"Doesn't sound like it," Karen grumped.

Far more beautiful than Camille with her boyfriend Mack. It stung to think of her. My guilt about what happened faded as the days passed but I doubted it would ever go away. I'd probably feel as if I failed her for the rest of my life.

Donna threw so many questions at Linda G she must've felt she was on trial. I got my answer—they'd used a condom—and a new set of questions. If Donna was so anxious to pop her cherry, why hadn't she done it already? She'd been talking about doing it since the minute I'd met her, and though she flirted with a ton of guys, she never seemed to find the right one.

Will popped into my mind, a Mr. Right if there ever was one. Could he ever like me as more than a friend?

A tallish, prettyish, curvy-ish Black girl passed our table, carrying a teetering stack of books of at least a thousand pages each. I blinked in recognition and shot out of my seat, rushing toward her.

"Yolanda."

She stopped walking and spun toward me, surprised. "Deidre."

"God. I haven't seen you in, what? Two or three years? You look good." She always had, and today she looked even better in jeans that hugged her butt and a dark red turtleneck. I gestured to her pile of books. "Looks like you've got some light reading there."

"Finals. They're a bitch."

I nodded, like *yeah, I know*, though finals at the fancy school she'd gotten a scholarship to attend were probably way harder than the ones non-honors student me would be taking. "I see you're growing out your hair."

"Oh, yeah." She touched her hair. She used to wear braids pinned down with barrettes. Now she sported a puffy afro style like Angela Davis, with reddish highlights almost the same color as her top. "I graduate from the academy in three weeks. They can't tell me how to wear my hair anymore." She looked me over. "I'm off to Dartmouth in the fall. What about you?"

I didn't know anything about Dartmouth, but if they accepted Yolanda, it had to be a good school. "I've got a few offers. Not surc which to take."

Yes, I was a liar, with my pants thoroughly on fire. I'd received three more thin white envelopes in the mail, polite and oh-so-sincere rejections from colleges I didn't want to go to anyway. The only one left was State U, and that would likely be a nope too. But I didn't want Yolanda to know that.

"That's great," she said. An awkward silence followed as we stared at each other. "How's your dad?"

"Fine. How's yours?"

"Good."

More silence, more staring. Our dads worked at the same factory two benches apart, where they could have a much livelier and in-depth conversation about how they were than this stilted exchange.

Yolanda shifted her book burden from one arm to the other and looked at her watch. "Hey, I've got to go. Those finals won't study themselves. Nice to see you. Good luck."

I wished her well and she strode off. It occurred to me that I could've asked Yolanda about her mom and four brothers or if she knew Pammie had a baby or any of the dozens and dozens of other things we would've talked about back when we were friends.

It also occurred to me that I probably would never see her again.

Chapter 24

You've Got A Friend

I GOT THE SHOCK of my life when I got home from school Tuesday afternoon. A white envelope—a *large* white envelope—with the state university's return address sat atop the pile of mail on the floor. The mailman had folded it so he could squeeze it through the slot in the door.

My heart thudded as I picked it up. It felt heavy and thick, as if stuffed with papers. I stared at it as if it would suddenly melt into nothingness. This *had* to be a yes.

The storm door squealed open and Rusty flew inside, beating a straight path to the kitchen. Cupboard doors banged open and shut as he hunted for a snack. Dad would get dropped off soon and rifle through the cabinets for something else. And Chrissy would dawdle in at some point. It would get awfully crowded in here.

Me and my envelope needed our privacy.

I hightailed it upstairs to my bedroom. I switched the portable record player's speed button from 45 to 33 and put on Elton John's *Madman Across the Water* album. I sat on the floor, my back against the wall, the envelope on my lap. I moved the needle back three times to listen to "Tiny Dancer" and "Levon" again and again, getting lost in the music and the words and the stories and imagining myself creating something half as beautiful someday.

When I was a writer.

If this envelope said what I hoped it said.

Time to rip off the bandage. I tore open the seal and pulled out the packet inside. One word blasted off the cover page.

Congratulations.

I shoved the envelope into Mom's hands the second she got home from work.

"Didn't I say you'd get accepted?" She skimmed the first page with a satisfied grin. "You're a smart girl. There's no way the school would've said no."

"Exactly what Will said." I couldn't wait to tell him tonight at rehearsal. Couldn't wait to see him after we'd been apart so long.

"I'm gonna spit in that goddamn guidance counselor's eye," Dad said. He sat at the table, still in his uniform, a beer in one hand, a cigarette in the other and an ashtray in between. He'd been cackling with glee since I announced the news, as if he'd personally arranged for me to be accepted to the university instead of trying to pop my hope bubble at every turn.

After Mom got dinner started, she removed the paperclip from the packet and spread the papers across the dining table. She pored over the entire thing like she was looking for coded messages. The financial aid numbers made no sense to math illiterate me. Luckily, she seemed to get it.

"Pell grant, other grants, work study," she murmured, totaling up the amounts. She straightened and stepped away from the table. "Almost there. Still not enough, but we'll find a way. Jay might lend a hand."

"Jay?" My brother worked a thousand hours a week and saved every penny of his salary for a car and that almighty first, last, and security deposit so he could rent a place of his own. How could he have any extra money to give to me?

"Jay knows this is important. He paid for your class ring, didn't he?"

My eyes popped. "He did? I didn't know that."

"I wasn't supposed to tell you. He didn't want you to know. He's kind of secretive."

"Kind of?"

"We'll find a way to pay— Oh!" Mom dashed to the stove and the spaghetti sauce bubbling over from the pan, splattering across the stovetop like a murder scene.

I tidied up the papers and shuffled them together the way Pete shuffled his deck of cards. *Jay.* The brother I never really knew. I glanced at my dad, staring into his beer as if it would tell him his future. The brother who sometimes seemed more of a father to me than this guy, sitting five feet away.

That night, I pushed through the Apostles and extras thronging the stage and shoved Marilyn and Carl aside to get to Will.

"Will, I got in!" I beamed. "I got accepted to State U."

He digested this information, then he beamed too. A smile as bright as a million-watt light bulb. "Was there any doubt?"

I punched him lightly on the shoulder. "Yes, there was. So, so much doubt. But I got in and now..." Now I have to find a way to pay for it. I brushed that gloomy thought aside. I'd think about that tomorrow. At this moment, I let myself wallow in my happiness. "Now I'm going to college. It's a big deal. I'm the first one in my family to go and..." *Stop babbling.* "Enough about me. How was your trip? How'd your dad take the news about you not going to BC?"

Marilyn stiffened in surprise and shuffled closer to eavesdrop.

"It went as well as I expected." Will's face clouded. "He won't listen—"

"Alright people, bring it in," Bushy Beard bellowed.

"Tell you later," Will whispered in my ear as he moved to join the others.

I couldn't move at all, seeing as how that whisper turned my knees to jelly. Several giddy moments later, I recovered enough to get into place for what Bushy Beard called dress rehearsal. Not much dress involved, since none of us had brought our costumes.

I started the show by opening the curtain then took my place, and *action!* Our intrepid director had played his guitar during rehearsals, but this was the first time he'd plugged it into a speaker. He was good. We were not. In fact, we were terrible.

It'd been two weeks since we'd last practiced and it showed. Everyone stumbled over their lines and cues as if they'd never read the script before. Marilyn's voice cracked four times on her solo. Carl smashed into Pete and half the other cast as if trying to tackle them.

I flubbed every word and fumbled each step. Partly because my left-handed brain told me to do everything opposite, like looking in a mirror. More likely because visions of college and whispery-voiced sugarplums named Will danced in my head.

My brain still reeled a couple hours later when we finished and left the church. The whole mob of us mingled outside, saying goodnight, waiting for rides, and chattering about Thursday night, when we'd perform the show for real.

"I've got the car tonight," Will said. "Can I give you a lift?"

He stood with me at the wall, with Donna and Marilyn close nearby. He hadn't settled his gaze on anyone in particular when he asked that question, dashing my hopes that he meant me, alone, and not everyone within earshot of his invitation.

I was going to wait for Jay to get out of work but couldn't pass up Will's offer. I nodded enthusiastically and Donna crooned her thanks.

Will led the way toward his father's car. Marilyn dragged her feet beside him, all mopey and annoyed. Probably because Will giving me a ride home meant driving into—horror of horrors—the Project. Or maybe she was angry he hadn't told her what he'd shared with me about his parents and his college plans.

Whatever the reason, I couldn't help a petty smirk at her discomfort. A smirk that died a sudden death as the shriek of sirens cut through the night. I swiveled and saw several police cars and two firetrucks bomb into Foley Plaza across the street, their lights flashing wildly. The vehicles screeched to a stop in front of Cully's Department Store.

My chest squeezed. "That's where my brother works." Jay could be in trouble. Maybe he'd fallen off a ladder trying to get something down from a shelf. He could be injured. "I have to go help him."

I spun around, about to dash across the street when Will grabbed my arm. "I'll drive you," he said, his voice urgent.

Seconds later, the Lincoln flew into the plaza's parking lot, with me in the front seat, Donna and Marilyn in the back. I twisted my hands together. Will tore past other cars and slammed to a halt as close to Cully's as he could get. I jumped out before he'd killed the ignition and ran mindlessly. His footsteps pounded behind me, followed by the others.

The firetrucks blocked the view into the store. When I got close enough to see around them, I skidded to a halt. A pain as sharp as a knife stabbed my belly. Smoke filled the store and billowed out of a busted window. Inside, firemen rushed about, silhouetted by the smoke. Water gushed from the overhead sprinklers and several men aimed a pulsing stream from a hose at the flames flickering deeper in the store.

"Where's Jay?" I cried, frantic. My lungs constricted. I couldn't breathe, imagining Jay trapped inside, choking. Suffocating.

"I think he's safe," Will said hurriedly. "Looks like everyone made it out."

He pointed to a large group gathered at the edge of the sidewalk near one of the police cars. I searched the crowd, my eyes stinging from the smoke. Finally, I spotted Jay. My knees went weak. Thank God and Jesus and every deity that ever existed he was okay. He stood talking with several cops, with Shirley by his side.

I whimpered in relief. Will moved closer but Donna shoved between us. She wrapped an arm around my shoulders in a bruising clinch.

"Poor you. It's okay, I'm here," she said, her voice so loud three people nearby turned to stare.

Jay spotted me and held up his hand. The policemen ebbed away like a waning tide as he strode toward me, his long, skinny legs moving fast. Shirley raced to keep up.

When he got closer, Marilyn screamed.

I froze, expecting some new terror, until I realized why she'd shrieked. *Jay.* She screamed at my brother. Like he was a monster. Donna stared at him too and even Will seemed a little stunned, but neither of them gazed at him with Marilyn's look of...

There was no other word for it. *Revulsion.*

Bile rose in my throat. "Get her out of here," I said, locking eyes on Will.

He hesitated. "Can I do anything?"

"No," I said with finality. "Please, Will. Get her out of here before I slap her."

"I might slap her for you," he said between gritted teeth. He led Marilyn and Donna away as Jay and Shirley reached me.

"What're you doing here, Deedee?" Jay snapped. His skin was paler than pale, his face and clothes smoke-stained and his expression as serious as bad news.

"What happened?" I demanded.

"Go home."

"Jay," Shirley said gently. "She's worried. We're all worried."

He looked at her a long time. Then he sighed and turned to me. "There... There was a fire, as you can see."

"Not your fault," Shirley put in quickly.

"It was, Shirley. I'm in charge. It happened on my watch. Started at the lunch counter. The grill, or the French fry machine sparked and caught fire. It spread fast. People panicked. I thought..."

His voice wobbled. He sounded like a scared kid. The breakable boy Mom talked about, laying in that hospital bed day after day and year after year, waiting for her to come see him on her day off. A million emotions flooded me and I would have hugged him if he'd let me.

Shirley put her hand on Jay's arm. "It's okay. Everything's okay now."

"Yeah." He released a heavy breath. "Fortunately we got everyone out safe."

"Your brother's a hero." Shirley looked from him to me, her voice soft, awestruck. "People ran for the exits when the alarms went off. He wouldn't leave until he was sure everyone was out. He even checked the dressing rooms and the bathrooms."

"Always wondered what the ladies room looked like," he said, with some of his usual wit. Making fun of the bad things, a family habit. Taking the blame for things we couldn't control. Another thing we excelled at.

"You should come home." I struggled to hold back tears.

"I can't. I have to deal with this. I have to finish talking to the police and firemen." He sounded stronger now. Focused. "It may be a while. You should take the bus. *Don't* say anything to Mom. I'll tell her when I get home."

Jay marched back to the store but Shirley stayed. "Can I walk you to the bus stop? You must be shook up."

"Was it my chattering teeth or trembling legs that gave me away?"

She smiled. A nice smile filled with patience and warmth, the right kind of smile for dealing with Jay and the rest of his messed up family.

She looped her arm through mine and we talked as we cut across the parking lot. Well, she talked. About her family, two sisters, two brothers. About her fondness for travel (she'd been to four states and three countries!). About being a Black girl growing up in lily white Oakhurst. And she talked about Jay a little too. I listened, calming down some.

She turned to me before leaving me at the bus stop. "Let me know if there's anything I can do for you."

"Thanks." I watched her dodge cars on her way back to Cully's. My anxiety and fear evaporated as giddiness and joy mingled in my heart.

All I wanted from her was a happily ever after for my lovely brother.

The people waiting at the bus stop grumbled. Number 26 was running late.

I shifted from foot to foot, wishing I'd gone to the bathroom before leaving the church. The light in the nearby phonebooth blazed down on a woman who'd been yapping on the payphone for a while, feeding Ma Bell's voracious beast a stack of coins. I looked toward Jay's store. The police had gone, leaving only the fire trucks on the scene.

A sleek Lincoln Continental glided up to the bus stop. Much to my surprise and a giddy flash of joy. Will jumped out of the car and ran around the front to open the passenger door.

"Get in," he said. "No argument."

I peered into the empty back seat. "Did you drop off Marilyn and Donna?"

Dumb question. Of course he did, unless he pitched them both off the Bancroft Lake bridge, a watery fate Donna didn't deserve but a fitting end for the horrible Marilyn.

"I took them home. Now I'm taking *you* home."

He touched my arm and urged me to get in. I did. I dropped my handbag on the floor and sank into the plush seat as he closed the door.

"What happened? Do they know what started the fire?" he asked, steering the car out of the plaza onto Adams Street. I told him the few details I knew and he nodded. "I'm glad everyone got out. And I'm glad your brother's okay."

"Me too. He's strong. Not to look at him. His body's breakable. That's what my mother says. But inside he's strong." I laughed a wobbly laugh and flexed my extremely un-muscular biceps. "Strong like bull."

"He sounds like someone I'd like to meet."

"Oh, you'd like him. He's the best." I sat back, relaxing a little. Simon & Garfunkel's "Bridge Over Troubled Water" drifted from the radio, encouraging me to relax even more.

Will stared out the windshield at the road a moment before speaking again.

"Deidre... I'm sorry about Marilyn." He sounded angry, not sorry.

"Don't do that, Will. It's not your job to apologize for her." Oh, irony, thy name is Deidre. How many times had I taken the blame for everyone and everything not my fault? "She's the one who should say she's sorry."

"I doubt she'll apologize. She never does. Never admits she's wrong or made a mistake. She..." He waved his hand. "...moves on."

She seemed a lot like Karen, who'd rather fight to the death than admit she was wrong. Maybe Marilyn's mother was like Karen's, a perfect little bitch who demanded her daughter be as perfect as she was. Maybe both of her parents were. Perhaps all rich people were. That would explain Marilyn's condescending attitude and superior sneers. And the pitying way she spoke about Will and what she called his *problem.*

And why she screamed when she saw my brother.

I tucked my anger away to unpack later when I could properly plot my revenge, and, like Marilyn, I moved on.

"You gonna tell me how it went when you talked to your father?" I said, remembering Will's whispery "tell you later" that had ignited my ankle socks earlier.

"Now?"

"Yes, now. I know a lot's happening. I could use the distraction. And I really want to know."

"Not much to it. I told him I wanted to make my own decisions about college and my future. I said he has to trust me. They both have to trust me." His expression turned grim. "He didn't listen."

"I'm sorry. You know, he could learn something from my mother. Jay went through a lot growing up. Mom shielded him when she could, but she knew she couldn't protect him forever. She had to let him stand on his own, make his own decisions. And mistakes. Well, she drew the line on that motorcycle he wanted to buy. We can't afford a second car and the motorcycle was dirt cheap, but a *real* piece of crap and she was afraid he'd get into an accident. They had big fights about that until Jay gave in and now he's saving up to buy a car... Uh, where was I? I guess I'm saying your father should be like my mom and back off. Let you make your own choices, right or wrong. If he won't listen—"

"Spit in his eye?"

"Cute, real cute." Something he was not. Cute was fleeting, a passing fad. Will was handsome and timeless and a lot stronger than he thought he was. "You could be right, though. You can yap at your father until you're blue in the face, but there's something to be said for taking action. Show, don't tell, as the writing gurus say. Some spit in the eye could do the trick."

We reached the Project and he turned in, looking thoughtful but far less troubled. "What happened with the girl you work with? The one you thought you got fired."

I sighed. "I not only got her fired, I got her arrested."

His eyebrows shot so high they launched into space. "Arrested?"

"Yup, arrested."

I told him the whole Camille story in all its heart-rending detail. I hadn't intended to, but once it came out, it came out, like one of Will's yips. I stared out the windshield at the streetlights and the buildings flashing by and spilled every painful moment.

By the time I got to the end, we'd reached my block. He executed a perfect three-point-turn to park in front of my house. He turned to face me, his gaze steady. He hadn't said anything as I spoke. Not "I'm sorry" or any of those empty words people think they have to say to make you feel better. He didn't call me weird like Donna did or give me that critical, prune-faced look like Karen. He just listened.

"You must think I'm a terrible person," I said. "And a shitty friend."

"Nope. Not even close."

He took my hand and laced his fingers through mine. I blinked in utter surprise. He seemed surprised too. Elton John's "Your Song" came on the radio as he gazed at me, his eyes glimmering in the dashboard light.

"Deidre." His voice sank as deep as a well. "I think you're too hard on yourself. You're honest and one of a kind. And I think...I think..."

A couple of yips tripped him up before he blurted, "You're a good friend."

Oh, that word. It burned. I nodded as if he'd given me the best compliment in the world, but really, what girl wants a guy they were interested in to call them that? While he's holding her hand and staring into her eyes?

I squeezed his hand and gently pulled out of his grasp though I wanted to hold onto him all night. And kiss him, too. He shifted, seeming uneasy. His gaze shifted from me to a point over my shoulder. I turned to see Dad in the picture window, poking his nose between the curtains, watching us.

"That's either my dad or a peeping Tom looking in the wrong direction."

Will gave a muted laugh. "You rarely mention him. You talk about your mother but not your father. I thought he wasn't in the picture."

"Oh, he's very much in the picture." If that picture was taped to a bullseye at the shooting range. "The less said about him the better."

He tensed. "Didn't mean to pry."

"No, no. It's not you, it's... Okay, you know how they talk about the nuclear family on TV? Well, picture the Daly family like that, only in perpetual meltdown, ready to explode like that other kind of nuclear. Fueled by good old fashioned whiskey."

Oh god, did I just say all that? In exactly that way? I'd meant to be funny but ended up sounding completely *not*.

"I get it," he said and I thought he did. Because he got *me*. He understood. Though he lived in upper Chisholm and tooled around in an expensive, ten thousand dollar car, we were the same in some ways. A lot of ways. Two awkward dorks with troublesome fathers who were bad at Catholic-ing.

"I better get inside before Dad calls the cops on us. Good night, Will. Thanks for coming back to get me and for...well, everything.

I couldn't have gotten through tonight without you. See you Thursday for the really, really big shoe," I added, doing a terrible imitation of Ed Sullivan.

I told him not to get out and opened the door myself, sliding out fanny first so the last thing he saw as I departed wouldn't be my butt mooning him.

He watched me until I got to the door. I waved and he drove off. I drifted inside, still feeling the warmth of his hand in mine, the subtle pressure of his fingers. This past hour had been a whirlwind of emotion, up and down, swirling and tumbling every which way, with Will as the solid center I could hold onto.

"Who's the fella that dropped you off?" Dad asked, his eyes on the TV, like he'd been watching the detective show *Mannix* all this time and didn't have his nose pasted to the window snooping on us two seconds ago.

"He's nobody," I murmured. The opposite of nobody. He was everything.

"You couldn't ask this nobody in to meet your old man? You ashamed of me?"

Yes sprang to my lips, and there it died. Why give him the fight he wanted?

"Good night, Dad." I climbed the stairs to my room, trying to rein in my wild thoughts and racing heartbeat. That song, "Baby Don't Get Hooked On Me" played in my head. *Too late.* I was no longer in danger of falling in love with that boy.

I'd fallen. All the way.

If only he'd love me back.

CHAPTER 25

Superstar

MISS FRENCH LICKED HER thumb and freed some papers from the stack, handing out the last of the stories she'd selected to read in class. She looked me in the eye as she gave me my packet. Before I could skim the pages to see if my story was there, Ruthie Cullen bombed into the room and fell into her seat, nearly knocking Miss French over.

Ruthie muttered something apologetic, looking sullen. Perhaps she'd overslept *the smorning*. Today she wore bib overalls with one strap unhooked and a pair of scuffed-up construction boots Will would envy. Miss French dropped a packet onto Ruthie's desk, then returned to the front of the class.

She cleared her throat for our attention. "The first story today is called 'Freedom.'"

I went still. Inside and out. I lowered my gaze to the packet's first page and the handwritten, mimeographed words scrawled across the page with a left-handed slant.

My handwriting. My story.

The night Camille got arrested, I sat up in bed with my notebook on my lap while Chrissy slept, struggling to write. What happened with Camille filled every space in my mind and squeezed my emotions. Exhausted, wrung out, no story idea would come. I considered tossing the notebook out the window and skipping school the next day, but I wanted so desperately to prove I could write something good. Not for Miss French. For me.

Write what you want to understand, Will had suggested. Which was a lot. Camille's despair, her desperate, aching search for love. My father's quest to kill his brain cells and alienate his family. How my mother endured it. Will's parents and those other parents who built boxes for their kids and got angry when they couldn't make them fit into it.

And most of all, I wanted to understand myself.

But how could I get any of that down on the page? Random words and half-baked thoughts flitted around my mind like hummingbirds, zipping out of reach when I tried to catch them. Then, just before dawn, an idea came.

I called my story "Freedom." A guy on a motorcycle bombed down a dark, winding road. He loved the wind in his hair, the growl of the gears, the roar of the engine. He leaned into each turn, taking the curves with ease. His body pulsed with power. He felt free. Invincible. He drove faster. The road began to take over. It led him down a more treacherous path. He couldn't see ahead. He got scared. He struggled to keep control, fearing he couldn't.

I'd left the ending uncertain, letting the reader decide. Who would win, the rider or the road?

A question for us all. We all fought a battle with that road. Camille, Pammie, my father with his nips, Will and his hiccups. Me with my insecurity and emotions and food. Would we keep control, hang on and steer to the finish, or would we crash in a fiery, bitter end?

Miss French read in a tough guy, Jack Nicholson voice. She even crouched like she straddled a Harley Davidson and reached out to twist the handlebar's throttle. The whole class pinned their eyes on her as she acted out the story, weaving fear, danger, and emotion into each word. An Academy Award performance.

I stared down at my desk and squeezed up into myself. I had to, so I wouldn't explode into a million pieces of joy. My words. She read something I wrote.

Miss French finished. No one spoke. A faraway lawn mower and the ticking of the classroom clock were the only sounds. Then... Everyone clapped. They hadn't clapped for any of the other stories.

I looked up to see Lawrence Tetro and Dale Frijon whispering to each other, looking my way. A second later, everyone turned and stared. I went as hot as the sun.

"Shit, Ruthie," Lawrence said, breaking into a broad grin. "Your story's *amazing.*"

Murmurs of agreement made their way around the room, followed by congratulations.

"What'd I do?" Ruthie said, stunned.

Not as stunned as me. I sank down in my chair. Not angry or embarrassed. Okay, a little of both. But mostly amused.

Leave it to me to write a show-stopping story and someone else get the credit.

Miss French gave me an A-plus and an enthusiastic *well done* underlined three times. Needless to say, my head barely fit through the church door when I arrived for the show that night.

I hoped to corner Will and brag to him about my success and thank him for his writing advice. And for his generally wonderful Willness. But with showtime minutes away, everyone crowded the stage, getting ready and we didn't have time to talk.

We'd been allowed to raid our favorite hippy friend's closet for costumes. As a result, the cast wore a combination of tie-dyed shirts, granny dresses, and old bellbottoms. Some of the boys wore fringed vests. Marilyn twirled around, showing off a gorgeous seafoam blue gown with a wide belt. Barry looked more like Jesus than ever in a white robe tied at the waist with a macramé rope. I'd chosen a flowered smock top and a purple maxi skirt with fringe along the hem that tickled my ankles.

And Bushy Beard? I'd never seen a chicken run around with its head cut off, but I imagined it would look like him. He darted about in a tizzy, checking costumes and yelling at people to find their places. When Father Young came in and handed him a note, I thought he might keel over from a stroke.

"This is tragic," he wailed. "Brian's bailed on us and now we have no one to play Apostle John. I need one of you gents to volunteer."

None of the gents did. They shuffled their feet and stared at the floor.

Suddenly, Will stood at my side. He wore a brown vest over a white pirate shirt with puffy sleeves for his costume. He looked nice. He also looked agitated.

"I'm thinking of playing the role, but..." He glanced at Bushy Beard across the stage, tearing his hair out. "I don't know. I can't act. Or sing."

"Come now, William. Have you seen this cast in action? Nobody else can act or sing either. You'll be in good company."

He grunted and flexed his fists. I could feel his agony. People would be watching him. Grendel might barge in and mangle his every word.

"I get it, you're nervous," I said gently. "So's everyone else. Did you know most people are more afraid of speaking in public than running into the grim reaper saying your time is up?" He didn't laugh. Not even a lip wiggle. "Besides, it's only a couple lines. They'll be over in a flash." I offered him an encouraging smile. "You can do this. I have no doubt."

That was too much for Marilyn, who'd been standing in the wings, her nosy ears tuned to our conversation like a radar antenna. She stomped over. "Are you crazy? What if you mess up?"

"Then again," I said sweetly. "What if he doesn't?"

Will's gaze bounced between us. She expertly fed his doubts and stoked his fears, something I suspected she'd been doing the whole time she'd known him. He was wavering. I kept my mouth shut. He'd been looking for a way to take action and prove himself. Now was his chance. But he had to make up his own mind.

He took a breath and then came the most satisfying words I'd ever heard. "I'll do it."

"I hope you're happy," Marilyn snapped when Will jogged over to tell Bushy Beard he'd take the part. "He's going to embarrass himself and it'll be *your* fault."

"You know, for someone who's supposed to be Will's friend, you sure like the idea of him screwing up."

Her head snapped back as if I'd punched her, which I'd been dying to do since she'd screamed when she saw my brother. Since I first met her, actually.

"We'll see what Will's parents think." She huffed away, her gown fluttering.

I gulped. I hadn't thought about Will's parents. My mom would be thrilled if I took a chance like Will was about to do. Well, Mom would cheer me on if I told her I was going to walk to the moon without an oxygen tank. Will's parents were *w-a-a-a-y* different. I hoped they wouldn't be too mad at him. Or embarrassed.

Now doubly nervous, I went to the bathroom then returned to the stage and took my place at the curtain ropes. People began to arrive. I peeked around the curtain to see Bushy Beard escort a petite, very pregnant woman to one of the folding chairs. His wife, I presumed. The Fathers Old and Young took their seats. Carl's football team friends and most of the coaching staff crowded into the back, knocking into each other like clumsy cows.

I waved to my mother and Chrissy as they sat down. And Rusty, who'd probably been bribed to be here tonight. No Dad. There'd been a snowball's chance in hell he'd come, though I'd had a flicker of hope.

"Earth to Deidre," Donna said.

I snapped toward her. "Huh?"

"You're always daydreaming. I asked, how do I look?"

"You look great." She also looked uncomfortable, in spiky high heeled shoes that squished her toes and blue jeans so tight they gave new meaning to the phrase hip-huggers.

"I'm so scared." Donna's teeth chattered, underscoring this declaration.

"Just picture everyone naked," I suggested. Dumb thing to say. I immediately looked to Will, pacing the stage, his lips moving as he practiced his lines, and I pictured him without a stitch of clothing.

"You're so weird, Dee."

Bushy Beard approached. "We have a problem."

"The curtains?" I asked. "I was a little late on my cue in dress rehearsal. I'll do better tonight."

"Not the curtains." Impatience laced his voice. I feared his head might explode all over the place. "Your glasses. They catch the light. Can you take them off?"

I pulled them off and dropped them into the pocket of my smock. "Better?"

He let out a sigh, heavily scented with the sausage and onion pizza he'd had for dinner. "Yes, better." He eyed me and did a double take. "You know, you have such a pretty face." He moved away and yelled, "Places everyone. Places! It's showtime."

Donna scurried away. Thumping footsteps and nervous voices filled the air as the ensemble assembled and got into position.

Bushy Beard plugged in his guitar then nodded at me. I yanked on the ropes and the curtain swished open. The mutter of conversation in the hall stopped.

As Carl/Judas croak-sang the opening number, I moved into my place. Close to Will, though without my glasses, far enough away I had to squint to bring him into focus. He stared out at the audience, scowling, concentrating. Determined to show he could do it. Worried he might screw up. I prayed he wouldn't. Because if he did, Marilyn would be right.

And I so wanted her to be wrong.

The show went on, and it went on well.

Barry's Jesus was a revelation (ha—Bible joke!). Carl portrayed Judas as both treacherous and conflicted. Marilyn's performance as Mary Magdelene was as perfect as she was. With one key thing missing. *Emotion,* Miss French might say and underline twenty times. Marilyn hit every note perfectly, but she didn't *feel* it.

Except that one moment when she sang, "I Don't Know How to Love Him," and glanced at Will. She truly didn't know how. Maybe not yelling at him and telling him he'd mess up would be a good start.

Will's moment came. He stepped onto his mark, clenching and unclenching his fists. I nearly bit a hole through my bottom lip, praying he could pull it off. The room seemed to fall silent as he opened his mouth. His parents were out there somewhere, watching.

The lines came out clearly, if badly out-of-tune. One yip. *One.* He'd done it. I let out my breath. I thought Marilyn did too.

It ended. The curtain swished closed, I opened it again and we bowed. The crowd jumped to their feet and I thought they were going to beat a hasty exit when they began to applaud. And cheer. And stamp their feet and whistle.

Excited, I hugged Will. I quickly hugged Barry and Donna and twelve other people so Will wouldn't think the hug meant anything. I even hugged Carl. He shouted excitedly into my ear as he hugged me back, clutching me against him too long and too tight, as if trying to scope out my bra size.

A roar of voices filled the basement. The passthrough window in the kitchen clanked upward and refreshments appeared in the opening. The smell of fresh brewed coffee cut through the scents of hairspray and cigarettes. Both priests made the rounds, mingling and shaking hands. For some reason I didn't get, the kids stayed away from Father Young, but the parents swarmed him like delighted bees.

"Wonderful show," Mom said, coming up to me. "I was riveted."

She looked happy and I was glad. The fire at Jay's store had scared her. He'd been transferred to another Cully's across town, working the registers while his store underwent repairs. Mom worried he'd lose his assistant manager position and the salary that went with it. And my chance to pay for college.

I worried about that too, but not tonight, not now. My heart sang like a chorus of angels. Donna grinned, equally happy. She'd glommed onto my family because her own hadn't come.

I searched for Will and spotted him with a gray-haired couple I suspected were Marilyn's parents. That trapezoid mouth must've been passed down for generations.

"You were very brave, Will," Mr. Marilyn said in a somber tone.

"Yes, very brave," Mrs. Marilyn echoed.

Will looked like he very bravely wanted to punch them both, but his better nature—and me dragging him away from the pity fest—restrained him.

"I thought you did great," I said.

His eyes crinkled. "I bet you say that to all the Apostles."

"Don't be modest, mister." I steered him toward Donna and my family. "Mom, I'd like you to meet Will Hovey. The best Apostle in the whole bunch."

Mom looked him over. "I enjoyed your performance. Your interpretation captured the hesitancy and inherent doubt any of those real men of the time must've felt."

Will beamed. "Thanks. I was just trying not to pass out."

Mom's Mr. Spock eyebrow popped up. "Well, you did a good job of that too. Excuse me."

She stepped away as a neighborhood lady tapped her on the shoulder and asked how she could get her kids into the free breakfast program. Chrissy found a friend and left too. Rusty waded into the football pack, to shoot the shit or pick their pockets, or maybe both.

"Your turn to meet my family," Will announced.

He led Donna and me across the room. I giggled nervously, worried about how his parents had taken his star turn on stage.

Marilyn had gotten there first. She did one of those European double kisses on the cheeks of a woman who looked a lot like Will—slim, same tan skin, similar bone structure and windblown hair. She wore a creamy-green wraparound dress and matching shoes, and she carried a boxy pocketbook that looked like it cost more than our car when it was new. The tall, sandy-haired, granite-jawed man next to her projected an attitude like he'd been ready to leave an hour ago.

Ignoring Marilyn, Will turned to his parents. "This is, these are my friends, Donna and Deidre."

That word again, friend. Plural this time, with Donna in the mix.

Will's dad gave us a cursory nod. Mrs. Hovey was more friendly. "Pleasure to meet you both," she said, in a French accent as beautiful as she was.

"*Enchantée*," I blurted, because saying stupid things was my *raison d'être*. I managed to stop myself from doing a little bow, so...progress?

Amusement flashed across Mrs. Hovey's face and she studied me a moment. "My, aren't you a pretty girl."

Her examination had stopped at my neck so I thought she might mean it. Will's face turned several shades of red the Crayola company hadn't invented yet. I didn't know why he blushed when she'd said that to me, but he did.

"You were all marvelous tonight," she continued before I could say something even more ridiculous in response. "Especially William."

She turned such a glowing smile on her son he blushed again, and even his dad unbent enough to mumble something approving. I flashed a *take that* look at Marilyn and gloated inside.

After that, people began to leave.

"Hey gang? My wonderful, wonderful cast," Bushy Beard called. "Before I lose you, bring it in one last time."

I'd promised to give Donna a ride home, so I told Mom we'd meet her in the parking lot and joined the circle around our director. I tried to get next to Will but several people butt in between us, and I ended up squished between Carl and Barry.

"This show has been *the* most important and satisfying experience of my life." Bushy Beard's shining gaze touched on each of us and not on his pregnant wife, who stood with the priests, looking exhausted and anxious to go home. "Who would've thought our scraggly little group could've put on such a worthwhile and truly amazing production? If you take away one lesson from our time together, it's that you have the power to do whatever you set your mind to."

I checked in with Will on the other side of the circle to see if he'd learned this important lesson. Our eyes locked. A short time, no more than a tick of the clock, but his fierce, almost gloomy expression sent my pulse flying into the stratosphere.

"Go home now," our director continued. "Be good to yourselves, love your friends and family. I wish blessings, brotherhood, and peace to you all." He flashed a peace sign with both hands and everyone cheered.

"Don't forget, cast party at Will's on Saturday," Marilyn chanted like the hostess with the mostest as the circle broke up.

Oh, I'd be there, with bells on. Whatever that meant.

I lost track of Will as the whole mob of us surged toward the exit. Everyone squeezed into the stairwell and we thundered upward. I got caught in the middle.

Suddenly, a male voice spoke into my ear. "I think you're beautiful."

The group shifted and swept me up the stairs. Heat raced over me. Stunned, I twisted and swiveled, trying to pinpoint whose voice had said those incredible words. Aching, desperate words, like the speaker couldn't bear to go on living another second without saying it. Like he really, really felt it.

The mob spilled out into the night and dispersed, rushing to their cars to head home. He was gone. Nowhere to be found. My secret admirer remained a secret.

I inhaled a deep breath of the warm, sweet April air. Light and joy swirled through me, along with an emotion I couldn't name but felt like champagne bubbles of pure happiness popping all over.

I hugged myself with a giddy grin. This had been the best day of my life.

Part Five

May 1976

CHAPTER 26

That Gauche Girl

I ARRIVED AT WILL'S house for the cast party to find a bunch of guys clustered around a black two-door Ford Mustang hardtop in the driveway. They whistled and groaned over the car as if it were a gorgeous girl.

Were any of them my anonymous admirer who thought I was beautiful?

I'd tortured myself over the guy's identity for two days. I desperately wanted it to be Will, but the voice didn't seem to match his. No one from the show's voice matched. A low, growly whisper that had soared through my veins and wrapped around my heart.

Determined to listen closely to every guy here today and figure it out, I headed toward the house, an elegant, three story Colonial painted yellow, with green awnings over the windows.

Donna sat on steps leading up to an enclosed side porch, watching the guys. She scrambled to her feet as I approached. The evening was cool, but she wore cutoff jean shorts, platform cork shoes, and a white halter top, as if it were the middle of summer.

"That's Will's car," she said enviously. "He got it for his birthday. I got a watch when I turned eighteen. Wonder what they'll give him when he graduates."

Not anything he really wanted, I bet. "I got a pair of socks for my birthday."

She gave me a quick hug. "Yeah, well, you're poor."

We climbed the steps and entered what Donna called a mud room. Coats hung on hooks with shoes lined up neatly underneath and not a speck of mud anywhere. Except on Will's boots, tossed haphazardly on top of the other shoes, as if he'd run into the house and kicked them off as he flew past.

I followed Donna into a huge living room/dining room space our entire apartment could fit inside, with wall-to-wall carpeting, claw-footed furniture, a massive dining table, and a gleaming china cabinet against the far wall. So many ornate vases and cherub figurines sat on side tables and shelves I felt like a sightseer on tour at the Vatican.

Not a single book or bookcase, though. Will must've hidden his stash in his room.

Aerosmith's "Dream On" played from hidden speakers, nearly drowned out by the roar of voices. Most everyone from the show had arrived. Will's mother perched on a stool at a counter in the big kitchen off to the left, observing the guests. She wore a daffodil yellow dress and a white apron, and she sipped from one of those tiny coffee cups like in a French café.

I spotted Will. He'd traded in his usual scruffy jeans for dress pants and a collared shirt I figured he'd been forced to wear as the party's host. He placed a tray of veggies on the dining table with the other goodies. I thought of the cherry tomato disaster the night we met and giddiness stole over me. Butterflies disco danced in my belly.

Anxious to see him, I abandoned Donna and rushed over.

"Hey." I beamed with a voltage so bright he probably wished he had sunglasses.

He smiled back. "You made it."

"Well, I didn't have anything else on my schedule, so..." I pulled a gift I'd bought for him out of the pocket of my new jeans (yup, I could finally find jeans in my size). "I have something for you. Sorry for the giftwrap. As a girl born in December, I'm fundamentally opposed to wrapping birthday presents in Christmas paper, but it was the only stuff we had in the house. Happy late birthday." I handed it to him. "It's not as fancy as a new car, but I hope you like it."

I rushed through this explanation and ended with an awkward bubble of noise that was supposed to be a laugh.

He thanked me, not meeting my eyes, then tore off the red paper dotted with dancing reindeer to reveal a bookmark. He turned it over to look at the illustrations on both sides—a wizard wearing a pointy hat.

"Cool."

"A *Lord of the Rings* bookmark is not cool, Will. It's nerdy, that's why I thought you'd like it." I giggled. "Hey, I got an A-plus on my story. I've been meaning to tell you since Thursday, just haven't had a chance. I listened to you and wrote what I wanted to understand and it worked." My voice bubbled with a joy that matched my happiness inside.

"Fantastic," he said, and not in the sarcastic way the Saint Stephan's boys always said it. Like he meant it. "I'd like to read it. If you'll let me."

"Hey gang, it's showtime," Bushy Beard bellowed as he pushed into the room.

Will groaned. "Sorry, I've got to say hello. I'll be back. Don't. Go. Anywhere."

Dizzy, flushed with warmth, I watched him stride away. I wouldn't move a muscle, even if the house was burning down.

Marilyn sidled up to me. "You're being really obvious."

"What?"

"I said, you're so obvious." She plucked a Ritz cracker from a tray and nibbled daintily. "It's so clear you have a crush on Will. Everyone can see it. You're practically drooling. It's gauche."

Gauche? Did anyone really use that word in conversation? Well, maybe the Holy Mother of God girls did, if they had a French teacher who actually taught French.

"I'm left-handed," I said, wanting very much to spit in her eye. "Which makes me gauche, I guess."

She snickered, not at all amused. "I'm trying to give you advice, if you'll listen. You're making a fool of yourself. Will's *not* interested in you."

My happiness balloon not only popped, it disintegrated. "How—?"

"How do I know? He told me. Will tells me everything. We're very close. He's had a rough time of it, poor guy." She lowered her voice saying that, like my dad did when he called Jay a cripple. "Will doesn't need any more stress in his life, and frankly, you're not a good influence for him."

"Why, because he enjoys himself when he's around me?"

"Oh, he had fun with you at the show. He thinks you're nice in an odd way, but a little much sometimes. He says he likes you. As a friend, nothing more."

My shoulders drooped all the way to the floor. *Friend.* I officially hated that word.

"I'm telling you this to help you, Deidre. You don't want to embarrass yourself more than you already have." Her gaze raked over me, head to toe. Her lip curled in that superior sneer. "And you've got to admit, you never had a chance. You're not Will's type. You're too...different. You don't fit in his world. At all."

She snatched up a couple more crackers and wandered away with a satisfied smirk.

That's when I saw the bookmark on the table. A giant rock plopped into my stomach. Will had put it down and forgot about it two seconds after I'd given it to him. What had I expected him to do with it? Wear it around his neck? Frame it? The gift had been special to me but hadn't meant much to him. Just something a friend gave him.

His gauche friend. His gauche, loud, embarrassing, and completely not his type friend.

Wrong size, wrong side of the tracks, wrong for Will.

Wrong in every way.

Carl squeezed his broad shoulders through the door half an hour later. He slapped Will on the back and said, "Hey buddy," like he didn't know his name or that this was Will's house.

"Hey pal," Will replied. Hostile, but at least he didn't call him Judas.

Marilyn and Donna joined them and Carl fell on each of them with a sloppy embrace. Donna giggled. Marilyn detached herself from his squeezy hug with a frosty rebuke that made him pout.

I watched the scene from a secluded spot across the room. After my not-so-friendly conversation with Marilyn, I'd tucked myself into a corner with an enormous potted plant that looked like a palm tree, determined to stay as far away from Will as possible.

Luckily, he was so busy playing host he didn't have time to chat, and the few times he stopped to say hi, I'd kept it cool. Decidedly not obvious. The last thing I wanted was for him to know how much I liked him. Bad enough Marilyn had figured it out.

Carl waded into the crowd and the party rolled on. I sipped from a can of Tab I'd found in an ice-filled bucket of sodas. Jane perched on one of the window seats, chatting with Barry and Pete. Bushy Beard made the rounds, sampled everything on the refreshment table, then left, presumably home to his wife. And Donna talked with (or more likely, talked *at*) Will by the record player, where he sifted through a pile of albums and 45s, playing deejay.

He put on a song called "Fooled Around and Fell in Love" and a hot, bitter sensation swept through me.

I was that fool.

Will's not interested in you. He told Marilyn that, because why wouldn't he? They were friends. They'd grown up together, part of the same world. People who went to private school and traveled to London on Easter break and gave their kids Ford Mustangs for their birthday. A world where I didn't fit. Where I'd never fit.

Jane and some Holy Mother girls came by to check out the snacks. Jane drew me into their conversation, which centered on a girl's favorite topic this time of year. *Prom.* Rose and Iris both announced they'd been invited to three proms each.

"I still don't have a date and our prom's coming up soon," Jane said, far from her perky self. "How about you Deidre?"

I sighed. "I doubt I'll be going."

Marilyn joined us, nibbling on another cracker like a dainty parakeet. "Never say never," she chirped. "There's still time."

That sounded more ominous than hopeful. "Crocodile Rock" began hopping and bopping on the stereo. Marilyn hurried off with Jane and the other girls to dance in the center of the room. I stayed put, preferring to be miserable, and not even Elton John could lift my mood.

The bookmark I'd given Will still sat on the table. Hurt, I scanned the display of cookies and sweets and French patisseries, tempted to gobble up everything.

"Watch out for the cherry tomatoes," Will said, suddenly beside me. "They're lethal weapons."

Every part of me tingled, but I played it as un-obvious as I could. "Yeah, deadly," I murmured.

His eyebrows drew down. "Something wrong?"

"Nope." I grinned, despite my misery. "Nothing at all. I guess I'm glad the show's finally over. Now my nights are free for more important stuff." That came out kind of annoyed, though I meant for it to sound all ha-ha jokey.

"I dunno. I had a lot of fun hanging out with you. Uh, and everyone."

"Want a snort?" Carl staggered between us and stuck a silver flask under my nose.

I looked at the flask, then at Carl. He was wasted. His eyes defined the word bloodshot and he smelled like he'd fallen into a vat of whiskey. I knew booze couldn't cure what ailed me any more than food could. If it did, my dad would've been cured long ago. But it sure could ease the sting.

I took the flask and sucked down a huge gulp. It burned like lava pouring down my throat. I coughed and choked.

Will frowned and Carl guffawed. "You're such a fucking lightweight."

I wiped my mouth with the back of my hand. *Lightweight?* Compared to my dad, the nip disposal factory, I supposed I was. And my martini loving grandparents. In fact, compared to most of my family I was a teetotaler.

I took another, smaller sip then tried to pass the flask to Will. He waved it away, his expression gloomy. "My mother doesn't want us to drink."

On cue, his mother sailed into the room. "Who's hungry?" she *tra-la-la'ed.* She held up a silver tray filled with deviled eggs, looking like my home economics teacher's dream of the perfect housewife.

"Better hide the evidence," I said and threw the flask into the potted plant. It landed spout down and the whiskey *glug-glugged* into the dark soil. I tossed Will an apologetic look. "Oops, sorry."

A smile flickered across his face before the gloom descended again.

His mother didn't notice my attempt to murder her plant. A hungry horde flocked to her like birds to a feeder and pecked the platter clean in four seconds flat. She wandered over to us, carrying the empty tray.

"Are you enjoying yourself?" she asked, her eyes on Will. He mumbled something and she lifted her free hand to smooth down his hair. Well, she tried to. I doubted that mop could ever be tamed.

"*Mom.*" Will flicked her hand away.

She *tsk-tsked*. "You have *such* pretty eyes. Why do you insist on hiding them?"

Carl snickered but I cringed in sympathy. I'd be completely mortified if my mother said that in front of other people, and I wasn't a guy.

Will's mom returned to the kitchen and he drifted away, leaving me with the former object of my desire. An interesting predicament that once would've ignited a hormonal bonfire inside me. Now, I could not care less to have Carl Werzbicki, drop dead gorgeous football god with the tight jeans and lazy smile, standing so close I felt his breath on my hair.

❋ ❀ ❋ ❀

The party wrapped up, and so did my brief infatuation with Will Hovey.

I had to move on. At least, that's what I told myself. Watching him say goodbye as people left, my chest hurt as if a python wrapped around it and squeezed. I knew the truth. I'd never get over him. Never.

When it came time for me to say farewell, I made it quick.

"Bye, Will. It's been nice knowing you." I forced a cheery smile. "You were an awesome Apostle John. And—" I gaped. He'd put the bookmark in his shirt pocket, over his heart.

"And?" His face lit up with an expectant look.

"And I'm sorry I murdered your plant."

I turned to go. He called after me, but I pretended not to hear.

CHAPTER 27

It's Her Party & I'll Cry If I Want To

MOVING ON FROM WILL proved difficult. I missed him. Terribly. I doubted I'd ever see him again. Unless I crashed afternoon vespers at Saint Stephan's, waving and shouting his name.

Worse, I didn't have anyone I could talk to about him. I'd be embarrassed to admit my pathetic crush to my school friends and there was no one at work I could confide in. Valerie was an old married lady and the new girl she'd hired to replace Camille didn't like to chat.

So I wrote down my feelings, trying to understand. I revived my Revolutionary War story. I dumped the heroine's soldier boyfriend and made her fall in love with the local innkeeper's son. He was loyal to the king and he did *not* love her back. Putting the tragedy and tears of unrequited love on paper helped me feel better. A little.

At school, prom fever ratcheted up. Of our group, only Linda G had landed a date, which didn't take too much landing, since she and Stew were connected at the hip these days. The rest of us were sadly date-less.

"Why do we need dates at all?" Barbie griped, loudly sipping milk through a straw. "Why can't we go together, as friends?"

"Are you nuts?" Karen bit into an oatmeal raisin cookie as if it'd offended her. "We'd look monumentally ridiculous."

"That's an old-fashioned attitude," Barbie said. "The world's changing. Women don't have to conform to society's expectations anymore. We can be who we want to be. And we sure don't need guys to make our lives complete."

Donna gasped and Jane laughed. "I always knew you were a secret women's libber," she said.

Karen snorted. "You've lost me. I *want* a date. I'm not going alone. It's embarrassing."

"Alright, that's enough." Donna spread her arms like a traffic cop trying to prevent a thirty car pileup. "I'm going to get prom dates for *all* of us. There's these guys I work with. They love to party and they're available. I'll fix you up with them."

Jane began singing the matchmaker song from *Fiddler on the Roof* and Barbie said, "Count me out."

I laughed, kind of bitter. "Are we gonna line up at your store's checkout and take the next cashier who becomes available?"

"Dee." Donna huffed in annoyance. "Do you *always* have to make a joke?"

"I don't always joke. I take Sundays off." Donna grumbled some more and I relented. "Okay, I'll stop. What's your plan?"

"Marilyn's having a party on Saturday night. I'll bring the guys from work with me and you can meet them."

I perked up. If Marilyn was having a party, Will would be there. Then I sagged. "Small problem. Marilyn didn't invite me. Or any of us."

Donna waved airily. "She probably forgot. I'll bring you as my guest. All of you can be my guests. Marilyn won't mind. Come on, it'll be fun."

I thought Marilyn would mind me crashing her party a whole bunch, but the prospect of seeing Will pushed all my qualms out the window. "Wait, there's three of your work friends. That's three guys for four girls. One of us will be the odd woman out." Me, probably. Wasn't it always me?

"Don't worry about me." Donna gave a funny little giggle. "I've got someone else in mind."

Work dragged on Saturday. The new Camille, a bony little lady of about forty named Wendy, didn't chatter or complain about her boyfriend or anything else because she didn't talk at all. We worked together in silence all morning, giving me plenty of time with my thoughts. Thoughts that kept straying toward Will, whether I liked it or not.

I took extra care getting ready for Marilyn's party and brushed my hair a thousand strokes until it shone as bright as polished gold. Jay drove me there, with Shirley beside him. I got more and more nervous as our Impala wound along the wide roads of the tree-lined development off upper Chisholm.

"You sure you wanna get dropped off at such a dump?" Jay said when he pulled up in front of Marilyn's gigantic house, an English country manor right out of an Agatha Christie mystery. I could absolutely see someone getting murdered in the conservatory here. Probably me when Marilyn found out I crashed her shindig.

Jay and Shirley left, promising to pick me up at my usual Cinderella time of midnight. I climbed a thousand stone steps to the front entrance, expecting Marilyn to slam the door in my face.

No one answered my knock, so I went in. A pile of shoes greeted me. I took the hint and kicked off my marshmallow shoes (which had seen better days), immediately losing a couple inches of height.

The smell of beer, peanuts, and cigarettes conjured semi-fond memories of Saturday afternoons at Hickeys Bar when I was a kid.

While Mom visited Jay in the hospital after one of his surgeries, Dad would take us downtown on the bus to see the sights. Sights that mostly consisted of drunk guys playing cards and smoking cigars while Joe Hickey stood behind the bar and poured pints for customers.

I steered toward the sound of voices and the lilting tune, "Baby I'm-a Want You." I entered a spacious den with wide chairs, a plush sofa, a combination TV-stereo console with a beer keg on top, and a wall of windows overlooking a patio area.

The room was stuffed with people, some I knew, most I didn't, most likely Marilyn's devoted friends from school and the neighborhood. The girls wore wrap dresses and hairdos that had spent considerable time in the company of a curling iron. The guys wore creased slacks and polyester shirts with the ugliest patterns ever invented—bold geometric designs, giant rhododendrons climbing a trellis, and what looked like electric eels splashing in water.

I frantically searched the crowd for someone I knew. I relaxed when I spotted Pete and Barry, and even Carl. One face I *didn't* see was Donna's. Or Karen and Jane's. Where were they?

Marilyn's laughter drew my gaze to the patio door. She slinked inside as Elton John's "The Bitch is Back" piped from the stereo and I blessed the gods of good timing for their excellent choice of music. She wore a sarong dress dotted with purple and white flowers, her glistening golden hair draped over one shoulder, and a plastic sunflower tucked behind her left ear.

Will followed her, dressed in jeans, his Puma sneakers, and a tan tee shirt with brown trim around the sleeves and collar. My heart did the tango, the jitterbug, and a waltz all at the same time.

They saw me. Marilyn's mouth went flat. Will's reaction hurt more. Pained, like he'd gotten a sudden toothache. Carl and some of his football friends muscled up to them. Marilyn said something and they all turned as one entity to look at me. Will's toothache got worse. I cringed, feeling like the world's biggest jerk for crashing this party.

Ready to turn tail and flee, I stopped when Barry and Pete waved me over. They stood near the TV console with the keg on top as if guarding both. At least I could say hi before leaving. I swam through a sea of people to get to them. They both held plastic cups filled with frothy beer and greeted me like a long lost and extremely wealthy relative. I doubted this was their first drink of the night.

"If it isn't my favorite curtain-puller." Barry gave me a one-arm hug. "Glad to see you."

"I'm happy somebody is." I couldn't stop myself from glancing toward Will, still with Marilyn. "What are you two turkeys up to tonight?"

Pete swigged his beer. "Drinking, what else?"

Barry plucked a cup from a stack by the keg and pushed it into my hand. "Join us. You look like you need a drink."

He gave me a push and I got into a long line. When my turn came, I pressed the toggle and got mostly foam.

"Tip the cup," Barry yelled. "You'll get more beer that way."

Good advice. Beer, and lots of it, was what I needed right now. I filled my cup and joined the guys again, chatting and watching the crowd, always coming back to Will. He leaned against the wall, drinking what I thought was beer. Since when did Will drink beer?

"Finally," I muttered when Karen and Jane sailed into the room. I waved to them but it took a week for them to get to me because Jane had to stop and greet everyone like she was Jimmy Carter running for president.

"I don't know where Donna is," I said before either of them could ask.

Karen frowned. "Will Marilyn be pissed that we're here?"

I replied with a shrug. I figured she'd be fine with Karen and Jane being here. Me? The mouthy, fat kid from *that* neighborhood who'd encouraged Will to embarrass himself on stage? The gauche girl who didn't fit into Marilyn's perfect little world? The girl she kept staring at and whispering about from across the room? The one she did *not* like.

Probably not.

"Get a drink," I said. "We'll figure it out."

When they got through the line at the keg, I introduced them to Barry and Pete, two fine prom candidates. Well, not really. Barry was an amazing dancer, but he didn't seem interested in flirting. Neither did Pete. But the guys greeted them warmly and we hung out like one big, happy family. Karen chugged her beer, Jane sipped daintily, like drinking Earl Gray at a tea party.

A few minutes later, Marilyn sailed up to us, towing Will in her wake. I waved but he didn't look at me. Why? Why wouldn't he at least look at me?

"Good evening," our hostess said sweetly. Her gaze took in all three of us, lingering on me. "I'm so glad you could come tonight."

The sheer weight of sarcasm in her voice could've sunk a ship. I chose not to be as petty. "Thanks, Mar." She cringed at the nickname. Okay, I could be a little petty. "Donna invited us to tag along with her—"

"Hey, guys." Carl shoved into our little group and honored me with a grin. "There you are my fainting girl."

He grabbed me into a hug that surprised a shriek out of me. A really loud shriek. The hubbub in the room cut off and everyone stared. Will's expression went sullen.

"I don't mind that you're here," Marilyn said when Carl finally let me go. She flashed the fakest of fake smiles. "You're my friends. I should've invited you in the first place. Enjoy yourselves."

She wiggled her fingers in a cheeky wave then moved on to her other guests. Her fake smile faded, replaced with an expression that defined the phrase *the cat that ate the canary.*

I had the sick feeling *I* was the canary.

Twenty minutes, two beers, one album by a band named *Boston,* and a song called "Born to Run" later, Donna breezed in. Trailed by one lonely coworker. I didn't have to be a math genius to know one didn't divide into three and we were up shit's creek where potential prom dates were concerned.

"Where've you been?" I said, trying to sound more concerned than mad, despite wanting to smack her.

Reason number 271 not to trust anyone. They ditch you at a party you weren't invited to. An odd and uncomfortable party, with Will ignoring me and Carl Werzbicki not. In fact, Carl had stayed after Marilyn left, hovering over me and calling me his fainting girl until I lost it and told him to take a hike. He'd obliged with a pout, staggering off to join his football buddies.

"I ended up working late," Donna said. "I called your house. No one answered. Must've been no one home."

More like Dad conked out and Mom far, far away in Narnia or somewhere. No doubt Chrissy was home, but she'd never answer the phone, because that would mean talking to someone. God my family was loony.

"I'm here now," Donna added as if that absolved her of blame. "Everyone..." She shoved her coworker forward. "This is Freddie Gallstones. Freddie, this is everyone."

I recognized him, the guy I'd seen stocking toothpaste at Donna's store. Tall and burly, with a roundish face and Brillo pad hair, he wore corduroys and a white knit sweater like the sailor in the Old Spice commercials. Way too hot for this steamy room.

He mumbled a bashful hello, looking a little hunted. Couldn't blame him. Three girls desperate for prom dates were panting in his face. Make that two girls. Jane put her mostly full beer cup on a side table and promptly announced she was going home.

Karen moved in. "So, what do you do for fun, Freddie?"

More mumbling, something about building model airplanes and bicycling. Karen frowned and I braced for an argument. She could never say something neutral, like, "That's interesting." She always had to jump down a person's throat, tell them they were dumb and so was their hobby. That was Karen, I supposed. She couldn't help it, just as Donna couldn't help being so boy crazy. And I couldn't help being the tacky girl who crashed parties no one wanted her at.

Not even Will.

Donna nudged me. "Ask him," she whispered.

"Ask him what?" If his last name was really Gallstones? Because that was a question I needed an answer to.

She choked in exasperation. "Ask him to the prom. Ask him before Karen does."

"I can't do that. I barely know him."

"You're not gonna marry him."

"Don, you need a drink," I said, which really meant I needed a drink.

"In a minute. There's Will." She pointed toward him across the room, where he stood drinking another beer and watching Pete perform card tricks for a group of girls. "You go make friends with Freddie. I'm gonna say hi."

She pushed through the crowd over to Will, greeting him with a smile. He flicked a glance at me over her shoulder, finally meeting my gaze for the first time tonight. He eyed me with an odd expression, hard to describe. Angry? Or maybe disappointed. Whatever, it was gone in a flash as he looked away.

Confused and hurt, I drained my beer and went to refill my cup. Or tried to. When my turn at the keg came, I thumbed the toggle and the liquid coming out of the tap sputtered and spit.

"Keg's empty," someone cried and everyone groaned.

Carl stepped into the breach. He strode to the bar and opened some secret doors in the wall behind it like he'd been here a hundred times before, revealing liquor bottles of all shapes, sizes, and proofs. A cheer went up and I joined the crowd thronging toward the booze.

"Here's an extreme amount of mud in your eye," Barry said, hoisting a shot glass and toasting me.

I usually glommed onto food when trying to smother my pain, to dull the hurt in my belly and fill the hole in my heart. To make myself feel better. But tonight I soothed my wounded soul the Daly way. We don't cry, but we sure do drink.

I lifted my shot glass and downed the liquid in one gulp. Whiskey, my father's booze of choice. And my choice, for tonight at least.

Like father, like daughter.

The night wore on. Olivia Newton-John's "If You Love Me Let Me know" thrummed from the stereo. I was feeling no pain, as the saying went. Except that dull ache of loneliness that never seemed to go away. My time hanging out with Will had helped ease that ache a little, a bittersweet thought that only made me hurt more.

I spotted Karen with Freddie at the snacks table, piling brownies and cookies onto paper plates. The thought of eating anything turned my stomach. A strange predicament to be in. Karen caught my eye and gave me a thumbs up. Mission accomplished. Prom date secured. I'd missed my chance, not that I cared one whit about Freddie or prom or anything else at this point.

I drank a little more and moved in and out of conversations. I lost track of time. Lost track of my friends. And Will. He might have gone outside to play basketball in the driveway with the other guys. Each time the music lulled, the *thump, thump* of the ball and the chatter of white boys who thought they were NBA champions cut through the room.

Karen and Freddie started making out. Barry got so drunk Pete had to hold him up. Laughing, they plopped down beside each other on the couch, arms entwined. I steered away from Marilyn and Carl having what looked like an argument and ended up in a group of Holy Mother girls. One of them had a Dorothy Hamill haircut so stiff with hairspray you could skate on it. I nodded, pretending to be fascinated by their conversation about guys and diets and clothes.

A long time later, I squeezed through the crowd to find a bathroom. I felt my way along a shadowy corridor, looking for some sign of a place to pee.

I heard the murmur of voices down the hallway. Donna's voice. Who was she with now? Another cherry-popping candidate? The guy she had her eye on as a prom date?

The bedroom door stood ajar. A faint light slipped out. I shimmied closer and reached out with my foot, giving the door a gentle push. It whisked open, revealing two figures in the dim light, standing close together.

Donna. And a guy who leaned against the wall. A guy who loved leaning on walls.

My breath hitched.

Will. My Will.

She whispered something giggly I couldn't hear. He gazed at her a moment then shifted, as if making a decision, and drew her into his arms. She tipped her head back. He tightened his embrace—and lowered his lips to hers.

A whimper rolled up my throat. Anguish seared my stomach. How could he kiss her? How could he like a girl like her? Self-centered, shallow, always hunting for attention. Donna couldn't make him happy. Not even Marilyn could do that.

He needed a girl who'd get him. Who understood him. Who listened to him. A girl who loved him.

He needed *me*.

But he didn't want me.

CHAPTER 28

It Takes Two To Tango

A DALY DIDN'T CRY. A. Daly. Did. Not. Cry. I would stick by that motto if it killed me.

I found a bathroom in a closet under the stairs and stayed in there a long time, long after I took care of my needs. My thoughts tumbled and whirled. Will and Donna. Kissing. I bet he kissed good. I bet his lips tasted as sweet as cotton candy. Emotion lumped in my throat. I balled my fists and jabbed my fingernails into my palms. I would *not* give in to the tears that tried to fall.

What happened? I'd been so focused on Marilyn and Will, I'd barely noticed Donna moving in to steal him from me. No... That wasn't fair. He'd never been mine to steal. I had no claim on him besides being a girl he hung out with during rehearsals. A friend he'd shared two intense rides home with. Intense to me anyway. He'd probably already forgotten about them.

Someone banged on the door, rattling the hinges. Just like home. Which was where I wanted to be. I wiped my leaky nose, washed my hands and flung open the door to see Karen.

"What took you so long?" she snapped and I whooshed by, ignoring her.

Back at the party, I snatched a random bottle from behind the bar. I vaguely registered Marilyn huddled with Carl nearby. Her harsh laughter rang in my ears as I staggered across the room. Someone had tapped another keg and people clustered around it.

261

The comedy show *Saturday Night Live* was on the TV, the volume turned way up, doing battle with "Bad Moon Rising" playing on the stereo.

I fell into an open chair, a wide thing with soft cushions my butt could sink into. Staring at nothing, I sucked down a big gulp. I laughed bitterly at the taste and looked at the bottle's label.

Tango.

"Move over." Carl flopped his massive self into the chair and nearly crushed my right hip. He smelled like the back room at the Kentucky Derby. I probably did too.

"This isn't a love seat, Carl." I shifted, trying to get out from under him. "There's not enough room for two."

"There would be if you didn't have such a big rectum."

"Rectum?" Funny way to tell me I had a fat ass. My amusement faded when I spotted Will crossing the room, his eyes on me. Donna floated beside him. I lifted the bottle in a flippant toast and gulped a big swig. His expression hardened and he took Donna's hand.

I didn't want to cry. I wanted to scream.

Carl snatched the bottle from me and glugged half of it before giving it back. He wiped his mouth with the back of his hand. He gazed at me with glassy eyes, his expression softening. "You have a pretty face."

I bleated a laugh. If he'd said that to me two months ago I would've melted into a puddle. "I bet you say that to all the girls."

"Not all. Only ones with pretty faces." He turned a little toward me. "You going to the prom?"

"No." I gulped more Tango.

He twirled a finger through my hair. "Wanna go with me?"

A million emotions shot through me, chased by the fifty varieties of alcohol flooding my veins. What was happening? "The prom's in two weeks, Carl. Don't you already have a date?"

"Nope." He glanced at something over my shoulder then back at me. "I will now." That lazy smile spread across his face. "If you say yes."

I had the hangover to end all hangovers the next day, but I still went to work. We Dalys took our drinking seriously and our commitment to our jobs even more so. That's why Jay worked a million hours a week and my father hadn't missed a day in forty years, despite his babies being born and Jay's surgeries and Dad probably suffering from hundreds of hangovers as bad as mine.

For the first time, I was glad the new girl, Wendy, didn't like to chat. I needed quiet for my headache to subside, and I needed some time to think.

Last night, Carl and I sat together on that big chair like Tweedledum and Tweedledee until I had to leave. We didn't talk much. Because we had nothing in common except for the bottle of Tango we passed back and forth.

And the fact that we were now prom dates.

I couldn't believe I said yes. Couldn't believe he'd asked me. I'd made him ask me ten more times before I believed it, and only because he wrote my phone number on the palm of his hand and promised to call me to work out the details.

I didn't see Will or Donna again before I left the party. I laughed at how cruel fate could be. Going to the prom had been my goal, going with Carl my dream. I'd gotten what I wanted. And I didn't really want it.

I wanted Will.

A Tango-flavored sourness still bubbled in my stomach on Monday, back at school. I feared this hangover would last a year.

"Guess what? I have a prom date," Donna burbled when I joined her and the others at our table at lunch. "It's Will." Her gaze bopped from Karen to Barbie to Linda G. "Will Hovey, a guy from our play."

"It's a *show*," I said, as tart as Karen in a fighting mood. I couldn't help it. Hearing Donna and Will were officially prom dates hurt like hell. "You don't call a musical a play. You call it a show. A play has no music."

Donna giggled. Not the whispery giggle I'd heard with Will. Kind of defensive. "You're so weird, Dee."

I guess I was. A big ol' weirdo Will would never look at twice, especially with slinky, skinny Donna on the scene. *Oh, snap out of it.* It wasn't Donna's fault he liked her better.

"Will's your date?" Jane sliced me a glance. "I thought he liked—"

"Wait 'til you see my dress," Donna sing-songed. "It's lavender, with spaghetti straps, and cute little butterflies." She patted her chest. "And just barely covers my *you know whats*."

I gagged, wishing she'd just shut up.

"Now we've both got dates," Karen said. "What about the rest of you?"

"I have a date," Linda G said, miffed she'd been left out.

"I do too." Everyone gaped at me as if I'd declared I'd brokered peace in the Middle East. "I do. I'm going with Carl Werzbicki."

"Werz?" Donna practically screamed. "I *knew* it. Everyone was talking about you and Werz at Marilyn's party, saying you two are going out."

"I wouldn't go that far. He asked me and I said yes, that's all," I muttered, as joyless as I felt.

I went to my locker after lunch, bracing for war. The combination dial won the first round, refusing to open. I counterattacked, spinning it fast enough to make it pop off. The damn thing squeaked, as if laughing at me.

Frustrated, I kicked the door. The metal twanged from the impact. I kicked it again. And again. And one more time, swinging my foot with all the fury and hurt and anger that had built up inside me since seeing Will kiss Donna and even earlier, going all the way back for years and years.

The metal pinged and groaned and finally gave up with a rattling gasp. The door popped open. I blinked in surprise. After all this time, with only weeks to go before graduation when I'd be sprung from my schoolhouse jail forever, I finally figured out the secret to opening my damned locker.

Kick it to death.

I clenched my fists and raised my arms. "Victory is mine!"

"Congratulations," Stew Baines said as he rushed by.

On Saturday after I got out of work, Mom drove Donna and me to a place called Shopper's World and the three of us went shopping for my prom gown.

A process that quickly became more complicated than landing a date. Though I'd lost almost thirty pounds, and had dropped several dress sizes, I *still* couldn't find a dress that fit. Apparently the fashion gods had decreed any girl above a size eight was too plump for prom, so they didn't bother to make dresses in larger sizes.

"I'm sorry," one saleswoman sniffed after we'd hunted through every nook and cranny of her shop. "The young lady is simply too big for our clothes."

We heard the same thing at two other stores, in that same sorrowful voice, tinged with scorn.

We'd almost run out of options when we stumbled upon a shop called Lane Bryant, hidden in a corner on the second floor.

I walked inside—and stepped into a dream. Pants and blouses and undergarments and dresses, dresses, dresses in my size and bigger. *Way* bigger. Nice dresses, too, not garish muumuus or baggy tents spattered with gaudy flowers.

"Where have you been all my life?" I whispered, diving in.

A heavy-set Black woman wearing a hundred jingling bracelets and necklaces approached us. She looked gorgeous in a patterned blouse and slacks with flared legs, clothes she'd probably bought here in the store. She invited us to check out the merchandise and followed us around, chatting with my mother.

The plastic hangers squeaked and clacked as Donna and I pushed them back and forth on the racks, pawing through the clothes.

"I'm so happy we're going to prom together," Donna said, examining a wrap-around blouse that tied in the front. "We're going to have so much fun." She peeped over the rack, checking to see if my mother was out of earshot. "Do you think you and Werz are gonna do it on prom night?"

"Not if I have to call him Werz." I moved away, less to avoid the subject, more to avoid Donna gushing about doing it with Will. I did *not* want to know.

Funny joke on me to have Donna help me find a gown, when I ached to be going to prom with her date. If only we could switch. She and Carl would be the perfect pair. Except Carl *wanted* to be with me, when Will...

Water under the bridge, as Grandma would say, though in her case it would probably be Beefeaters Gin under the bridge.

Time came to focus on dresses. Donna and I cooed over the vast selection in my size. Mom only looked at the price tags, her eyes growing wider and wider. Yes, this place was expensive. But I'd decided to use some of that money I'd been saving for a college

I probably couldn't afford and splurge on the nicest gown I could find.

No surprise to discover Donna was an excellent judge of fashion. When I plucked a contender off its rack and held it up, she'd look the gown over and give a thumbs up or thumbs down like a Roman emperor choosing his gladiators. She turned two thumbs down on a flouncy thing the color of a purple popsicle, much to my relief.

I took the thumbs up gowns into the dressing room, slipped one on, then stepped out onto a small platform in front of a three-fold mirror. I twirled around. Not quite right, Donna or Mom and sometimes even the salesclerk would say. I'd change into the next gown and try again. The fifth dress, Mom clasped her hands together. Donna bounced on her toes, giggling.

I'd found *the* dress.

Made from a smooth, luscious fabric the salesclerk called chiffon, the gown was sky blue and brought out the color of my eyes. The sleeves clung gently to my arms, with small silver buttons on the thin cuffs. The neckline plunged in a V that showed just the right amount of cleavage.

And the skirt... *Sigh.* Like something a goddess on Mount Olympus might wear. Best thing of all, the dress had a waist. The fabric pulled in, accentuating my hourglass figure, then draped elegantly over my hips down to my ankles.

"*Gorrrrgeous,*" the saleslady said, getting emotional. Over how good I looked or in anticipation of a nice commission, I couldn't tell. "It'll look even better with a girdle. We have a wide selection in our foundations department."

"No," Mom said firmly. "She looks perfect. Beautiful."

Beautiful. *I think you're beautiful,* my secret admirer had said.

I examined my reflection a long time, almost beginning to believe it myself.

CHAPTER 29

The Most Tragical Night of the Year

THE NEXT TWO WEEKS brought some order to my usual school day chaos.

My locker opened whenever I banged on it, like Fonzie smacking the jukebox to make it play on *Happy Days*. Stew and I worked out a schedule, so no more run-ins. Mrs. English continued her daily news commentary while Mr. Meager toned down his insults, as if he'd had a Talking To from the principal.

And we moved on to poetry in English, not my favorite thing, but after that A-plus and enthusiastic applause for my story, I put up with it.

Prom night finally arrived. Funny how all my dreams of this special evening had flopped. No seventy pounds lost, no skinny-mini me waltzing into Oakhurst Country Club with my dream date, no happy ending. No Will.

But I had a gorgeous gown, so *c'est la vie*. I had no idea what that meant, though it sounded appropriate for the moment.

I took my time getting ready. I soaked for fifty hours in the bathtub and nobody banged on the door yelling for me to hurry up. I washed my hair, sprinkled baby powder over every surface of my body that could sweat, doubled up on the deodorant, squeezed myself into a pair of L'eggs pantyhose and hoped they wouldn't run, and put on one of Mom's long slips.

Then the dress, and the shoes, a pair of light blue, low-heeled pumps I'd found on sale at Cully's.

I checked my reflection in the mirror on my bureau, something I didn't do much, because I rarely liked what I saw gazing back at me.

Tonight, I did.

My pimples were gone (except for a rogue zit on the side of my forehead) and my hair glowed. I left it hanging loose. As flat and straight as a Kansas highway, it didn't hold a curl, anyway. I'd even cleaned my glasses, giving me a clear new perspective on the world.

And my beautiful, beautiful gown.

Chrissy clapped when I came downstairs and Dad let out one of those cartoon wolf whistles. Or tried to. Nothing but wind came out of his toothless mouth.

"You look stunning." Mom said, snapping a picture with her Instamatic camera.

I squinted from the flash. She thumbed the film advance button and the silver flashcube on top of the camera turned with a jerk. She took three more pictures, until the flashcube ran out, then put the camera down and went to get her pocketbook and car keys to drive me to Jane's.

My father narrowed his eyes. "Isn't that Polack gonna come pick you up?"

I regretted, immediately and forever, telling him Carl's last name. Dad had been calling him *that Polack* ever since, and I wasn't even sure Carl was Polish.

"His name is Carl, and we already planned to meet at Jane's house with the rest of our friends."

He snorted. "He should come *here*, so I can look him in the eye."

"Why, do you want to challenge him to a duel?" I tugged at the uncomfortable waistband of my pantyhose, annoyed. Dad hadn't shown this much interest in my life since... Well, never.

He dragged on his cigarette then gusted out smoke in an irritated sigh. "He should show you respect and come here. Not make you go to him. He's not much of a man to use you like that."

I waved him off. Dad was full of shit. And completely right. There was something off about this whole date, but I didn't want to think about that now.

"Did you go to your prom?" I asked Mom after we got in the car and headed toward Jane's house on the east side of the city. "Did they even have proms in those days?"

"We did. We rode to the prom on dinosaurs." She flicked me an impish grin. "It wasn't *that* long ago, you know. It was called a promenade, and it was held in the school gym, not a country club. The senior boys built an arch in shop class and covered it with flowers. Each couple walked under the arch while the master of ceremonies introduced them and everyone applauded. Then the dance began."

"Sounds quaint. What was your gown like?"

"Not as pretty as yours. It was the war. Fabric was rationed and we had to make do. Some of the boys had already enlisted and wore their uniforms instead of suits."

"Oh." It may not have been that long ago, but the world sure was different then. "Who was your date?"

A secret smile touched her lips. "A friend. A boy in my class. He was a gentleman." Her smile faded and she gave me a quick, serious look. "As I expect *your* date tonight to be."

She didn't say anything else the rest of the drive. We got to Jane's, a shabby but cute Cape Cod-style house, green, with metal awnings over the windows. Mom stopped me before I could climb out of the car. She flipped open her pocketbook, pulled out a twenty dollar bill, and handed it to me.

"Safety money. A girl should always have money in case she needs it." She fished around in her purse again. "Here." She stuffed a small, square package into my hands. "In case you need *these.*"

Condoms.

My cheeks burned hotter than fifty suns. My parents sure were full of advice and surprises tonight. Really uncomfortable surprises. Mom hesitated and I braced for whatever instrument of embarrassment she'd pull out of her bag next.

"Use your head, Deidre. Don't do anything you don't want to do."

A lump suddenly lodged in my throat. "It's okay, Mom. You don't have to worry."

She snorted. "It's a mother's job to worry. Don't you know that?"

I watched her drive off, then put the condoms in my clutch purse and slid the twenty into my shoe. I followed the sound of voices to the rear of Jane's house, where everyone had gathered.

I saw Donna first, standing on a small wooden deck off the back door. She wore a slinky spaghetti strap gown that clung to her hips and *ooh-la-la* boobies.

Will stood on the grass, gazing up at her. His rumpled hair seemed to defy gravity and he looked delicious in a sober black tux, white shirt, black cummerbund, and polished black shoes, with laces properly tied.

That lump took residence in my throat again. I thought I was prepared for seeing him tonight. But nope. Especially him standing there, with his shoes all boring and tied like everyone else's and not like Will at all.

He saw me and his eyes widened. I thought he might say something when Donna spotted me too and let out a delighted shriek that scared birds out of trees for ten miles around.

"Dee! You finally got here. You look gorgeous. But your face is naked. Why don't you *ever* wear makeup?" She waved furiously toward the door. "Get in here and come up to Jane's room. I'll get you prettied up for Werz." Will scowled the foulest scowl I'd ever seen on a human face and Donna clucked. "Now, don't be impatient Will. We'll only be a minute."

Only a minute turned into fifteen. Neil Diamond's "Song Sung Blue" played on the radio, followed by "Silly Love Songs" by Wings, Barry Manilow's "Mandy" and five other sappy songs as we chattered and got ready.

Donna sipped Tango while she painted my lips orange-red and shellacked sixteen coats of blue eyeshadow onto my lids. The smell of perfume and burning hair filled the room as Jane and Linda G took turns using a curling iron. Karen separated the globs of mascara congregating on her eyelashes with the sharp point of a large safety pin. I prayed a passing car wouldn't suddenly backfire and make her poke her eye out.

We finally spilled out of the house. Donna made a beeline for Will and I went in search of my date. I found him by a fake wishing well, chatting with a man I figured was Jane's father by his severe military haircut.

"If you're thinking of joining up after graduating, go Army," I heard Mr. Jane Austin say as I approached. "Best choice I ever made. They pay for school. Lots of benefits." He swigged a Schlitz beer. "Lots of poontang."

Carl's crude chuckle defined *poontang* for naïve me and he smacked his own beer can to Mr. Austin's.

I cleared my throat, interrupting the recruitment talk. "I'm here, Carl," I said, somewhat surprised to discover him here too. "You look nice."

He did not.

He wore a bright orange tuxedo the identical color of the downtown Howard Johnson's roof, with brown trim on the jacket's broad lapels, a brown cummerbund, and a bow tie so wide you could spin it as a propeller. Whatever villain had talked him into that ridiculous suit should've been boiled in oil and poured down a castle wall.

I gave up waiting for him to return my compliment and we joined the others near the in-ground swimming pool.

The evening was warm and sticky. Massachusetts' official and most annoying insect—mayflies—were out in full force, zooming into our eyes and up our noses. Some parents had come to take pictures, except Donna's and Carl's. And mine. Mom would've been here for certain if I'd known our parents were invited.

Jane's mother arranged us under a tall oak tree with a yellow ribbon around its trunk. She took so many pictures she had to put a new roll of film into her Instamatic. Will's dad had a fancy camera with a big lens. Will posed with his arm around Donna while the camera's shutter clicked a dozen times. For some reason, he didn't smile. Not even when his father told him to.

"What do you mean no pictures?" Karen's mother complained when Karen's date Freddie threw his hand in front of his face and refused to be in the pictures.

He wouldn't even join in for a group photo. Karen stood off to one side, arms crossed and pouting. I anticipated they'd have their first fight before we left Jane's back lawn.

I ended up next to Will in the lineup, with Carl on my right. "You look nice," I said to Will, meaning it this time. He looked like an old-time movie star in that slick tuxedo.

He gazed at me a long moment, something unsettled in his eyes. "So do you," he said finally, like the words had to force their way out.

Pictures done, we traipsed around the house to the front and got into the various cars hauling us to the country club. Donna settled her shapely butt into the front seat of Will's Mustang with a satisfied smile. I bit my lip and got into Carl's Buick, determined to stash my hurt into the deepest pocket of my heart and enjoy myself.

Carl sipped one of the beers Mr. Austin had given him for the road. "Want one?" He dipped his head to indicate the six pack on the seat between us.

I shouldn't. Carl shouldn't because he was driving. But I figured drinking was part of the prom experience and I had to indulge. I pulled the beer's ring tab and choked down several gulps. The liquid sloshed into my almost empty stomach and in seconds a tickling heat spread to my limbs.

We set out along Jane's street with car windows rolled down, a convoy of whoops and cheers, horns beeping. Minutes later, we reached the highway. Carl zoomed his car to the front of the pack and the rest of our merry band fell behind. He drove scary fast. And quite reckless. I held my breath as he bombed up behind other cars, inches from their bumpers, before he tore past them.

We left the city and I could breathe again as he turned off the highway and had to slow down. We reached Oakhurst Country Club well before the others, though a lot of cars already clogged the parking lot. Carl pulled into a spot with a nice view of the pond and the golf course beyond. The sun had dropped and the sky blushed a pleasant pinkish red.

Carl chugged the last of his beer and got out. I hesitated. Should I wait for him to open my door? Will would've already done it.

After a moment of indecision, I pulled the handle. The door stuck and I had to push and push before it popped open with an ear-splitting squawk. Careful not to step on my skirt's hem,

I walked beside Carl toward the function hall. Close, but not touching.

"You got the tickets, right?" he said, tossing me a glance.

Probably should've asked that question before we'd driven all this way. "Yeah, sure." I patted my purse, stuffed with tissues, Lifesavers, a year's supply of sanitary napkins in case MDP decided to crash the party. And the condoms.

We crossed a lobby done up in gold sconces and paneling then entered a huge ballroom with big windows and a glittering chandelier over the dance floor. Red, white, and blue streamers draped across every surface, and large crepe paper Liberty Bells dangled from the ceiling, swaying in the breeze from the air conditioners. Dozens of tables ringed the room, with a bar by the wall near the kitchen entrance.

Fancy. Not as fancy as the White House where President Ford's daughter Susan had her prom, but fancier than any place I'd ever gone to.

"What're you drinking?" Carl asked after we found a table.

What was the closest thing a country club would have to Tango? "A screwdriver, I guess."

He left, joining some of his football buddies at the bar. They wore tuxedoes in every color of the rainbow—mustard yellow, mint green, Necco wafer brown, Lawrence Tetro's robin's egg blue, my date's creamsicle orange, and Billy Boner's pink monstrosity with matching pink shoes.

Carl said something to his friends and they aimed curious looks my way. That got my suspicion meter pinging again. Was this a legit prom date, or did Carl plan something nefarious? A joke on the scale of Stephen King's book *Carrie*?

A ridiculous thought. But I looked up to see if there was a bucket of pig's blood in the rafters over my head, just to be sure.

If the color of 1976 was orange, the style of the year was halter dresses adorned with buttercups and daisies, and tuxedos with lapels wide enough to land an airplane on.

I knew this because, after we ate a meal of rubbery chicken, Carl had agreed to dance exactly one dance and get our picture taken together then deserted me for his football pals. I now had ample time to study the outfits my classmates wore while I watched them cavort.

At least I had my friends. Or most of them. Linda and Stew sat with me. So did Karen, who'd spent the whole night bickering with Freddie like they'd been married for forty years. Finally, he threw up his hands and stomped off to the bar. Barbie had yet to show, and Jane and her date, Hank Tilney, who was in as many clubs and committees as she was, barely perched on their chairs for more than three seconds before they rushed off to mingle.

The only friends not at my table were Donna and her date.

"Will says he wants to sit over there," she explained shortly after they'd arrived. She nodded toward a table on the other side of the room. "Some people he knows from his neighborhood are sitting there. Says he'll be more comfortable."

So what if he wanted to be with his snooty pals rather than me? It was one of the rare moments when Carl had planted his fanny beside me. I placed my hand over his, my eyes on Will.

"Fine by me," I said, forcing a cheery tone.

They'd toddled off and I told myself, Will out of sight, out of mind would be a good thing. Except I could hear Donna laughing and shrieking, as if starring in her own movie. And he sure wasn't out of sight when she dragged him onto the dance floor to gyrate against. He danced like the nerdiest white boy of the century, all flailing arms and out of tempo feet, providing me with my only genuine laugh of the night.

Barbie waltzed into the room well after our dessert of crushed strawberries and vanilla ice cream. Several girls followed her, including my gym class pal, Competitive Carol. All of them were dressed in tuxedos or men's suits.

Karen's eyes narrowed. "*What* is wrong with them?"

"Nothing," I said. "I think everything's right."

Barbie floated across the room to us. "What do you think?" She spread her arms wide and twirled around.

She wore a black tuxedo like Will's, with silky lapels and cummerbund. Red, white, and blue eyeshadow sparkled on her eyelids and she'd twisted her dark hair and piled it as high as Dolly Parton's. She looked gorgeous, and I said so. Linda G echoed my sentiment, and even Karen managed a compliment.

Not everyone was so generous. Some people stared and snickered. A bunch of girls fooped together like metal shavings to a magnet, buzzing with harsh whispers. The deejay stopped the song "Boogie Fever" mid-note and played "Walk on the Wild Side."

"I can't believe you did it," Jane said, hugging Barbie.

"You like it?" Barbie ran her hands down her sides, her face wreathed in a happy grin. "The tuxedo store wouldn't rent to girls so I gave my cousin Ricky the money and he rented this tux for me." She tugged at the seat of her pants. "I love it, but it's a little snug."

Competitive Carol came up beside her. She wore a walnut brown suit from the 1950s, with thin lapels, an equally skinny tie, and her short hair as slick as Fonzie's.

"It's my dad's wedding suit," she said, then greeted everyone at our table, getting to me—as usual—last. "You're here with Werz, huh?" She nodded toward Carl, laughing with his friends and shoving each other around by the bar. "I dated him once during my lost years. Before I figured things out." Her gaze lit on Barbie then back to me. "You're nice, Deidre. Too nice to go out with a putz like him."

I blinked, surprised. "If I'm so nice, why'd you always pick me last in gym?"

"Because I wanted to win." The deejay cued up "Jive Talkin'" and she slapped Barbie playfully on the arm. "Come on, Barbarella, let's dance."

"Join us," Barbie said as Carol tugged her away.

I waffled a moment. Hadn't I vowed to try and have fun tonight? But here I was, contributing to my own misery. Sitting and fretting about Will, steaming over being ignored by Carl. Why not get out there and enjoy myself?

I plunged into the undulating mob. I wiggled and twitched through the rest of "Jive Talkin'," KC and the Sunshine Band's "Get Down Tonight," and Hot Chocolate's "You Sexy Thing." I perked up, felt better. Until the slow song "I'm Not in Love" came on and Donna dragged Will onto the dance floor. She fell against him. His arms came around her. The song's lilting, almost bitter words burned into my heart.

I fled.

I escaped to the bathroom, where I had to wait a long time. Girls *always* had to wait, while boys walked in, *splish-splash*, and they were done. Toilets flushed, stall doors squealed open and shut, and I tapped my foot, impatient and annoyed. And angry with myself.

Barbie had more courage than I ever would. If I had any guts, I would've admitted my feelings for Will instead of hiding them. I would've ignored Marilyn's *you're too obvious* warning and marched up to him at his party and told him how I felt. At least then he would've *known*, even if he didn't like me back.

Afterward, back at my table, I sipped my watery screwdriver and watched my friends dance to "Lady Marmalade." Barbie and Carol did the bump. Karen had dragged Freddie onto the dance floor and they bopped around, never making eye contact. Donna had abandoned Will. She flit about in a wild, arm-waving frenzy that looked more like drowning than dancing.

The music faded and the deejay put on Elton John's "Your Song." The song that had played in Will's car when he held my hand. That startling moment when our eyes met and I hoped, for just an instant, that there could be something more between us. Something special.

Then it was gone and he'd asked Donna to the prom and I had to nod and smile for weeks while she went on and on about his good looks and his cool car but saying nothing at all about Will himself.

I sighed, then swore. And belched. Real loud.

As Will sat down next to me.

I raised my eyes heavenward. Why, for the love of Jesus and little baby ducks, did Will have to witness each and every one of my most embarrassing moments?

"Deidre. You're not having a good time."

To my dying day, I would remember Will Hovey, King of Obvious Observations. "I'm having a great time. I'd like to go to a prom every night of the week and twice on Sunday." He didn't laugh. Neither did I. I glanced at Carl, chugging his fifth or twenty-fifth beer of the night. "Why are guys such jerks?"

"We're not *all* jerks."

"No, not you," I murmured. "You're perfect."

"You know I'm not." He sounded miserable.

My heart flipped over. To me he was perfect. To me he was everything. And it crushed me. "What do you want, Will?"

That rattled him. "I saw you sitting here alone. I felt—"

"You felt sorry for me." I crossed my arms, fuming so hard he could probably see the steam coming out of my ears. "The poor fat girl ditched by her date. How nice of you."

"That's not why—" He cut off with an aggravated scowl. "Why are you with him? Why'd you come here with him?"

The question I'd be asking myself for the rest of my life. "Why did you come with *her*?" I jerked my chin at dancing Donna, swaying to the music.

His face went gloomy. "*She* asked me."

Yup. My fault. If only I'd asked him, things would be different. If only I'd had the courage.

"Deidre." He reached out but didn't touch me. "I don't get why you're going out with him."

I stiffened. I swore I would track down whoever started that rumor about Carl and me and beat them to a pulp. "We're prom dates, nothing else. We're not going out."

"You're not?" For some reason, that news got him even more miserable. "Then why did she say...?" His jaw went tight and a spark of anger lit his eyes. "Everyone said you were together."

"Everyone was wrong."

He flexed his fists. "All this time, I thought you were into him."

I snorted. "Put another check in the wrong column, William."

"Deidre, I think we need to talk. I mean, really talk." He flashed a glance toward Carl, then Donna. "Let's go outside."

I didn't want to talk. I wanted to kiss him. Wanted him to kiss me and hold me and *be* with me. But he didn't want that. "Why can't we talk right here?"

"Because... Because I'm not sure I can say what I need to say in here."

His gaze held mine, staring at me as he had at Jane's earlier tonight, an intense, unsettled look that set my heart pounding like storm waves against a cliff. My spine tickled and my belly flipped upside down and all around.

Damn him for making me feel this way.

"That's your problem, isn't it, Will? Saying things. Speaking up. Well, I'm done listening to you and your complaints. Go tell Donna your tale of woe and leave me alone."

His head snapped back, his expression shocked. Wounded.

Time froze and the world stilled. The chatter and laughter in the room faded. So did the final notes of "Your Song." There was only me and Will and my harsh words hanging between us. Hurtful words I didn't mean, but words I'd said. Because that lump in my throat had become a boulder with a thousand tears crowded behind it. Anguished tears centered around one thought.

He'd hurt me and I wanted to hurt him back.

I opened my mouth to apologize. Too late. He shoved back his chair and stood. With one long and utterly final look at me, he left.

I watched him stalk across the room to his table, taking the last shreds of our friendship with him.

Chapter 30

Big Girls Do Cry

The deejay wrapped up the most wonderful night of the year with the prom favorite, "Stairway to Heaven" then he booted the Class of '76 out into the night.

Outside, couples made their way to their cars. Karen and Freddie had left long ago. Linda G and Stew sat on a swing on the club's porch, holding hands, chatting with Jane and Hugh. Barbie and Competitive Carol disappeared around a corner into the shadows.

I saw Donna and Will veer off toward the other side of the parking lot. She danced around him in a circle, giggling, her skirt flaring out. She took his hand and dragged him to his stupid little car. I supposed she'd get her wish tonight and her cherry would be thoroughly popped.

Carl suddenly became a gentleman and opened the car door for me. The hinges squawked, scaring some sleeping birds out of the nearby bushes. He climbed into the driver's seat and let out a heavy sigh.

"Did you have fun tonight?" he asked.

If having him ignore me all night, watching my best friend hang on the guy I really liked, and hurting that guy and completely ruining our friendship was a fun time? Why, yes.

"A night I'll never forget," I muttered, gazing out the windshield. The moon was nearly full. Its light rippled over the pond. Very romantic. Carl must've thought so too because he sneaked over toward me. He reached out and caressed my neck. The night was steamy, his hand warm, but a chill crept up my arms.

"I had a good time, too," he said. "I'm glad you said you'd be my date."

He sounded sincere. Too sincere. "You're welcome," was the only response I could think of.

He pulled me into his arms and kissed me. It was a good kiss, though not as amazing as I'd imagined it would be all those months ago. His lips were smooth and he tasted like beer. He paused to peel off my glasses and toss them onto the dashboard. I shivered. That gesture seemed more intimate than his mouth on mine.

He kissed me again, our tongues touching. His hand found its way to my breast. Horniness wrapped in misery flared inside me. Carl hadn't come through with the other prom night ingredients, no slow dancing, no holding hands and being together, but he sure wanted to cash in on the *doing it* part.

Did I? I had to get it over with sometime, and Carl probably knew what to do like an expert. Everyone else would be having sex tonight. Will and Donna were going to. How, I didn't know. His car was so small Donna's legs would stick out the window.

Will. A pitchfork suddenly stabbed my heart. Carl was *not* Will.

I pulled away. "No. Not here."

"Why not? There's no better place. Everyone else is."

I glanced around and saw lots of fogged up windows and bouncing cars, proving his point. He moved in and kissed me again.

"You like that," he said against my lips.

Not a question. A statement. Something he'd probably said to all the Holy Mother girls and all the girls before that who sat where I sat. He shifted his kisses to my neck and further down. He took my hand and guided it to his crotch. His dick pushed against the orange fabric, begging to be set free from its polyester prison. He groaned.

"Take off your underpants," he whispered urgently.

First of all, was there any less romantic word than underpants? And secondly, was there any less romantic place for me to *do it* than the front seat of his rusted, busted Buick? Or a worse guy to do it with.

I snatched my hand away. "No, Carl... I..." I scrambled for an excuse, because a girl couldn't just say no. Guys needed a solid reason. "I can't. I don't have any protection." Well, I did, but Mom said not to do anything I didn't want to, and I certainly didn't want to do anything with him.

"I got some condoms in the trunk. You're not gonna make me go get them." His gaze dipped to the bulge in his pants. "Not in *this* condition."

He said that like a boner was a disease he was about to die from. He reached for me again and I shoved him away.

"Give me the trunk key, *I'll* get the condoms." *And then I'll run far, far away.*

"Christ." He let out the most self-pitying sigh I'd ever heard, and I'd grown up with the king of self-pity. "Alright, just give me a blow job." He reached for his zipper.

Ick. "No."

Now he pouted. "You can't leave me this way. I'll get blue balls and never have children."

"That's horseshit." I grabbed my glasses and shoved them back on. "Jesus, did you ever pay attention in health class?"

He heaved another sigh, angry this time. "Your loss, sweetheart."

He turned the key in the ignition and the car's engine started with a disgruntled roar. Deep Purple's "Smoke on the Water" blasted from tinny speakers. My cue to leave. I had my emergency money, more than enough for a cab if I couldn't get a ride from one of my friends.

"Well, it's been fun. Let's never do this again—" Before I could shove open the sticky door, he tore out of the parking lot at a speed that threw me back against the seat. "Hey. Stop. Let me out."

He did neither of those things. "I didn't want to take you tonight," he spat. "There's hundreds of other girls I coulda gone with."

"Then why'd you ask me?" Curiosity trumped my anger. A little.

"I made a mistake," he said with a bitter snort then floored the gas pedal.

I hung onto the seat as we blew through a red light and up the highway onramp at a reckless speed my school bus driver would applaud. Icy prickles stabbed my spine. I had more serious things to worry about than trying to decipher what I *made a mistake* meant.

"Carl, slow down. You're going too fast."

He seemed not to hear me. He glared at the road, his jaw clenched. His face looked old and ugly in the dashboard light. Our speed increased. Eighty-five, ninety. My stomach cramped like MDP squeezed it full force.

"Please slow down." My voice came out in a frightened squeak.

No response. Terror exploded inside me. He was drunk and angry. At me for not putting out, or something more? The mistake that fueled his bitterness?

My gaze locked on the speedometer. Ninety-five, a hundred, a hundred and ten. The Buick shuddered and shimmied. I trembled just as much. Carl squeezed the steering wheel and pushed the car to one-fifteen. Newspaper stories of post-prom car crashes flashed into my mind. Was I about to become a statistic?

My mouth dried out. I knew how the guy in my motorcycle story felt for real. Petrified. Blinded with fear. Out of control.

"Stop the car," I screamed into Carl's ear, a desperate attempt. "Stop. This. Fucking. Car."

It worked. He let up his foot and the car slowed. He steered into the breakdown lane and stopped. He breathed heavily, like he'd run a fast mile, his face pale and coated with sweat. He looked at me with a stunned expression, as if he'd left his body for a second and was surprised to see what happened while he'd been gone.

"What the fuck?" I punched his arm. Hard. "What were you thinking? Driving like a lunatic because I wouldn't fuck you? Asshole." I punched him again. And again.

"Whoa." He flung up his arms, as if to block a tackle. "Stop. I'm sorry. I didn't mean it. I do stupid things sometimes when I get mad. I'm sorry."

Apologies weren't going to cut it, any more than my frantic *I'm sorry* to Camille what seemed like a lifetime ago or any apology I could cobble together for what I said to Will. But Carl's pathetic mewling snapped me out of my heated rage. After a struggle, I heaved the door open. It squealed like fighting cats. I grabbed my clutch purse and scrambled out.

"Where you going?" he demanded.

"Anywhere but in a car with you."

I marched down the breakdown lane as fast as I could. Vehicles whizzed by on the highway, making my skirt snap. The fabric caught on a guardrail and ripped. I didn't slow down. Anger and every scrap of frustration that had been building up inside me for months propelled me forward. I wished I'd stayed home. I wished I'd said no when Carl asked me to the prom. Wished I'd never heard of Carl Werzbicki.

He rolled the Buick along beside me, badgering me to get back in the car all the way to the bottom of the off-ramp, then he sped up and shouted, "Bitch," as he roared past.

"Fuck you," I yelled even though he couldn't hear me.

I trekked along Canal Street, hoping to stumble across a payphone so I could call home. Some cars slowed as they puttered by and the drivers peered at me. My pulse sped up and so did I. My comfortable pumps weren't so comfortable now. My pantyhose puckered like wrinkles on an elephant's legs. Sweat trickled down my back and pooled under my arms. My head ached and so did my heart.

What was supposed to be the best night of my life had been a disaster from start to finish. Who was I kidding? My life was a disaster. End of story.

I rounded the corner onto Milltown Street, steering toward Hot Dog Benny's, a cheap eats place open twenty-four hours. I planned to spend every penny of that twenty bucks Mom gave me on chips and hotdogs. Minus a dime for the payphone.

The pulsing beat of disco music thumped from inside a nightclub I passed, a place called The Hammer. A door padded with red leather swung open. Heat, smoke, and the spirited dance tune "Love Machine" spilled out. Two young men stood framed in the doorway, their arms around each other, and not in a *we're just buddies* way. They broke apart the moment they stepped out of the club.

It was Barry and Pete.

Barry's eyes widened when he saw me. "Hey Cinderella. Are you off to the ball?"

I burst into tears.

"I'm so embarrassed." I dabbed my wet eyes with the napkin Pete handed me. "I never cry. Crying's illegal in my family, so I have to keep everything in."

We sat in a booth at Hot Dog Benny's, waiting for our order, me on one side, Pete and Barry on the other. One of the overhead lights flickered. The place was as steamy as July, the air thick with the aroma of French fries, onion rings, and hotdogs sizzling on the grill.

"Keeping it all in is my specialty," Barry said.

"I plan to major in it at college." Pete looked up at the stout guy in the greasy apron and paper chef's hat who placed a tray of food on our table. "Thanks Benny."

Benny mumbled something that might've been *you're welcome* and slipped back behind the counter.

"Okay, Cinderella." Barry squirted enough mustard onto his hotdog to drown it. "You gonna tell us what you're doing in this part of town at midnight?"

"And in that fantabulous dress," Pete added, attacking his chili dog with a knife and fork, a wise decision given its condition as more chili than hotdog.

I told them my sad prom tale and recounted my wild ride in Carl's car as we ate. I saved the more intimate details of my front seat wrestling match and Carl's blue balls for the girls at lunch. I didn't say one word about Will, or how mean I'd been to him.

"What a felon," Barry said when I finished.

"Will never trusted the guy." Pete wiped chili from his chin. "Will called him a selfish prick. All ego, he said. Fragile ego he needs others to feed. Especially girls."

Will sure had Carl pegged. While I'd been mesmerized by Mr. Lazy Smile's pretty package, Will had seen the real guy from the start. Hadn't he always called him Judas, and in a bitter, resentful way?

I finished eating. Unburdening had helped. I felt, well, not happy, but not as unhappy as I'd been earlier. I pushed my plate away and studied Barry and Pete. They wore dressy slacks, shiny polyester shirts, platform shoes, and gold chains. Nightclub clothes, for a place called The Hammer.

"So, are you two, like, a couple?" Of course they were. I should've seen it sooner and maybe would have if I wasn't so focused on my own drama. They were always together, always smiling at each other. Like two people in love.

"Don't tell anyone." Pete scanned the restaurant and the sparse number of customers. "My family's sort of okay with us. Barry's parents would take the news bad."

"Like, throw me out of the house bad."

I put my thumb and forefinger to my lips and mimed turning a key in a lock. I could keep a secret. The thing my family was best at. "Gotta say I'm happy for you." My smile broke into a wide grin. "You're so cute together."

Barry lit a cigarette. "Don't get mushy on us, Cinderella."

I grinned again and wiped my mouth with my napkin. "Now, without further ado..." I tipped my head toward the payphone on the wall. The telephone book hung suspended from a chain, its multitude of pages fanned open like flower petals. "I need to make a call."

Mom waited until we were well on our way home before speaking. "Do you want to tell me what happened?"

"Not really." She hit me with that Spock eyebrow and I relented, giving her the *Cliff's Notes* summary of the story, which, as a reader who lusted after the entire book, she surely hated. "Safe to say, I won't be riding off into the sunset with Carl." Or anywhere else, after that horrifying demonstration of his driving skills.

"I'm sorry your night turned out so bad," she said when the flames of her outrage had cooled. "I think life throws lemons like him at a girl so you'll know the right guy when he comes along. I sure dated my share of stinkers in my day."

"Mom. Really?"

"Really. I know it's hard to believe I was once your age. I had my admirers. None were right for me. Except for one fella..." That secret smile touched her lips.

"Your prom date?" It felt funny to think of her young and mooning over a guy who wasn't my dad. "What happened?"

She sighed. "We were young. Too young. Our families were..." Her voice turned gloomy, hushed. "We came from two different worlds. It never would've worked. We had to go our separate ways."

I pictured Mom like Juliet on her balcony, with her prom date Romeo gazing up at her, declaring her as bright as the sun. Before Gramps had bullied her into breaking off the romance. I thought of Jay and Shirley. And Barry and Pete. And I hoped against hope they'd get the happy ending my mother was denied.

We rolled up to a stop light and she pressed the turn signal. The *click-click* of the blinker filled the silence.

"Life goes on," she said as the car puttered forward again. "That sounds like an advertising slogan, but it's true. We move on and make the best of what we can. If I hadn't met your father, I wouldn't have you." She aimed an affectionate smile my way. "Don't despair, there's someone out there for you. Someone who'll see you for the beautiful girl you are."

Beautiful. I smoothed the skirt of my ripped and smudged and now mustard-stained gown. There was only one person I wanted to see me in that way.

I turned to stare out the window. Mom hadn't taken the highway. Thankfully. I'd had enough of *that* road for one night. Instead, I got a tour of the city's blue-collar neighborhoods that would probably scare Marilyn to death to drive through so late at night.

"I messed up, Mom. I said some mean things to a friend tonight."

She digested that a long time. "Sounds like you know how to fix that. Say you're sorry. If this person's really your friend, they'll forgive you."

I let out a heavy breath, full of regret. Will had been exactly that from the start. A friend. Even if the stars had aligned and we could've been something more, he still would've been my friend. One of the best friends I'd ever had.

And I'd ruined everything.

Part Six

June 1976

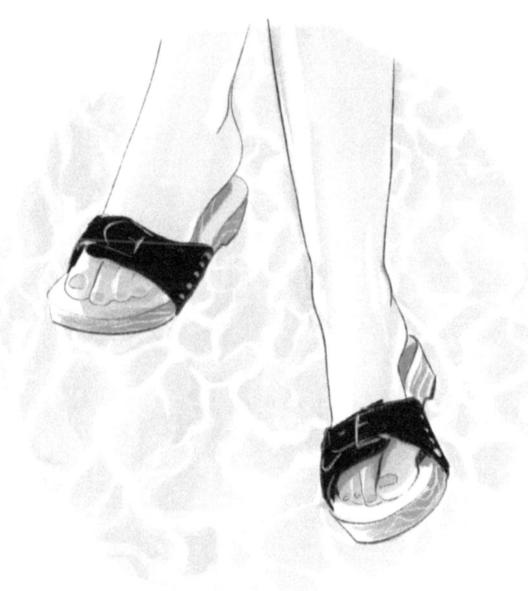

Chapter 31

School's Out

With the last week of school and graduation dead ahead, I put the prom—and Will—behind me as best as I could. Which meant I tried not to think of him, while still thinking about him all the time.

Senioritis kicked in, for us and our teachers too. Every one of them seemed to have adopted Mrs. English's teaching style and they sat at their desks reading the newspaper, teaching nothing. In science, we watched film strips from the 1950s while Mr. Meager laughed at the poodle skirts and beehive hairdos.

Figuring Mrs. Baker would be glad not to give me one last chance to burn the school down, I skipped my last home ec class to hang out in the school library with Linda G instead.

"You'll keep in touch, won't you?" I said. We stood near the spinning metal bookracks lined up along the windows. "I want to know what you think of the books I suggested."

I'd convinced her to do the Bicentennial thing and switch from reading about the Civil War to the Revolutionary War. She'd started with Howard Fast's *April Morning* as an appetizer, would move on to *The Adams Chronicles* as her main meal, and end with the sexy and soapy *The Bastard* for dessert.

"Of course I'll stay in touch." She spun one of the racks like a roulette wheel. *Carrie, Go Ask Alice,* S.E. Hinton's *The Outsiders, To Kill A Mockingbird* and dozens of other titles flashed by. "I'll write to you from... Wherever Stewart and I end up."

Stewart meant Stew, who'd enlisted in the Navy. I assumed there was less poontang available for a Navy man at sea than for an Army guy on land, but to keep him from temptation, he and Linda were getting hitched. He'd proposed after the prom, giving her a diamond ring. Well, not a full diamond, more like a shiny chip you needed to squint to see.

Mom would have some choice words about Linda G giving up college to become a Navy wife, but my irretrievably smitten friend just wanted to be with her man. Hopefully the right decision, and hopefully, as the Captain and Tenille's hit song went, love would keep them together.

The last day of school arrived. The last lunch period of my high school life. We'd gotten our yearbooks in homeroom, a thick tome with an illustration of a Revolutionary War Minuteman on the cover. I tucked the book under my arm as I moved my tray along the line. I flashed my free lunch card to the sourpuss at the register one last time and took my hockey puck hamburger and soggy French fries to our table.

"This is it, our last day," Donna squealed as I sank into my seat. "Will you sign my yearbook?"

"If you'll sign mine."

I opened to the page with my photo and slid it over to her. My picture came out good, a nice closeup of my pretty face. My name however... *Doodre Daley.* Daly I could see misspelling, but I congratulated whoever had screwed up the spelling of Deidre so badly it seemed a work of art.

Donna pushed the yearbook back to me and I skimmed her inscription, *To my bestest friend and a good kid. Thanks for putting up with me. Love always, D.*

A sweet note that activated a flood of guilt. A week ago I hated her, and resentment still simmered in the pit of my stomach. But she didn't know about my feelings for Will. I had to remember that.

Karen stomped up and tossed her tray onto the table. She fell into her chair.

"What's got your knickers in a twist?" Barbie asked.

"What doesn't do that?" Linda G said, with the sweetest smile.

Karen turned a furious glare on Donna. "Thanks a lot. My prom date, Freddie, the guy *you* fixed me up with? I found out he's married. He's fucking *married.*"

Donna's mouth gaped like a fish in a tank stuck to the glass. Linda G clapped her hand over her mouth. Barbie hooted. I laughed, and eventually everyone did, including Karen.

"I hope my mother never finds out," she said, in between gasps of laughter. "And thank god I didn't fuck him."

That sobered me up and my giggling turned forced because... Will. And Donna. I was sure they'd done it on prom night and every night after, though she never talked about it. Not ever. Odd, though I supposed I should be grateful she didn't blab non-stop about finally popping her cherry, because I didn't think me or my bruised heart could stand to hear it.

Jane rushed up, balancing her tray on her yearbook. "What'd I miss?"

"Nothing," Karen gurgled, wiping her eyes with a napkin.

"Where've you been, Jane?" I asked.

"Getting everyone to sign my yearbook."

My lips twitched. "Everyone? Like, all twelve hundred students and office and guidance staff everyone?"

"Pretty much. You girls need to sign too, and vice versa."

A flurry of pens scribbling followed, then everyone abandoned their lunches to join the mob of seniors bopping around the room, crossing cliques and cajoling classmates they'd never spoken to in four years of high school to autograph their yearbooks like they were their best friend.

I was about to do the same when Jane stopped me. "Deidre, wait. I've got news. About you and Werz, and prom. And it is *juicy*."

I sat back down, all ears. My friends had exploded with outrage when I'd spilled the story of what happened with Carl. Jane latched onto what he'd said about making a mistake asking me to go with him. She put on her Lois Lane reporter's hat and went hunting for answers.

She leaned closer, her eyes gleaming. "Werz only asked you to be his date because Marilyn told him to."

I lifted an eyebrow, surprised yet not surprised. I should've seen Marilyn's evil hand in that whole prom debacle.

"It's nuts, huh?" Jane said. "I talked to Iris. She's one of Marilyn's closest friends and she says Werz is *crazy* in love with Marilyn and he'd do *anything* to get her to go out with him. It's not like with the other girls. He just wanted to sleep with them. My dad would call him a horndog, getting notches on his bedpost, which is really gross. Anyway, Marilyn wouldn't give him the time of day. Of course that made him want her more. Guys are like that. They could have a dozen girls piled up by the door, but they always want the one who ignores them. Like they have to prove something."

Especially Carl. Will had called him an ego needing to be fed and a lot of girls were eager to do just that, even me for a while. Not Marilyn. She'd been the hard-to-get holdout. It must've driven him bonkers.

"At Marilyn's party, Iris heard her tell Werz to tell everyone he was dating you, and to ask you to the prom. Werz didn't like that, thought it was a stupid prank, but she sweet-talked him into giving in."

My belly twisted. I imagined that sweet-talking involved a coy promise from Marilyn to give Carl the poontang he was after—*if* he would do this one tiny favor for her. Which led to him falling into that chair beside me at Marilyn's house and asking me to be his date.

How dumb could I be? I should've known something was up at the cast party at Will's, when I said I wasn't going to prom and Marilyn stepped in with a falsely sweet, "never say never." And her cat-that-ate-the-canary attitude at her own party practically announced she had a diabolical plan in mind.

"The whole thing's weird," Jane said. "Marilyn can be kind of bitchy, but that's just mean. Why pick on you?"

I shrugged, though I had an inkling of the truth. Good ol' Mar hadn't played prom matchmaker because she wanted to do something nice for the gauche girl with the misguided crush on Will. She despised me. She hated the idea of Will and me being friends even more. She didn't set me up with Carl to do me a favor.

She did it to hurt me.

But why? Was she jealous of the time I'd spent with Will and hoped to drive us apart using Carl? She knew Will disliked Carl. Did she think cooking up a romance where there was none would do the trick?

Well, she needn't have bothered. I ruined my friendship with Will quite handily, all by my own little self.

The bell rang. Jane squished me in a hug then flitted off to class. I did the same. My yearbook filled up with signatures of people I barely knew and would probably never see again as I moved from class to class.

Later, on my way to English, the last class ever of my high school career, I spotted Carl in the Desert, hanging out with Billy Boner and some other guys.

Our eyes met. He gave me a wary look. I gave him the finger. With both hands. I shot the rest of the guys there the bird too. To my surprise they cheered and clapped. Impressed with my audacity, perhaps. I considered taking a bow but thought I'd leave them wanting more.

English class flew by. Miss French read some poetry no one listened to. Not even Lord Byron, who'd written that flowery codswallop, would listen to it. The bell rang and everyone stampeded toward the door.

"Deidre, hold up," Miss French called as I made to follow. "I'd like to talk with you a moment."

I stiffened. What could she possibly want to talk to me about today of all days?

I glanced outside at my bus, the motor running and Gus's foot hovering over the gas pedal, ready to take off. I dragged to the front of the room, bracing for the worst.

"I want to wish you good luck, Deidre," she said and flashed a motherly smile. "And keep writing. You're quite talented. I hope to see your name on the bestseller list someday."

It took five solid minutes for her words to sink in. And for me to speak. I murmured some semblance of a thank you and sailed out of the room and out of Northside High forever, grinning like a fool. Funny how a few kind words could make someone feel so good.

"What're you so happy about?" Gus muttered as I floated onto the bus.

I gave him a smirk and said, "I suppose I'll miss you least of all."

CHAPTER 32

I Can See Clearly Now (Mostly)

"YOU ARE NOT LEAVING this house," I heard Mom holler as I came downstairs.

She stood with her back to the kitchen door, a reverse image of her stance when Camille came calling nearly two months ago. Then, she blocked Camille from coming in. Now, she stood as firm as a solid wall, keeping Rusty from racing out.

"Why not?" he demanded. "Jimmy Three-Finger's gonna fight Danny Kolbus and he needs me to back him up."

Mom shook her head. "First, I do *not* want you hanging around anyone named Jimmy Three-Finger. Second, you know how these fights go. Two guys turns to twenty and before you know it, there's a riot. I do *not* want you in the middle of it. Third, hurry up and get ready for Deidre's graduation. I do *not* want to be late."

Rusty grumbled but didn't argue. When Mom emphasized her *I do not wants* like that, we knew we'd never win, so why bother to fight? He expressed his frustration by slamming into me as he stomped past on his way to the stairs.

"He doesn't have to come to the ceremony," I said, following Mom from the door into the kitchen.

"Yes he does." She gazed into the mirror over the washing machine and pulled a hairbrush through her shiny hair. She looked pretty in an above-the-knee, short sleeved cotton dress dotted

301

with rose petals. "Rusty's coming whether he likes it or not." She turned and ran a critical eye over my outfit. "You look very nice."

Nice, *and* comfortable. For the first time in Northside High's history, girls were allowed to wear pants instead of dresses or skirts under their graduation robes. I'd thought about putting on my new jeans, but I knew Mom would voice a strong *I do not want* at the idea of me wearing something so casual, so I compromised with dressy brown knit slacks, my marshmallow shoes, and a tan-and-white checkered blouse perfect for the mild weather.

Soon we were ready to go. Everyone except Dad. He still wore his uniform, though he'd been home from work for hours and had plenty of time to change. He sat in his chair with a beer on the table beside him and a cigarette smoldering in the ashtray.

"Uh...is that what you're wearing?" I asked, scowling.

"I'm not going." He rubbed his hands together in an agitated manner. "I'm no good in crowds. Besides, I got a cold." He let out a hacking cough to prove it, though he didn't have to. He'd been coughing and sniffling for days.

"Not going to my graduation?" I could see Rusty skipping the ceremony, but my father? That hurt. "Are you serious?"

"I told you. I got a cold. You don't want me there, passing on my germs."

I fumed. "Good, *don't* come. Everyone would stare at you, anyway, staggering and puking in the aisle."

He glared, a look that went from cold to glacial. "Go on Princess. Go get that piece of paper. Show up your old man and rub my face in how good you are."

"That's enough, both of you," Mom said, her voice like steel. She tugged my arm. "Get moving."

Chrissy and Rusty waited for us in the car. Jay was getting out of work early and he and Shirley were driving to the auditorium in her Gremlin. I flopped into the Impala's front seat and slammed the door.

"I hate him," I muttered.

"Deidre..." She started the car and pulled away from the curb. "You don't hate him."

"No. He hates *me*. He resents me and he always has."

"It may seem that way, but it's not *you* he resents. It's...life, I guess. Your dad had to leave school at sixteen to work in a factory after his father died. He never graduated. Never had a chance at college or anything else, not even the Army after he was classified 4-F for his flat feet. He sees you getting everything he didn't have. Opportunities he never dared hope for. That's difficult for a man to face."

"Oh." My anger fizzled, replaced with confusion. "I guess I get it, but that doesn't make it okay to pick on me."

"No it doesn't. None of that is okay. The way he acts, his resentment, his mood swings, what he'd probably find out is depression if he ever went to a doctor, it's all a symptom of his disease, the compulsion that makes him drink." She took a deep breath and released it with a sigh. "Well, the truth is, your father's an alcoholic."

That wasn't news to me or anyone riding in this car, but to hear her say it, to hear her finally admit it sent chills down my back.

"He's tried to stop," she said, turning the corner at the bottom of our street. "He fought it, a couple times. When Jay was born, when you kids were little. But now... He's simply given in."

Those words came out stark, emotionless, and clear in their meaning. He'd given in, and she'd given up trying to help him.

"I don't want you to think I excuse his behavior, because I don't." She gave me a wry, somewhat pleading look. "But I want you to try to understand where it comes from."

Understand. That word again. It followed me and haunted me. And challenged me.

I looked over my shoulder at my siblings in the back seat. Chrissy played cat's cradle with an old shoelace tied at the ends, intently focused on her hands. Rusty clenched his jaw, his fists balled, ready to wallop any convenient target he could find.

The perfect illustration of how they each coped with our family's drama. Chrissy withdrew, Rusty lashed out. Jay coped too, with his secrets and guarded emotions. And me, with humor and Twinkies and putting myself down.

I glanced at Mom, who focused on the road ahead. Even she found a way to cope, escaping into her books and ignoring the very large elephant in the room.

Maybe someday I'd understand everything, but at the moment, I understood only one thing. Quite well. Alcoholism was a disease. A contagious disease. It not only afflicted the drinker. It hurt everyone around them.

The buzz of excited voices and the smell of cigarettes and perfume filled the auditorium's cavernous lower concourse. Teachers and office staff wound through the crowd of five hundred seniors, handing each of us graduation gowns in Northside High's colors, vibrant blue for boys, a dull yellow for girls. They gave us those flat, square hats called mortar boards too, and a tassel with a little gold '76 dangling from it. The gowns and mortar boards we had to give back, the tassels we got to keep.

Donna flew up to me. "We're graduating!" She pulled me into a rib-cracking hug and jumped up and down, making me jump up and down with her until she forced a smile out of me. A smart doctor ought to bottle Donna. She worked better on lifting a person's spirits than any drug ever could.

Within minutes, Karen, Barbie, and Linda G had joined us and we all babbled in excitement. As usual, Jane rushed in late.

"Look what I have." Jane handed each of us an envelope emblazoned with logo of the Fotomat Drive-Thru kiosk at Foley Plaza. "My mother got the pictures she took at our house before the prom developed. I had her make copies for everyone."

I pulled a stack of four-by-six photographs from the envelope she gave me and skimmed through them. I paused at the picture of all of us lined up by the old oak tree with the yellow ribbon. I zeroed in on Will.

Jane peered over my shoulder. "Aw, look at Will. He's so cute. A shame you two never got together, Deidre. I thought you'd make a perfect couple."

"What?" Donna cried and I cringed. *Have a little tact, Jane.*

"It's so plain Will likes you," Jane went on. "You can see it every time he looks at you."

"*What?*" Donna again.

My heart went on a rampage as soon as the words *Will* and *likes you* came out of Jane's mouth, but I wished she'd shut up. I doubted Donna wanted to hear the guy she was seeing was hung up on someone else. Especially since it wasn't true.

"C'mon, Jane. Will does *not* like me."

She laughed. "Yes he does. See? See that look?"

The others crowded around me to examine the photo. Karen *hmphed.* Barbie whistled. "That's a like look if I ever saw it," Linda G said.

I stared intently at the picture. While I dutifully smiled for the camera, Will gazed at me. His expression made my heartbeat thunder like a summer squall.

Could what Jane said be even remotely true? I pored through the memories of these last months. Will always hanging out with me at rehearsal, always offering to drive me home. That time he helped put my coat on. The movie date-not-a-date. Laughing with him, how comfortable we were together, and how much he seemed to enjoy being with *me*. An insecure girl so convinced that he could never, ever like me that I didn't allow myself to consider well, why wouldn't he?

I grinned as wide as the universe.

"You get it now." Jane straightened her mortar board. "He likes you. And I'm pretty sure you like him too."

"What?" Donna cried for the third and loudest time. She swung on me. "You? And Will? Why didn't you tell me?"

My elation shriveled like a balloon losing air. "Because you two are dating. I'd never get between—"

"We're not dating. We never were. Sure, we went to prom together, but I haven't spoken to him since."

My turn to *what*? "Does this mean you didn't...?"

"No way. He's got style and a nice car and he kisses like a five-alarm fire. But..." She shrugged. "He's kind of boring. He doesn't like to have fun. I had to *force* him to dance at prom. All he wanted to do was talk. *Oh*." She slapped her forehead. "My dad's right, I *am* stupid. Will *only* wanted to talk about you. Like, all night. He was moody and in a funk and talking about you. Now I get why. He wanted to be with you and was mad you were with Carl."

A switch flipped and the proverbial lightbulb flashed on. That explained why Will had been so unhappy at Marilyn's party. *I thought you were into him*, he'd said at the prom. He'd heard Carl and I were going out. Probably Marilyn had told him that herself. Because she knew Will liked me and that's what set Operation Use Carl and Make Deidre Miserable into motion.

Damn it, Will. Fate, my inability to keep my mouth shut, and a petty girl named Marilyn had worked overtime to keep us apart.

"Glad we finally got *that* straightened out," Jane said, immensely pleased with herself. "He likes you. Now, what're you going to do about it?"

"Time to line up. Alphabetical order by homeroom," Miss Dolan called before I could answer, and the buzz of conversation became a roar as everyone rushed into place.

"Deidre," Barbie said, squinting at Miss Dolan. "Did you know you sort of look like her?"

Laughing, I gave her a hug. I hugged Donna too and everyone else within arm's reach then we all scattered like ladybugs in platform shoes.

We trooped up the marble steps to the main auditorium. I practically flew. Upstairs, once everyone quieted down, the processional began. A sound like soft thunder rumbled through the room as our families and guests stood. We filed through the doors and down a broad aisle toward our chairs at the front.

I spotted my family in the balcony, third row up. Good location with a great view of the stage. I imagined Mom sending Rusty ahead to elbow people out of the way to secure that spot. Jay was there. He was always there. He waved. So did Shirley and Chrissy. I waved back, feeling light and full of stars and possibilities, my father's woes and my anger forgotten.

I moved into my row, took my seat, and the ceremony began. The guest speaker delivered a droning lecture about our duty to the future, followed by our valedictorian Lars Quigley's equally dull speech. I'd hoped Lars would talk about being a Project kid and how The Man oppressed the poor and oppressed poor minorities in particular and maybe our duty to the future would be to fix that. But no, he dumped a bucket of clichés on us about remembering these, the times of our lives, and stepped off the podium to tepid applause.

I barely listened. Jane's words sprinted through my mind like an 8-Track tape on repeat. *Will likes you. What're you going to do about it?* What could I do? I'd destroyed any chance we ever had with my careless words. I would apologize up, down, and sideways if I ever got a chance to talk to him again. Would he forgive me?

The time came to get my diploma. Mr. Anger called my name in his whispery voice, but at least he pronounced it correctly. Cheers and a respectable amount of applause erupted from the crowd. Linda G and Barbie waved to me as I passed them in the National Honor Society mob, seated on stage like a lineup of teachers' pets.

Then it was done. Deidre Daly, high school graduate. College bound (if I robbed a bank or won the Irish Sweepstakes). Now, to figure out a way to see Will and ask him if what Jane said was true.

CHAPTER 33

Candle In The Wind

SUNDAY, JUNE SIXTH, D-DAY. Also G-Day—the day of my graduation party.

My relatives breezed into our house at precisely three o'clock. The booze made an appearance exactly one minute later. The gin and vermouth and the martini shaker seemed to appear out of thin air. I'd like to say that's when the serious drinking began, but Dad had them beat by several hours.

My grandparents, aunts and uncles, and various hairy cousins greeted my father with their usual unenthusiastic niceties then pretended he wasn't there. Though he was hard to ignore. He sat in his chair in the living room, wearing an old button-down shirt, his work pants, and his slippers, hacking and coughing as if he had the worst case of galloping consumption this side of the tragically doomed Fantine in *Les Misérables*.

My guests and I steered away from the contagious zone and mingled in the dining room, nibbling on carrot sticks and tuna salad sandwiches Mom and I had made. Marco sniffed around between people's legs, looking for dropped crumbs and generally getting in the way.

"From me and Uncle Wilfred," Aunt Sigrid said, tossing an envelope into the basket for cards and gifts on the kitchen table. "Twenty dollars, for your college fund."

She said that like I should be impressed. I kind of was. Every dollar I got would shave a buck off the amount we were going to have to beg, borrow, or steal to pay the rest of my tuition.

Aunt Polly called me over and introduced me to her new boyfriend, a guy with silver hair named Albert, who wore a plaid sport coat and looked a little like Johnny Carson.

"He owns a dry cleaners in Oakhurst," she said. "I won't have dry cleaning bills with him around."

As I was about to cut the cake, Shirley arrived. She added an envelope to the basket then pulled me into a squeezy hug. Jay watched her. Affection lit his face, his tightly locked vault of emotions seeming to finally wedge open.

"Congratulations, Deidre," Shirley said. "I know you'll do great things in years to come."

"I'll be happy to do things, never mind great." I thanked her, and Jay led her into the living room so she could meet Dad.

Mom came up beside me. "Shirley's a catch. But I worry about those two."

I watched Dad shake Shirley's hand. "Jesus you're a tiny thing," he said. "Wanna borrow my stilts? *Haw-haw-cough-cough.*"

"I don't know," I said. "Dad seems on his best behavior with her."

"It's not him I'm worried about. Not everyone they meet will approve of them together."

"Mom. This isn't Mississippi in the fifties."

She frowned. "No, it's Massachusetts in 1976. Where white people are rioting to stop Black kids from being bused to their schools. And you remember what happened with the flag."

How could I forget? In April, a photograph of a violent scene at a Boston busing protest had exploded into the news. A white guy snatched up an American flag on a long pole and lunged at a Black man, as if trying to impale him with it.

I shivered. Mom had a point. But Jay and Shirley had a point too. They liked each other, despite, or maybe because of their differences. Shouldn't that be the only thing that mattered? "Does that mean you're going to tell Jay to stop seeing Shirley?"

"No, never. He needs to live his life. I would *never* interfere. I'd never interfere in any of your lives." A bittersweet note laced her voice, and I suspected she thought of the boy her parents wouldn't let her marry. Then she flashed a grin. "With the exception of Rusty, I suppose. That boy needs a kick in the pants, every hour of every day."

Soon, the party ended, everyone toddled off (or staggered, quite honestly), and our house grew quiet. Mom ignored the paper plates and other trash, grabbed a book she'd gotten from the library, *Interview With the Vampire*, and made her way upstairs to the bathroom. Rusty vanished and Chrissy retreated to our bedroom to calculate Pi or something. Jay kissed Shirley goodbye and she puttered off in her green Gremlin.

I sliced myself another piece of cake—it was my graduation after all—and settled on the couch with the basket of gift envelopes to count my loot. Jay sat in the chair near the stairs with a happy sigh and the evening newspaper. Dad slumped in his own chair, alternately smoking, drinking, and coughing.

"Gee, you're rich," he said, eyeing the pile of bills stacked in front of me.

"That's for college," I said, like, *don't even think of stealing it.* The first direct words I'd spoken to him in days.

He laughed, which ended in a wracking cough. Then he went back to watching the Boston Red Sox take on the California Angels, aided by the skillful pitching of a guy with the giggle-inducing name of Dick Pole.

I nibbled on cake and tallied up my gifts while plotting how to get in touch with Will. The simplest way would be to call him, though

I feared his scary dad might answer the phone. I could do the old fashioned thing and write him a letter. Or I could show up outside his house and bellow for him to come out and talk. None of these options seemed even slightly acceptable.

Dad gurgled an odd sound. I glanced over and ice filled my veins. His face had turned as white as his hair. He held his arms stiff, sticking straight out, like a wooden soldier. His legs stuck out too. His head and his body twitched in a spastic dance. His tongue thrust in and out of his mouth. It was blue.

"Dad?" I squeaked, jumping up. Cake crumbs and twenty-dollar bills went flying.

Jay dropped the newspaper and scrambled over, his expression frightened, his mouth gaping. "Dad," he cried. "Dad."

I crouched beside my father and took his hand. His fingers grasped mine, his skin sweaty but as cold as winter. His body convulsed, head to toe. His tongue pushed between his lips. Spittle greased his chin. I whimpered.

Jay didn't call out to Dad again. He screamed for Mom.

Somehows filled the next terrifying minutes.

"Call an ambulance," Mom shrieked and somehow I managed to do it. My hands shook so much I had trouble sticking my finger into the number hole—0 for Operator—and turning the rotary dial. A woman answered. Somehow I remembered our address. Somehow I managed to hang up the phone.

Somehow the ambulance found our apartment in the sea of identical buildings. The sirens screamed, the lights flashed, and the whole neighborhood thundered toward our house to gawk at the spectacle. A hundred silent faces watched the ambulance guys rush my father's stretcher out the door, with Marco barking and nipping at their heels.

Jay rode with Dad. Somehow I didn't crash the car as I drove my frantic mother to the hospital. Didn't panic as she dug her fingers into my arm and moaned, "I can't lose him," over and over. Somehow I didn't cry when a nurse shepherded us into a sterile, white room to wait.

And somehow, I made it through that horrifying moment when the doctor came in and told us my father was dead.

The wake was decidedly not Irish. No booze, no food, no keening women. Just Chrissy sobbing, Mom staring vacantly, Rusty fuming like he wanted to punch a wall, and Jay looking broken.

I didn't know how I felt. Kind of empty. Sad. A wasted life. The heart attack had killed him, the doctor said. Aided and abetted by the disease he couldn't conquer, the doctor didn't say. And the thousands of cigarettes he'd consumed during his sixty years of life.

We stood in the funeral parlor's viewing room, lined up near the coffin like the Von Trapp family ready for inspection. Mom first, then oldest to youngest, Jay, with Shirley beside him, me, Rusty, and Chrissy.

The room smelled like embalming fluids and the mix of flowers in the sympathy wreath Dad's labor union had sent. Weepy orchestral music droned from unseen speakers. People came and went, expressing their condolences in hushed voices as they moved through our line of mourners.

I saw my father die.

Those stark words repeated in my head like a needle stuck on a record. He was gone. No more. I should've been blubbering all over the place, but I hadn't cried at all. Not a single tear.

Our neighbors shuffled through the line, people Mom had helped, people who promised to help her if she needed anything. My boss Valerie came, followed by several guys from Dad's factory, including Yolanda's father. He gripped Mom's shoulders and whispered at her for a long time. She dabbed at her eyes and nodded, thanking him for coming, as she did for everyone who paid their respects.

A spare elderly woman in a coal black dress crept into the room and tottered up to the casket. Jay and I exchanged looks. "A Daly," he mouthed and I nodded. One of our many Daly cousins we never saw, unpacked from their crypts to come out for wakes and funerals.

The old woman bent her head and prayed over Dad, then she made her way down the line. She grabbed Jay's wrist with a skeletal hand. "You poor, poor boy," she whispered in a reedy voice. "With everything you must face, and now the loss of your father, poor thing."

Jay didn't say anything. He let his eyes do the talking, rolling them so hard they were in danger of popping out.

She moved on to me. "I'll pray for you," she said, more of a threat than a promise. She squeezed my hand, her skin dry and papery, then she was gone. Until the next Daly funeral.

The ordeal continued. Mom's side of the family showed up halfway through the calling hours and parked themselves in the front two rows. I almost didn't recognize my grandparents without a martini glass in their hands.

Grandma signaled to me to come sit beside her. Her watery brown eyes found mine and held on. "I have an inkling how you feel."

I doubted it, though I nodded like *yeah, we're grief buddies.*

"I lost my father at a young age, too." A heavy exhale of stale gin and mouthwash followed. "He also died of a heart attack. He was younger than your father. Was on his way to visit my sister Violet. She was a piece of work. She'd just ditched her fourth husband and Dad went to talk her out of looking for number five. Anyway, there he was, walking down the street, and he dropped dead." She snapped her fingers. "Here one second, gone the next. I guess bum tickers run in both sides of your family."

Great. Now I had that to worry about. "Thanks, Grandma. Very comforting."

She patted my knee. "You'll be okay. It'll take some time, but you'll move on. You'll smile again. Life is like that. It goes on and we have to find a way to appreciate that. To embrace the day and treasure what we have now."

Interesting words. Wise words, in a way.

I excused myself and returned to the receiving line when I saw my friends file into the room. Donna, Karen, Barbie. Linda G holding Stew's hand. Jane with Barry and Pete.

And Will.

They paid their respects to Dad first. Donna knelt and crossed herself. Tears gushed down her cheeks though she'd never met my father. They came over and spoke softly to Mom, Jay, and finally me. Their hugs and sympathetic murmurs comforted me. Will hung back until the others moved along.

"Deidre, I'm so sorry," he said, his voice pitched low. "How're you doing?"

I lifted a shoulder and parroted Grandma's folksy wisdom. "I'll be okay. It'll take time, but I'll move on."

He tilted his head, gazing at me intently. "Deidre," he repeated gently. "How are you doing?"

I shook my head and my bottom lip quivered. *I saw my father die.* I desperately wanted to tell him that, to release the pain, but I couldn't. The words got stuck behind the tears clogging my throat, tears I'd been holding back since my father died and for years and years and years before that.

Suddenly, he folded me into his arms. He whispered my name and it all fell into place. I was with the boy I could depend on. The boy who was always there when I needed help. The boy who understood me, in all my messiness.

And the boy who made me feel it was okay to cry.

I clung to him and bawled my eyes out.

❀ ❁ ❀ ❁

I made my way to where my friends clustered, looking at pictures displayed on a table. There weren't many. My family had so few photographs and almost none of Dad. Will had joined the group after I'd cried on his shoulder for a long time, while he'd held me close in his strong and comforting embrace.

I approached him, dabbing at my eyes with a tissue. "Thanks for what you did. That..." Strangely, I couldn't say the word *hug.* "I feel better. Well, not *better*, better. But better."

He laughed softly and picked up a picture of a pudgy blond girl wearing a cowboy hat, standing by our front stoop. "Is this you?"

"Yeah. I was seven. Wasn't I adorable then?"

"Still are."

I flushed, and maybe blushed. "Will, why are you so perfect?"

His expression turned rueful. "You know I'm not."

"So you say." I hesitated, needing to bring up a sticky subject, not sure how. "Listen, about what happened on prom night."

"Let's forget about that night."

"I can't." I looked toward Dad's coffin, seized by regrets over what I'd never said to my father, devastated by what I had, especially my angry last words. "I *have* to make it right. You said I speak my mind, which is good, but not always. Not with the people I care for." A hopeful expression lit Will's face and I hurried on. "I say whatever pops into my head. Speak first, think later, you know? And sometimes what I say isn't very nice. Like with you that night. I said something that hurt you, and I'm *really* sorry. Can you forgive me?"

He stepped closer and gazed deeply into my eyes. "There's nothing to forgive."

New tears threatened as a thousand emotions crashed into me at once.

"Deidre... We've wasted too much time. *I've* wasted time. Because I couldn't speak. Because I was afraid of your answer. Now..." He lifted a hand and touched my cheek, a soft brush that stilled my breath. "There's only one thing I want to hear you say."

He stiffened and snatched his hand away when Father Old bustled into the room, dressed to perform funeral rites. Mom had asked him to come send Dad on his way, since my father was a man without a church. I silently cursed the interruption, though even a gauche girl like me knew flirting at your father's funeral absolutely wasn't done.

After the priest commended my dad's soul to God's tender mercy, I walked my friends to the exit, wishing I could make my escape with them. A solemn-faced funeral parlor employee in a black suit watched them leave like he expected them to pilfer an urn on the way out.

Will turned to me at the door. "Whenever you're ready to talk, I'll be there. Just let me know." He gave me a lingering look as he stepped out into the June heat.

The remaining relatives and mourners murmured their way out the door after that and the wake ended. As the funeral home guys ushered my family from the room, I crept up to the coffin to take a last look.

Dad looked small and frail in his Sunday suit, the only one he owned, bought when my parents were married so many years ago. Gray wool trousers and jacket, with a gold cross pinned to the left lapel, over his heart. The rosary beads he'd clutched when he prayed at the kitchen table before each of Jay's operations were woven between his fingers. He didn't smell of booze or cigarettes or sweat anymore. He smelled like science class.

I touched his cold hand. I wasn't the best daughter. Wouldn't even rank in the top one hundred. But I was there with him when he needed me. At the end, when he left us.

Grief flushed through me, along with sadness and regret. I wished we'd had more time. I wished I understood who he was. Wished I'd known him when he was young, when he was sober. Now I would never know him at all.

One of the funeral guys wafted into the room. "Everything alright, Miss?"

Which really meant, we want to close up shop, so move it, girl.

I gave the guy a distracted nod. Then I leaned down and kissed my father's ashen forehead, saying goodbye.

CHAPTER 34

Pick Up The Pieces

THE FIRST DAY OF summer arrived hot and sunny, bringing the entire neighborhood out to celebrate.

Down the hill, several families gathered for a cookout. The tangy smell of barbecued ribs permeated the air. Someone had toted a record player outside and Bachman-Turner Overdrive's "You Ain't Seen Nothing Yet" blasted from the speaker. Kids played jump rope or drew hopscotch squares with chalk on the sidewalk. Mr. McMahon drove his rusting Chevelle up onto the sidewalk, popped the hood, and stuck his head inside, while a good number of his fifty kids swarmed around him.

I took advantage of the warm weather too. I sat outside on the stoop, reading Jane Austen's *Persuasion* for the thirty-sixth time. I wished Anne Elliot could give her annoying relatives a big piece of her mind and a healthy dose of her middle finger, but I knew that type of impropriety simply wasn't done in those more buttoned-up times.

Chrissy perched beside me with her nose stuck in a book called *Silent Spring*. She'd tied Marco's leash to one of the stoop's railings. He snapped at flies buzzing around the garbage pail, hoping for an afternoon snack.

Inside the house, the telephone shrilled.

Mom was out and I knew Chrissy would let the phone ring from now until doomsday, so dutiful daughter me closed my book and

319

went to answer. I braced as I picked up the receiver. Surely the bill collectors wouldn't be calling now, looking for the money we owed, not so soon after their number one customer had shuffled off this mortal coil.

To my relief, the caller turned out to be someone more welcome. Donna.

"Are you coming to Jane's graduation party Saturday?" she asked. "I mean Jane's graduation and going away party, since she's moving next month. Please say you'll come. It'll be fun." She gasped. "Oh. I shouldn't mention fun right after you lost your dad. I'm sorry."

"It's okay," I said with a muted laugh. "Life goes on."

It did, surprisingly. Two weeks after our world tipped over, we were learning to move forward. Rusty had vowed to ditch his nefarious friends and find a job this summer. Jay and Shirley were talking about moving in together.

Even Mom was coming out of her funk after slumping on the couch for days and days, doing nothing, not even reading. Yesterday, she packed up dad's clothes and shoes. Today she brought them to Goodwill. Monday, she was going back to work.

I was moving on too. Slowly. As Grandma said, there would be good and bad days on the road ahead, and I'd have to deal with each as best as I could. The shock had worn off, and reality seeped in bit by bit. Dad was gone. Absent from our lives forever. Didn't mean I'd have to get over it, but I would have to get used to it.

"Does that mean you'll come?" Donna said. "It's a pool party, so you'll need a bathing suit. I almost forgot. Will's gonna be there."

My pulse kicked up. My anxiety level jumped too. I weighed the pros and cons. On the one hand, I had a constitutional aversion to appearing in public in a bathing suit. On the other hand...

Will.

I'd gotten a sympathy card from him last week. A brief note of condolence, signed *Sincerely, Will Hovey*. No declaration of undying devotion. Well, how could he profess his love for me in a sympathy card? That would be beyond gauche.

He'd said we could talk when I was ready. I was ready. Eager, in fact, to see him and ask him if he wanted the same thing I wanted. To ask if we had a future. To ask if I'd ever taste his cotton candy lips on mine and feel his arms around me and not when I was crying my heart out in grief, but when he was holding me as he kissed me and kissed me and kissed me.

Yeah, I was ready. And that outweighed *all* the cons I could throw into my own path.

On the day of Jane's party, a wall of humidity hit me when I walked out of the motel after work. The temperature hovered around ninety. That put an end to my dithering about what to wear. Too hot *not* to wear a bathing suit, and way too hot to wear jeans over it to hide my legs, as I would've done in the past. Surprise, surprise, I didn't care anymore what people thought about how I looked (mostly).

I arrived at Jane's in a pair of purple pleated shorts and a cotton blouse dotted with lilacs and, shockingly, on time. Probably everyone Jane had met in her short stay in the city had shown up. People from school and from our show splashed around in the pool or mingled nearby, others tossed Frisbees around on the patchy lawn.

Will wasn't here yet. Disappointing. I was eager to see him. Eager to be with him.

A Beach Boys song, "Good Vibrations," played as I crossed the grass to my friends, who'd gathered under the oak tree. I felt slightly overdressed, with Jane and Karen in Jantzen one-piece swimsuits, Barbie in a halter top and cutoff jeans shorts with the pockets sticking out, and Donna in a bikini.

Jane stuck an ice-cold Tab into my hand. She gave one to Donna too, who declared she'd sworn off Tango forever, and we drank a toast to our absent friend Linda G.

"I've been thinking about you, Deidre," Barbie said, nibbling on a grape popsicle rapidly melting in the heat. "You doing okay?"

"Yeah. I'm good. Good enough, I guess." Donna put her arm around me and squeezed, boosting my spirits. "What's happening with you guys? Seems like forever since graduation. What's new?"

"Well..." Barbie glanced toward a group clustered around a rowdy game of lawn Jarts, with Competitive Carol taking a turn hurling metal arrows with sharp points at the bullseye target. "I'm dating a girl."

Karen snorted. Not a classic Karen snort. Not derisive at all. More like amused, affectionate even. "Tell us something we *don't* know," she said.

Donna didn't know, judging by the way her eyes popped. I didn't know either, though if I hadn't been so occupied with my own romantic woes, maybe I would have. I was glad to know now, because Barbie sounded—and looked—so happy.

"My news isn't as big," Jane said. "We leave for El Paso in two weeks. Do you know they have cockroaches the size of baseballs there?"

I predicted she'd make friends with every single one of them as soon as she arrived in Texas.

"My parents are getting divorced," Donna blurted. "It's for the best. They plan to sell the house and my dad's gonna rent an apartment for me near the community college, so I guess I've gotta go there. On the plus side, I've heard *lots* of cute guys go there and I plan to scope out every one of them."

We all laughed. Except Karen. "Looks like I'm going to community college too." She sounded unhappy but resigned. "Can you believe I didn't get into *any* of the schools I applied to? Not one. My mom's pissed at *me*, like it's my fault. But you know what? I decided I don't give a shit about making her happy. And I told her so." She laughed now, a gush of relief. "Donna, you got an extra room in that apartment for me? I think I'm gonna need a place to live."

Someone put Joni Mitchell's "The Circle Game" on the record player, a bittersweet song about growing up and moving on. Donna's gaze touched on all of us, her eyes welling. "Girls, promise me we'll always be friends."

My eyes misted too. If this was one of my stories, I'd write a future where we did stay friends, forever and ever. I'd write a world where Pammie and Yolanda were still part of my life, and not fading memories and a picture on the windowsill. Where Camille had a family that loved her. Where Barry and Pete could have a happily ever after, and not in secret. Barbie too. Where my mother could've married the boy she loved or even gone to college.

And, most of all, I would've written a meaningful moment between my father and me, a final scene where we got to say goodbye.

But life wasn't as neat and tidy as that. Life steered you in a direction you never expect, and as my wise old martini-swilling grandma said, all we could do was enjoy what we had now.

But that wasn't what Donna wanted to hear. "We sure can try," I said and impulsively hugged her. I hugged everyone else too. Me, a child of the most anti-emotional, anti-hugging family to grace the earth, had become as touchy-feely as a hippie.

"Uh-oh, here comes trouble," Jane said as Marilyn strolled into the yard and sashayed over to the Holy Mother girls hanging out at the pool. Jane looked at me. "One of her school friends must've invited her. I sure didn't, not after what she did to you."

"Maybe it's payback for us crashing her party." I forced a laugh. "Don't worry, I don't mind. In fact, now's our chance to have a chat." I handed Jane my empty soda can and headed for the pool. "Wish me luck."

"Let us know if you need backup," Barbie called after me.

The pool's metal gate squeaked as I opened it and stepped inside. I strode toward Marilyn, my sandals clacking on the concrete. She stood with a gaggle of girls close to the pool's edge. They jumped out of the way when they saw me, leaving Marilyn alone.

"Hey, Mar, how've you been?"

She frowned, demonstrating the awesome properties of an acute trapezoid. "I have nothing to say to you. *You're* the reason Will won't talk to me anymore."

"You're blaming me?" I usually folded at the slightest hint of a fight. Not now. I lifted my chin, eager to go toe-to-toe with the girl who'd made my life—and Will's—so miserable. "*You* set up that whole thing with Carl. You used him, used me. You hurt Will. Deliberately. No wonder he's angry with you."

Oh, the sneer that greeted those words. "I had my reasons. You're bad for him. You bring chaos to his life. You bring chaos *everywhere*. You make Will do things he shouldn't, things that make people laugh at him. I thought if you were with Carl, Will would forget about you and move on."

"Move on to what? You?"

"You don't get it. I'm not interested in Will in that way. Never have been. I'm his friend. I want to help him."

"A friend wouldn't mess with his life like that. Or act like you do toward him. Like you pity him. That's not a friend. That's called being superior, which is one thing you're *really* good at."

A crowd had gathered to watch us spar. Donna and the rest of my friends had rushed over too. Everyone let out a collective "ooh" at my snide dig.

Marilyn narrowed her eyes. "Think whatever you want. I did what I did to protect him."

"Protect me from what?"

Marilyn's startled gaze shot over my shoulder. I spun around. Will plowed through the onlookers and strode toward us. He wore a pair of jean shorts, an Aerosmith tee shirt, and a furious expression, directed at Marilyn.

"From..." She jabbed a finger at me. "From her. She..." Her voice caught. "She wants you to make a fool of yourself."

"She wants me to be *me*, Marilyn," he said, irritated, completely out of patience. "That's why I like her. One of the many reasons I like her." He turned to me and his anger evaporated. "And I'm hoping to hear she feels the same way about me."

He flashed the brightest, most million dollar smile I'd ever seen. It lit me up like a thousand stars. My answer sang in my heart and trembled on my lips.

Yes. A million times yes.

Before I could speak, Marilyn let out a furious roar—and shoved me into the pool.

Chapter 35

Some Kind of Wonderful

I'D ALWAYS WANTED TO make a big splash. Today I got my wish.

People shrieked and paddled out of the way as I bellyflopped into the water. I held my breath. Too late. I went under and inhaled a bucket of chlorinated water.

Choking, it took a moment to gather my wits and swim upward. I almost broke the surface, when some asshole pushed me back down, laughing like drowning me was a joke. I thrashed and wriggled, trying to break through the mass of people in the water, banging into legs and torsos, and getting shoved back and forth as if in a pinball game.

Unable to breathe, wreathed in fear, panic set in and I swallowed more water. Suddenly, a pair of strong arms clamped around my waist and brought me up. I burst out of the water, spluttering, gasping. And still panicking. I fought to break free of his hold.

"Whoa. Deidre. *Whoa*."

I blinked water out my eyes. It was Will. He'd jumped into the pool to save me.

He guided me to the shallow end and helped me climb up the ladder. I straightened my glasses, which had miraculously stayed on during my impromptu swim. Then I bent over and coughed up sixty gallons of chlorine.

People gathered around, chattering, some amused, some concerned, but all I saw was Marilyn. Laughing. At *me*.

Weirdra Deidre, the gauche girl who brought chaos everywhere she went.

Shame and fury burned in me brighter than an exploding star. I snatched a can of Coke from a nearby ice-filled bucket and hurled it at her with the velocity of Fenway Park's newest southpaw pitching sensation.

Everyone instantly froze with a collective gasp of shock. I froze too. The soda can hit a target, but not the one I meant. It hooked to the right and smacked Will square between the eyes. He jerked back with a pained *oof* that shot across the yard, across the city, and maybe all the way across America.

I didn't stick around to find out.

Dripping wet, still coughing, heart hammering, I bolted to the front of the house and down the sidewalk. Heading where, I didn't know, just *away*. I slowed to a walk, mostly because my soaked sneakers were hard to run in. My wet cheeks burned in humiliation. How could I have done that? Will had saved me from drowning and I'd put his eye out with a Coke can. Jesus, I was a world class mess.

"Deidre, wait." Will trotted up from behind me.

"Not now, Will. I'm...busy."

"Busy? Stop. Come back to Jane's house before you freeze to death."

I stopped and swung toward him. "It's a thousand degrees out, how can I freeze?"

"It doesn't work that way. You're all wet."

"Yes I am. In both a literal and figurative sense. So are you."

His Pumas and his clothes were sopping wet. Rivers of pool water streamed down his face. His beautiful hair was plastered to his head. And he looked gorgeous. Except for the ugly red spot that had bloomed between his eyes where the soda can had nailed him.

"Crap." I touched the spot gingerly. He winced. "I'm sorry. I meant to hit Marilyn."

"I know you did. If your aim had been better, I would've cheered. Everyone would've cheered."

No one would've cheered. He was being nice. He was *always* nice. "I don't need your pity."

"That wasn't pity. That was pain."

I sighed, then shivered. He was right. I was cold. "Why do you hang out with me, Will?"

"Seriously? Why wouldn't I? You're fun. You're wicked funny. And you literally know how to use a word like literal. You're real. You speak your mind. You crack me up. You know who you are, and you like who you are. You've got the sweetest eyes. Your smile makes me happy. *You* make me happy. And..."

"And...?"

"And I think you're beautiful."

My heartbeat accelerated to six thousand beats a second. "It was you, that night at the church. Someone said that to me and I didn't see who. I hoped it was you, wanted it to be you but I wasn't sure and..." Tears gushed from my eyes and spilled down my cheeks. "All this time, it was *you.*"

"Hey. Don't cry."

"What else is there to do except cry?"

He kissed me. Well, okay, there was that.

He wrapped his arms around me and pulled me to him. I blinked away the tears and basked in this new, wonderful, and wondrous sensation. His lips on mine were soft and warm. They tasted exactly like I'd hoped. Cotton candy and starlight and sweetness and *Will.* Who liked *me.* Who thought I was beautiful.

We parted (*way* too soon) and he smiled into my eyes.

"Will." I sighed, the sensation of his kiss still tingling on my lips.

"Deidre. I've been wanting to do that forever. Since we met."

"Really?"

"Really. I tried to ask you out for months. I thought you might be interested, but I wasn't sure. You seemed to be into Carl. Then, at Marilyn's party, she told me he was your boyfriend. That broke my heart. He didn't deserve you. I got stupid mad. I said I'd be Donna's prom date, thinking to get back at you, but really so I could be near you. *Big* mistake. I had to watch you sit there all night, while that asshole ignored you. I wanted to hold you and kiss you and if you'd come outside with me when I asked you to, I would have."

He punctuated this passionate speech with a series of yips that stole my heart. We kissed again, our lips blending, our tongues tangling in a heated rush. Donna was right. He kissed like a five-alarm fire that burned every inch of me, right down to my toes.

We broke apart but he kept his arms around me. "I wasted a lot of time being afraid." He kissed the tip of my nose. "I wish I'd spoken up. Wish I'd told you how I felt a long time ago."

I brushed his wet hair out of his eyes and traced my finger along his jaw. "Me too. I thought you could never like someone like me."

"Are you kidding? I love everything about you." He pulled me close and whispered in my ear. "Even when you throw things at me."

I shivered all over, and it wasn't from the cold. "And you don't care that I'm..."

I pulled the words back before they could slip out. Will didn't care about my weight. He liked me for *me*. He liked me because I liked myself. And I did. It had taken a long time to get here, with too many detours along the way. Now I knew who I was. A positive girl, comfortable with myself. Unique. A little weird. The one and only Deidre Daly. Me.

And Will liked that me.

"I mean, you don't care that I'm from the Project?"

"Do you care that I'm from upper Chisholm?"

I giggled. "Will, how'd you get to be so perfect?"

"Deidre, you know I'm not," he said, different this time. Pleased. Happy.

He glanced back to Jane's house. Through the water spots on my glasses I saw Jane and my other friends on the front lawn, watching us, grinning in excitement.

"Now, will you come back with me so we can dry off?" he said. "Then we can talk about you and me, going out."

"Like on a date?"

"Yes, on a date."

"Can we kiss one more time first?"

He laughed and lowered his lips to mine. As we kissed, I heard Donna shriek with the happiness I felt in my own heart.

Part Seven

July 4, 1976

CHAPTER 36

Our Song

TODAY, ON AMERICA'S BICENTENNIAL birthday, all my dreams came true.

I sat in Schaefer Stadium in Foxboro, Massachusetts, minutes away from Elton John taking the stage. Live, in concert. Something I never imagined I'd see. I gazed at Will, sitting next to me. Another dream come true, though a dream I didn't know I had at first.

Will knew I loved Elton and he bought the tickets as a surprise. We had good seats in the stands, with a great view. The smell of beer and marijuana battled each other for supremacy in the open air. Thousands of people milled about down on the field, pressing close to a stage bookended by metal scaffolds, huge spotlights, and a hundred giant speakers.

The opening act had just finished. The sun was going down. The musicians tuned up and roadies moved Elton's piano into place. I grabbed Will's hand and squeezed. He squeezed back then he kissed me. He kissed me as often as he could, and it still wasn't enough.

He'd met my whole family and they heartily approved of him. How could they not? Things were changing at home. Rusty got a job, Chrissy had come out of her shell a little, and Mom seemed stronger every day, planning for a future without my father. Jay and Shirley were apartment hunting.

And me? Off to college in the fall, thanks to Dad in a roundabout way. Turns out he had a life insurance policy through his union

333

at work. Not a ton of money, not even a half ton, but enough to pay my tuition bill, with money left over for first, last, and security deposit so Mom could move out of the Project if she wanted.

I hadn't shed a single pound since June and seemed to settle at Bicentennial minus thirty. A hundred percent okay by me. If my body decided that was where I should be, who was I to argue? As long as I was healthy and happy.

A hush fell over the field, then a ripple of excitement. Music swelled and Elton burst out onto the stage, dressed in *the* most perfect costume for America's birthday—the Statue of Liberty. Will and I shot to our feet along with everyone else, clapping and singing along to "Grow Some Funk of Your Own."

I sneaked another glance at Will's happy face. We spent every minute we could together, hanging out. Laughing. Talking. About everything. I told him about my dad and he held me when I cried. We talked about his father and how he was slowly loosening up, though both he and Will had a long road ahead.

My mother had convinced Will to come pitch in at the free breakfast program, though, honestly he wanted to help and didn't need much arm-twisting. I'd get a chance to put the cut of my jib to the test next week, when Will planned to take me sailing on his family's boat. Not a yacht as I'd once thought. I used to think everyone who didn't live in the Project was rich. Now I knew rich was a relative term (still, his family had a boat).

We were Romeo and Juliet with a happy ending, from two different worlds but our hearts beat the same. Yeah, horribly cliché. I'd have to rewrite it, but the sentiment was true.

Later, Elton played "Your Song" and Will drew me into his arms. That was *our* song. It played at a happy moment, in Will's car when he held my hand, and at a terrible moment, when we'd fought at the prom. The perfect song to help us remember there would always be ups and downs, and we would make it through together.

I think you're beautiful.

Will had told me that several times since that first time on the stairs at Saint Mary's when I didn't know it was him. What better words could a guy say to a girl than that? Well, maybe *I love you* and *will you marry me*, but let's not put the cart before the horse. I mean, we hadn't even discussed the *doing it* thing yet. We planned to take things slow, no big rush. The time would come when it was right.

I think you're beautiful, he'd said.

And you know what? I thought so too.

Author's Note

I hope you enjoyed your visit to the Bicentennial year with Deidre Daly and her friends. Please help others find Deidre's story by spreading the word about her far-out adventure and/or leaving a review at the review site of your choice.

If you'd like to learn what's coming next from Evie Kelley and discover more about the pet rock and platform shoes era, please visit my info page at Linktree. https://linktr.ee/EvieKelley

Acknowledgements

Bringing Deidre and her marshmallow shoes to life wouldn't have been possible without the support, encouragement, and occasional tough love of my first readers, Jeanne Oates Estridge, Katherine Decker, and Lauren Espe.

Thanks to my writer friends Kari Lemor, Sharon Healy-Yang, Barbara Wallace, Suzanne Tierney, and Jean M. Grant for their continued friendship, support, and their patient answers to my occasionally (okay, often) stupid questions.

Also, thanks to my family for always laughing at my jokes (no matter how groan-worthy). To my siblings—no, these characters aren't based on you. To my friends in the Class of '76, Terry, Barbara, Linda, the Cindys, and myriad Karens, these characters aren't based on you either, but your spirit, humor, and sometimes un-groovy fashion sense were and are always an inspiration. Finally, to those unfortunate fellow students I pranked all those years ago because they thought I was my lookalike social studies teacher, I'm sorry you got an F on your assignment.

Evie's Books Written as Janet Raye Stevens

The Beryl Blue Adventures in Time
Beryl Blue, Time Cop
It's Been A Long, Long Time
Every Time We Say Goodbye
The Suitcase: A Beryl Blue Time Travel Short

Time Travel Suspense
The Titanic Time Heist

WWII Historical Suspense
A Moment After Dark

Romantic Suspense with a Supernatural Twist
The Fateful Knight

Mystery & Suspense
Clues & Chills: New England Stories of Mystery & Murder

Contemporary Holiday Romance
Cole for Christmas

About the author

If she can't live in the 1970s or a galaxy far, far away, Evie Kelley figures she might as well write about them.

Evie scribbles angsty YA sci-fi and stories set in the era of mood rings, platform shoes and the eternal debate of who's cuter, Starsky or Hutch.

Evie also writes WWII-set historical mysteries, suspense, and romantic time travel adventures as Janet Raye Stevens.

www.ingramcontent.com/pod-product-compliance
Lightning Source LLC
Chambersburg PA
CBHW022308310726
48973CB00001B/263